THAT FIRST moment

A Moments of Us Novel

Stefanie K. Steck

This one is for you.

And you.

And you.

All of you.

This journey has been absolutely wild, and I couldn't have
done it without you.

And you.

And you.

I love you.

The Moments of Us Series is highly inspired by songs –
specifically songs by Thomas Rhett.

Elliot and Jamie's story is inspired by
Unforgettable

It's worth a listen, trust me!

Chapter One

-Elliot-

F*ive Months Ago*

I belonged on the stage.

I loved every single part about being on stage—the guitar strings on my fingers, the sweat on my brow, the mic against my lips, the lights.

Especially the lights.

When the spotlight hit my band, we blew up; we became who we were meant to be. Normally the lights were hot, beating down on us, but tonight there weren't a lot of lights focused on us as I sang. My band wasn't the focus tonight—the bride and groom were. With a makeshift stage set up on the Oregon coast, it was cooler and a completely different setting than I was used to. Still, I sang every song with the same passion I always did as I watched my best friend, Milo, dance with Madeline, his new wife and the woman of his dreams.

And thankfully, tonight, no one seemed to notice how many times I stumbled over a word or two.

I couldn't help myself—she was always in my line of sight.

Jamie Gaines . . .

The one that hadn't left my mind since the first time I saw her months ago at The Piano Bar. And tonight, her strawberry blonde hair fell over her shoulders in waves—her gray eyes sparkled when she smiled. Even from the stage, when I heard her laugh, I had to focus *not* to laugh with her. Her personality was contagious.

Jamie sat with Clay and Ophelia, her chin in her palms as she smiled at them. Then, when Ophelia turned her head to kiss Clay, she turned away, and for a moment, her eyes met mine. I held onto the note, pushing through to the end of the song, before quickly turning away to grab my water bottle.

"What's next, Ell?" the drummer, Chase, asked, his drumstick flying through his fingers.

I swallowed. He had the set list right in front of him. He only asked because he knew I was getting distracted.

"Um, yea . . ." I fumbled, trying to remember what was next. Normally I had the set list memorized. "'Grave.' Clay and Phe's favorite. Let's get those two other love birds on the floor, shall we?"

Chase gave me a cheeky grin and put his hands on his knees, knowing he wouldn't be needed for a while for this particular song. As much as the kid loved to bang on the drums, sometimes he just liked to sit back and relax while Bennett, Jameson, and I did all the work. The start of this song was just me, and me alone, and the others joined me after the first verse.

As soon as that first line left my lips, I noticed Ophelia. She leaned into Clay, and in an instant, he stood, leading her out to the dance floor. I watched my friends for a few moments, simply enjoying the fact that the once grump had finally found his sunshine, but as soon as the band picked up and there was more depth to the song, my eyes began to wander.

Where did Jamie take off to?

Milo and Madeline were pressed against each other, Holly danced with her grandpa Wallace, Clay and Ophelia were giving each other small, sweet kisses as they swayed, and Jamie was . . . alone. She had moved to a different table, her phone staring back at her as she scrolled. Every now and then she would sit up, raise her phone to the crowd and smile as she presumably took a photo of the happy couples on the dance floor.

For the first time since I started my singing career, I found myself wishing I wasn't on the stage. I wanted to walk up to her, one hand in my pocket, the other, extended to ask her for a dance. She would accept, of course, and then we would sway to the music— to whomever was singing because it wouldn't be me. I would sing along for her though, so only she would be able to hear my voice. And then at the end of the song, I'd lift her chin and kiss her.

But alas, I was on the stage.

I pulled my focus back into the song. With the guitar solos almost over, and Bennett's backup ending, it was my time to shine again. I didn't have much longer on this stage, and I needed to pull myself together to enjoy it.

Pull through your set, Elliot. Then you can talk to her.

Ten more songs. That's all it was . . . ten more songs.

Man, they felt like the longest songs on the face of the earth.

"Congratulations, Milo and Madeline," I said, slightly out of breath as I finished the last song, pushing the sweat off my brow. "Now, if everyone can, please give the bride and groom a few minutes before we see them off. Please grab a tube from the basket and line up so they can do the cheesy run through thing while we shower them with bubbles!"

I flung my guitar over my shoulder, unplugging it from the amp to jump off the stage. Chase, Bennett, and Jameson followed, a larger skip in their step as they made their way toward the bride and groom.

Everyone—and I mean everyone—grabbed a tube of bubbles. The newlyweds held hands and began to slowly walk to the truck— which turned into a run as soon as the soapy bubbles began to fly through the air. Everyone laughed as Milo used his hands to brush the soap out of his and Madeline's hair before giving his bride one last kiss as they climbed in the car.

The crowd began to disperse, leaving the wedding party and event staff to fold the tables and pick up. I stuck to the stage, wrapping wires around my arm as Jameson and Chase worked on his drum set.

Bennett came up, slapping my shoulder as he passed to where his guitar sat. "That was a great set, Elliot."

"Yeah, Madeline picked great songs."

"We can move on from country music now, right?" he asked. "As fun as that was, can we go back to our sound?"

I nodded. "Yeah, yeah. I have a few other lyrics to hand off."

Bennett had been my right-hand guy ever since high school. It had been just me and him, playing in his garage. Five years ago, we found Chase and Jameson and the band came together, flawlessly—we've been together ever since. Now, I'd hand Bennett some chicken scratch I called lyrics, and he would fine tune them to make a song. We had a few we would sing at each gig and, surprisingly, the crowd always seemed to enjoy those more than the covers. A part of me wanted to pursue something more—something other than just karaoke bars and unpaid gigs.

"Great! Are they slower tunes or—"

Bennett began to ramble, always wanting to start another project as soon as possible.

Meanwhile, Clay and Ophelia had folded up all the tables, and Jamie worked on the chairs. She'd pulled her hair up in a ponytail and thrown a hoodie on over her bridesmaid's dress. She stacked the chairs and sighed, giving Clay and Ophelia a wave as they left hand in hand.

"Elliot?" Bennett said, his tone making me think he had said my name several times.

"Yeah, that all sounds great. Listen, I'll be right back." I dropped the wires and leapt off the stage, making a beeline for Jamie.

"Do you need any help with the chairs?" I coughed as I approached, the idea of Suave Elliot completely gone.

She turned suddenly to face me, her hair hitting her shoulder as the ponytail flung around her head. "Oh," she said in surprise. "No, I think I got it. The staff said if I folded them up, they'd take them to the trailer."

She waved her arms around, motioning to the multiple stacks of chairs then to the trailer on the road.

I inhaled, stuffing my hands in my pants pockets.

"Do you uh—" I stammered. She didn't need help; we just established that. There was no more music for a dance. My mind went completely blank. What in the name of all that was holy could I offer this woman?

"I loved the set, better than The Piano Bar and the party. You really upped your game." Jamie shifted on her feet, sticking her hands in the pockets of her hoodie.

I smiled. "Thank you. I kept messing up, though. Bennett had to poke me a few times." I looked back at my band, who all stood on the stage in a line, watching me. Jameson had his arms folded and brow furrowed. "I think they want me to get back to packing up."

"I can tell." She laughed as she looked at each guy then trailed her eyes back to me. "For the record, I didn't notice any mistakes. It was flawless."

Her eyes grew as she smiled. They had depth, a gray stillness to them that somehow managed to distract my entire focus.

She hummed, filling the silence that fell between us. "Well, I came with Ophelia, and she just took off with Clay in the car I arrived in, so . . ." She shook her head and pulled out her phone. "I'm going to call an Uber and finish up. I'm sure by the time they get here I'll be ready."

"I can take you home," I blurted. I finally figured out what this woman needs—she needs a ride. "Clay came with me, so I'll be more than happy to take you back to Portland. I just need to help the guys . . ." I pointed my thumb over my shoulder, turning my body slightly back toward them, my feet still firmly planted in front of her.

Jamie lowered her phone and looked at me, narrowing her eyes as if she was thinking.

Come on. Say yes. I desperately want to spend time with you . . .

"Sure, yeah . . ." she finally muttered. "That works great actually. I'll just . . . um . . . finish with the chairs while you break down the stage. Just let me know when you're ready?"

I grinned, holding back a small laugh that was sure to make me look like a creep. "Great, just give me twenty minutes?"

She gave a single nod as I turned back and ran to the stage, giving the guys a smile as they each shook their heads at me.

"We could have been done by now," Jameson argued.

"Well if you idiots hadn't been watching me, then you could have been. Come on, let's load up—I gotta take her home."

Jameson raised a single eyebrow before turning back to his keyboard. I went back to the mic, twisting apart the stand, making sure Jamie was doing okay as she folded up more and more chairs.

Once everything was packed and the guys were driving off with the trailer full of equipment, I met Jamie back at the tent. She sat in the only chair left, her thumbs steady on her phone screen.

"Texting Madeline already?" I asked as I approached. I mentally slapped myself on the forehead.

"Madeline is most likely in a situation where she is away from her phone." Jamie chuckled. "My sister actually." Tilting her head, she looked up at me, locking her phone and standing. "Are you sure you can take me home? It's a long drive, so I don't mind calling an Uber."

I folded the chair she'd been sitting on and handed it to the waiting event staffer. "I'm heading that way anyway. I live in Portland, so it wouldn't make sense for you to pay for an Uber when I'm offering a free ride."

She let out a long breath. "Okay, where's your car?"

I matched her stride as I led her to my Jeep, opening the passenger door for her. She bowed her head and climbed in, instantly buckling up. Walking around the back of the Jeep, I gave myself a small pep talk.

It's just a ride home. Chat with her, get to know her a little bit, then ask for her number. Oh yeah . . . Clay gave it to you. Okay well, she doesn't know that. Ask for it anyway and pretend like you don't have it. In fact, delete it so you're not lying. And stop being an idiot.

Chapter Two

-Jamie-

"So, tell me about your band," I said, breaking the silence that had lasted for forty minutes of the drive.

Elliot turned to look at me, his eyebrows raised as he opened his lips to talk. But no sound came out. This guy—who I had met a few times before, who people have told me has asked about me—was stiff. I couldn't tell if he was nervous, or if this was just who he was. His shoulders were squared, and his hand was firm on the gear shift. There were a few times I could tell he wanted to talk, but it was like the moment he entered the car, he forgot how to. Almost as if he didn't *want* to. His eyes were focused on everything but me.

"How long have you been in a band? Do you always play covers? Do you have any more gigs coming up?" I asked rapid-fire questions, hoping to elicit a response.

I would be the first to admit, Elliot was breathtakingly handsome. I thought so from the first time I saw him at The Piano Bar. His hair is clean on the sides, but a mess on top. A five o'clock shadow defined his jaw and gave him that rockstar look. His green eyes would captivate anyone—and I'm sure they had. Elliot Whittaker was extremely sexy, but, ultimately, that night he hadn't been in my line of sight—that was all Clay. And even then, I knew Clay wasn't interested, even though I made it obvious I was. I was told that Elliot *seemed* interested. I even knew he had my phone number, but no texts were sent, no phone calls were made. To me, that didn't really scream, *interested*.

So why should *I* be?

But that didn't mean that friendship wasn't a possibility. If only I could get the man to open up and find out.

He let out a small cough. "My band, um, well . . ." He swallowed, his eyes narrowing. "We've been playing together for about five years. Bennett and I started it up. We throw in a few popular covers in our set, but mainly try to stick to our originals. We do about five or six shows a month. One at The Piano Bar and the rest as smaller venues."

"So, Bennett is . . ." I trailed off.

"He plays guitar and sings backup vocals. Jameson is bass, keyboard, and pretty much any other instrument we need—that guy can play anything. He'll sing too, but it's not his favorite. Chase is drums, and there's no way in hell we can get that guy to sing."

As he talked, his shoulders began to loosen, and his thumb tapped the steering wheel.

"Have you always been the lead singer?"

He nodded, his lips forming a crooked smile. "I've always loved music. Started playing the piano when I was seven, and it took off from there."

"And you write your own songs?"

"What's with all the questions?" He raised a single eyebrow, and a smirk that actually lit up his face.

"I'm just making conversation. You're kinda stiff."

"I am not," he mumbled, wiggling in his seat.

"This is the most-high strung I've ever seen you. Where's the guy from the stage? I want to talk to him," I teased.

He furrowed his brow and scoffed. "Hate to tell you, sweetheart, but I'm the same guy. The only time you'll see me stiff is when I'm at the office and I'm forced to be."

I rolled my eyes. The guy in the driver's seat was definitely not the man who was on stage. "Okay. If you say so."

My phone dinged in my bag and Elliot's eyebrow twitched in my direction before he returned his attention to the road. I unlocked the screen and found a text from my sister.

Jillian: *Let me know when you're home. I don't like the idea of a random guy driving you.*

I sighed and shook my head.

Me: *He's not a random guy, Jilly. I met him at the wedding. He lives in Portland and is just being nice. I'm. Fine.*

"Everything okay?" Elliot asked once the light from my phone died.

"Yeah." I shoved my phone back into my bag. "My sister tends to worry a bit more than necessary. She just wants to make sure her twenty-five-year-old sister makes it home safely."

"Twenty-five?" Elliot asked, his voice a little lower than normal. "I wouldn't have pegged you as twenty-five."

"And how old did you think I was?" I leaned away from him, glaring at him through the darkness.

His eyes widened. "I'd rather not say. I know assuming a woman's age gets you in trouble."

"You thought I was closer to Maddy's age, right?" I asked.

Elliot shrugged but didn't say anything.

"You can say you thought I was older; I won't get offended," I egged him on.

"No, I . . ." He coughed. "I thought you were younger."

"Oh, good, well I'll take that. And you?" I relaxed back in my seat.

"Thirty-six."

"I think I knew that."

"It's Google-able."

"Google-able?"

He nodded. "Yeah, if you look up the band. We're easy to find—all our information is there"

"I'll be honest, I don't even know what your band is called. I don't think Madeline has ever told me."

"Did you not see the giant logo on Chase's drums?"

I clenched my teeth and shook my head. "Sorry, I was too busy paying attention to Milo and Maddy."

"Fair." He sighed. "I'll tell you, but you can't laugh."

"Why would I laugh?"

"Jameson thought of it." Elliot took a deep breath, "We're called *Savaged Whittakers*."

"Savaged . . . Whittakers?" I bit back a smile. "Explain, please."

"Bennett Savage, Elliot Whittaker. *Savaged Whittakers* sounded better than *Whittaker Savaged*." The corners of Elliot's lips twitched, like he was holding back a grin. "Jameson came up with it when we were stuck. He said that since Bennett and I started the band, it made sense."

"I guess it does. I always wondered how bands got their name."

"It's a mixture of things."

"What's harder, naming the band or writing the songs?" I twisted so I leaned on the center console, loving how he was loosening up. Maybe he wasn't how I initially pegged him. My mind went to a hot-headed rockstar—one who could get anything and any*one* he wanted. But maybe I was wrong. Maybe the rockstar persona was only one side to him.

"Definitely naming the band." He laughed. *Okay, I like that laugh.* "I guarantee you it almost caused a breakup."

"I'm pretty sure you would have figured out how to make it work." I smiled, having a feeling he wouldn't be able to stay off that stage for long. "And the tattoo?" I asked.

He lifted his hand from the steering wheel and rotated his forearm. I saw the sketch of a guitar, the pick board, and sound hole, complete with bridge and string, leading up to an unfinished neck.

"It's just a part of the band," he answered, his smile widening. "So, it's your turn. You work with Madeline?"

I nodded. "I do."

"And you're her assistant?"

"I am."

"Do you like working in the dental field?"

"I wouldn't be working in it if I didn't like it," I replied sarcastically. Thankfully, Elliot got it. He shook his head and let out another laugh. I needed to keep him laughing. I loved his laugh. Loved? No . . . just really, really liked his laugh.

"Okay, that's fair. What do you like about it?"

"I like working with my hands. I can do everything in that office. I even have a dumb nickname because I literally can go anywhere that's needed."

"And what's the nickname?"

I let out a loud, *Ha!* "The Octopus."

"The Octopus?"

I nodded. "Doc gave it to me because when I get going, it's like I have eight arms. I move at the speed of lightning in that office. I'm everywhere all at once, and I've been forced to fit in tight places." I was talking way too fast, but by the look on Elliot's face, I could tell he was keeping up. He laughed, following along with the story of how I had to squeeze into the small opening in the wall to open the doctor's office.

Once I got this man talking, it was easy to keep the conversation going. Elliot was easy to talk to, easy to laugh with, and simply just easy to be around. Before I knew it, we were coming into Portland. It was only midnight, and I wasn't ready to let him go quite yet.

"You wanna grab a drink?" I asked boldly.

He raised a single eyebrow and turned to me. "Sure, that'd be great."

"Cool."

"Of course, The Piano Bar!" I exclaimed as we parked. Truth be told, this was my favorite place; they knew how to make a perfect mango-rita.

"I get free drinks."

I raised an eyebrow. "Will I?"

"Maybe, if you're lucky. It helps that you're cute." Elliot turned off the Jeep, giving me an eyebrow wiggle before jumping out of the car, and I followed suit.

The air in Portland was warmer than in Depoe Bay, reminding me I was still in my bridesmaid's dress. Before closing the door, I removed my hoodie and threw it on the front seat. Elliot was still dressed in his tux, the top few buttons of his shirt undone, and his tie was loose around his neck. He looked perfectly disheveled.

Walking in front of Elliot, I made my way to the bar, taking a free seat and turning to watch Elliot. He waved to a few people he knew, and stopped to shake hands with someone, then finally sat next to me. Elliot, at this moment, was the lead singer of *Savaged Whittakers*—Rockstar Elliot Whittaker.

"You're popular around here." I sighed as he removed his suit jacket, placing it on the back of the chair.

"Not to toot my own horn . . ."

"Toot it!" I shouted.

"I am. This is my favorite venue." He tilted his head, getting the bartender's attention, who instantly came over, placing the circle cardboard coasters in front of us. "I'll have my usual, and for the lady—" With his palm up, Elliot turned towards me.

"A mango-rita, please." I smiled. The bartender nodded and turned away. "You knew that."

"I was going to order for you but then decided against it. You never know how a girl will react."

"I'm not one to react like a crazy person." I patted his shoulder. "You're safe to order for me. Mango-ritas. Always mango-ritas."

Elliot nodded. "Noted."

"Do you think they will ask you to sing?"

Elliot groaned. "I hope not. I love it, but I just sang for three hours, so I'd probably say no. Besides, it looks like the pianos are going to duel tonight."

The bartender came back, placing my orange drink in front of me and a beer in front of Elliot. I took the mango slice off the rim and bit into it.

"I love dueling pianos. It's not too late for that, is it?"

"Oh, hell no," Elliot scoffed. "They will play until last call."

"We picked a good night to come then, huh?"

"Cheers to Milo and Madeline." He raised his cup.

Pursing my lips, I raised mine and clinked the glasses. "Cheers."

We each took a drink, Elliot pounding back his beer faster than I could even think to sip my margarita.

"Whoa, slow down, you need to drive me home still." I laughed.

"One beer is fine; I'll be your DD don't worry. I'll make sure you get home safe." He set his half empty glass down, giving me a cheeky grin.

"I'm the one and done drinker. After this glass I'll be ready to go home and hit the hay." I ran my fingers up the stem of the glass, trying to keep my eyes off of Elliots.

"I'm sorry, but are you Elliot Whittaker?" A platinum blonde approached us, with a skimpy dress on as she and two of her friends closed in on Elliot. "From *Savaged Whittakers*? We come see you whenever you play here . . . we love your band." She giggled. *Giggled.* I held back a scoff and picked up my drink. "I'm Sofia, and this is Heather and Justine. Can we get a photo with you?" There was that giggle again.

Elliot gave them a crooked smile, raised his eyebrows but kept his body angled towards me. "Um . . . ladies . . ."

He was too attractive for his own good, and I think he knew it, too. The way his eyes lit up when he turned to them told me he was in his element. If Madeline was right in saying that Elliot was interested in me, this, right here, is why it would never work. He was Rockstar Elliot Whittaker, and I was simply Jamie, the girl who'd rather stay at home or hang out with her girlfriends than sit and wonder if her boyfriend was going to call.

Was Elliot a boyfriend that never called?

Forcing myself to ignore them, I spun towards the bar in the chair, concentrating on how many ice cubes were in my drink. I didn't need to think of Elliot as a boyfriend anyway. Friends, Jamie . . . *friends*.

"Not to be rude, but I'm with a friend. The guys and I play again next Friday, why don't you three come and meet us after the show. We can do a meet and greet kinda thing," he said politely.

I was shocked for two reasons. One, did he just agree to hook up with them later while I was sitting right here? Not that it would matter—I was just a friend. And two, did he really just say "no" to adoring fans so he could pay attention to me?

I found myself staring at him as he shook each of their hands and told them he'd see them in a week. The girls gave off whining noises as they made their way past him, only to burst out giggling once they got to their table.

"*Oh Em Gee, we just met Elliot Whittaker!*" I heard one of them shout.

"That was fun," I say, taking another drink. "I think I can go my entire life without hearing another giggle."

"It comes with the job. I bet if those girls knew I was a businessman in real life they'd run away." He turned, rolling his eyes, and resting both arms on the bar top, reaching for his beer.

"I bet they wouldn't. Girls read books about billionaires to experience that. And think, if you and your band ever sign a label and do major tours, it may get worse." I patted his shoulder.

He let out a long, exasperated sigh. "Unfortunately, it will always come with the territory, but I'll also have bodyguards to protect me," he joked, his grin fading, "Nah, the guys will have fun with those three on Friday night. Remind me to text them."

"You're all single then, huh?"

He shook his head. "Jameson has a girlfriend, but the other two are enjoying the attention they get from a band. Me . . . well . . . I just love to sing."

"What, no mic bunnies?"

"What?"

"You know, like the rodeo has 'buckle bunnies,' you don't have any super fans or"—I lifted my fingers to air quote—"Mic Bunnies?"

His jaw dropped slightly, and his eyebrows pinched. I couldn't tell if he wanted to laugh at me or tell me I was right and that he currently had a girl in the back waiting for him.

Finally, he let out a laugh and shook his head, while his eyes studied me. He smiled as he held my eye contact only to drop his gaze to my lips. He raked his bottom lip with his teeth and turned away. The tension that was radiating off this man could be cut with a knife. "With running an architecture firm and being the lead singer of a band, I don't have a lot of time for 'mic bunnies.'"

"Friends though? Do you have time for friends?"

I could hear the gears in his head turning, then when it clicked, he nodded slowly. "Friends. I always have time for friends."

Sticking to our one drink rule, Elliot and I made them last, and I kept thinking about how much I was thoroughly enjoying his company. Not once did he make a move on me or try to push anything other than friendship. Getting to know one another—that's all this was. The tension eased as we talked. Laughs and stories were shared, and Elliot was...growing on me. When I felt those flutters, I had to stop myself. Friend-zone. Stay in the friend-zone.

Elliot paid our tab and placed his hand on my elbow, leading me through the crowd and out to his Jeep. He opened the door for me, going through the same motions as before, and walked around the back of the Jeep. Once the Jeep was on and my address was in his GPS, he drove off.

He was more relaxed in the seat this time, a slouch to his posture and his free hand animated as he kept talking. I felt calm watching him, not even really paying attention to what he was saying, just listening to his voice. His singing voice was one thing, but his regular voice was just as enchanting. I watched as his fingers gripped the steering wheel, wondering how his calloused fingertips would feel against my chin. Or how his lips, that have sung so many lyrics up against the microphone, would feel on mine. I licked my lips and looked out my window.

What were these thoughts? Where the hell were they coming from?

I took a deep breath and exhaled through my lips.

It was just the alcohol talking at this point . . .

This is why I was a one-and-done kinda girl . . .

He stopped the Jeep, turning it off as he pulled up to my complex. "Here, I'll walk you up." He unbuckled and hopped out of the Jeep, walking in front of the hood to open my door.

"You don't have to. It's literally right there." I pointed to my front door. Being on the bottom floor had perks.

"What kind of gentleman would I be if I didn't walk you to your door." He furrowed his brow and waited for me to step out of the Jeep. I draped my hoodie over my shoulders and grabbed my bag, taking the steps towards my apartment door, with Elliot right next to me.

Fifteen steps, that's all it was. Fifteen, long . . . silent . . . steps.

"Thank you for the ride, Elliot, and the drink. It was great getting to know you tonight—knowing the man behind the microphone." I smiled as I reached in my bag for my key.

"I had a good time, thank you."

He pinched his brow and took a step closer to me.

"If uh…if you would allow me to be honest here . . . I'd like to be . . ." he muttered.

I swallowed. "Okay . . ."

"I'm sorry if this is a bit forward but . . . you've been on my mind, Jamie. I kept skipping words tonight at the wedding because I noticed you were alone and I just wanted to talk to you, spend time with you and dance with you. Truth of the matter . . . I've wanted to kiss you ever since that first night at The Piano Bar." His voice was soft, barely a whisper as he leaned in towards me.

My stomach jumped and my breath faltered.

"I know we said we would be friends, but I'd really like to kiss you now . . . if you'd let me."

I raised myself up on my tippy toes and closed the gap between us, my lips crashing into his. He was stunned at first, his lips tense but as soon as his hand found my waist, they relaxed. His tongue slightly separated my lips, deepening this amazing, carefree, whimsical kiss. I ran my hands up his chest and drank him in, feeling his body twitch under my touch. His fingers found my neck, feeling exactly as I thought they would, bringing shivers down my spine. When girls talk about a kiss that changed their life . . . that was this kiss. *Elliot's* kiss.

Elliot . . . Whittaker's . . . kiss.

What the hell are you doing Jamie . . .

I gently pulled away, ignoring the nagging voice in my head, and looked up at Elliot. His eyes were heavy and his lips were plump. I was tempted to kiss them again, but instead, I pursed my lips and swallowed. I ran my fingers through his hair briefly and then stepped away.

"Good night, Elliot," I said softly.

He let out a breath of air. "Good night, Jamie."

I stepped into my apartment, shutting the door instantly, closing the kiss and Elliot out. I leaned against my door and listened for his Jeep to start, my fingers on my bottom lip as the feeling of Elliot's lips lingered.

What the hell Jamie, the last thing you need to do is get involved with Rockstar Elliot Whittaker.

Chapter Three

-Elliot-

Present Day

"So how big of an idiot am I being?" I leaned back in my office chair, raising my hands behind my head as I grinned at the computer screen.

Once a week I had a virtual meeting with Clay. He would start by going over any finances and accounts that needed to be handled, but it would always turn into us rambling about whatever we were up to. In less than a year, Clay had become one of my best friends. It didn't matter that he lived in New York, and three time zones separated us, he knew more than my bandmates. Possibly knew more than Milo.

His glare shot through the screen, aimed directly at me. I just widened my smile.

"I cannot stress enough . . ." he began, keeping his teeth clenched as he grumbled at me. "If you accept that offer, you will go bankrupt and lose everything you've worked for." He put his right hand on his forehead. I could *feel* his stress through the computer.

"I'm not saying I'm selling to Anthony. I'm just saying I *think* I want to sell. Anthony just put it in my head." I put my feet up on my desk—true relaxation at its finest.

"How much did this 'Anthony' offer you?"

"Half a mil." I wiggled my eyebrows.

Clay let out the loudest groan I'd ever heard, and I chuckled as he dropped his head and hit his desk. Behind him, Ophelia came into view. Those two were attached at the hip now. He ran his growing business from home, and Ophelia had moved one of her desks in his office. If he was there, she was with him, sketching away. If she was at the boutique, he worked from the studio that was above the warehouse. I'm not sure how they weren't sick of each other yet, but wherever one was, the other wasn't far away.

"Hey, Ophelia!" I shouted.

She arched her back and dropped her pencil, turning towards the computer. "Hey, Elliot, please stop trying to give my husband a heart attack."

"Yeah, can we talk about that again."

Shortly after Milo and Madeline tied the knot, Clay and Ophelia did too. A private ceremony the day before her boutique opened. They still hadn't told many people, but since Ophelia insisted I sing their song at the ceremony next year, they spilled the beans to me. I wasn't mad or annoyed that I wasn't there, but that wasn't to say I wasn't going to give Clay grief over it. He was fun to tease.

Clay's head rose and he twisted his torso to face his wife. She shrugged her shoulders and went back to her drawing. Using his left hand this time, he ran his fingers through his hair, his black wedding ring hitting the camera just right. I smiled. I loved that they were finally living their lives together.

"I told you . . ." Clay started, ". . . we're having a ceremony . . ."

"I know, I know. And I'll be there to sing that song . . ."

"It's called *Grave!*" I heard Ophelia shout from the background.

"I know," I whispered into the camera with a grin. "I just like giving her hell."

"Well stop. I gotta live with it so, stop. When you finally get married, I'll make sure to give your wife a hard time over everything," he grumbled, his voice low enough to make me think he was keeping it secret, but high enough to know that Ophelia was listening to everything. "But seriously you are not selling your business for only half a million dollars."

"Well, that's why I brought it up, isn't it? To figure out how much I can sell it for." I pulled my feet down and leaned on my desk.

Clay blinked a few times before his eyes began to move. The man worked off of one computer, always working in the background as he had a video call up. I knew he was pulling up my file and, after a few moments of silence, he heaved a sigh.

"Your stocks alone are worth more than half a million, and still tend to do relatively well. If you give me a few days I can contact an appraiser and we can work on getting it up for sale, but . . ." He ran his hand over his face, "Have you talked to your dad?"

"My dad doesn't even know who I am." I sighed.

"Your mom then. I understand you have total control over the company and its assets, but it was fifty years of your dad's life. It may be a good idea to at least get their approval before you sell."

I took a deep breath, running my hands against my desk before flopping back into my chair with my exhalation. I bit my bottom lip, looking away from my computer to the frames along my wall— my dad with his first design as an architect, him and the building when they first opened, the new office, and finally, me and him the day he retired.

I got a degree in business for this. This was supposed to be my life; even though it wasn't what I wanted. I had worked with my dad for three years now and had been the CEO of the company for, going-on-two years, although I still wasn't sure if I could really keep doing this. So, when an offer appeared out of nowhere, it was almost as if a light bulb went off. Selling the company seemed to be a way out for the family—a way out for *me*.

"I'm going to mom's tonight, I'll talk to her," I finally said.

Clay gave me a single nod. "That's all I ask. Text me an update."

"It's date night!" I heard Ophelia yell.

I smiled at him.

"I may not answer," Clay responded.

"I wouldn't expect you to." I chuckled. "If I don't text you tonight, I'll talk to you tomorrow."

"You're playing this Friday, right? How are the guys?"

"They're good, and not this Friday, next week. Craig has been hinting that a talent scout may show up one night, but nothing yet. We've been practicing, doing sound checks on the new songs and fine tuning them." I sighed, folding my arms over my chest. "They're secretly hoping we will get signed to something huge."

"That's what you want right?"

"Well, that's the ultimate dream, but who would handle my finances?"

"Elliot," Clay groaned. "I know you very, very well. When you are in rockstar mode you drop one-hundred-dollar bills on the counter like they are candy . . . even if you get signed, I will still handle your finances."

"Damn straight. I'll talk to you tomorrow?"

Clay gave me a smile and nod. "Talk tomorrow."

I waved at the camera and closed the meeting.

Silence filled the room. Heaving a sigh, I stood from my desk and stretched my arms to the side, arching my back. It was a motion I had seen my dad do numerous times after a meeting—a way to pull him back to the here and now. For me it was simply copying his mannerisms; I wasn't hunched over at a desk all day, so there was no need to really stretch my back, but here I was, twisting my torso just like Dad.

The rest of the day went by in a blink. I sent a few more invoices Clay's way and showed a new client the building. Everyone loves the design floor, and I especially love it when there are architects working there as I lead the potential client through—being able to show them our process, and then landing their business before they leave.

But they always leave, and so do all my employees, while I'm always the last to leave the building, making sure to lock the doors on my way out. The lights that hit the glass make the smaller building shine even when the winter weather keeps the natural light away.

The cold air hits my skin as I pull my coat to my neck, readjusting my bag on my shoulder. It's only the beginning of the year and I'm already done with the winter. I'm ready for Spring— for longer days and the warmer weather. I'm ready to leave this behind and move forward.

I just need to take those steps.

And Clay, as much as I hate to admit it, is right. I need to talk to my parents before locking this building for the final time.

After scraping the ice off of my windshield, I sat in the cold Jeep. Shivers ran down my spine as I reached for my phone. A message had arrived when I was out in the cold, and it was my brother who wanted my attention.

Jacob: You're coming to dinner right? Mom has news about dad.

I sighed.

Dad.

Ever since he was forced into retirement he had gone downhill faster than the doctors expected. Even Jacob, with his Ph.D., was baffled that his memory had faded so fast. Whenever I visited my dad, I had to remind him who I was. He called our mother the name of his old secretary, and my sister was nowhere to be found in his mind. Normally when mom had news on dad, it wasn't good. The last time we all sat down to dinner, she told us she was moving him into a home for constant care. My mind automatically went to the worst.

Me: *I'm on my way now, is everything ok?*
Jacob: *Everything is fine, Sydney's already here so we're just waiting on you.*
Me: *On my way.*

I pulled in the driveway thirty minutes later, my siblings had left me with just enough room to squeeze my Jeep in between their cars and the road. Making my way into the warmth of the house, I rubbed my hands together, instantly regretting leaving my gloves in the car.

"Elliot's finally here," I heard my sister, Sydney, call from the dining room.

"You're staying too late at the office honey," my mom's voice followed.

"Yeah well . . ." I took my coat off and hung it on the stair railing. Who needs a coat rack anyway? "Someone has to close up the building."

Both my brother and sister were already sitting at the table, and Jacob's son was settled on his lap, enjoying the snack puff that was put in front of him.

"Where's Andrea?" I asked, looking around for Jacob's wife.

"At home with Kenzy. She brought something nasty home from school, so Wyatt gets to stay with grandma." Jacob began to bump his knee up and down. My nephew began to giggle as his hand tried to stay steady to get the snack.

"He's always welcome," My mom came over and scooped up her grandson. "Well now that we are all here . . ." she trailed off, giving Wyatt a kiss on his cheek. "Your dad was lucid today, for about an hour. He didn't know where he was—he was kind of scared—but by the time I got there he had calmed down."

Sydney sat up straight. I think out of all of us, dad's memory loss has affected her the most. "What was . . ." she stammered. "What happened?"

"He was confused. Worried he would forget again. I tried to tell him as much as I could, even though I couldn't tell him everything . . . but he wrote it down."

Sydney's bottom lip quivered as she slumped back into her chair. I put my arm on her back and rubbed lightly, bringing her some source of comfort.

"Why didn't you call us on your way?" Jacob spat. For the first time since Mom had taken Wyatt, I looked over at him. He was hunched over, his elbows resting on his knees, his gaze focused down. "We could have made it there."

"I was at the salon," Sydney sniffed.

"You three have more than enough on your plate. Sydney, your salon is taking off and Jacob, you were telling me about a surgery you had today. I knew Elliot was close, but he was busy at the office."

My eyes darted towards her, biting my lip to stop myself from saying anything. Now was obviously not the time to bring up selling.

"We listened to one of your songs, Ell," she said softly.

I let out a sarcastic chuckle. "Oh, I bet he loved that."

Giving me a soft smile she nodded. "He wrote down *'Elliot's wasting time singing'* in his notebook."

"Oh, that makes me feel so good about my life choices," I added. I went into business for my dad. I followed the path *he* wanted me to follow.

"Mom." Jacob's voice was harsh again. "Next time he's lucid, I don't care what I'm doing, I need to know." Jacob stood and reached for Wyatt.

"Oh Jake, I know you—"

"Mom." Jacob interrupted. "Next time he's lucid, I don't care what I'm doing. You need to call me. I need to know," he repeated himself, as if she didn't get the message the first time.

He stared at our mother, standing taller than her. My mother though, as broken as she was sometimes, still stood strong. She took her grandson back and glared at her son.

"I don't care how old you've gotten, Jacob Dalton—you do not talk to me that way. I went and saw *my* husband. We talked. He's proud of all of you. He'll read his notebook tomorrow, just like he always does, and maybe when we go visit on Sunday, he will remember something. He remembered today, and that's something." Her glare never once left Jacob. Even at the age of forty-two, you could tell Mom still made him quake. "Now, I am going to go play with my grandson. Sydney, Elliot, can you two please set the table."

"Sure thing, Mom." I smiled, not taking my eyes off of my older brother.

"Of course, Mama." Sydney stood and walked to the kitchen.

Once my mom and sister were out of ear shot, I looked over at my brother.

"You good?" I asked.

Jacob's jaw was tense. He let out a breath and I could see his entire body relax, that jaw, however, stayed stiff.

"I know a hygienist that wouldn't like how you're clenching your teeth," I mumbled.

"She should have called us."

"I know, but, Jake, she just wanted to see her husband." I sighed. "You're still a part of that study . . . right?"

Jacob nodded. "Yeah, nothing new to report there. I just . . ." he sighed, "I wish I could have talked to him."

I stood, pushing myself off the chair to stand next to him, "It wasn't the first time he was lucid, and it won't be the last. Don't be mad at Mama, she just wanted to see the love of her life."

Jacob's jaw tensed again, and he nodded, the tears welling up in his eyes.

"Relax the jaw, Bro." I slapped his shoulder.

His lips opened as he turned to glare at me. "I'm not your bandmate."

I gave him a crooked smile. "Go easy on Mom, okay?" I slapped his shoulder once again and let him go to help my sister.

I understood why he was upset. He's the first born, dad's pride and joy. He and dad had a relationship that Sydney and I didn't. I knew dad loved us, he made sure he told us, but he was always proud of how far Jacob had gone. Mom didn't specifically say but I knew he had asked about Jacob first, and then the company - and then Sydney and me. Those were dad's priorities.

Shaking off the thought, I switched my mind to focus on the here and now. Dinner with my family, a sound check tomorrow night, performance on Friday and the potential of selling the one thing my dad loved almost as much as us.

I was in for a wild ride.

Chapter Four

-Jamie-

Ding, ding, ding.

I was going to tear that stupid bell from the wall.

I put the denture I was working on back on the counter and walked into the operatory. All four rooms had a patient in them. As I walked past them, I noticed that Dr. Brenner was focused on his patient, and Madeline was busy talking about oral hygiene. They didn't ring the bell. That only left . . .

"Jamie," I heard Kelli's voice muffled by her mask. "I need that other scaler—the purple one—can you grab it from sterilization?" She turned her body to look at me.

"Sure thing, Kelli," I took the few steps to the sterilization room, and found Drew standing by the sink, his hands deep in soapy water as he cleaned out the lab bowls.

"Oh sorry, Jamie. Kelli needs something?" he asked, twisting his body as he watched me walk in.

"Got it." I waved the scaler in the air and went to give it to Kelli. That's when I noticed Dr. Brenner stand up and walk to Madeline's room. "Exam?" I asked as he passed me, knowing he would most likely want me in the room with him for any notes to be taken.

"Maddy's got it. You reline that denture." Dr. Brenner slapped my shoulder as he passed.

I saluted, "Yes sir." I set the scaler down on the tray for Kelli saying, "There you go."

"Thanks, Jamie."

"Hey, Jamie."

I spun to face Dr. Brenner's assistant Claudia. She was masked and gloved up, her hair a mess as usual and a look I knew all too well on her face.

"Can you sit with the patient so I can use the restroom? He's on nitrous . . ."

"You got it, go." I waved her off and went to take her chair next to the patient who had his eyes closed as he breathed in that elusive "laughing gas." I glanced at the clock on the computer that was mounted to the wall: 3:24 p.m.

Only an hour and a half left to go.

A few moments later I was pushed back out of the chair, with Claudia arriving just in time for Dr. Brenner to return from the exam. Meanwhile, Madeline passed me with her patient, taking her up to the front desk to check out, and I returned to the lab where the denture was still waiting for me.

I enjoyed all aspects of my job, but working in the lab, and with my hands, was what I loved the most. It reminded me of the sculpting clay I would mold as I sat and watched TV, or the paints and easels that sat waiting for me in my room. I knew it was a strange comparison, but working with the 3D Printer, bleach trays, and dentures in the lab brought a tad bit of creativity to the dental office.

"Hey," Madeline's voice broke the silence moments later. "There's a book signing at Powell's next Saturday, wanna come?"

"Where's Milo?" I asked, knowing that she and her husband were glued at the hip.

"He'll be working. You, me, and Holly. Girls' day. You in?"

"I'm in. I could use a new book or two. Who's the author?"

"Brooke Easten-Turner."

I gasped. "The girl you found in Colorado? Her new book is out already?"

Madeline nodded. "It came out last week and she's on her tour. I knew she was coming to Powell's so I've been impatiently waiting to buy it. Next Saturday at eleven?"

I gave her a nod and smile, turning back to the denture. "Sound's perfect. Meet you there? Too bad it's too cold for the food trucks."

"Olive Garden after."

"Perfect plan." I held the finished denture up and studied it, looking at Madeline. "Pray this fits . . ."

"I'm praying." Madeline laughed as I passed and went back into the operatory where my patient patiently waited for her teeth.

I dug in my bag for my phone as soon as I got into my little Toyota, the defrost was not working fast enough, not to mention, I didn't have a scraper with me and instantly regretted it. A credit card could only do so much and my fingers were freezing. A text from Jillian was waiting for me once I pulled my phone free from the mess that was my purse.

Jillian: *Call after work! *smiley face**

Putting my earbud in, I called Jilly. She answered on the first ring—the same time I put my Toyota in reverse.

"Jamie! How was work!" Her voice rang through my ear.

"Hey, Jilly. Good, busy."

"What do they call you? The Octopus?"

I rolled my eyes at the nickname I was given by the office manager. "Ha...yeah, the Octopus. What's up?"

"Will and I are trying to get our final plan for February going, you're coming right?"

Once a year my family had a reunion of sorts in one of our favorite places: Park City, Utah. Since we all lived in different states, and had mix-matched schedules, holidays were, sadly, never a possibility for us. As much as we tried to take time and visit during the chaos, it never happened. So, we came up with the plan to spend three weeks together in February. We would celebrate Christmas, my mom would make massive meals every night, and we'd simply just be together. It was one of my favorite times of the year. My parents would rent out a cabin in Park City and we would call it home. I had to use all my vacation time at once, but it was always worth it to see them.

"Of course, I'm coming. Time off was approved a year ago." I smiled.

"Great, when's your flight? Will thinks we can coordinate and meet at the airport at the same time. Save money on an Uber to Park City." Jillian was talking fast, her two kids in the background demanding her attention. "We don't really want to rent a car . . ."

"Actually, I think I'm going to drive this year. It's not too long of a drive, and that way I won't be stuck in the cabin. There's an arts fest this year, right? They started a winter one?" I asked, knowing very well the city had decided to host a second festival. The big one was in the spring—the one everyone knew about—while this one was supposed to be smaller for it being its first year. A trial of sorts.

I had this crazy idea this would be the year I entered a piece. I knew the painting I wanted to put in the show, but the overwhelming imposter syndrome crept up and settled in my chest, telling me I wasn't good enough for a Park City art's fest.

"I think they did, and why are you driving?"

"Well, I've been considering entering a piece . . ." I trailed off, my voice falling as I turned on the freeway.

"Seriously!? We've been trying to get you to enter for years! What changed? Was it Daxton?"

Daxton?

Oh shit . . .

Yea . . . Daxton . . .

I had forgotten about my imaginary boyfriend.

I winced and tried to remember what I had told my sister about my "boyfriend" Daxton. All that came to my memory was that I met him at Madeline's wedding, and we connected.

"Oh yeah, uh no. I just think I finally have the right piece to enter. Right timing you know," I stammered, hoping the topic of *Daxton* would fade.

My siblings had all gotten married relatively young and were still going strong in their relationships. My brother Holden had married right out of college, currently owned three restaurants, and his wife stayed home with their three kids. Jillian got married while in college, then had her twins after her career was established. Her husband, Will, stayed home with the kids while she worked as a social worker. Then there was me and my younger brother Harrison—perpetually single. Harrison decided to be a drifter of sorts—traveling everywhere he could, on the least amount of money he could. He's managed to backpack across Europe, twice, on less than $50 a day, which still baffled me. And then there was me, although I preferred my carefree life in Portland, working with people, and creating whatever came to my mind.

But considering my sister often asks if I had met anyone—if I had come any closer to "settling" down—one day I let it slip that I had. Her scream was louder than I expected, and the story kind of spiraled from there. Every now and then I would say I was going out with Daxton, or enjoying a night in with him, but I never sent any other information other than that.

And apparently it showed in my short-term memory because I had to think about who *he* was.

"You're still with Dax, right?" Jillian asked.

"Oh, yeah, we were out just the other night actually. He hasn't seen the painting yet."

"Why not?" she asked, a sternness to her voice I had thought was only reserved for his kids.

"We um . . ." *We what!? Come on Jamie, keep it together.* "We normally met up at his house. You know my one bedroom is a little too crowded for two."

"Right with all the easels and pottery wheels," she scoffed. "You should bring him . . ." Her thought was quiet at first, but then as if she had heard exactly what she had said, she gasped out loud. "Oh my hell, Jamie, bring Daxton! You've been together long enough now, I'd love to actually meet the man, and I'm sure mom and dad would be just as excited to have him."

My eyes went wide. Bring a man, who didn't exist, to a family function that lasted three weeks. *Sure . . .*

"I mean I'd love it if he could come, but he may not be able to take three weeks off from work, and it's kind of late notice . . ."

"Have you seriously not told him you're going to be away for three weeks?"

"No . . . no . . ." I pulled into my parking spot and shifted the car in park, my hand instantly rubbing my forehead, trying to force lie out. "He knows."

"Even if he can come for a week, you know we have a couple nights planned. You wouldn't have to 'date' Harrison to get the discount."

Okay . . . I did love couples night. The four siblings and their spouses, using up the Park City two-for-one on a meal. Harrison and I always pretended to be the third couple to get the discount.

"I'll talk to him, but don't get your hopes up."

"Oh, I'll get my hopes up. I need to meet the man who captured your attention at a wedding." Jillian's voice was sweet, I could hear her smile. "Speaking of hopes, how have you been feeling? You had your annual checkup right?"

I rolled my eyes. Not only did my sister and mother think they could weasel their way into my romantic life, they also constantly asked about my health.

"Yes, Jilly. I'm still fit as a fiddle—that's the term, right?"

Jillian laughed. "Yes Jamie, I'm pretty sure that's the saying. I'm happy to hear that, you know we always—"

"I know, I know. And before you ask, I updated mom already."

Jillian let out a sigh of relief. "Perfect, I know she'll be asking when she sees you. Okay, so . . . back to plans . . . you'll be driving . . ."

She began to talk my ear off faster now that the conversation wasn't focused on my health, or me and my imaginary boyfriend. I had three weeks to find a boyfriend, or come up with an excuse as to why he wasn't able to come. Because—you know—those things were a lot easier than *actually* telling the truth.

As soon as Jillian and I finalized our travel plans with each other I plopped on my sofa. My apartment was small, with plants galore, and art supplies occupying every single corner. I loved my little space. Even though it was on the first floor, natural light still found its way in through the windows. Every single picture that hung on the wall was painted by me, making it so the apartment literally screamed, *"Jamie Gaines Lives Here!"*.

I closed my eyes and rested my head on the back of the couch, trying to picture who Daxton was in real life. What would he look like if I had found someone to at least *pretend* to be him? What would we do when we were together? What would his job be? What would his kiss be like?

Elliot . . .

Snapping my eyes open I pushed myself off the couch and into my kitchen. I hated to admit that Elliot Whittaker had entered my mind more often than I would like, and it always went back to that kiss. I could still feel that kiss on my lips. He had texted a few times, but fear crept in, and I went out of my way to ignore them—not even opening the messages. I was so scared . . . nervous . . . ashamed, maybe, that I even went as far as to check the Piano Bar's listing before making any plans. I didn't want to put Elliot on a pedestal he didn't belong on. I didn't know him enough to trust that. Elliot Whittaker was not the kind of man I saw myself with. He may have been different than I expected that night, but I simply couldn't get involved with some who had—what did I call them, Mic Bunnies coming up to him every night.

But he turned them away . . . remember?

I shook my head, trying to keep myself away from that train of thought and focus on the new problem at hand.

Daxton.

Pulling out my box of Kraft Mac 'N' Cheese, I grabbed my phone and downloaded a dating app. Maybe, just maybe, I would find Daxton there and get Elliot out of my head once and for all.

Chapter Five

-Elliot-

Craig Masters', the owner of The Piano Bar, phone number lit up my phone. I furrowed my brow and looked at the small clock on my computer: 10:48 a.m. . . . on a Tuesday? Why would Craig be calling me on a Tuesday?

Grabbing my phone I swiped that green bar, "Hey, this is Elliot."

"Hey Elliot, I was hoping you'd answer." I could hear Craig's smile as his deep voice rang through my phone's speaker.

"For you Craig, I'd always answer," I replied, leaning back in my chair, spinning to face the window. My office sat on the ground floor, so the first thing I saw was the parking lot, but the trees—currently covered in snow—were always what my eyes were drawn to. "What brings you to call me on Tuesday?"

"Well," he began, "I have it on good authority there will be a talent scout here this Friday."

I sat up right in my seat, my jaw dropping slightly.

"From Pacific Sound Records," he finished.

"A California label," I said, shock filtering through my voice.

"The one and only."

Pacific Sound Records wasn't a large label by any means, but it was one that I'd had my eye on. If we could get picked up and signed by them, there was a good chance we could go further in the music world with record sessions, local gigs, and maybe even tours. Wouldn't it be something to see my face on a t-shirt? I let out a heavy breath and flopped back on my chair.

I did a quick mental check of my calendar, only to groan when I realized...

"Only one problem Craig, we don't play this Friday." I ran my hand through my hair.

"We can rearrange to get your guys on the stage. Call Bennett and Jameson, make sure they're available Friday. And Chase too."

"Ha, yeah, can't forget Chase. I'm down to play, and I guarantee the guys will be too, especially if there's a scout in the crowd. The Piano's won't mind the switch?"

Dylan and Tate were the best piano players The Piano Bar had to offer and when we weren't on stage, they were.

"They've already agreed. So, we will see you Friday at the same time as always."

"Sound check at four, performance at eight." I smiled, a rush starting at my toes and trailing up to my stomach. Butterflies formed as the news finally seemed to hit. I smiled, the widest grin, and only my computer was there to see. "I'll call the guys and shoot you a quick text. Thanks for this Craig, I owe you one."

"When you make it big, do your first paying gig with us. That'll cover everything. See ya Friday, Elliot." Craig didn't give me a moment to say goodbye before the line went dead.

I didn't even hesitate. Before my phone could close down, I dialed Bennetts number.

"Bennett," I said as soon as he answered, "you're not going to believe this."

To say the guys were in disbelief would be an understatement. They all showed up at my office faster than I anticipated. We sat in my office, Bennett sitting at the visitor seat, Jameson on the small sofa, and me behind my desk. Chase paced the room running his hands through his hair so much so that the sweat from his palms made it stand on end. Bennett instantly started writing the set list, even throwing a new song idea my way, and Jameson was rapid fire texting everyone he knew.

Bennett shot up from his seat and handed me the crumbled piece of paper full of his chicken scratch. He had about twenty songs on the list, half covers, half ours.

"This is more than we play in a night, this is a full blown concert." I looked up at him, "We only have a few days to get things together, maybe we should stick to five or seven songs."

"We normally do fifteen," Bennett retorted.

"It's not our normal night, a shorter show will give the scout a taste so they want more."

"I agree with Ell," Jameson said, hitting the lock button on his phone, placing it face down beside him and falling onto the back of the couch. "Macy says we may want to cut the show in half, and invite everyone we know, get a huge crowd there to back us up."

Macy, Jameson's girlfriend, worked in marketing—she knew how to sell things, and, apparently, she could add band marketing to her resume.

"Give them a taste," I repeated. "So, let's cut this list in half, five originals and two covers. You think we can agree to that?"

"What if they don't like us?" Chase asked, his voice shallow.

"Then they don't like us and we keep playing at our normal venues. Nothing changes," I stated. "It's as simple as that."

Bennett let out a long breath. "Why wouldn't they like us? We'll do what Macy suggests and get a crowd there. Have Craig post it on the website that we're playing. Hype. It. Up."

"Hype *us* up," Chase corrected, yet again running his fingers through his hair. "This is really happening isn't it? An agent. An *agent* agent. An actual agent from an actual record label is coming to listen to us."

"Fucking finally," Jameson said, a breath leaving his lungs as he leaned himself forward. "Five years you guys. Five long years and we are finally getting our break."

Our break.

After the guys left, leaving me in my office alone, I stayed to finish my actual work. I didn't get anything done after the phone call from Craig, and my mind was still swimming. Clay had sent over an email of numbers—all ways to appraise the business, with the causal reminder to talk to my mother, and Craig had sent over information on the scout coming. Add those two emails on top of the new contracts and multiple messages from the band and my plate was officially full.

This was something I wanted—something that I had been hoping for so long. I knew that if we were to get signed, I would leave this company and never look back, finally becoming who I was meant to be. This office—this building my dad built from the ground up—had nothing on the stage. The stage was where I belonged.

I knew the guys had felt the same. Bennett hated his nine-to-five, and Chase wanted out of his customer service job. Jameson wanted to travel, and this was his way of doing it. Of course, Macy would join him—those two were tighter than Clay and Ophelia—and having her come along would actually be fun.

I fell back in my chair and spun to look out the window, the snow had started to fall gently, dusting the sidewalk. I took a breath and closed my eyes.

Would we have a tour bus, or fly everywhere and stick to one side of the US? Would we tour aboard? Would we have number one hits that made it on Billboard?

So many what if's to consider.

So many possibilities.

Chapter Six

-Jamie-

Okay, so, *maybe* a dating app wasn't the best idea I'd had in a long time. I swiped right on a few guys and got a few matches—mainly creeps—and the messages consisted of *"Hey Girl, when can you hook up?"* to *"You look smokin' hot in those scrubs."* Needless to say, I didn't respond to any of them. That is, until Rick Johnson messaged me. He had dark hair, an amazing smile, and blue eyes that put Milo's to shame. His profile photo was that of him behind a bar top, leaning against it, showing off the tattoos that trailed up his arms.

I never responded so fast to a message before.

Rick and I talked non-stop for two days. We had so much in common, and he asked me so many questions—seeming to be completely focused on what I was saying. I mean, as much as one can through text. He was easy to talk to. He owned a restaurant and said he was able to set his own schedule, all he had to do was shift a few things around and, before I knew it, we had a date lined up for Friday. I wasn't going to get my hopes up, I had to date the man first, and then casually bring up my family's trip. If we hit it off, who knows, maybe he could be the Daxton I was looking for. He sure as hell looked like a Daxton.

After work on Friday I rushed home to get ready—choosing a simple, black dress, one with a high neckline and no sleeves. Rick and I agreed to meet at the Piano Bar, so he could stay at his restaurant for a few hours before leaving for our date. I showered and curled my hair, feeling nervous. The butterflies rose in my stomach as I slipped on my shoes and locked my front door.

To my surprise the Piano Bar was a little more packed than I thought it would be. I checked the website, I knew the Pianos were playing tonight, but they didn't normally bring in this big of a crowd. I sat down and waved the bartender over, ordering my normal Mango-rita. I quickly glanced at my phone, only to see no new notifications. I was a little early...not to worry, Rick would definitely come.

My drink was placed in front of me and I lightly touched the stem of the glass, pulling it toward me. Tapping my phone screen to life—still no notification—I then turned it face down. This was not the time to overthink.

The lights softly dimmed around me, giving me the indication the pianos were going to start. I took a sip of my drink, and then the guitar notes hit my ears. I coughed and turned towards the stage.

Elliot strummed his guitar, a large smile on his face, with the hair on top of his head—longer than I remember, but the sides still trim around his ears. He winked at the crowd as he began to sing and my stomach fell. I had been avoiding this man for five months. I had checked the schedule of the Piano Bar's website. I had turned down any invitation that was thrown my way for *Savaged Whittakers* nights . . . and my successful streak had officially come to an end.

And Elliot was still as handsome as I remember him being.

I took a deep breath and watched their performance for a moment, hoping that because I was sitting at the bar he wouldn't see me—or if he did see me . . . what would happen. He was singing, his sets were longer—he wouldn't break his groove just to come talk to me.

I scrunched my nose at the thought.

But then again, he might.

If I still think about that kiss . . . he has to think about it too.

It was a damn good kiss.

I turned my back to the stage and unlocked my phone, pulling up Madeline's text thread.

Me: *You would have mentioned if Elliot was playing tonight, wouldn't you?*

The dots began to dance . . .

Madeline: *I didn't know he was. Next Friday he is. Milo and I have a date night - can you watch Holly?*
Me: *Yes I can - but no, he's definitely here tonight.*

I turned back to the stage and raised my phone, snapping a photo. It was a good shot, Elliot was turned to look to his left, the smile wide as he sang. He was definitely in his element. I sent the photo off to Madeline.

Me: *See . . .*
Madeline: *Well apparently Milo knew. He said Elliot mentioned something about adding a night to their set. Want us to come down?*
Me: *No! I'm meeting a date and don't need the perfect married couple to make me nervous.*
Madeline: *Oooo a date! Fill me in tomorrow? Book signing?*
Me: *You bet.*

I scrolled back up to the photo of Elliot and gave a small smirk at it. I would delete it later, maybe go up and show him after the show. It was a good picture of him, honestly. I could send it to him and maybe they could post it on their social media accounts.

The clock in the corner told me I had been waiting for twenty minutes, and still no sign of Rick. I opened Tinder and looked for his message thread. He hadn't mentioned being late or anything, and after three songs I knew I was being stood up.

I twisted in my chair and brought the salted rim to my lips.

Since I'm here . . . I might as well watch the show.

I watched Elliot as he moved with the music, playing something other than country—his voice filling the room just like I remember from the wedding. A voice I wouldn't mind hearing on the radio from time to time—flawless and smooth. He turned his body towards the bar and in a flash our eyes met.

I pursed my lips to avoid smiling. But that didn't stop *him* from smiling. He gave me a grin before winking and pulling himself back to the crowd—never missing a beat.

"Jamie?" I heard a deep voice come from behind me while, at the same time, a thick, hairy arm fell on the bar top next to me. I turned to look at the arm, recognizing the tattoo from the profile picture, but as my eyes trailed up the arm and to the man I was assuming was Rick.

I wanted to burst out in laughter.

The man behind me was *not* the man from Tinder. Well he was, technically, but at the same time, he wasn't. He was heavier, with a full beard, and his breath smelled like gum disease. The tattoo though was the exact same as Tinder.

I had been catfished.

"I'm sorry," I mumbled, "you must have me mistaken with someone else."

"Jamie Gaines right, from Tinder? I'm Rick. I know I look a little different but—"

"I'm sorry, sir." I lied through my teeth. "I'm meeting someone here, so if you don't mind . . ."

"Right, you're meeting me."

"I'm sorry, sir, I don't even have Tinder."

I glanced down at my phone, making sure the screen was black. *Thank the LORD I locked my phone.*

"Jamie Gaines, right?"

"Sir . . ."

How many times could I say, "sir" before he got the picture?

Rick took the seat next to me and I watched his shirt ride up his middle a little bit, the hem falling from his pants where it was tucked in.

"You're gorgeous by the way, your photo doesn't do you justice." Rick smiled and, being the dental assistant I was, I instantly looked at his crooked smile. Nothing was wrong with crooked teeth—but when they were stained yellow, there was definitely something wrong.

"I'm sorry, Rick, was it? I'm here with my boyfriend and he'll be back any moment, so I really suggest you leave his chair, now."

"Does your boyfriend know you're on Tinder?"

"I'm not on Tinder."

"Oh, but you are. We've been messaging all week. You work as a dental assistant and they call you the Octopus because you do everything in the office. You like to paint, and you have a family vacation coming up."

Shit. Why did he have to ask so many questions about me? All I really knew was that he owns a restaurant—which I was now questioning—and that he liked dogs and played football—which I was also questioning.

I tried to hide any giveaway on my face and pinched my brow.

"Listen, Rick, my boyfriend is on that stage, and he's going to join me for a drink after he's done. Maybe *then* you'll believe that I'm not on Tinder. I don't work as a dental assistant—teeth are gross—I don't paint, I'm not going on any kind of vacation, and I'd really appreciate it if you left me alone."

I hoped I sounded convincing. He narrowed his eyes at me, but lifted the corner of his mouth to a smile.

"It's because I look so different, huh? Truth be told, that's my brother in the photo. We have the same tattoo. I used to have a profile but I never got any matches."

Huh . . . I can see why . . .

"But the moment I made a new one with his photo, I had multiple matches."

"I have no idea what you're talking about. For the last time, I've never used Tinder."

Rick winked at me and waved the bartender down, "Sure you haven't. It's okay. I won't tell your 'boyfriend' you have a dating app on the side."

"I do not—"

"Is this man bothering you?" Elliot—my knight in shining armor—appeared at my side, his guitar slung on his back, sweat beads dropping from his hairline. Gorgeous as ever. He placed his arm around me and focused his eyes on Rick. I looked at him, hoping my face didn't show complete shock. I didn't even hear the music stop.

I blinked . . . snapping out of the trance I had found myself in. I leaned into him, placing my hand on his chest. *Relax . . .* I reminded myself.

"See, Rick, I told you my boyfriend was on the stage. Now, if you could please leave me alone."

Elliot didn't say anything. He just raised his eyebrows at Rick and pulled me closer to his body. My grip tightened on his shirt.

Rick looked from me to Elliot, his eyes narrowed. He groaned and stood, giving Elliot one more look over.

"I hope you know your girlfriend is on Tinder." Rick gave me one final wink and turned to head down the bar. Elliot stepped behind me, forcing me to turn around to look at him, my back to Rick.

"Thank you," I said breathlessly.

"You're on Tinder?" Elliot asked, his eyes locking with mine—the look on his face turning to pure lust. He kept his smile on his lips and his hand on my shoulder, pushing my hair over my shoulder, letting his fingers linger a little longer.

"Um . . . maybe. Why are you looking at me like that?" I asked, trying to keep my voice steady.

"Because your date is still watching us and, apparently, I'm your boyfriend." He bit his bottom lip.

"Thank you again, I know that wasn't exactly what you wanted to come over here for." I shifted in my seat and scooted a little closer to him. If Rick really was still watching, I had to play it off too.

What's with me and fake boyfriends? I was definitely way in over my head here.

"Not really, I honestly was going to ask why you ghosted me for five months, but now I need to know the story here. After I go talk to the agent, okay."

"An agent?" I widened my eyes.

Elliot gave a small nod. "Yea, can you believe someone may be interested in us?" He leaned in and kissed my forehead, only to step back, leaving his hand on my neck for longer than he should have. "I'll be right back; can you order me a beer?"

I gave him a hum and nodded, watching as he gave me a smile and walked back to the stage.

What the hell *Jamie!?*

Chapter Seven

-Elliot-

I wasn't expecting to see Jamie, so the second our eyes met I began counting down the minutes until the last songs were over. She may have ghosted me, but hell . . . she was sitting right there at the bar, and she was still just as gorgeous as I remember. I could still taste her lips on mine. And I mean, I couldn't not go talk to her, especially not when I saw that guy approach her. Her body language was screaming for him to leave her alone, and he was clearly not taking the hint, so I knew I had to step in.

What I didn't expect was for her to tell him she was my girlfriend.

I kissed her on her forehead—all for show of course—my lips tingling from the skin contact, before turning back to the guys. We were told to act as if we didn't know there was a scout in the audience, but I had made eye contact with him a few times during the performance. He knew, I knew, what he was there for.

I met up with Bennett, who was buzzing with adrenaline as he unplugged from the amps.

"We can go talk to him right, or should he come to us?" he asked, his voice shaking.

"Let him come to us, we were awesome, I'm sure he liked what he heard."

"Good call going with new songs." Jameson jumped off the small stage and stuck his hands in his pockets. "Album material."

"Elliot, Bennett, Jameson, Chase—" Craig came up to my left, in between Bennett and I, while another man approached and stood next to him. *The agent.* "This is Liam." He held out his palm towards Liam, the agent, who gave us a slight nod and held out his hand.

I took it first, shaking it with power, just like my dad taught me. "Great to meet you Liam, did you enjoy the show?" I asked.

Liam shook the guy's hands, giving each a small nod before turning back to me. "I really did, actually. I'd love to meet up with you guys again, talk about the possibilities of what I can do for your band."

I furrowed my brow, reminding myself that I wasn't supposed to know who he was. I tightened my lips to a thin smile.

"Oh, right, I'm an agent with Pacific Sound Records and I've seen you guys on YouTube, so I had to get out here to see you for myself. I love your sound, it's just what we are looking for," Liam added, laughing at himself for forgetting his pitch first thing.

"I would be lying if I had said I didn't know why you were here." I laughed, looking behind him to Jamie at the bar. She was sitting as stiff as a board, her back still to Rick, who had thankfully moved on to someone else. "I'm glad you liked it." I turned my attention back to him and smiled.

"It was all new material," Bennett blurted out.

"That's perfect." Liam reached in his coat pocket to take out a business card, handing it to Bennett before taking my hand in his once more. "I'm leaving town tomorrow, but like I said, we're very interested in you."

Bennett looked at his card and then to me, giving me the biggest grin imaginable. It was as if he transformed into a five year old.

"We'll be in touch," Liam said, giving Bennett a nod.

Liam gave Jameson and Chase another nod and handshake before Craig led him back to the bar, who turned to give us a huge thumbs up before disappearing with Liam in tow. Once they were out of eye and ear shot, Bennett slapped me hard on the back while the guys turned back to the stage, grabbing their guitars and wires.

I, on the other hand, went straight back to Jamie. She watched as I came close, her eyes drifting to my forearms as I rolled up my sleeves.

"Your beer," she said smugly once I approached, sliding the mug towards me. "Great set."

"So, tell me this story." I wasted no time, grabbing the handle of the mug to raise the beer to my lips. It wasn't my first go-to drink after a gig, but it would do. "Who's Rick?"

"You don't want to talk about talking to an agent just now?" Jamie nodded her chin towards the stage where Bennett and Chase were still acting like school boys.

"We can talk about that in a minute . . . I want to know who Rick is?"

Jamie rolled her eyes and twisted her body back towards the bar. "Obviously, some guy I met on Tinder."

"*Obviously*, but there is so much more to the story."

"Honestly, you don't need to know."

"Oh, but I *so* do."

"Can't a girl just meet a guy on a dating app?"

"If you were purposefully meeting him here, then why did you introduce me to *Rick* as your boyfriend?" I raised an eyebrow at her.

She let out a sigh and then unlocked her phone, opening her Tinder app and showing me the photo of Rick. I furrowed my brow and, suddenly, the reasoning became very clear.

"You were bamboozled."

"I'm sorry, what? The term is catfished." Jamie pulled her phone away and locked it, setting it face down on the countertop.

"Same thing." I smiled at her, holding in my chuckle as I took a sip of my beer, keeping my eyes on her.

She heaved a sigh and shook her head. "I don't need this from you, too." She grabbed her handbag and shoved her phone inside, standing up from the bar stool, "I would say it was great to see you, but it wasn't. Thank you for saving the day and your set was great. See you later, Elliot."

"It wasn't great to see me?" I asked as she began to turn away. "So you *have* been ghosting me?"

"Ghosting is a relative term," she grumbled over her shoulder.

"Five months with absolutely no contact is pretty much the definition of ghosting."

"How old are you? Forty? And you're the one holding a grudge over it?" She turned back to me, her eyebrows pinched and anger in her eyes.

"I'm thirty-six, and I honestly think I have every right to know what I did that warranted the silent treatment?"

Our eyes locked on to each other. She glared. I glared. Jamie was the first to break the staring contest and she slumped her shoulders as she let out the longest groan I had ever heard. This groan even topped Clay's, and Clay has given some pretty epic groans.

Staying silent, I raised an eyebrow and watched as she plopped her small bag on the bar top and flopped back onto her stool.

"Listen," she began, "maybe some ghosting did happen but that doesn't mean it had anything to do with you."

"Ghosting has everything to do with the person being ghosted—"

She held up a finger to stop me. I bit my lips together and waited.

But she didn't continue. She rolled her eyes and turned her body away from me, facing the bar. Her Mango-rita was still on the counter in front of her and her fingers found the stem, lightly rubbing up and down.

"Okay, so then . . . can I know the story with Rick?"

"It's long."

"Well, the guys are done packing up and I don't have anywhere to be." I grabbed my mug, raising it ever so slowly. Maybe if I kept her eye contact, she'd give in. She opened up five months ago, she could open up again.

She raised her glass and took a small sip before taking a deep breath. "I have a family reunion coming up—it's this big, long event and I go every year. Everyone does. My sister and her family, my brother and his family . . . my other brother who stays as far away from everyone as possible. We're all there. For three weeks. And I . . . months ago . . . told my sister I had a boyfriend, and now they expect him to come to the reunion."

I pieced the rest of it together from that. She didn't even have to say anything else. I shook my head and chuckled, "So you're in need of a boyfriend?"

"No, I'm not actively looking for a boyfriend. I just thought . . . maybe I could find someone to pretend to be my boyfriend for the family vacation." She laughed at herself. "It sounds insanely stupid now that I'm saying it out loud. Madeline would be very proud of me."

"For becoming a book trope?"

Her eyes fluttered over to mine, before a roll took them back to her drink.

"So"—I put my mug down, a bang hitting the counter louder than I intended—"you're leaving for a family reunion, and your family thinks you have been in a long term relationship, when you haven't, and they expect to meet him there?"

"That sums it up. Ugh. I'll just convince Milo to let me call him once a day and send him photos. I'm pretty sure Madeline would let me borrow her husband."

My mouth moved before my brain could stop it. I was still drawn to Jamie, even though she clearly had no interest in me, maybe that would be the excuse I would tell myself for the rest of time.

"What's my name going to be?"

Her head spun in my direction. Her hair flipped and her eyes were literally bugging out of her head. "I'm sorry, excuse me?"

I cocked my shoulder. "I figured, since I've already pretended to be your boyfriend once tonight, I can do it again, in front of your family. But I'm assuming that this fake boyfriend of yours already has a name. So . . ." I elongated the "o", "What's my name going to be?"

Chapter Eight

-Jamie-

What the *hell* did he just say? Did he just ask me what his name was going to be?

"You've got to be kidding me." I said, a chuckle in my throat.

Elliot cocked a smile, that stupid grin of his staring me down. "Not at all," he answered.

"There is no way on this earth that *you* are pretending to be my boyfriend for my reunion. It's not happening."

But wasn't he the first person that popped into my head when I even thought about finding a boyfriend? Wasn't he the one I envisioned when I created a fake boyfriend? He could be Daxton . . . couldn't he? I furrowed my brow and scrunched my lips.

"Oh okay, I'll go get Rick. I think he's still talking to that other girl who paid him attention—" He began to stand up, his finger pointing behind me to where I assumed Rick would be.

Out of impulse—possibly—I grabbed his left wrist. I looked at my fingers wrapped around his skin, the tattoo of an unfinished guitar making me pause. I kept my hand on him, pulling him back down to the bar stool, where I finally looked up and met his gaze.

"I take it you don't want me to get Rick?"

Biting the inside of my lip, I shook my head.

"Listen," he sighed, putting his free hand on top of mine still holding onto his wrist. "I don't quite understand why you don't like me, but I still very much like you, even as just a friend. I have a job that allows me to step away from a few days—"

"Weeks," I corrected him.

He chuckled, and looked down, shaking his head before looking at me again. "Weeks," he repeated. "And I'm serious, I can help you out. I just need to know what my name is."

With a long sigh I let go of his arm, the warmth from his hand leaving mine as I slapped my palm on my lap. "Just don't laugh, okay."

"Have I laughed yet?"

"You just did."

"That doesn't count. Jamie . . . what's my name?" he asked again, his tone becoming nothing but serious.

"Daxton."

Then, as if all cards were off the table and he had forgotten everything he just told me, Elliot burst out in laughter, his chin falling and his shoulder shaking. I watched him, my jaw open as he laughed, using his fingers to dry his eyes. He lifted his head and his smile widened. My previous thought of "it's not happening" entered my mind again. I couldn't believe I even contemplated the thought . . .

"Yea, thanks for this, but I'm not going to sit here—" I grabbed my bag from the bar top and began to stand.

"No, no . . . Jamie," Elliot stammered, trying to get the words out through his laughter. "I'm not laughing at the name; I'm laughing at the coincidence."

I furrowed my brow and sighed. "The *what*?"

"Jamie. My name is Elliot D. Whittaker. Elliot *Daxton* Whittaker." He smiled, watching the realization finally hit my brain.

"Daxton is your middle name?"

He nodded, a small laugh leaving his throat. "It's fate. I'm meant to be your fake boyfriend."

I heaved a sigh and looked up at the ceiling, letting out a long, well overdue groan before looking back to Elliot.

"I can't believe this."

"I can. It's going to be a blast."

"So, wait." Madeline furrowed her brow as we moved forward in the line. The author she so badly wanted to see was sitting at the table surrounded by other women, her husband standing behind her—willing to stop and take photos for her fans. We were further back in the line and, as Holly was engrossed in her Kindle, I told Madeline everything—starting with the kiss after the wedding, to creating a fake boyfriend, and Elliot being so willing to take the role. "Elliot is going to be your fake boyfriend for three weeks? And you're totally okay with this?"

"No I'm not okay with it, but he's insisting, and I'm desperate. I was close to asking Milo if he would pretend via the phone." I folded my arms over my chest, embarrassment settling in. In reality, this entire thing was stupid.

"You know he would have too, but your family knows Milo." Madeline gave me a sideways glance, her brain practically buzzing.

"It would just be a few phone calls here and there and letting me send random photos too, but not that it matters anyway because Elliot is going to pretend to be Daxton. Oh, and get this - his middle name *is* Daxton."

Madeline shook her head and let out a small laugh. "You do know he's going to love this don't you? He always asks about you, and then told us he was pretty sure you were ghosting him."

"I wasn't ghosting him. I was just . . ." I trailed off, knowing full well that Madeline knew, from Elliot, that he hadn't heard from me in months. Granted, she didn't know until just now that I had gotten a ride home from him—and a kiss—but Elliot had let it slip that I was avoiding him. "Busy," I finished.

"Jamie," Madeline sighed. "I know for a fact you weren't 'busy,' and you would always turn down going to see his band play. I wasn't blind to it. I knew something was going on, I'm just glad you finally told me . . . but now we need to figure out this fake boyfriend scenario."

"There's nothing to figure out. We said we'd meet in a few days and go over logistics and then we're off to Park City. He owns a business, I'm pretty sure he won't stay the full three weeks, and then there's the agent he talked to last night . . ." I motioned towards the line as it moved forward, Madeline took a few steps, placing a hand on Holly's shoulder so she'd stay with us.

"An agent?"

I nodded. "Yeah, one from a record label. Apparently, they want to get signed and they seem to have a label interested enough to come to the Piano Bar. We didn't talk about it much . . . he was more interested in—"

"That's amazing!" Madeline interrupted, shouting louder than she meant to. Others in line turned to look at her, scowling in annoyance. She scrunched her shoulders and clenched her teeth. Turning to me she said, softer, "They deserve it, I know that's been a dream of Elliot's for a while now."

"But he owns a business, how will he get signed to a record label if he's working at his company?"

"That's something to ask him. I'm assuming you'll have to get to know him a little before the vacation. You can't go in pretending to know a man you've been dating for five months. You two need to get your story straight." She raised her finger in the air proving her point.

"Which is why we will be meeting, but again, I'm not worried. I know enough about Elliot to sneak through. I'll just have to tell him my family's names and remind him, constantly, that his name is Daxton," I told her, taking a few more steps to the table. "It's almost your turn."

"You know enough to 'sneak through?'" Madeline turned towards the table. "So, tell me . . ." she began. "What's his band's name?"

"*Savaged Whittakers.*"

"And what kind of company does he own?"

"Um . . ." I thought. "A . . . paper . . . company?"

Madeline pinched her brow. "He doesn't work for Dunder Mifflin. What kind of car does he drive?"

"Easy, a Jeep."

"And how does he take his coffee?"

I looked at her, shrugging my shoulders when her glare deepened.

"What's his favorite TV Show? What kind of books does he prefer? Does he like dogs or cats? What's his favorite color? What brand of shoes does he wear most often?"

"Maddie . . ."

"These are the kinds of things couples know about each other. I've read enough fake dating tropes to know that if you don't ask him these questions, it's not going to end well. You two need to get your story straight if you think your family is going to believe you at all."

I looked at her, our eyes locked. I knew she was right, I just didn't want her to be.

"It's your turn," I said slowly as the person in front of her left, opening the path to the author.

Madeline spun and walked up towards the table. Madeline had met Brooke Easten Turner during their honeymoon, and, by the sounds of it, Brooke remembered her. She stood from the table and walked around to give Madeline a hug, her husband giving them a smile as he raised his phone to snap a picture of them. They chatted, and Brooke even asked where Milo was.

I stood with Holly as Brooke signed her books and her husband, Caleb, stood behind her. He kept his hand on her shoulder, his eyes were heavy on his wife, a faint smile on his lips as he watched her interact with Madeline and other fans. Once Madeline said her goodbyes and shook Caleb's hand, he leaned down and kissed his wife's cheek, whispering something in her ear. Brooke turned and kissed her husband on the lips, giving him a sweet, *"I love you"* before she turned back to her next admirer.

I followed Madeline to the register where she purchased her books, glancing back at the author and her husband one last time. It was obvious that they were in love, the sweet looks he would give her and the subtle touches—reassuring themselves the other was there. The look in Caleb's eyes was the same look I had seen Milo give Madeline, and Ophelia give to Clay. Love and longing—pure happiness.

Even though I knew it was far from happening, I wanted that look too.

I looked away, making sure Holly was next to us as we made our way back into the hustle and bustle that was Portland. The air was cold, and clouds began to cover the blue sky—another storm was coming.

"When are you meeting with Elliot?" Madeline asked, bringing me back to reality.

"I'm not sure, I need to text him," I responded. "We just said 'soon.'"

"You leave in a few weeks right? No time like right now to start dating your fake boyfriend."

I furrowed my brow and grimaced at her. She reached out for Holly's hand as we made our way to her car. We went to Olive Garden for lunch and then back home to text Elliot . . . I rolled my eyes. Madeline caught my eye roll and chuckled.

"I don't get what you have against him," Madeline said through her small laugh. "He's a great guy."

"I get that," I responded, "I just . . ." I sighed. "I don't know."

Chapter Nine

-Elliot-

Me: *We should get together sooner rather than later - this requires you texting me back.*

It had been five days since seeing Jamie at the Piano Bar. Which means it had been five days since agreeing to be her fake boyfriend, and I was being ghosted . . . again.

I looked at the texts I had sent her since we met that night, all gone unanswered. At one point she had begun to respond, I watched as those little dots jumped up and down on my screen, but then they stopped and no text came through. I had even tried to call her, but only reached her voicemail.

I scrolled back down to the bottom of the thread before closing my phone, shoving it into my coat pocket and turning off my Jeep. I left the office early, still dressed in my slacks and tie. The only indication I was off work was my rolled-up sleeves. My mom was expecting me, and I would be lying if I said I wasn't surprised when I saw Jacob's car in the driveway next to hers. When I called and told her I needed to talk to her—about something important—I knew she would call Jacob. He was the eldest in the family, the most wise, and the one who would have way more to say about dad's business than Mom did. I had a feeling Mom would give me her blessing in selling, but I didn't think Jacob would react the same.

I could only hope.

I opened the door, closing it loudly behind me, taking in the instant smell of home. Mom was baking something, and my stomach instantly reacted with a growl. I could hear Jacob's voice, talking to her about his latest visit with Dad. He had made it a point to visit him at least once a week, both for family purposes and research. I knew that, while he sat there with Dad, he talked to other doctors, and even nurses, who attended to Alzheimer's patients on a daily basis. From the sounds of it, Jacob was able to talk to Dad about things Dad remembered, like his wife and young kids and his favorite thing: work.

I took a deep breath and prepared myself for the worst. If Dad was recently talking about his business, it was going to be harder to want to sell it. I glanced at my phone one last time before walking in the kitchen.

Still nothing from Jamie.

Elliot . . .That's the least of your worries right now.

"He was drawing," Jacob said as I entered the room. His back was to me, as he leaned against the counter, facing Mom, but when her face lit up, he stood up and turned. "Dad was drawing, Ell."

I smiled. "I heard, that's great news. You went and saw him?" I pulled out the chair next to Jacob and sat down, folding my arms in front of me. "How's he doing?"

"Fine, I guess. He thought I was one of his doctors so we talked about things. It was just good to sit with him. You should go." Jacob nodded at me.

I inhaled. "Yea, I need to. I haven't been in awhile."

"He'll want to know how business is going." Mom smiled.

"It's going great." I returned her smile. "Probably better than before. I know our profit has gone up, and I have a few meetings this week with a few other clients, but then I need to hand things over to Kevin for a few weeks while I go remote."

"You're going to be working from home?" Jacob turned to look at me. He knew I worked at the office, and *only* the office.

"Just for a getaway with a friend, I mean, once I get details about the trip. I can work from anywhere as long as I have good WiFi—easy breezy. Technically they don't even need me there." I wiggled my eyebrows at mom, hoping she would understand that the company didn't need *me* to run. Unfortunately her answer was the exact opposite of what I hoped for.

"Oh yes they do." Mom turned her back and grabbed a glass from the cabinet. She filled it full of water and then placed it in front of me. "You have run that business so well, your dad knew what he was doing when he left it to you."

"I was the only one who could take it," I retorted, sliding the glass towards me.

"It was always your dad's dream to keep it running in the family, and when he saw how creative you were turning out to be, he knew it'd be you."

"Yea, Jacob was too busy dissecting worms in the backyard."

Jacob chuckled. "I was always meant to cut something open, wasn't I?"

I shook my head, blinking a few times to remember exactly what I needed to talk about, "Well the business is actually why I'm here."

My Mom's eyebrows furrowed instantly, worrying being her first train of thought. "Is everything okay? You said you have meetings . . ."

"Yes, Mom, everything is great. So great, in fact, that I've had a few people approach me."

"For?" Jacob asked, his voice going monotone.

"You've heard of Anthony Rummer right?" I looked at Jacob and Mom as they both nodded their heads. Anthony was a fellow architect that went to school with Dad. "He offered to buy the company from me."

Jacob let out a long sigh, his head tilting away from me and Mom. She pursed her lips and kept nodding.

"I declined the offer; it was way too low . . . but it got me thinking about really selling it. I talked to Clay and he's going to look into the value of the business. I really think I can sell it for a decent chunk and—"

"And what?" Jacob interrupted. "Dad wouldn't sell it."

"Well, Dad's not really able to make that decision, is he?" I turned to Jacob, my voice coming out more forceful than I meant. His eyes met mine before he blinked and turned to the counter, his body turning stiff.

Mom took a deep breath for, by my count, seven seconds, then let out a long exhale. "What would you do if you sold?" she finally asked softly.

"Well . . ." I swallowed. "I'd do music. I'd use a part of the money to pay off your house, take care of any expenses you would need and then I would hire a decent agent and maybe pursue the band a little more."

"The band?" Jacob muttered, his gaze not flattering from whatever it was focused on. "You would sell something that dad worked so hard on, something that you just heard mom say was his dream to keep in the family, just so you can play your guitar?"

"It's not just playing guitar, Jacob. We have something with the band, and we could become big if we tried. We had a talent agent come to the Piano Bar the other night and he wanted to meet us. He's interested in us." I held my ground. This was who I was, even if it wasn't who Dad *wanted* me to be.

Dad left me his architecture firm for a reason. He saw that I was the creative one—the one who saw things differently. The one who had a mind like his.

Except, I was never interested in drawing or doodling like Dad was. I wanted to create other things. I wanted to create sound. I was always banging on rocks and using trash cans as drums. When

I was seven mom enrolled me in piano lessons and it exploded from there. Music became my world. I played the guitar in high school and then gave lessons to others. I would play and make Milo listen to all my song ideas during slow nights in an ambulance while I studied business in college—boring myself to death simply because I knew that's what my Dad wanted me to do. I wasn't creative in the way he wanted me to be creative. I found my own voice and own rhythm, only to have it pushed aside . . . again . . . when I had to take over the company.

"Elliot?" My mom's voice brought me back to earth. "Are you saying you could get a record deal?"

"Potentially. I mean it's a huge possibility. But I can't do that *and* run the firm. If I sell, I can focus on my dream—what I *want* to do."

Jacob scoffed and pushed himself from the counter, turning his back to leave the kitchen. I watched as he stormed out, taking the tension with him. As soon as I heard the front door close, I turned back to Mom.

"Don't mind him," she whispered, a faint smile forming.

I locked her gaze, knowing without him she would listen, and understand. "I'm serious, Mom, but this is a big decision, and, honestly . . . it involves the entire family. Jacob has every right to be upset."

"Elliot, you know I'm proud of you for everything. You took over the company even when it was the last thing you wanted to do. You still went to the office with your father with a smile on your face and learned the ins and outs, and look what you've done with it since he's retired. But I can see when you're here, and I hear it when you play me a song. Your passion lies with that band of yours, not behind that desk." Her voice was soft, very maternal, and just by the look in her eyes, I knew she meant every word. "I'll support the sale, but you need to promise me something first."

I raised my eyebrows, taking a deep breath.

"Your father left *you* the company. The house has been paid off for years, I'm set with my retirement and savings I have. I don't need any of that money."

"Mom." I stopped her. "Clay is looking into the numbers. I know it's worth more than half a million—that's why I declined Anthony's offer—but I couldn't take all the money for myself."

She pursed her lips. "I'll only take one percent."

"Mother."

"Elliot Daxton."

Daxton. Jamie.

I reached my hand down, placing it in my pocket to feel for my phone. Did I miss a notification during this?

"I know you hate it when I use your middle name." My mom laughed, reminding me that checking my phone was the least of my worries. "But it got you to shut up."

"What happened to the sweet mom I had five seconds ago?" I asked sarcastically.

"Elliot, even though Jacob stormed off, you have my blessing to do whatever you want—or need—to do with the company."

I stood, feeling a weight lift from my chest, and walked around the counter, wrapping my mom in my arms. I was just tall enough that my chin could rest on the top of her head as she nestled herself into my arms.

I stayed a while longer and we talked, mainly about the company now that I had her go-ahead to sell, and, after we decided it was happening, we both agreed I would be the one to tell Dad.

"I'll be leaving in a few weeks for a vacation"—*maybe*—"I need to figure out the plan though, and then when I get back I'll finalize all of the plans. I'm not expecting all of this to happen fast—we have plenty of time. I can visit dad this Sunday and talk to him." I rubbed the back of my neck as I made my way to the door, with Mom following me every step of the way.

"A vacation? You haven't taken a vacation in a long time," she said as she grabbed my left arm, taking a look at my tattoo. "Aren't you ever going to finish this thing?"

I looked at the unfinished guitar on my arm and smiled. "I like it like that. Sunday? Visiting dad?"

She hummed. "Sunday, around noon."

I inhaled. "By then I'll have my vacation figured out. Like I said . . . I have time."

I stepped out onto the porch and grabbed my keys from my pocket, unlocking the Jeep as I turned back to my mom. She leaned against the door frame and folded her arms.

"Where are you going?"

"Um . . . not sure yet," I admitted. "Wherever she wants to go."

"*She*? Elliot Daxton, are you hiding someone from me?"

I laughed and shook my head. "Not yet, Mom. But don't worry, she's one I'd want you to meet if I can ever get her to answer me."

Turning the Jeep on, I waved goodbye to my mom, then checked the clock on the dash. Almost five—I knew exactly where to go. One obstacle was out of the way, now onto the other.

I pulled up to the building, knowing very well it was closing time. If I played the clock right, I could be walking in as soon as Jamie was walking out. And if she was still in the office? Well . . . I needed a teeth cleaning anyway.

I swung open the glass doors, hearing voices as I came close to the stairs. One of them I knew belonged to just the person I wanted to see. I stuck a hand in my coat pocket and slowed my stride. Casual. Cool. Collective.

"Ah." I smiled as soon as Jamie and Madeline came into view. "Just who I wanted to see."

Jamie's eyes grew wide as she froze in place, while Madeline came up and gave me a quick hug.

"Elliot! Good to see you," she said into my shoulder.

"Good to see you too, Mads." I hugged her back, taking her in for a moment before releasing her and turning back to Jamie. "But I really came here for Jamie."

Madeline laughed as she turned to face her friend, who was still frozen.

"Oh I know, *Daxton*. Milo got a kick out of that by the way." Madeline patted my shoulder. "I'll see you tomorrow, Jamie. Have fun. Bye Elliot."

"Bye, Mads, tell Milo I'll call him." I waved as Madeline left, leaving just Jamie and I in the lobby. I gave Jamie a smile. "I had to get a hold of you somehow."

"By stalking me?" Jamie finally said.

"It's not stalking if I simply came to make an appointment." I smile.

"Elliot . . ."

"Come on, Jamie. You can't keep ignoring me if I'm going to be your fake boyfriend. So, let me take you to dinner and we can figure this whole thing out."

"I . . ." she stumbled. ". . . have plans."

I raised an eyebrow, lowering my chin slightly. We stared each other down for a few seconds, her body tensing up more and more as mine grew relaxed. I laughed, thinking about the first time I had actually talked to Jamie—when I was the one who was tense. I was the one stumbling over my words, simply trying to get everything out. And now here we were, months later, roles completely reversed.

Jamie took a quick breath, shuffled her feet and slumped her shoulders. "Fine, I don't have plans." She walked towards me, patting my shoulder as she passed. "But I'm choosing the restaurant, and you're paying."

I smiled, turning to follow her. "I wouldn't have it any other way."

Chapter Ten

-Jamie-

Elliot sat across from me, his arms folded in front of him and that same smirk on his face. I chose a burger joint for dinner—something simple, nothing fancy, and nothing that served hard liquor. I kept my hands in my lap, my tongue running over my teeth as I tried to find words . . . any words to say. Elliot just waited.

I took a deep breath and raised my hands onto the table, my fingers playing with the silver edge on the linoleum in front of me.

"Okay, I'm sorry I've been avoiding you," I start.

"Ah, so you admit it?" Elliot's smile grew.

"Yes, okay? I admit it. It's an awkward situation," I defended myself, my hands flying back into my lap.

"Not if we talk about it and get the details out of the way."

"What details?"

"Well, for one, when are we leaving? Where are we going and staying? Your family is going to be there too, I take it? They will expect me to know something about them . . ."

He kept rambling, listing off facts that I knew I would have to give him, but my brain only focused on what Madeline had told me a few days earlier: *"You two need to get your story straight if you think your family is going to believe you at all."*

"Okay, okay, I get it." I stopped him. I had begun to tune him out, but my sudden "okay" stopped him. His lips formed a line, and he leaned back into the seat.

"Let's start small." He leaned back into his seat. "Where are we going?"

"Hey, you two, I'm Jordan, I'll be taking your order this evening. What can I get you?"

I looked at the man who stood at the end of the table. Jordan stood with a large smile on his face, his eyes fixed on me. His eyes roamed my face, stopping on my lips a few times, and traveling farther down my body. I was still in my scrubs, my plain, black shirt with a white tank underneath. My hair, still in a loose ponytail, fell over one shoulder, most likely looking like a tangled mess after work. I was tired and uncomfortable and sitting at the table with Elliot, but Jordan didn't seem to mind that as he checked me out. I shifted in my chair and lifted my hands back to the table. At this moment, I wanted to hide. I could feel Elliot's eyes on me and then suddenly he moved his arm across the table, taking my hand in his.

"Burger and a coke, babe?" Elliot asked me.

I looked from him to Jordan, who was now looking at anything *but* me.

Babe?

"A lemonade." I hummed.

Elliot smiled. "Two burgers, two orders of fries, and two lemonades, please."

Jordan nodded. "You got it." And then he was gone.

I half expected Elliot to pull his hand away, but he didn't. His calloused fingers lightly rubbed my palm and his thumb pressed into the back of my hand. It was warm, comforting, and I didn't want him to let go. *Why didn't I want him to let go?*

"Where are we going?" he asked again, his voice gentler than before. No longer sarcastic and snarky, but instead, kind and comforting.

I looked at our hands and blinked, bringing my attention to him. "Utah. Park City."

"Oo . . . a ski town. Are we going to go skiing?"

"We could, but I like to ice skate, or there is a tubing park. My brother will probably ski though, so you can go with him."

Any nerve that was filtering through my body seemed to drain as Elliot's thumb kept pressure on my hand. Almost as if that one pressure point was the release of all the tension. The ease of talking to him came naturally, and damn . . . I loved the feeling of his hand in mine.

"I'll go if you go. I can ice skate too." Elliot smiled. *That smile.* "Park City, Utah. When do we leave?"

"In two weeks," I said softly, my eyes meeting his.

"Oh wow. Two weeks?"

"That's too soon, isn't it?" I pulled my hand away and hid it back under the table. His fingers dropped to the table but stayed in place.

"Here's your lemonades." Jordan came up and placed the two drinks in front of us.

"Thank you," Elliot mused, gently moving his hand to grab the straws Jordan placed on the counter.

"Your burgers will be right up," Jordan said, his voice not as enthusiastic as it was the first time. Thankfully, this time, his eyes didn't land on me.

"No—" Elliot tapped the straw on the counter and slipped it into his drink. "Two weeks isn't too soon. Gives me plenty of time to prepare the team and the band, get some things in order with Clay. You said it was a three-week adventure?"

I nodded, "Yes, three weeks with my family."

"Tell me about them."

"Who?"

He let out a small laugh. "Your family."

"Well . . .there's my mom and dad, two brothers, and sister. My nieces and nephews will be there too."

"So, I call them mom, dad, brothers, and sisters?"

"Don't be a jerk . . . no. Mr. and Mrs. Gaines for my parents, unless they tell you otherwise. My brother, Holden, is the oldest. His wife Carrie and their three kids will be there. So will my sister, Jillian, and her husband, Will, and their twins. And then there's my brother Harrison, he's not married but he will be there." I listed them off on my fingers, totaling the ten bodies not including my parents.

"Holden, Jillian, Harrison. I like the H and J theme your parents went with."

"Believe it or not I don't think it was intentional."

He cocked an eyebrow and took a long swig of his lemonade, his lips still smirked even with the straw between his lips.

"What? I really don't think it was. It goes, Holden, Jilly, me, and then Harrison." I chuckled, surprised the sound left my lips. "My mom always said if it was intentional, I would be an H name and Harrison would be a J name."

Taking a quick glance around the restaurant, I caught sight of Jordan. He stood behind the bar top, waiting for some plates to run to various tables, but his eyes were fixed on us.

"Our waiter is watching us," I whispered.

"I know," Elliot whispers back.

"Is that why you grabbed my hand?"

"Just playing the part."

I lifted my chin. "Getting into character?"

He nodded. "Holden, Jillian, and Harrison. Mr. and Mrs. Gaines. What else? Tell me about Park City."

I roll my lips between my teeth. "My family rents out these cabins in Deer Valley—three total. My parents, Harrison, and I normally stay in the big one, and then Holden and Jilly each get their own for their families. Jilly normally takes the small one with the loft because her kids are still little—they can share a blow-up mattress—but I'll be honest they mainly sleep with my parents in the big cabin."

I could just picture the cabins in my head. It would be snowy, with footpaths going from cabin to cabin. The larger one sat in the middle, making it easy for everyone to gather there. I mainly stuck to the main cabin. Harrison and I would find something to keep us busy while Holden and Jilly took care of their kids—a fire with card games, some wine, and travel stories from Harrison. A quick glance at Elliot gave me a glimpse of the future—him sitting next to me as Harrison told a crazy story. His arm draped on the back of the sofa, possibly his fingers brushing my shoulders, chills running down my spine as his fingers would find my neck and hair, not caring that Harrison was in the room with us . . .

I blinked away the thought. That wasn't what this was.

"Deer Valley? Isn't that fancy?" Elliot asked, leaning closer on the table.

I reached for my lemonade, taking the straw and mimicking Elliot from earlier. I was suddenly very thirsty. "Very, but we enjoy it while we've got it. We go to Main Street and we'll take some trips to Salt Lake—have you ever been?"

Elliot shook his head, a single corner of his lips raised. Was this man always smirking?

"I think you're going to like it. Oh, and there's an art's festival happening while we will be there, I'd love to go to that a few times."

"So, I can go?" He raised his eyebrows and leaned in on the table.

"Here's your burger's guys, enjoy." Jordan put the plates in front of us, taking one glance at me.

"Thank you." I gave Jordan a quick smile and then scooted my plate to the side, bringing my hand up to grasp Elliot's. "I think you're in too deep *not* to go, don't you agree?"

He laughed, his thumb pressing on the same spot as before. "Agreed." He loosened his grip on my hand to lean back into the chair, "In that case, we're going to have to meet up more often. And please, stop ghosting me."

I furrowed my brow and scrunched my nose. "Okay. I'm sorry. No more avoiding or ghosting. We have two weeks to figure out how to pretend to be a couple."

Elliot popped a French fry in his mouth. "Two weeks. Like I said before, it's going to be a blast."

Elliot dropped me back at the office, watching as I got into my car, and even followed me out of the parking lot. As soon as I walked in the door, I called Jillian. I had to act excited that Elliot—I mean Daxton—would be coming to Park City.

"Hey, Jame," Jillian's voice echoed in my ear.

"Hey, Jilly, just thought I'd give you the good news. I talked with Dax and he's down to come to Park City with me."

"You're kidding!" she screamed. "Oh, mom is going to be thrilled."

"He's excited." I kicked off my shoes and turned the light on. "He wants to go skiing, so I hope Holden and Harrison are up for it."

"Have you seen the snowpack Utah got this year, Holden is definitely wanting to ski. Not sure about Harrison, but Holden wants to take the kids. He's already rented the gear from the resort . . . well he has it reserved."

"Oh perfect, I'll tell Ell . . . Daxton and I'm sure he will want to jump right in on that day."

"You sure he'll want to spend time with the kids? I thought you would want to show him around Park City."

"Oh, I will, but I know he wants to ski. I'm sure he won't mind the kids."

I bit my bottom lip. We never went into detail on my nieces and nephews. I lowered my phone and put Jilly on speaker, pulling up Elliots text thread for the first time since the wedding.

Me: *How do you feel about kids?*

"My kids are tough. Add Holden's into the mix and that's a whole other ball game," Jillian said.

Elliot: *Well isn't that funny - all of your messages just turned to "read." I love kids. I have nieces and nephews of my own. We'll have a snowman building contest.*

"Dax just said he's totally in love with kids," I responded as I typed out my answer to Elliot.

Me: *You sure you want to ski down a mountain with them?*
Elliot: *100%. As long as I get to choose the bar afterwards.*

I laughed.

"What?" Jillian asked. "Is Daxton there? Can I say hi? FaceTime? I need to meet him!?"

"No, I'm texting him. He said he's happy to go skiing with kids as long as he gets to pick the bar afterwards. That's fine right? Mom and Dad can watch the grandkids and we can all go out for a night?" I closed the text thread and put my phone back to my ear. "We always do anyway . . ."

"Oh, that's definitely happening. I need to spend time with this Daxton, make sure he's good enough for you. Speaking of—"

"I'm *fine,* Jilly," I interrupted her. "I updated Mom and everything."

Jillian let out a hum, "Okay, okay . . . you know I just have to ask."

"I know, but trust me, when something—anything—changes . . . you guys will be the first to know." I sighed.

"I know, James . . . you know we just worry."

"I know, I don't blame you. But listen, I'm fine. Daxton is great, and I'll see you in two weeks."

"Two weeks."

We said our goodbyes and, once my phone was free, I instantly went to the Spotify app. It had my usual song preferences on the home page, but my mind went to Elliot and his band. I typed *Savaged Whittakers* in the search bar and instantly the band profile came up. Elliot stood in the middle, his hands stuck in his jean pockets, his lips forming a thin, tilted smile—his eyes hyper-focused on the camera with a single eyebrow raised. The others—I couldn't remember their names—stood around him, all with the same demeanor.

I chuckled at the photo and hit the green PLAY button—shuffling all their songs that were loaded onto the app. The first one was called "Cosmic," and the next thing I knew, the melody and Elliot's voice filled my apartment. They sounded different than they had at the wedding, and the few times I had heard them at the Piano Bar. This wasn't exactly country, wasn't exactly rock, but it had an edge to it, and Elliot's voice was the perfect sound.

While the *Savaged Whittakers* serenaded me, I turned on my shower and stripped off my scrubs. Dinner with Elliot had lasted longer than I thought it would, and my evening at home was now shorter than normal. I mean, my night of rewatching *The Office* or *Schitt's Creek* was cut shorter than normal. So, instead, I opted for music, a shower, and time to paint.

I glanced at myself in the mirror as the steam filled the bathroom. The simple scar that trailed down in between my breasts had never faded over the years, and had caused more anxiety than anything else had in my life. I lightly touched the end of it, feeling the rise of my skin. It had been twelve years since the surgery that saved me, and the scar would never let me forget it. But if it wasn't for this scar, I would have never picked up a paint brush.

Shaking my head I turned from the mirror, taking a quick glance at the canvas on the easel that sat in my room. The landscape of the Utah mountains, surrounded by sunflowers—my favorite painting I had ever created. The one I planned to load up in my car and enter it in the art's festival—all because of a little scar. It made me wonder, as the warm water hit my scalp and as Elliot's singing filled my bathroom, if something like that had happened to Elliot to bring him close to music, or if it was always in his sights. Painting was always my hobby. It wasn't anything I wanted to make a career out of, but the more time I spent with my brushes and canvas, the more I wished I could do *only* that.

Only time could tell what would happen with my paintings. I wasn't expecting much to come from the art's fest, just seeing it on the wall of a gallery is all I needed to feel like I achieved something. Once that was done . . . only time would tell.

Chapter Eleven

-Elliot-

"So, that means, I'll be selling the company, as soon as possible." I shoved my hands into my slack pockets and looked at the team of architects sitting around the conference table. A phone sat in the middle, where I knew Clay was silently paying attention. Each and every soul in this building, and their eyes, were fixed on me. The tension was real, and I wanted to swipe it away.

"What does that mean for us?" Sharon asked. I knew she would be the first to ask something. She had worked for this company since the beginning and was one of the most well known architects here. Currently, she has three projects going—all of which were for big clients.

I shrugged my shoulders. I talked briefly with my mom about this, telling her I'd take care of everyone before I left. My dad wouldn't want the team he worked hard to build over the years to be let go simply because of a new owner.

"It will be written into the contract that the team keep their jobs and current salaries."

"You're not selling to Anthony are you? He's a scumbag?" Michael folded his arms and leaned back into his seat.

"No. No I'm not—"

"Don't worry, Mike, I put a stop to that real fast," Clay's voice echoed through the room from the phone, interrupting me. The team chuckled at Clay's response.

"He did put in an offer, and that's what started the idea, but I'm not going to take the first offer I'm given. I'm going to make sure you guys are taken care of," I offered.

A few people nodded, one even gave me an understanding smile.

"It's not going to happen overnight—hell it may take years. But I'd like to get the ball rolling as soon as I get back from a three week remote trip. Clay is going to be working behind the scenes with me in New York, helping appraise the business and finding the perfect agent to help. Once I get back I'll start seriously looking into putting everything up for sale, and . . ."

"Are you going to pursue music full time?" a team member asked who sat in the back. He had his eyebrows raised and a smile on his face. I had seen him at a few of my shows, but we had never talked about that here. He knew I preferred to keep things between the office and the band separate, but I couldn't help returning his smile.

"If all goes well, then yes," I answered simply. "Until then, we still have clients to meet with and projects to complete, now Sharon, tell me about the VanGurt project." I slid my normal seat out from the table, relaxing into the chair.

Sharon began to tell me all about the project she was currently working on, then it went to Michael and the others. The tension that had filled the room the moment I dropped the news I wanted to sell seemed to dissipate and we were back to business as usual.

Even when Clay gave his run down on the current finances for the projects, and when Ophelia made a guest appearance bringing him his cup of coffee, the entire team chuckled at his change in demeanor.

Once the meeting ended and everyone left to go their separate projects, I retreated to my office. Now that *that* big news was out of the way, I had to call Bennett and tell him I would be out for three weeks. I could hear his voice now . . .

"As long as you give me more lyrics and learn the new tunes, I don't care where you're going to be . . ."

I chuckled at the thought of how my friend's brain works, but before I could dig my phone out of my pocket to text Bennett, my office phone rang in my ear. It was loud and shrill—the perfect ring tone that you had to answer.

I hit the speaker button as I sat down. "This is Elliot."

"Do I need to come there and stop you from taking a two week sabbatical right before you start a huge, life-changing decision!?" Clay shouted into the room. His voice was loud. So loud that I noticed a few people turn their heads to me.

I waved at them and grabbed the phone, bringing it to my ear. "It's not a sabbatical. I'll just be working remotely for three weeks."

"Three? Did you just say three weeks?!"

"Yes. I've worked remotely before, you heard me in that meeting—"

"A warning would have been nice . . ." he grumbled. I pictured him reaching for his water glass, running his hands through his hair.

"I have Kevin prepped and ready to go with approvals and meetings with clients. It's not like I'll be gone forever, just three weeks."

"And where are you going for three weeks?"

"Utah."

"Utah!? What the fuck is in Utah?" Clay's voice was getting harsher, the new stresses that were coming with his new company finally showing and the news of his first client—and highest paying client—was leaving for a few weeks *while* selling his company probably didn't sit well with him.

"Jamie's family."

"Jamie?"

"Yea, I'm going as her boyfriend for a family reunion."

"Boyfriend? Family reunion?"

"Yes, in Utah. I'll take my laptop and make sure I get work done."

"Utah. You're going to take your laptop to Utah and work remotely?"

"Are you going to keep repeating everything I say?"

"Only until you fill me in on what's actually going on."

"I *am* filling you in. Jamie needed a boyfriend for her family reunion, and I volunteered."

"You *volunteered?*" Clay practically screamed so loud I would have been able to hear him from New York *without* my phone.

"Wait, what? Elliot did what?" Ophelia's voice faded through the background. "I've heard you say Jamie, Utah, and volunteered?"

"Tell Phe I say hi," I muttered.

"What's going on?" Her voice was stronger. I envisioned her yanking the phone from Clay's hand, him dropping his arm to the desk in defeat and taking a few deep breaths. I knew he always had a neck issue when he worked in Seattle . . . perhaps he rubbed his neck out of habit.

"I'm going to be working remotely for three weeks and your husband is freaking out," I replied.

Ophelia let out a long sigh. "There's more to the story than that so . . . here—" there was a pause and a fumble, no doubt Ophelia moving the phone, "—you're on speaker now. Tell. Us. Everything."

I heaved a sigh and started to explain the entire story. Every now and then Ophelia would give a little "Yup" or "Mmhmm" while Clay remained silent. It sounded insane, being the first time saying it out loud. Jamie had caught my attention the first moment I saw her, and I simply saw this as a way to get to know her. No more ghosting or purposefully avoiding me. This was my chance.

"Your middle name isn't Daxton." Ophelia laughed, disbelief practically flooding the speaker on my phone.

"I happen to know it is," Clay mumbled. "I asked while filling out the client paperwork. I had to know what that D stood for."

"Elliot Daxton Whittaker at your service." I was tempted to take a bow, but I was already getting funny looks from my team members, so I refrained.

There were a few beats of silence from my friends, and then Ophelia asked, "You're really excited about this aren't you?"

I smiled. Yea, I was excited. This was an adventure. "I'm excited to see a place I've never seen before. Jamie even mentioned going to an art's fest."

"She paints you know," Ophelia added point blank.

"No, I . . ." I stumbled. I had no idea Jamie painted. We had talked about my band and her family, but not once did I ask *her* questions. With as much as I wanted to know her, you'd think I'd ask her something about *her,* but I never had. I heaved a sigh. "I didn't know she painted."

"I wonder if she wants to submit one, oh that would be a complete dream for her." Ophelia's voice faded, more than likely because she was stepping away from the phone with her eyes in a daze. Ophelia was the one to follow dreams—she was the one you wanted to be there as you followed yours. Sprinkle in some tough love from time to time and Ophelia was the perfect cheerleader.

"Can I talk to Elliot again? It's great that he's finally getting Jamie's attention, but we have business to talk about now?" Clay's voice was harsher than I expected, and the chuckle that Ophelia let out brought a smile to my lips. I rubbed my forehead and peaked my eyes out into the office. Everyone had returned back to their own desks—most seemingly getting their work completed.

Three weeks away from this building was something that I needed.

"Clay"—my hand trailed to the back of my neck—"we talked about selling the company before. You're the one who told me to investigate it. And before you ask, yes, I talked to my mom. She gave me her go ahead and we will be telling my dad this weekend."

"You, selling the business I don't mind, it's the leaving for three weeks that's bothering me."

"I will—"

"I know, you'll have your laptop, and you will get some work done but are you sure this is a good idea?"

"When has a vacation ever been a bad idea?"

"Not the vacation. The fake . . . boyfriend . . . thing?" he drew out his words. I knew Clay. I could envision him circling his hand in front of him, that look of concentration on his face.

"It's a brilliant idea, don't overthink things Clayton!" Ophelia shouted in the background. "You know he's liked Jamie since day one."

"Phe . . ." Clay sighed. "I get that but if he wants to date her, he should go about it the right way, not by posing as her 'fake boyfriend.'"

"Listen, Jamie has no interest in dating me, she made that abundantly clear when she ghosted me for five months. We can be friends, and friends help each other out. And for some reason she needs a boyfriend and I happen to be single, *and* my middle name just happens to be Daxton."

"No, no, no. I'm going to need to see your driver's license. Or birth certificate." Ophelia laughed in the background.

Shaking my head I grabbed my wallet from my desk, flipping it open to look at my ID. The name *Daxton* was right there—clear as day. "I'll send you a picture. Look, Clay, it's going to be great. The vacation will be good for me and once I get back, we can meet with agents and sell this dump."

"It's not a dump," Clay mumbled.

"Ha, I know. Doesn't mean I can't wait to start something new."

My mom met me at the assisted living home, and as we walked in the door the rush of cold air hit me in the face. As much as I loved my dad, coming here always had that *feeling* to it. The nurses sat at the check in counter, waving to my mom and I as we walked past them into the living areas. Other residents mingled together or with their families, and when I spotted Dad—sitting across from a nurse playing a game of chess—I smiled.

Even though I knew he wasn't who he used to be, he still looked like my dad. His gray hair was thinning on top of his head, brushed back and tucked behind his ears. His glasses perched on his nose as he lifted a skinny finger to move the pawn. I knew he was concentrating, his eyebrows gave that away. Finally, he picked up the piece and moved it one space ahead. I let out a small laugh, so much concentration for such a small move.

"Good morning, Graham, honey," my mom said softly as she came up to him, leaning over and giving him a sweet kiss on the top of his head. He looked up, blinked a few times and then smiled. It was always fifty-fifty on if he remembered my mom and it looks like today he did.

"Good morning, Harriet."

Harriet? Aunt Harriet? His sister? Oh—perhaps he doesn't remember today.

My mom gave him a sigh. "No, honey, it's me, Linda. I have Elliot with me." She placed her hand on his shoulder and glided it past the back of his neck. My parents' love story could almost be from a book. They were loyal to each other, high school sweethearts from the beginning. The touch she gave him was one she would do often as he sat at the table waiting for dinner, or as he hunched over his desk drawing yet another building. It was a touch that always gained her his attention.

"Hey, pops," I said, pulling the seat out next to him.

He blinked a few times at my mom and looked over at me. "Oh yes, Linda." He smiled. "How are you, dear?"

"I'm wonderful, thank you."

"How's your chess game? Who's winning?" I asked, looking at the board. Clearly, seeing the nurse was winning.

"Oh, I can never win this game, not unless that doctor comes by. He always lets me win." He sighed and turned back to the board, noticing it was his turn.

"Jacob? Dr. Whittaker?" I asked.

"I think that's his name. He always asks me questions as we play. I think it throws him off." He picked up the knight and moved it, only to lose his bishop to the opponent's Queen. "Damnit," he mumbled under his breath.

"Dad, I have something I want to talk to you about," I started, leaning forward on my knees. "It's about the company."

He scrunched his eyebrows and looked over at me. "Company?"

I let out a sigh and looked up at my mom. She scrunched her nose and shook her head.

"Not today, huh?" I asked softly.

"Well today's a good day so far," he smiled. He actually smiled. "I'm Graham by the way, what's your name?"

"It's Elliot," I answered, pinching my brow. I had lost count of how many times I had introduced myself to my dad. My heart broke a little more each time. He would nod and hum and then return to whatever it is he was doing. Sometimes he would ask me if I was another doctor, but today, his response shocked me.

"Elliot. I've always liked that name."

I could feel my chin quiver, and I forced myself to hold back tears. I knew he was the one to name me, but I had never heard him say that about my name. My mom always told me the story as to how he honored one of his friends growing up by naming me after him. He could have given my name to Jacob, but he gave it to me instead.

"It's a good name." I sighed, keeping emotion out of it for now. "Can I play the next game?" I asked the nurse. He nodded and gave me a smirk.

He rose from the chair, glancing at his watch. "I'll be right back with your meds Mr. Whittaker, your son is going to step in for me okay, or maybe you can start the game over?"

"I don't know, this one looks smart enough to take me. He could be an architect." He started to move all the pieces back to their spaces. I slid over to the empty chair and Mom took the one next to Dad, sliding her hand into his.

"I'm kind of an architect," I answered back, moving a pawn two spaces ahead.

"In school?" He moved a knight.

I shook my head. "No, I own an architecture firm. My dad left it to me."

"Smart man." He furrowed his brow as I moved another pawn, then he moved one too.

"He is a smart man, but I'm nervous because I want to sell it. I don't want to own it anymore."

My mom glanced at me, tears welling up in her eyes.

"Well, why not?"

"It's not what I want to do—be in charge of it anymore. It's just not who I am. I want to sing."

"Sing? That other doctor talks about a singer." His pawn took mine and then he looked at me. "Singing is an empty career."

I chuckled. "That's what my dad says too." I stole a pawn with my knight and he let out a low hum.

"Graham, honey, Elliot is an amazing performer. He'd love being on the road. It's what he does," my mom explained, placing her hand on his, her thumb rubbing his knuckles.

Pinching his lips, he reached forward and moved another pawn. "Well, then the best thing to do would be to talk to your father. If it were me, I'd try to encourage my son, even if I didn't approve of his career." Lifting his chin he studied the chess board, no doubt trying to guess my next move.

But I was frozen. I never expected my dad to say something like that to me. He didn't even know it was what I needed to hear—

his encouragement, his approval—above anything else. That's all I needed.

"Really?" I stuttered.

He hummed. "I would want my kids to excel at whatever they were best at. I may be hard on them on the outside, but I would always be proud of them on the inside." He chuckled. "But this is all just me thinking of a future I may never have. If you really want to waste your life singing, you just need to talk to your father. He may be more supportive than you think."

I smiled, still in awe. He had moved his piece and was waiting patiently for me to take my turn.

"It's your move son," he mumbled without even looking up from the board.

I glanced at my mom, blinking a few times before turning back to the board. "Thank you, Dad, I'm pretty sure you're going to beat me."

After he had indeed beaten me at three games of chess, he announced he was tired. He gave my mom a hug and shook my hand, giving me another hint to "talk to my father" before he left and went to his private room. Once we got to our cars, I flashed my mom a smile.

"He'll never know what he gave me, will he?"

"He knows," she replied.

Chapter Twelve

-Jamie-

"Okay so if we leave early Saturday morning we can potentially be in Park City that same night." I showed Elliot the map on my laptop. "It's a ten-hour drive, but I figured with stops it will be closer to twelve. How early do you want to leave? You have a show on Friday, right?"

Over the past few weeks Elliot and I had at least tried to form a friendship. He would text me everyday, and I would respond. We even FaceTimed a few times as we did silly tasks around the house. If nothing else, it helped us become comfortable talking with each other. Most of the time, while I was home doing the dishes, he was still at the office finishing up a few things. I would watch as he would throw his coat on and, once he was outside, we said our goodbyes. The conversations were light, but had become routine. We never asked each other personal questions, and didn't say anything that even remotely hinted that we were going to be taking a three week vacation together soon. It was just as if he was a long-time friend who just wanted to catch up.

Like I said. Comfortable.

The FaceTime we had planned for tonight, to talk about our route, ended up with Elliot sitting at my dining room table. He had his chin resting in his palm, looking at the blue line that led from Portland to Park City. He quickly lowered his hand and turned the computer to face him.

"Well yea, but can't we just fly?" Elliot furrowed his eyebrows at the screen.

"No, we can't. I plan on taking a painting with us and driving will be easier to transport it and make sure it gets there safely. Plus, my Corolla gets pretty good gas mileage." Pulling my computer back towards me, I looked at Elliot as a single eyebrow raised.

"Do you have four-wheel drive?" he asked simply.

I met his gaze. "No."

"Utah has been having a heavy winter, so we may want to take my Jeep. It will be safer."

"I guess you have a point, my sister mentioned the snowfall being heavy." Once again, I looked at the Google map on the screen. 790 miles, and that was just to Park City—that didn't count the driving we would do around town. "I'll help pay for gas of course, and I guess there will be more room for the painting."

"Are you entering it in the art's fest?" he asked quietly.

He began to take in my apartment, observing all the paintings on the wall and art supplies scattered about. He left the table and walked around, slipping his hands in his jean pockets. Walking up to my large desk that faced the large window in the living room, his concentration was focused on everything that lay on the table. Completely covered with sketch pads and paint brushes propped up in cups, he lightly ran his fingers along the bristles. Next to my desk sat my pottery wheel, and a giant bag of clay next to that.

"I plan to." I swallowed, finally breaking the silence.

"How long have you been painting?" he asked, turning his body to look back at me.

I took a deep breath. Did I really want him to know this information about me? Did he *need* to know? A part of me was saying no—that was too personal—but the other part said he needed to know so if my family were to ask, he would know the answer. I could give him a vague answer–he didn't need to know the real reason.

"Since high school really. I found a paint brush and it took off from there."

Vague. Nice.

I watched him as he nodded, turning back to a painting of a woman holding a bouquet of roses. Her blonde hair flowed down from her large straw hat, creating the perfect shadows that were a bitch to paint. It was one of my favorite paintings, and seeing Elliot admire it put small flutters in my stomach.

"Did you paint all of these?" Elliot asked.

I hummed a yes. "Every one."

"I feel like I need to know more about you in order to pull off being your boyfriend." He twisted suddenly, no longer stiff and uncomfortable.

His face lit up as he walked back to the small kitchen table where I sat. I could see in his expression that he wanted to know. If I let him, he would sit and listen to me talk all night long. He would probably never lose interest. Any girl would love to have this kind of attention on them, especially Elliot's, and, even though I loved how his focus was on me, and me alone, I knew it wasn't real. He was just trying to learn his role as Daxton. That one thought popped me back into reality. The fact that we had to leave on a road trip in three days and he had a show to do before then . . . we didn't have time for the normal get to know you questions.

"Well, it's a good thing you're going to be stuck in a car with me for twelve hours isn't it, we will have plenty of time to talk then." I cleared my throat.

A corner of his mouth lifted, showing off a glimpse of his white teeth and one eyebrow cocked up. "Yea, I guess. These two weeks flew by didn't they? Until then . . ." Elliot wiggled his shoulders and sat up a little straighter. "Is there anything you need to know about me?"

I narrowed my gaze at him. I could ask that man so many questions. We could go back and forth, a truth or dare if you will—except without the dare. Elliot had years on me that were filled with whatever he had accomplished. I knew he owned a business, I knew he sang, I knew he was friends with Milo, thanks to his time as an EMT, and that he and Clay talked almost every day. But other than that, this man was still a mystery.

"Tell me about your tattoo," I blurted out.

"I already told you about the tattoo." He rolled up his sleeve, showing off the black unfinished guitar.

"You only told me it was a part of the band. You didn't elaborate. Most tattoos have meaning. Does this one?"

Running his palm over the ink, he grinned and nodded. "Bennett and I got them together once the band was formed. Chase has drumsticks on his shoulders and Jameson has music notes on his thigh. Bennett and I got them at the same time, and we picked the same design, except he finished it once we completed our first year. His guitar goes up to his shoulder." His palm ran from his forearm all the way to his shoulder, his muscles twitched as he touched the fabric.

I blinked, pulling my eyes from his arms to his eyes, "You never wanted to get it finished?"

He scrunched his nose and shook his head, "Nah, I like it this way. Ben's always on my case to get it done but I never will. It's perfect just the way it is." Rolling his sleeve down again he continued, "I have a lot of long sleeve shirts, so if your parents don't approve of tattoos, I can keep it out of sight. My dad never cared for it."

"I don't think my parents will mind. Tell me about your family. You know mine, so it's only fair I know yours."

He smirked. "Don't we have an entire twelve hours ahead of us to talk?" He wiggled his eyebrows once, giving me a wink.

I shook my head and sighed, releasing a small chuckle. I had a feeling Elliot would make me chuckle a lot over the next three weeks. He was free, and he was fun. My family was going to fall for him.

"Are you coming to the show tomorrow? Milo and Maddy are going to be there, I think Hannah and her husband will be there, too," Elliot said softly.

"All you need is Clay and Ophelia and your entire posse is there."

"Milo will FaceTime Clay for sure, but I want to know about you? You're not avoiding the place anymore, are you?" He pinched his brow, his eyes heavy.

It was a punch in the gut. I was avoiding the Piano Bar while he played, ever since that night we kissed. I didn't think I could trust myself to not want to talk with him again. He wasn't the one I wanted to get involved with and yet, here I was.

I rubbed my lips together, giving him a small nod. "I'll be there. Just promise me lots and lots of coffee Saturday morning."

He laughed, his perfect laugh that filled the room. "Deal. Speaking of, you said we needed to leave early . . . hopefully not *too* early."

"Finally!" Madeline pulled me close for a hug as I sat next to her on the small round table. "You become Elliot's fake girlfriend and you show up to a show."

"Fake girlfriend?" Hannah, Milo's ex-wife, asked. She sat next to Madeline leaving a chair open for her husband, who was currently up with Milo ordering drinks.

The stage was dark, the illuminated logo for *Savaged Whittakers* hanging behind the drum set the only light on the stage. The black lettering and half guitar looked amazing—something I had never noticed before. All of the guys' names were under the guitar: *Bennett, Elliot, Jameson, Chase.* I squinted, keeping the thought that Elliot's name should be first to myself.

I shook my head and looked at Hannah. "He's just helping me keep my family off my back. Are you guys here just for the night?"

Hannah nodded. "Yeah, Holly gets the next week off school so she's coming up to Seattle, we'll leave in the morning." Hannah smiled, twisting her body towards the stage. "I've only seen Elliot play at the wedding, is he still singing country?"

Madeline shook her head. "Nah, that was just for me." She smiled.

"For us," Milo corrected as he came up behind her, dropping a glass of white wine in front of her.

Donald, who still looked uneasy and irritated, sat next to Hannah. I've never seen that man smile and, by the looks of it, he was annoyed he was here. If I had to guess, he was only here because Hannah wanted to be. Milo had been married to Hannah and, together, they had Holly. After a nasty custody battle, they formed a friendship and were able to co-parent from different states. But even though Hannah and Milo got along like old friends, Donald was still just along for the ride.

"He said he may sing some new things tonight. I guess he writes the lyrics and Bennett makes the music," I added, remembering that little tidbit from five months ago.

"For being the fake girlfriend, you seem to know a lot," Milo said, his lips forming a cheeky grin.

I rolled my eyes. "Well, your wife put it in my head that we needed to get to know each other. So, we've been texting and talking a lot."

"So, are you fake dating him, or are you *dating* him?" Hannah asked, raising her wine glass to her lips.

"At the moment . . . neither. He doesn't become Daxton until we get to Park City, and then we will be fake dating." I lifted my mango-rita and licked the salt off the rim. I closed my eyes and hummed.

The lights around us dimmed and then a few shouts came from the large crowd. I smiled, knowing Elliot was on his way out. Taking a quick inventory of the room, I noticed the same man from two weeks ago, the talent agent—the one who was interested in them. I lightly tapped Madeline's arm and pointed to him. She squinted and nodded, seemingly understanding what I was trying to tell her.

"Good evening!" Elliot's voice hit my ears and pulled my attention back to the stage.

Chase was settled behind his drums, his blonde hair messy as always. Jameson looked stoic as he lifted his bass over his head and Bennett looked as if this was his thrill. Elliot had his guitar strapped over his shoulder, his fingers already pressed against the cords, while the other hand grabbed the mic. He smiled as he pressed his lips up against the mic in front of him.

"I hope you're ready for a good night."

The crowd cheered as Bennett and Jameson started the beat and the song began—the spotlight hitting Elliot in all the right places.

I couldn't take my eyes off him as he moved to the music. He would close his eyes, his deep voice filling the room with confidence and charm. He was where he belonged—up on that stage—bringing music into the world. Every now and then he would glance over at our table, his eyes would catch mine and I would force the butterflies down, reminding myself that I didn't need that right now and he was simply just a friend. I swallowed, and even though his eyes told a different story, I told myself the truth: this was all for show.

I sighed and took the final sip of my mango-rita. Simply a friend.

Chapter Thirteen

-Elliot-

I pulled up to Jamie's house at 5 a.m. on the dot. Yawning, I parked the Jeep and rubbed my eyes. Why we decided to leave so early just so we could get to Park City the same day was beyond me, but for some reason Jamie insisted. In my head we could stay in Boise, split the trip up into two days. But she desperately wanted to be in Utah. I knocked on her door lightly, the porch light making it so I could barely keep my eyes open.

The show ended around ten. Bennett and I met with the talent agent again, talking about the possibility of traveling to the studio, and after that I had a drink with Milo before Madeline whisked him away. I made sure to give Jamie some of my attention, but she snuck out to get some sleep before the trip. It was oddly good to see Hannah again and then, when I got back home to see my suitcases packed and ready for me, I thanked Past Elliot for packing in advance. All I had to do was plop in bed and go to sleep.

The three hours of sleep I managed to get would be enough for a twelve-hour road trip . . . I hoped. I promised Jamie coffee and the Lord knew I would need plenty of it.

Jamie opened the door to her apartment, her hair up in a messy bun and a large canvas in her hands.

"Good morning." She yawned.

"Morning," I replied.

"Can you get my suitcases while I get the painting?" She motioned her head into her living room where two suitcases sat, a large handbag perched on top.

I nodded and stepped inside, tossing the handbag over my shoulder and using both hands to roll a suitcase out.

"Do you have everything?" I asked as I passed her.

She perched the canvas, which was wrapped up gingerly in a fabric tarp, on her knee. "Yup. I packed before the show."

"Great minds think alike." I yawned. "We should count how many times we yawn today."

Jamie let out a loud groan. "Let's not, that may be worse. Bring our attention to the yawning and how tired we are. Let's just go get coffee and dream about the beds we will get to sleep in tonight."

"We never mentioned sleeping arrangements." I opened the trunk to the jeep and lifted her suitcases inside. Jamie carefully slid the painting in the backseat, making sure it wasn't leaning the wrong way.

"Well," she sighed, fixing the fabric that was protecting it, "normally my brother and I share the main cabin with my parents, so I'm assuming you and I will be sharing a room."

"Ah, so I'll be on the floor Ryan Reynolds *The Proposal* style, huh?" I chuckled to myself. Not only was I proud that I knew to make that joke, but the face Jamie gave me in response was one in a million. It said *"Elliot you idiot"* while also saying *"I half want you in the bed with me."*

"You got it. Thankfully there's no blanket my parents call 'the baby maker.'" Jamie shut the door and yawned, yet again.

"That's two for you," I joked. "I have one if we aren't counting the yawn I had in the car before I knocked."

"Elliot, don't even," she began. "Of course it doesn't count, I didn't see it therefore, it doesn't exist."

I laughed as we both climbed in the car. I started it, typed in the address on my GPS and shifted the car in drive, starting to yawn which turned into a laugh as I counted in my head that we were now tied with yawns.

"Elliot Daxton Whittaker." Jamie leaned her head back on the headrest. "Take me to a Starbucks and stop yawning."

Once the sun was up, and we both had two coffees in our systems, we were well on the way to Utah. Jamie had texted her sister to let her know we were on the way, even including a photo of me driving so we could start "selling the relationship." I gave a grin but kept my eyes on the road. A text came through a second later, making Jamie laugh.

"She says you're cute."

"Oh good, already in good graces with your sister." I drummed my thumb on the steering wheel. "Jillian, right? And Holden and Harrison."

"Impressive." Jamie looked over at me and smirked. "And my parents?"

"Mr. and Mrs. Gaines," I answered, giving her a slight nod.

"Ha . . . good one. My dad's name is Howard, my mom's name is Janet."

"Again, with the H's and J's." I chuckled.

"Again, unintentionally." Jamie shook her head and unlocked her phone screen, "But unless they tell you otherwise—"

"Mr. and Mrs. Gaines," I repeated. I gave her a side eye and smirked. "That's what you told me a few weeks ago."

Jamie's smile grew as she typed out a quick text, then locked her phone, flipping the silent switch, and slipping it into her bag by her feet. Shifting her body to face me slightly, she asked, "Okay, what about your family?"

I grinned, hoping that questions would start flying. Ever since we talked the other day I've been wanting to get her alone for these twelve hours. I thought of all the questions I wanted to ask—and hoped she would ask me—the entire time I was on stage last night.

"Mom's name is Linda, Dad's name is Graham. Older brother is Jacob and younger sister is Sydney. Jacob is a doctor, specializing in Alzheimer's treatment. Sydney just opened her own salon and is insanely busy. Mom is retired and just spoils Jacob's kids all day," I answered.

"Are you close to them?"

"Sydney and I text at least once a day, but my brother is more focused on my dad and his family. He's busy and, as much as I hate to say it, he and I don't always see eye to eye."

Jamie's focus shifted. She turned her head towards the road once again.

After a deep breath, she said, "I'm close to Jilly. Holden is a typical older brother, very protective of us, and Harrison is always traveling. I can't keep up with him."

I nodded along with her. Closer to our sisters, more distant from our brothers. I knew eventually we'd find something we'd have in common, but I was hoping it would be our taste in music—something less . . . daunting.

"It's not that Harrison and I aren't close," Jamie added, almost as if she could hear my thoughts, "it's just that he's always traveling. He backpacks all over different countries. We only see him at this reunion. The man doesn't even have a cell phone."

"How do you keep in touch?"

"He calls Mom when he can, and sends postcards—I have a whole collection. My parents want him to settle down," she groaned. "Jilly and Holden have graced them with grandchildren, but Harry and I are the odd ducks—the ones that will forever be single."

"You're not single. You have your loving boyfriend right beside you." I leaned my body toward her, cocking an eyebrow.

"Ha ha. You're full of jokes today, aren't you? Enough about my family, you'll get your fill of them and then wish that you never agreed to this. What's up with Jacob? Why do you not see 'eye to eye'?" She threw her fingers up in air quotes.

I clenched my teeth and let out a low growl. My relationship with Jacob wasn't complicated, it just wasn't the best. He stepped in where Dad couldn't and gave the disapproving comments where he could. He hated the tattoo, he never came to shows, and now he was giving me the silent treatment since he learned I was selling the company. If he wasn't already a doctor, who was leading a new study, he would take over the company simply to keep it in the Whittaker name. Jacob was my older brother whom I once admired, now—even though I'm close to forty—all I saw when he talked to me was complete and utter disappointment.

"It's complicated," I answered. Simple and sweet.

Jamie hummed, accepting the answer. "Families can be a blast sometimes, can't they? But you and . . . Sydney?"

I smiled at my sister's name. "My baby sis. Sydney is creative and talented in more ways than I can fathom. I took on music, where she took up art and she decided to express it with hair and nails and she just . . . excels. She's a gem, you would like her."

"Maybe I'll make an appointment when we get back. Lord knows my nails could use some help." She held her hand out in front of her, showing off her short, plain nails. "I love getting my nails done, but the dental office keeps me from that."

I chuckled. "Okay so, why dental? You obviously have a passion for painting."

"I love to paint, but it's hard to make a career out of it. I've always loved going to the dentist, so I decided I could work at an office while finishing my degree, but when that didn't happen . . ."— she shrugged her shoulders—"I just stayed in the dental field. I get to work in the lab, and I love it because I get to work with my hands. It's not much different than working with clay. I can still do art . . .

just in a different way. Plus, thanks to that job, I met my best friend."

"I'll take that. Thanks to a job, I met Milo. And through Milo"— I looked over at her, catching and locking her gaze for a moment before having to turn back to the road—"I met you."

Jamie had a sharp intake of breath as she shifted in her seat. "Okay, well . . ." she stammered, "we have nine hours left on this adventure, what kind of music do you like?"

She began to busy herself connecting her phone to my Jeep, completely taking over the music selection. Once she opened her music app, I couldn't help but smile when I noticed that the last song she had listened to was one of mine.

Chapter Fourteen

-Jamie-

Nine hours with Elliot passed way too quickly. We stopped for lunch and some snacks while we got gas and, before I knew it, we were passing into Utah. In the time being in the car with him I learned his favorite band was Metallica, but would often go to more soothing music while working or trying to find inspiration for his own songs. We listened to a few of his songs on the drive—I claimed they just popped up with the shuffle of music—but the smirk and quick side-eye he gave me told me he didn't believe me.

He didn't need to know that I added all of his albums to my library and starred my favorite ones.

As soon as Salt Lake City came into view, I got butterflies in my stomach. My family was just twenty minutes away—just through that canyon. There was snow, seemingly a fresh layer, and a lot of it. More than I had seen in a long time.

I pulled my phone from my bag to text my parents, taking a quick mental note that it was almost seven; we would make it just in time for dinner . . . and then bed. But the moment my screen came to life I saw a text from Madeline.

Madeline: *Make sure you two set the "rules." You may have gotten to know him, but all fake relationships need those ground rules.*

"Shit. she's right," I muttered.

"Who's right?" Elliot asked, his eyes not leaving the road he was unfamiliar with.

"Madeline . . ." I sighed, locking my phone, and leaning my head back on the seat. "She reminded me we should set rules for the relationship."

Elliot twisted his lips and shook his head. "When does that ever work? I'm going to treat you like I would any girlfriend of mine, and you're just going to go along with it."

I dropped my jaw. "Excuse me?"

"Jamie, I will be holding your hands and I will be kissing you and giving you the kind of attention you deserve. I'll wrap my arm around you and pull you close to kiss your temple and I will be mushy and shit in front of your parents." He stopped. "No rules. They just make things more complicated."

"Complicated? What about this *isn't* complicated?"

"It's simple. Starting now, I'm your boyfriend and you're my girlfriend. If we add those 'no touching, no kissing, absolutely no sign that we are a couple' rules, that will make it complicated and we need to sell to your family that we are indeed a couple. I *will* want to kiss you, Jamie, and I *will* do it."

I pursed my lips and looked out my window. I don't know where *this* Elliot has been hiding, but those words rang through my head over and over.

I will want to kiss you . . .

I unlocked my phone again and quickly typed a response to Madeline.

Me: *Elliot says no rules, it will only make things more difficult. He's going to treat me as his girlfriend and I need to accept it.*

Madeline: *Oh - that's a new approach. Love it though. Keep me updated on how many times he touches you.*

I let out a low, uneasy, laugh before swiping back to my mom's text thread.

Me: *We entered Parley's Canyon, Dax is driving safe, and we should be there soon! Just in time for dinner. We. Are. Pooped.*

Mom: *So glad he's coming! We're just double checking to make sure everything is set up for you. Oh! We forgot to ask - is Daxton a vegetarian?*

I furrowed my brow. "You're not a vegetarian, are you?" I asked, not taking my eyes off my phone, still kind of in shock by his forcefulness just minutes before.

Raising an eyebrow, he turned and looked at me. "No, give me all the meat."

I took my attention back to my moms texts and responded.

Me: *No mom, he's not.*

Mom: *Ribs for dinner.*

I will want to kiss you . . .

. . . and I will.

I stayed silent for the rest of the drive—those nine words playing over and over again in my mind. He wanted to kiss me . . . again. He admitted it matter-of-factly. Had he been thinking of that kiss as much as I had?

It was too dark to watch the mountains, all I could see was the salt-covered road in front of the Jeep. Every now and then another car would pass and give me some indication of where we were, but that didn't help my thought process any more.

My mind was elsewhere.

Elliots fingers on my neck, finding my hair with ease, feeling the calluses, caused by the guitar strings, glide across my skin. Elliots lips on mine. The warmth and tingle they created. The energy and want . . . need . . . just from one kiss.

I will want to kiss you . . .

. . . and I will.

"I believe that's Park City." Elliot's voice caused me to snap back to reality, watching as the small junction came into view. "I would say let's stop and get McDonalds, but I'm assuming your mom cooked?"

I nodded. "Ribs."

"Perfect."

"Take this exit, and then follow the signs for Deer Valley, we're not far, maybe fifteen more minutes depending on the traffic," I mumbled, knowing for a fact that my voice was way too low for him to understand what I was trying to say. But he pulled off the exit all the same, turning off to the right and passing all the buildings I had grown to know. "I come here every year and something always changes."

We passed the Olympic Park entrance on the right, and the Redstone Shopping Center to the left. I could see the first barn come into view and the new Bill White Ranch off to the side.

I will want to kiss you . . .

I'll wrap my arm around you . . .

Taking a deep breath, I pulled my attention back out the window. The drive from the freeway into Old Town Park City was quick, with a few neighborhoods on the right, but light still illuminated the buildings I loved to see while vacationing here. Each one still looked the same—had that same feel to them—even though Park City was still ever-changing. The Park City Nursery, still full of trees, had their Christmas lights on even though it was February. The ski resort I still called, "The Canyons," despite the fact that it was sold years ago and now had a different name. The large Catholic church, St. Mary's, was before the iconic white barn, right before you passed the "Welcome to Park City" sign. I sighed, happy to see that sign still looked the same as it had.

I looked over at Elliot, his eyes still focused on the road in front of him while his thumbs still drummed the steering wheel to the beat of the music, so concentrated on the road he was missing all the sights that the drive to the cabins had to offer. Even if it was dark outside, the McPolin Barn still came into view, making me remember how much I loved this little town.

Starting now, I'm your boyfriend and you're my girlfriend .

. . . I will want to kiss you.

. . . and I will.

"Still following signs for Deer Valley?"

I snapped my eyes from Elliot, and looked back at the road. I cleared my throat. "Yes, not much further. We can go up Main Street if you'd like, it's stunning at night."

"We have three weeks to see Main Street. I don't know about you, but I'm exhausted." He sighed.

"Oh, right." Instant guilt hit my stomach. Out of this drive, I had driven maybe two hours. He closed his eyes for a few moments while I drove, and then offered to take back over. "And now you have to meet my entire family."

He tilted his head and hummed. "I'm actually looking forward to that." He chuckled. "But I'm really looking forward to making a bed on the floor and passing out for a solid eight hours."

"Oh, here"—I pointed to the roundabout—"go up to the left— the third exit."

Elliot followed my instructions, and once he turned down the final road to the cabin, the snow-covered trees made my heart lurch. I loved these mountains. The snow and the memories they brought with them. My family was right around the bend, and soon they'd all be meeting Elliot . . . meeting *Daxton.*

The large cabin came into view first. I saw the lights on in the main room, and I caught a glimpse of my mom's blonde hair in the kitchen. Jillian and Harrison's rental car was parked out front, and my dad's Tahoe was parked in his normal spot. The two smaller cabins sat dark, off to the sides, but I knew they were filled with their suitcases already. The kids had most likely already claimed their beds and made themselves at home. I smiled at the thought.

Elliot pulled the Jeep up next to the Tahoe and took a deep breath. He turned to me and smirked.

"Ready?"

Pushing out any thought that settled in my brain, I nodded. "We can leave the suitcases for now, let's have dinner and then we can get settled into the room."

Closing the door, he rounded the car to meet me in front. He instantly grasped my hand, linking our fingers together and I embraced it, feeling as natural as if he really was my boyfriend.

"Ready when you are, *Dax*."

My eyes met his as he pulled me closer to his body. His warmth enveloping me as his hand lifted free from mine and his arm draped around my shoulders.

I'll wrap my arm around you and pull you close to kiss your temple.

"Jamie, we see you two out there! Get in here!" I heard Jillian's voice through the door, and less than a second later the wooden door flung open and there was my sister. "Why are you just standing out here, it's freezing."

"Hi, Jilly." I smiled, leaving Elliot's warmth to give my sister a hug.

"Auntie Jamie!!!" a loud screech came from the living room followed by the trampling of feet. Within moments my youngest nephews, Phillip and Killian, had their little arms wrapped around my legs. They squeezed, their cheeks pressed against my thighs as they let out the cutest squeals.

"Boys, boys!" Jillian laughed, trying to pull them away from me, "Sorry Jamie, they've been asking for you all day."

"Oh Jilly, you know I love it."

"Auntie Jamie, who's the man you brought with you?" Phillip asked me as he backed away.

I smiled at him and reached back for Elliot. "This is my friend, Daxton." I grabbed hold of Elliot's arm and yanked him forward.

"That's a funny name." Killian walked up to Elliot and looked straight up.

"Oh yea," Elliot responded, "What's your name?"

"Killian. Mommy named me after a TV Show." Killian's face didn't change as he stared at Elliot. "How did your mommy name you?"

"My dad named me actually. He loved the name so much he gave it to me."

"Just like mommy loved that pirate so much." Killian turned away, giving me another hug before he went to join his cousins.

"The pirate?" Elliot asked, raising an eyebrow to my sister.

Jillian rolled her eyes and shook her head quickly. "*Once Upon a Time* was my comfort show while on bed rest." She waved a hand as if to erase the entire conversation. "I'm Jillian, nice to finally meet you."

Elliot took her hand and shook it, giving her the most irresistible smile. He reached for me again, pulling me back into the arm. "Nice to meet you as well, Jamie's told me so much."

"Jamie!" My mother's voice came from the kitchen.

"Hi, Mama."

My mother, radiant and as beautiful as ever, came from the kitchen. Her smile filled the room as she opened her arms and wrapped Elliot and me in a large hug.

"Oh, you're here!" she said into our necks. "Daxton, welcome! We are so thrilled you could join us!"

"I'm happy to be here, thank you for inviting me," Elliot replied. "It's wonderful to meet you, Mrs. Gaines."

"Daxton," my mom held him at arm's length, "please don't call me Mrs. Gaines, no matter what my daughter has told you, you can call me Janet."

Elliot's lips curled into a smirk as he gave her a quick nod. "Thank you, Janet."

"Where's dad? And Holden and Harrison?"

"Oh, they're getting the rooms set up. They'll be down for dinner, which is almost done, I'm just waiting on the rolls." Rubbing my arm, my mom turned and left for the kitchen again, "I hope you like ribs Daxton."

"I do, Mrs. Gaines," Elliot replied sweetly.

My mom spun, her eyebrows raised as she gave Elliot the all-knowing glare.

He chuckled, raising his hands in surrender. "Sorry, Janet. I really do like ribs, Janet."

I nudged him with my elbow as my mom smiled and walked back into the kitchen.

"One parent seems to like me," he whispered.

I placed my hand on his chest and leaned in. If he was going to treat me like his girlfriend, then I was going to act like I was. Physical touch wasn't out of the question, in fact his words still rang in my head. Physical touch was most likely Elliot Whittakers love language. He smiled down at me, our lips close enough to kiss.

"Just wait until you meet my dad," I whispered back. "He's a whole other ball game."

"Daxton," my mom called from the kitchen, "can I get your help here quick? Just help setting the table."

Elliot bounced his eyebrows at me, "Of course, Janet, be right there," he replied. His gaze never once left mine.

My hand fell from his chest as he turned to walk away, but I swear I could still feel his heartbeat.

Chapter Fifteen

-Elliot-

Jamie's family was the complete opposite of how I pictured them. When she told me I had to call her parents "Mr. and Mrs." until told otherwise, I was pretty sure they would hate me. Making sure to cover my tattoo as best I could as I helped cut the ribs, the thought crossed my mind that maybe Jamie was right and they wouldn't mind it. Janet had corrected me from the get-go, seeming to take to me quickly. Her dad, Howard, shook my hand and welcomed me to the trip, although afterward he remained stoic and quiet, still trying to get a read on me. As any father should when their daughter brings an older man to their house.

The five kids, who had all given me a hug and told me my name was funny, sat at the kitchen island after dinner. They had a board game set up and were immersed in that. The adults, on the other hand, sat around the kitchen table. I scooted my chair close to

Jamie and slung my arm around the back of her chair, trying to relax as much as I could.

Truth be told I was dead tired. I wanted to curl up on the floor with a pillow and fall asleep. Our suitcases were still in the car and with a glance at the clock I quickly counted how many hours I had been awake after sleeping so little the night before. It didn't feel like my show was just last night. I yawned and blinked my eyes a few times.

"Tired, Dax?" Harrison, Jamie's brother that sat across from me, asked. He was a carbon copy of his dad—messy brown hair and dark eyes, his face hidden by a thick beard. His skin was tan from the sun and his clothes looked like they had seen better days. He looked comfortable.

A second yawn escaped as I nodded. "Well, *someone* made me leave Portland at five this morning."

"FIVE A.M.!? Jamie, seriously?" Jillian asked, turning to look at the clock. "It's almost nine, no wonder Daxton is yawning."

"We've been counting yawns all day, haven't we Dax?" Jamie grinned over at me, giving me a wink.

I slowly blinked back, "We have. I'm pretty sure you're at fifteen."

"And this makes fifty for you."

"I have not yawned fifty times." I furrowed my brow and looked over at her.

Her lips were pursed and pulled into a tight smile. Her eyes were narrow and focused on me. Her hair was behind her ears, falling on her shoulders in the perfect waves. She was sexy as hell in the moment and there wasn't anything stopping me from pulling her close and kissing her.

Hell, I told her I would.

Instead, I stood up, stretching my arms out to the side, and I couldn't help but notice how Jamie watched my every move.

"I'll go get our bags and your painting. Do you know what room we have?" I placed my hand on her shoulder and gave her a slight squeeze. She took a deep breath and turned to point to the stairs.

"I normally take the second on the—"

"Oh," Mr. Gaines interrupted me, "we made a few changes to the sleeping arrangements."

Jamie's eyes widened as she slowly turned her head to her dad. "I always sleep in that room."

Janet stood, taking her husband's plate with her. "Well, we figured you and Daxton would want a little more privacy. Holden, Jilly, and all the kids will all be here in the main cabin. Your father, Harrison and I will be in the second cabin, and you and Daxton get the small cabin."

"The small cabin," I repeated. "Jamie, they're letting us have the cabin." I squeezed her shoulder again, a little harder this time.

I could feel her shudder. Her hair flipped as she turned back to me, giving me the fakest smile I had ever seen in my entire life. I bit the inside of my lip to stop myself from laughing.

"That's great," she mumbled.

After saying goodnight to everyone—Janet giving me another hug, Mr. Gaines giving me another handshake—Jamie and I grabbed our suitcases and the painting and made our way to the small cabin that sat off to the right. Janet had given me the key, and I fumbled trying to unlock the door, opening it to pure darkness.

"The light is off to the left," Jamie said softly, a hint of hesitation in her voice.

The lights were soft as they brought the house to life. A fireplace sat in the middle, a staircase going up to a loft behind the fireplace. A leather sofa and a few leather armchairs sat in the middle of the living room, and behind me, a large kitchen that, thank the Lord, had a coffee maker on the counter.

"Oh look," I broke the silence, "I can sleep on the couch."

Jamie heaved a sigh and rolled her eyes. "It's probably better than the floor in the main cabin, I never mentioned that it was hardwood floor."

"If I recall correctly, Ryan Reynolds sleeps on a hardwood floor, it would have been good for my back."

"Oh right, cause you're old." Jamie let out a joke, which only made my eyebrows raise.

"Yea, about that." I set my suitcase down behind the couch and turned to her. She gently placed the canvas up against the wall in the kitchen, making sure the fabric covering it was protecting it from the hardwood floor. "Did you tell your family how old I was?"

Furrowing her brow and shaking her head, Jamie stood up and crossed her arms in front of her. "I didn't think it was important. Why?"

"Well obviously I look my age—"

She laughed. "You do not look forty."

"Thirty-six, and yes . . . I really do, especially standing next to you, and I think your dad noticed."

She scoffed, turning her back to me and walking into the kitchen. She knew this place, I could tell as she moved toward the exact cabinet for two glasses that she then filled with water."We'll need to go grocery shopping tomorrow. I know my mom packed food and has meals planned, but we can get snacks and such." She took a long drink, handing me the second glass.

"Jamie," I persisted, "your father is not keen on the fact I'm older than you."

"I told you he was going to be harder to crack. But my mom seems to love you, so you have that going for you."

I rubbed my face with my palms, a long sigh coming from my lungs. I needed sleep.

"Okay, listen." Jamie's voice got closer to me as she grabbed my wrist, pulling it down from my face. "We can sleep in tomorrow, but my parents will want to go to breakfast at the Moose Cafe. You can talk your way into my dad's heart tomorrow morning."

I tilted my head, narrowing my eyes at her and parting my lips to say the comment on the tip of my tongue. *He's not the one who's heart I want to find my way into.* But thought better of it. Jamie didn't need—correction—Jamie didn't *want* that.

I nodded, still enjoying the feeling of her fingers against my forearm.

Nodding towards the staircase she dropped her hand. "The bathroom is upstairs. I'll grab you a few blankets from the linen closet if you want to get some rest."

She was still standing close to me, and even though the skin contact had faded, she remained where she was. I gave her, yet again, another nod, words seeming to fly out of my brain whenever I looked at her. Acting on boyfriend instincts, I leaned forward and gently kissed her forehead. I felt her freeze once my lips hit her skin, and then I left her standing there, making my way up the staircase to the bathroom.

Jamie let out a small cough. "Um, watch the top step. It's a little further away from the floor. Jillian called it the demon stair."

I chuckled and watched my feet, coming up to the "demon stair" just as she predicted. "I'm pretty sure if one of us walks down these steps at night we will fall to our death," I said before I turned and went into the bathroom.

I woke to the smell of coffee filling the small cabin. The Folgers commercial jingle rang in my head as I willed myself to sit up on the leather sofa, which was surprisingly more comfortable than I thought it would be. Draping my arm around the back of the couch I watched as Jamie moved flawlessly through the kitchen. She wore a light, cotton blue robe, her long blonde hair in a messy bun, flyaway's dancing around her ears as she moved.

"Morning!" I pulled myself to a standing position, picking up the blanket to fold it, before draping it over the couch. I grabbed my pillow and tossed it up to the loft, watching it clear the banister and land with a plop. I assumed her family would have no reservations about coming in unannounced, so I had to make sure it looked like I wasn't sleeping on the couch.

"Good morn—" Jamie turned and stopped. "—ing," she finished.

I gave her a smirk, not realizing what state she would find me in. I didn't sleep in pajamas, just my boxers. I lived alone, so it never phased me, but seeing Jamie's cheeks blush as she caught a glance, quickly turning back to the coffee mug, made me very aware that I was practically naked, standing in the middle of the living room.

I bit the inside of my cheek to stop from saying something completely stupid before turning to walk up the stairs.

"What time does everyone want to meet at that cafe?" I asked, trying to be completely natural.

She coughed. "Um, around ten."

I hummed in response. Last night I unpacked my bags into one of the dressers, storing my suitcase in the closet. Reaching into the closet, I grabbed a long sleeve button shirt, a clean pair of jeans and my towel. A shower sounded perfect, and then, coffee.

"It's only eight thirty, you didn't care to sleep in?" Jamie called.

"This *is* sleeping in. Thank you for making coffee." I leaned over the banister to try to get a glimpse into the kitchen, but Jamie had made her way to the living room, taking a seat in one of the armchairs. Tucking her leg under her, she brought her coffee mug to her lips. "Do you need to shower? I won't be long."

Raising her chin, she shook her head. "I'll shower after you, I'll just enjoy the quiet time for now."

Her cheeks were still red.

I showered, dressed, and ran my fingers through my hair in all under fifteen minutes, and it was a *glorious* fifteen minutes. Who knew that twelve hours in a car would make a person feel so dirty. Jamie was still in the same armchair when I came downstairs. I took a detour to the kitchen, filling my own mug with coffee, topping it off with a dash of creamer. By the time I had meandered my way back to the living room, Jamie was gone and the shower was already running.

My phone dinged next to the couch, still attached to its wireless charger. Plopping on the couch, I unlocked the screen.

Milo: *How's the cold?*

I smiled.

Me: Not cold at all. Quite comfortable, actually.
Clay: Please tell me you didn't sleep naked.
Milo: Elliot sleeps naked?
Me: Ah, the elusive group chat. Clay pops in when needed.
Clay: Only when I need to stop you from doing something stupid.
Me: Says the man who drives a Tesla named Tessa.
Clay: Hey. You leave Tessa out of this.
Milo: Ok, back to the subject at hand - you did not sleep naked, did you? I thought you were sleeping on the floor.
Me: We have a small cabin, so I got the couch. And no, I wasn't naked.
Clay: You have your own cabin . . .
Milo: What would Madeline call this?
Me: I'll make sure to ask Jamie at brunch.
Clay: Please don't.

I closed out of the group chat and logged into Instagram. Bennett and I shared access to the band's page and we both made a habit to check daily. We had people who would message us, and we always answered. Being an indie band, it was important to us to handle our accounts personally and I loved the fact that we were able to respond and interact with our fans. We made some amazing connections.

Bennett had posted some photos from the gig the other night, all of which were fantastic shots—despite the sweat coating my face. It never bothered me that you could see the sweat on my brow, honestly, it only proved that the lights were focused on us; right where they should be. The post already had a few hundred likes and a few comments, all of which Bennett had already responded too.

I swiped out of Instagram and opened Bennett's text thread.

Me: *Great photos. Thanks for responding. I didn't get a chance to log on yesterday.*

Bennett: *No problem. I'll have more to post soon - but you should post pics of Park City!*

Me: *Definitely. We're heading to a cafe today - I'll get to see the town.*

Bennett: *Send pics.*

The shower turned off, covering the cabin in silence. I sipped my coffee before standing up to leave, giving Jamie the privacy she needed to dress and get ready. Stepping out onto the deck I got my first view of Park City in all its morning glory. The sun was hitting the snow-covered mountains just right, other cabins peeking out from the trees. It was quiet—so quiet I bet you could hear a pin drop. It was absolutely stunning.

"Good morning, Daxton."

I turned at the sound of my middle name to see Harrison walk up with a thermos in his hand. The man was wearing a winter coat, snow boots and . . . shorts.

"Morning, Harrison, aren't you cold?" I asked. Considering I was able to see my own breath as I talked, I knew he must be very cold.

But instead, he shook his head. "Nah, I've slept in colder than this."

"You didn't sleep outside, did you?" I knew I was asking a dumb question, but I couldn't help but wonder.

Harrison laughed. "No, mom wouldn't let me even if I tried. You probably couldn't see the other cabin last night, but the parents and I are in that cabin." Using his thermos he pointed to the cabin up the road, closer to the main cabin we ate in last night. "Did you sleep well?"

"I did, thank you and woke up to Jamie making coffee." I smiled, bringing my cup to my lips to take a full gulp.

Harrison took a drink from his own thermos. "Where is Jamie? Mom sent me over here to tell you guys to get ready for brunch."

I nodded towards the house. "She just got out of the shower. Just thought I'd give her some privacy."

He nodded and then took a deep breath, closing his eyes and tilting his head back. "You'll love it here. Park City is . . . clean."

"Clean? Compared to?"

"Anywhere really. I've traveled a lot, but this is always my favorite place to come every year. And not just because my family is here." Opening his eyes, he took in the scenery. A chill air flew by, hitting our cheeks just right. "Ha," Harrison laughed. "I bet you your coffee is cold now."

"That just means I'll get to make more for Jamie."

Harrison squinted his eyes and looked at me. His bushy beard and hair covered most of his face, but his green eyes still stood out through the hair. He looked like a mountain man, one who went weeks without a shower, sometimes even food. There was no telling where this man had been in his years and suddenly, I wanted to know all about him.

He hummed. "Good response."

The cabin door creaked open, and Jamie stepped out, making both of us turn. Dressed in black leggings and a gray baggy sweater, her wet hair fell over her shoulders. She looked towards me and her brother. I could almost see the hamster spinning in the wheel. The many thoughts that could be going through her brain. I shifted my feet and reached out for her arm. Pinching her sweater between my fingers I pulled her close, wrapping my arm around her shoulders.

Was my PDA a little too much? Maybe, but honestly, if she was willing to take it, I would keep giving it.

"What are you two talking about?"

"Your boyfriend's cold coffee," Harrison replied.

"I was just about to make another pot." I raised my chin slightly and looked down at Jamie. Arching her back, she stayed close to me while looking up to meet my gaze.

Harrison let out a long sigh. "Actually, Jamie . . . dry your hair. We're leaving for the cafe soon. Dax can get more coffee there."

"Perfect." Jamie placed her hand on my chest and pushed herself off. "I guess I'll go braid my hair. Give me a few more minutes. Oh Harrison"—she pointed at her brother—"you took a shower, proud of you."

Harrison chuckled and looked down at his feet. "I shower."

"I need to know all about your adventures Harrison. Every. Single. One." I took another drink of my coffee, which was—as Harrison predicted—freezing cold.

He smiled, the white shining through his dark beard. "Those are bonfire night stories." He turned his back, stuffing his freehand in his coat pocket. "See you soon."

I watched as he trudged back through the snow, a foot almost falling out of his boot - but the man pressed forward until he was at the front porch. Before he went inside, he removed his boots, leaving them sitting by the front door.

I took one last glance at the mountains—pulling my phone out to snap a photo of the view, before instantly sending it to the group chat with Milo and Clay, and then I sent it separately to Bennet.

Milo: *Looks like Marble - only a lot bigger!*
Bennett: *Can you imagine playing there?*

Chapter Sixteen

-Jamie-

The Moose Cafe was on the complete opposite side of Park City compared to where we were staying. We had to take three separate cars just to get there for our reservation. Harrison opted to ride with us, while Mom and Dad split up between Holden and Jillian's vehicles. The fifteen-minute drive was interesting listening to Elliot and Harrison talk about the places they had both traveled. I wasn't aware that Elliot had been around so much, but I guess it made sense with his band. However, not once in the conversation did he mention the band.

I wasn't sure if I should mention them, or if we were pretending he wasn't the face of *Savaged Whittakers*. I raked my teeth on my bottom lip, regretting the fact that we didn't come up with our backstory, or even what to say when my family inevitably asked what *Daxton* did for a living. *Elliot* owns an architectural firm by day, and sings in a band by night. But I'm not sure what he wants me to say to my family.

We pulled off the freeway, taking a left turn into Summit Park where the small cafe resided. I pulled my phone from my pocket and typed a quick text to Elliot.

Me: *Do I tell my family about your band...or??*

I heard his phone ding, muffled by his coat pocket. Hopefully, the man would check it before we sat down and ordered breakfast.

We parked next to my sister, and my nephews were the first to jump out of the van, followed by my mom. Elliot unbuckled and situated himself before opening the car door and jumping out. He nodded to my parents and walked around to my door, opening it for me and extending his hand. With a light chuckle, I took his hand and let him guide me into the cafe.

"Aren't you going to check the text you got?" I whispered, stepping a bit closer to him.

Elliot scoffed. "Nah, it's probably just Milo or Clay. The group chat has been blowing up all morning. I'll silence it before we sit down."

"You should probably check your text," I reiterated.

"Ah." he laughed, catching on. "My girlfriend sent me a secret text, did she?"

"I . . ." I stumbled. "I . . . what . . . no. I just . . ."

"Jamie." Elliot squeezed my hand. "I'll read it."

"Thank you," I said under my breath.

"Looks like we have the cafe to ourselves this morning," my dad called as he opened the door. He held it open for everyone, my siblings and their families crowding in first. Elliot gave my dad a smile and nod as he passed him. "Morning, Daxton."

"Good morning, Sir," Elliot replied.

Sir.

The long table took up the entire restaurant, and even though my dad claimed we had it to ourselves, there were some locals enjoying their meal. Jillian instantly took her kids aside and reminded them we were in public, while Holden and his wife each took a seat between their three kids, splitting them up. Elliot pulled my chair out for me, waiting for me to sit before removing his jacket and sitting himself. I looked at him, raising my eyebrows, trying to send him a telepathic message to check his damn phone.

"Oh, right." He wiggled his eyebrows as he reached for his phone. He silenced it, and then quickly read my message. Once his phone was back in his coat pocket, he looked at me and shook his head slightly, giving his nose a good scrunch.

Okay, no band.

Once the waitress came and took our drink orders, the conversation started flowing. My mom focused her attention on her grandchildren, doting on her only granddaughter—Danielle was seven and welcomed the attention. Holden and his wife, Carrie, were coloring on the kids' menus with their two boys, Dustin and Dane. Dustin, being eleven, seemed more interested in the Nintendo Switch that he was forced to leave in the van. He sat with his arms folded as Holden tried to get him to play the game where you create squares with dots. Killian and Phillip were engrossed with their menu of games while Jillian and Will were busy reading the menus.

"We always get the pancakes and sausage. I don't know why you're looking at the menu," I said across the table, not even lifting my menu up.

Will raised his eyes up at me. "Maybe I wanted an omelet today, they seemed pretty good."

"I think I'm going to try the Cowboy Omelet," Elliot said, looking at his menu with extreme concentration.

Will dropped his menu and looked across the table at Elliot. "That sounds amazing."

Elliot raised a single eyebrow and looked up at Will. "It's right here. Ham, green and red bell pepper, onion, four eggs, and cheddar jack cheese. I wonder if I can add any ingredients to it?"

"What would you add?" I asked, looking at Elliot as his brows pinched.

"Jalapeños." Elliot's eyes met mine. He smirked and wiggled his eyebrows.

"Yep, that's what I'm getting." Will closed his menu and folded his arms. Jillian, who was still looking at hers, gave a small smirk and shook her head at her husband.

Will was the stay-at-home dad. He stayed with the boys while Jillian worked as one of the best social workers in the United States. Her job was hard—I knew she had seen some tough things—but she had Will to comfort her when she needed it. They were the perfect balance.

"I'll get the pancake combo and when you decide you are done being a cowboy, you can have some of my pancakes." She smiled, closing her menu.

Elliot laughed and leaned back in his chair, his arm wrapping around the back of mine just like last night at dinner. "The omelets come with pancakes."

Jillian looked over at him, her lips pursed. She was ready to strike back with a tease. Just with that little look from Jillian, I had it figured out that at least half of my family had accepted Elliot so far. My mom had welcomed him with open arms, but my dad still seemed to watch his every move. Holden had yet to really talk to him and Harrison seemed to love him so far.

Elliot was relaxed with my siblings, but the moment he noticed my father he took a sharp inhale and sat up straight in his chair. I could feel his arm slip from my shoulders and, as much as I knew it was for show, I also knew it could have been a bit much. I had to get my dad to talk to Elliot.

I racked my brain trying to find a topic of conversation that could get the two of them going, but alas, I was coming up short. The waitress came back, placing all the drinks on the table before taking our orders. Elliot reached for the coffee creamer that sat in the middle of the table and I watched him, intently. It wasn't every day you met a man who enjoyed sweeter coffee. I raised my orange juice glass and leaned into him to whisper in his ear.

"So, Daxton." My dad's voice stopped me before I even had a chance to talk. "Jamie has told us very little about you, what is it you do for a living?"

I widened my eyes. There it was. The connection. I internally slapped myself for not thinking of this sooner.

"Daxton actually owns his own business, Dad. An architecture firm," I answered for Elliot.

Elliot took a deep breath and looked over at me, his eyes wide.

"You're an architect?" My dad asked, more invested now.

"My dad was an architect, he retired about a year ago," I replied, not even giving Elliot a chance to say anything. I was hoping Elliot would catch my drift. Elliot may not be an architect, but that didn't mean Daxton couldn't be.

Elliot cleared his throat. "Yes, sir, I am."

Mental high five! Thank you, Elliot!

My dad smiled. *Let the bond begin.*

"And you own your own firm? At such a young age?" My dad laced his fingers together, his class ring on his right hand, and his wedding ring on his left, glistening in the lighting of the restaurant.

Elliot nodded. "My dad started it, sir, and when he retired I took over. I actually have work and meetings to do while I'm here."

My dad chuckled and shook his head. "The work is never done, is it? I used to love the design room. The light hitting that desk just right, nothing beats it, right, Daxton?"

Elliot let out a small laugh, shaking his head down towards the table. He reached for his coffee mug, giving me a side eye, a soft plea for help, perhaps? I licked my lips and emptied the silverware roll, placing the cloth napkin on my lap. Maybe this was the wrong idea. Maybe I should have made up a profession—Elliot would have rolled with it. Why wasn't my dad a recording producer or something to that effect? Elliot would be more comfortable, he could be more himself. I let out a small sigh and filtered the nerves that coursed through my body.

Elliot, though, didn't skip a beat. "Designing isn't even the best part, Mr. Gaines. Don't get me wrong, sir, but I love it when I get to show the client the model. The look in their eyes as they see their vision come to life. Nothing beats *that*."

My dad raised his chin, narrowing his eyes as he kept his focus on Elliot. The corners of his mouth raised as he concentrated.

"My building has three levels and the top level is the showroom, and I really enjoy giving the clients the full tour before they see the finished project. Whether I worked on it, or another team member, I absolutely love seeing their reaction. I have yet to see an unhappy client," Elliot continued, passion in his words.

I looked over at him, amazed that he was so smooth—so calm—when it came to talking about something he knew nothing about. He was a better actor than I gave him credit for.

"That is an amazing feeling, Daxton." My dad settled back into his chair, placing his hand on my mom's forearm. "I'm happy to hear you're still using 3D models, so many companies are switching to digital."

The conversation kept rolling—my dad and Elliot talking about elements in architecture that I couldn't even wrap my head around. The two really hit it off, talking about stories with their clients, and watching the drawing come to life on land. If only someone had asked me these kinds of questions about teeth, or paint . . . I could talk all day. Instead, I ate my pancakes, listening, and truly enjoying the time with my family and boyfriend. *Fake boyfriend.*

The table had gotten quieter as the food disappeared, even the kids were entering their food comma, and once his omelet was gone, Elliot reached under the table and grabbed my hand. He pulled it up to his lips, placing a small kiss on the back as shivers ran up my arm.

We arrived back at the cabins shortly after one in the afternoon. My siblings, with their half asleep children, retreated back into the large cabin, even Harrison followed them with Killian on his shoulders. Elliot grabbed my hand and waved to my parents as he pulled me towards our cabin. As soon as we were in the door, he pulled me close, wrapping his arm around my waist.

"You know," he whispered, "it would have been nice to know your dad was an architect. I could have talked about a lot more than *just* showing clients the building and animations."

At first, I was confused as to why I was in his arms for him to tell me that. Our bodies were pressed together, I could almost feel his heartbeat. He felt good—solid—as his hands roamed against my back, before finally resting on my waist. I slid my hands up his arms, resting them on his shoulders. He was close enough to kiss.

I let out my breath, trying to focus anywhere except his eyes. Outside, I saw my parents, sitting on the porch to their cabin, facing us.

Rolling my eyes, I took in the moment for what it really was— an act, just like breakfast.

"I'm sorry. He retired and I honestly didn't find it relevant until then," I whispered back, trying to act as if it were completely normal to be this close to Elliot Whittaker. "If it helps, you played the role very well."

He smiled. "Of course I did." He kissed my forehead, sending me down another spiral I had to pull out of. "I do know the ins and outs of architecture. I may hate it, but I know it. Let's just keep the fact that I'm selling it to us, okay? I can pretend to be an architect for three weeks."

Elliot moved, heading into the living room before taking off his coat and laying it over the sofa. He plopped down with a sigh and leaned his head back against the couch.

"Don't mention the band, or selling the company." I followed him, mimicking removing my scarf and coat, taking a seat next to him on the sofa.

"Is that our only meal today? That omelet was huge. So good, but I don't think I can eat again today."

I let out a laugh, falling back to turn and look at him. "Oh *Daxton*, we're just getting started on the food."

Chapter Seventeen

-Elliot-

On the third day in Park City, I woke up before Jamie. I folded the blankets and tossed my pillow on the landing at the top of the stairs, not wanting to take the chance the light *flop* would wake her. I could hear her breathing, still shallow and soft; she needed the rest.

I made coffee and popped some toast in the toaster, setting up my laptop on the kitchen island. I hadn't had the chance to log into my work emails, and my phone had been relatively quiet the past two days. But now that the week was in full swing, I knew that the messages would start to come in. Kevin was a great second in command, but there were still things that I was needed for.

Clay had sent an email—a few numbers that included some of the company's assets along with a meeting time for Wednesday. I replied back, pushing the meeting to a different day. Jamie had told me Wednesday was family day. Everyone was on board, and, even though I had no idea what we were doing, I was really excited for it. The kids were so excited that they were trying to get hints from their parents, but alas, they gave no information to them. I tried to tell them to just go with the flow and wait for the surprise, but no little kid wanted to hear that—Phillip and Killian especially.

After answering a few more emails and finishing my toast, I closed my laptop. I stretched and looked out the window towards the mountains. It really was gorgeous. Captivating and serene.

"Good morning," I heard Jamie's soft voice as she walked around the island, coming into my view. She grabbed a coffee mug and filled it, topping it off with cream before she smiled. "Did you get any work done?"

I nodded. "Yea, I answered a few emails. Clay says hi."

She let out a small laugh before taking a sip of her coffee.

"What's on the agenda today?" I asked, folding my arms in front of me and leaning on the counter.

"Well, I need to get that painting to the art's fest studio. I know the festival doesn't start until next week, but submissions need to be handed in before. Since we don't have much planned today, I was hoping you would like to come with me to drop it off?"

I raised an eyebrow, a part of me shocked she openly asked me to come. "I'd love to."

"We can see Main Street," she added.

"Sounds perfect. Anything else planned?"

She shook her head. "Not that I know of. I bet Harrison is going to go for a hike. Wednesday is a family fun day."

"Yea, about Wednesday . . ." I pushed myself off the island, walking around to where Jamie stood. She was wearing her robe again, her hair a mess from sleeping, and her face fresh with no makeup. She was naturally stunning. From the kitchen window I could see her parents step out onto their porch. Janet hugged her coat closer to her body as she stepped off the front steps.

Jamie hummed, her back facing the window, obviously to the fact her parents were headed this way. I slinked my arm around her and pulled her closer.

"I would love to have some kind of guess as to what we're doing on Wednesday." I kissed her temple. I heard her suck in a breath of air before she turned to me, her cheeks turning red, only to soften once she caught sight of her parents.

Blinking, she smiled, turning up her game. "Nope, Wednesday is a surprise."

"Do you have any idea what we are doing?"

Finally, there was a light knock, pulling our attention toward the glass door. Janet waved at us, a large smile on her face.

"I didn't sleep in that late, did I?" Jamie asked, setting her coffee down on the counter to go let her mom in.

Taking a quick glance at the clock on the stove, I responded, "You needed the rest."

"Good morning you two!" Janet said loudly once the door was open. Jamie placed a hand on her hip and tilted her head at her mom, still holding onto the door handle. "Breakfast in the main cabin."

"Janet—" I called, "I'm not used to eating this much. I ate some toast while I answered some emails."

Janet raised her eyebrows at me, sticking her head in the door, "Jamie should have warned you. I cook a lot."

"Oh, she warned me, but I wasn't at all prepared."

"Daxton," she lowered her voice, "breakfast in the main cabin."

Jamie turned to look at me. The look on her face was comical, almost as if she knew I had been caught by her mother. Janet's "mom voice" was stern, and the look in her eye was worse than any my own mother had ever given me. Janet meant business, and Jamie knew that. And by looking at Jamie I knew the minute she closed the door she was going to burst out in laughter.

I pushed myself off the counter and held up my hands in surrender. "Yes, ma'am," I said politely.

Janet gave me a nod and then her smile returned. "See you two soon."

Jamie gave her mom a hug and then closed the door, dropping her arms to her side and slowly turning towards me.

"I don't care what happens for the rest of the day, that was brilliant and I'm never letting you live that down."

"Yeah, yeah, yeah," I mumbled as I left the kitchen. "I'll go get changed and then get ready for breakfast. We can skip lunch, right?"

Jamie's laughter only grew as she followed me up the stairs and into the bathroom. I was definitely never going to live this down.

I hadn't seen Jamie's painting before today. She kept it well-covered as we drove to the studio and as she carried it inside, but once we got to the director, she removed the cover and I was frozen.

It was beautiful. I had taken a look at all the paintings she had hanging in her apartment, but nothing compared to this one. It was of a mountain range with a sunflower field, the colors completely popping off the canvas. The textures and the lighting she used made it seem surreal, enchanting in a way. If I didn't know it was a painting I could have sworn it was a photograph. I was mesmerized. The director soaked it in just as long as I had, pointing to a few things on it as Jamie nodded her head at him.

The director carefully took the painting from her and she watched as he took it in the back, assuring her he'd take great care of it until it was time for the festival. She had her thumb nail in between her teeth as she watched his every move before she turned to come towards me.

"I'm nervous," she said softly.

"Why, that's an amazing painting."

"It's my first time entering a piece and trust me, Park City festivals are brutal. I won't even get a participation ribbon." Jamie's hands fell to her side as she walked through the door, walking back into the chill air that filled Main Street.

Park City still had its Christmas lights hanging above the street, with wreaths hanging from the light posts. There was so much snow on the road that Main Street seemed to have become a one-way street, so others could still parallel park. I could see signs for some name brand stores, while others were clearly locally-owned. I reached my hand behind me for Jamie so we could take the walk up together.

"What are the awards?" I asked her as she came closer to my side, not taking my hand. She zipped up her coat and folded her arms.

Letting out a long sigh she said, "Best in show of course, best breakthrough, best landscape, best portrait . . . the list could go on and on."

"You're entered in?" I dragged out the "*n*" hoping she would fill the void.

"Landscape and breakthrough." Her voice was heavy, a hint of anticipation settled. "But did you see the others? There's so many phenomenal artists. It wasn't easy getting in, you know. There are over two-hundred artists entered this year."

"All oil paintings?" I asked, glancing in a window of a store that had cooking oils and vinegars. I stopped, grabbing a hold of Jamie's coat to pull her back to the store. I opened the door for her, letting the fabric slip between my fingers.

"Well, no," she responded as she walked through the door and up the steps. "There's photography, sculptures, paintings, and even jewelry. Why did we come in here? Are you wanting a gnome?" Jamie giggled as she picked up a small stuffed gnome.

I took the gnome from her and placed it back on the shelf with the others. "Ha, no. I saw the cooking oils and thought it would be a good gift for your mom."

"Really?" she asked, pinching her eyebrows together as her eyes widened.

"Well, yes. I can get her a gift, can't I?"

She softly nodded. "She loves this store. She always comes here to get oil. She's going to love it. And the fact that you thought of it is going to be even better."

She began to walk around the store, circling the tables to try a few of the oils and vinegars, searching for the perfect pair. Once again, I watched as she moved with grace, her attitude changing from when she left the gallery just moments before. She was stiff, biting her nails before, but now she seemed to flow from table to table—the thought of her painting being in the hands of someone else completely leaving her mind.

Main Street was the distraction she needed.

Once we chose the oil and vinegar, we went to the other side of the store, where featured items from locals were displayed as well as a lot of gnomes. Jamie would point them out as we passed them, even going so far as to find the ugliest one that sat on the top of the cabinet. After grabbing a book about Park City's historical building, we made our way to the cash register, and, before I placed the items down, I grabbed the gnome she had picked up when we first arrived.

"Are you buying the gnome?" Jamie asked as she watched me place it next to the book.

I wiggled my eyebrows at her and dug in my pocket for my wallet. "You liked him so much I figured he had to come home with us."

Giving me a small smile, she turned her head, letting out a gasp that caught my attention. "Look!" She held up a magnet that had a mountain with bright orange gondolas on it. "For Madeline!"

"She'll love it."

She chuckled, placing the magnet on the book. "And the book?"

"For my dad."

Tilting her head, her hair falling off to the side, she smiled up at me. "You're very sentimental Elliot."

I shrugged my shoulders, watching the older lady wrap up the bottles before swiping my card. "I know he would like it; he loves buildings."

"As any architect would."

"Would your dad like this?" I asked, taking the bag from the clerk.

"Believe it or not, he has it."

I scoffed. "Well, I'll have to keep looking for him then."

Jamie linked her arm with mine and laughed as we made our way down the stairs back to the street. It had started to snow—the perfect, fluffy snow that you only saw in movies, making Main Street look even more magical.

"Come on, I know a great place for some coffee." Jamie bumped into me as she used her weight to pull me along, keeping our arms linked together.

Atticus Coffeeshop sat on the lower, 'newer' end of Main Street, but still held the curb appeal that the older part of the street had. As soon as you walked in, you were hit by the smell of coffee and tea, and the amazing sight of used books. Tables lined the walls as locals sat with either their book or computer—sipping their coffees as they worked.

"Did we just step into a movie set?" I asked, taking in my surroundings.

"Ha, it seems that way doesn't it. You'll love this place, I promise." Jamie smiled as she tugged me towards the counter.

"I have no doubt."

Just like the rest of the morning, the coffee was perfect.

Chapter Eighteen

-Jamie-

I was a bundle of nerves handing over my painting, and then Elliot pushed them away. After our coffee at Atticus we headed back up to the cabin. It was snowing harder now, making the roads heading up to the cabin harder to navigate, but Elliot and his Jeep did it effortlessly. With him behind the wheel I felt safe, just like I did after the gallery. Elliot seemed to make all the uneasy feelings in me float away, as if they were never there.

Jillian and her family were out in front of the main cabin when we pulled up and parked. They were bundled in snow gear and Killian was attempting to build a snowman that was bigger than him, while Phillip was trying to build a wall of snow, most likely for a snowball fight with his cousins. One happened every year, and the pure fact that there was more snow on the ground this year called for a bigger fight.

Leaving the gifts in the car, Elliot and I headed over to the fun.

"Phillip, isn't it too early for the snowball fight?" I called, bending over to scoop up a palm full of snow. I began to pack it, getting ready to toss it at someone. I knew who I wanted to toss it at, and it wasn't one of my nephews.

Phillip giggled when he saw what I was doing and he gathered snow as well. "It's never too early, Auntie Jamie!"

"We still have so much time here," I replied. "How many fights are you planning on having?"

He tossed his snowball at me as his response. I ducked as it flew past my head, hitting a tree and bursting apart.

"You missed!" I called.

Jillian laughed and ran over to her son, crouching behind the snow wall with him. I could hear her whisper something to him, telling me a fight was on. I was still holding my snowball, waiting for the perfect moment to toss it. I kept packing it, making sure it was the perfect weight and shape to throw and hit my target.

Phillip and Jillian jumped up at the same time, a snowball in each of their hands before they tossed them. I took the moment, knowing my sister and nephew were a terrible aim and spun around to face Elliot, chucking my snowball in his direction. I watched as he cowered, lifting a leg and holding out his hands in defense as all three snowballs hit him in the stomach and shoulders.

Little arms wrapped around my waist as Phillip's laughter grew and carried through the air.

"Auntie Jamie!" he cried. "Uncle Daxton wasn't expecting that!"

Uncle?

I froze for a moment before laughing with him. I couldn't let the comment of a little kid get to me. "We weren't aiming for you!" Jillian called over the snow wall, "Daxton was always the target."

Elliot bent over, his eyes firm on me as he gathered snow in his hands and began to pack it together. "That was a dirty move,

Jamie!" he exclaimed. "Something you don't know about me is that growing up I held the title for snowball fights."

"Is that so?" I taunted. Pushing Phillip behind me, I placed a hand on my hip, cocking my body to tease him more.

"You three tossed a snowball at the wrong person." He pulled his arm back, like a pitcher aiming for the catcher's mitt, and the ball came flying through the air.

I turned my back to protect Phillip as the snow hit my shoulder. It was soft, not at all like I was expecting. I crafted another frozen mound before I tossed it at him, Elliot, however, wasn't planning on hurting me. I heard Jillian laugh and Phillip jumped up and down.

"You make as many snowballs as you can and go hide with your mom, I'll distract him!" I whispered to Phillip who instantly took off behind the fort wall. I turned back, making sure to grab a handful of snow, lumping it together as I ran towards Elliot.

He already had another snowball, tossing it towards me. I ducked and the ball flew past my head. I was gaining on him as he bent to pick up more snow, but I was faster. I tossed my snowball at him and hit him right on his cheek.

"Ah!" He laughed. I knew it didn't hurt too bad, I didn't pack it like before, but his acting skills were fantastic. He raised his hand to the side of his face, his eyes squinted and head back, a loud cry of "pain" escaping his lungs. His performance didn't stop me from running towards him, bending over to scoop up some more snow.

"Get him Auntie Jamie!" I heard Phillip yell.

"You better watch out Daxton!" Jillian called out.

The closer to Elliot I got, the more fake his performance became. He opened his eyes, dropping his hand from his face, taking a few steps back he hurled his snowball at me, but I was too close. I flung the loose snow in my hand at him and crashed into him. I wrapped my arms around his waist, and we fell to the ground. I could hear Phillip and Jillian laugh. Phillip said something about making the snowballs while Daxton was down, but all I could focus on was Elliot. Snow flew around us as we hit the ground hard, not only falling from the sky, but flying up from us hitting the ground.

He wrapped his arms around me as we fell, giving me a sense of security. I wasn't afraid of the fall. With Elliot's arms around my waist, I felt safe. Just like before, in the car, when the snow was falling so hard we couldn't see the road. Just like when he was able to pull my mind from the nerves that clouded them. Elliot just felt … different … then I wanted him to. I wanted him to be distant, I wanted him to be rude and selfish. But Elliot … he cared, and I didn't think it was all for show. He captured my family's attention, and now, with his breath on my neck and his stubble gently rubbing against my skin, he was one hundred percent capturing mine.

I nuzzled my face in his shoulder for a moment, taking in his scent before flinging my hair off to the side, pushing myself up to my elbow to look at him. I have always found him handsome, but at this moment, with the snow in his hair, and his eyes completely on me … he was perfect.

And to top it off, he smiled, and I had to force myself to remember to breathe.

"I told you, you tossed a snowball at the wrong person," he said, a playful softness to his voice.

The corners of my lips raised, giving him a crooked smile as I searched his eyes. I touched his cheek and leaned in close, our lips only millimeters apart.

"Oh, don't worry," I whispered against his lips, "I'm only the distraction."

"NOW!" Jillian screamed.

I rolled away from him, leaving him absolutely stunned as Jillian and Phillip came up with snowballs, pelting him with them, repeatedly. Elliot just laughed, trying his hardest to stand and gather some snow, but Phillip and Jillian outnumbered him.

Once Phillip and Jillian were out of snowballs, Phillip laughed, shouting over and over that he won, that he beat *Uncle* Daxton. I walked over and grabbed Elliot's hands, lifting him off the ground. He had snow all over him, his black coat was covered, and his hair was soaked. I brushed off his shoulders and his hair, only stopping when he reached up to grab my wrists, pulling them down to his chest.

"Are you okay?" I asked, a laugh escaping my lungs.

He nodded. "Never better."

I flattened my palms against his chest, feeling him rise and fall with each and every breath. I looked up at him, taking in him—feeling myself slip away.

"Okay you two!" Jillian called. "It's almost dinner time. That was fun, but let's go inside and warm up."

Elliot watched as Jillian gathered her family and walked back inside, turning his focus back to me.

"Do you want some hot chocolate?" he asked, raising his eyebrows and tilting his head towards the house.

"Race you?"

Without hesitation, Elliot took off towards the house, running past the kids and Jillian and through the door. Shaking my head, I followed, knowing that it wasn't a race, and I was starting to want to follow him anywhere.

After dinner, Elliot helped my mom in the kitchen and I helped my siblings get their kids ready for bed. Holden was working well with Carrie, getting their three off to bed, and I was in charge of the bedtime story. All five of the kids shared a room, with two sets of bunk beds and a twin bed up against the wall. The cousins seemed to be enjoying their time together.

I sat in the middle of the room, the book laid out in front of me and all ten eyes staring at me as I read the first few chapters of *Charlotte's Web*.

Closing the book once they all had drifted off, I closed the door and headed back to the adults. My parents had already escaped to their cabin, and my brothers and sister stayed with their partners and Elliot in the living room. I joined them, sitting next to Elliot on the couch, lifting my knees close to my body.

"All the kids are asleep. You're welcome." I bowed, looking at my brother and sister.

"In that case . . ." Carrie slapped Holden's knee. "I'm going to bed myself. It's not every night I get to read."

Holden stretched. "Oh, I'm coming."

"They won't be sleeping," Jillian mumbled. "Just remember you're already out numbered!"

Holden turned back to glare at Jillian, who only gave him an extremely cheesy grin.

"Thanks, Jamie," Carrie called, while Holden waved to me as he disappeared up the stairs.

"Night," I responded. "Are you two going to go to bed too? It's still early." I asked Jillian, leaning on the back of the couch, sitting a little closer to Elliot then I normally would.

Jillian twisted her face, furrowing her eyebrows to give me a look of either disbelief or confusion. "I'm not lame like Holden and Carrie. My kids are asleep and it's only eight."

Elliot laughed, his head tilting back onto the couch. I watched him as he relaxed. His jaw was defined, and his Adam's apple bobbed as he chuckled softly. His eyes fluttered back open with a sigh as he pulled himself back to the present. It was five seconds— and five seconds was all I needed to notice these things.

I blinked and took a deep breath. *It's. Not. Real.*

"Would you two be up for a few drinks?" Will's voice was heavy as he pushed himself off the couch. "I know Janet and Holden have wine and beer. What about you, Dax?"

Elliot leaned his head back again, following Will as he got closer to the fridge. "I'll take a beer, thanks."

"Jamie?"

"I doubt Mom has margarita mix in there." I smiled, running my hands through my hair as my gaze was still fixed on Elliot.

"You and your Mango-Ritas." Elliot's remark flew off his tongue, as if he was waiting to say it.

"Hey, they are delicious." I slapped his shoulder lightly with my hand, my wrist hanging off the couch.

The flirtatious vibes that were coming from me even shocked me. This is how I was with other guys, not with Elliot. I had never really flirted with Elliot—never really had the desire to. But yet, here I was, wanting all of his attention. Noticing those small things that I normally wouldn't have noticed on him. Even that night when he kissed me, the kiss that still entered my mind from time to time, I admitted he was attractive, but that was it. I had made the decision then and there he was a friend and nothing more.

Was it just because he made the day seem different? Main Street, the snowball fight, the small glances and looks he gave me all day. The *Uncle Daxton*.

Whatever it was, I needed to get it out of my head.

"There's no margarita mixes, but there is a mango Moscato," Will called from the kitchen.

"Oh, I'll take a glass!"

"Check the alcohol content," Jillian added. "Jamie's a lightweight."

I spun my head to glare at her, my jaw dropped as low as it could go. She was telling the truth, but I wasn't about to admit that. Whenever I went out with Madeline, I was a one and done kinda girl. It wasn't just for Elliot's benefit that night. I. Am. A. Lightweight.

"I am *not* a lightweight," I argued.

"Daxton, back me up here." Jillian turned towards Elliot. "You've seen our girl drink. You must know she's a lightweight."

"Yea, *Daxton,* choose who you back up." I turned my glare towards Elliot.

Raising both his eyebrows, he gave a smile. *One that said, "If I don't choose my girlfriend I'm screwed, but I always want to be loved by the family. So choose my words wisely."*

"I mean"—he shrugged—"I've seen you drink at the Piano Bar, and then that night after Madeline's wedding."

The wine glass appeared in front of me as I looked at Elliot. I began filtering through my brain, trying to find the lie I told Jillian all those months ago. How did I meet my boyfriend Daxton? Did we meet at the bar, did we meet at the wedding? I was pretty damn sure we met at the bar. In fact, I was certain of it. I took the glass from Will, watching as Elliot wiggled his eyebrows when he cracked the can of beer open. I lifted the rim to my lips and tasted the sweet mango.

"You two met at the wedding, right?" Jillian asked.

Shit.

Chapter Nineteen

-Elliot-

Jamie was, in fact, a lightweight.

I had pulled back two beers, and was nursing my third as Jamie topped off her glass of wine. There was no crazy party to be had, just four adults playing the random board games that we found in the closet. We played a round of Clue (it was Colonel Mustard with the Revolver), a game of Life (Will won that by a landslide), and now we were halfway through Monopoly and Jamie was drunk.

Very drunk.

I had gone to the kitchen, bringing her some bread and a glass of water, which, thankfully she took without question, but she still managed to drink the entire bottle of mango wine.

Once we were 90 percent done with Monopoly, with Will, once again beating our asses, I grabbed the basically empty wine glass from Jamie and stood.

"I think it's time I get this lightweight to bed," I said as I was leaving the living room, putting the empty beer cans in the recycling and Jamie's glass in the sink.

"I am not—" Jamie started.

"We know, we know . . ." Jillian laughed. "You're not a lightweight. You're just the one who couldn't remember how you met your boyfriend, even before you got drunk."

"I'm not drunk. I'm happy. And I know exactly how I met him."

I paused, placing my hands on the counter watching Jamie and Jillian through my eyelashes.

"I met him at Madeline's wedding and we went out for some drinks. Sooo," she drew out the *"o,"* her lips making the perfect circle. "We technically met at both—the wedding and a bar."

"And we go to the Piano Bar on occasion with Milo and Madeline, so it works. She only ever has one drink though." I pushed my palms off the counter, walked over to Jamie, taking her forearm gently. "So, yes, *babe*, you are a lightweight and it's time we take you back to our cabin so you can drink some more water and go to bed."

"Fine," Jamie gave in, "but we're bringing Clue."

"Jamie," I groaned as she pulled free from my grasp and walked over to the board games. "We don't need to bring Clue."

"Yes!" she shouted, only to be shushed by Jillian. "Oh . . ." She bent her back and raised a finger to her lips, grabbing the game and holding it close to her body. "The babies are sleeping." Her voice was a whisper now and then she turned back to me. "Yes, Dax, we *need* to bring Clue. I want to play again."

I chuckled at her, shaking my head as she walked past me to the door. "Okay, I guess we'll bring the game back tomorrow?"

Will waved. "Night, Daxton. Make sure she drinks some more water, or we'll hear about it in the morning."

"Ha, yes, please make sure she drinks some water," Jillian echoed.

"I'm not drunk," Jamie protested.

"Oh, but you are." I put my hand on her lower back, grabbed both of our coats, and gently pushed her through the door, through the snow, up the patio steps, and into our cabin.

It was dark, but warm, and once I flicked on the kitchen light and the living room glowed, I got the urge to light a fire. But Jamie stumbling into the living room, tossing the game on the rug, reminded me that I had a fake girlfriend to put to sleep.

"Okay you—" I started.

"One more game," she interrupted.

"Jamie, no, it's past midnight."

"It will be fast. Besides, I'm not drunk."

"Says the drunk person," I mumbled under my breath, grabbing a glass, and filling it with water. "This entire glass needs to be gone before you go to bed."

"How come you're not drunk?" she asked as she positioned herself on the rug in front of the board game. She sat on her knees and wobbled back and forth, trying to get comfortable in the most uncomfortable position ever. She laid the game board out and started matching the color pawns to their square. "You drank way more than I did."

"I can hold my liquor. You, apparently, cannot."

Holding the cards in her hand to give them a good shuffle, she straightened her back and glared at me. "I can."

"Okay, whatever you say."

"Sit, let's play."

Giving into her wishes, I sat with my legs crossed in front of her, watching as she carefully shuffled the cards. Once she started dealing them out, she looked to the empty place to her right, squinting her eyes, and slowly handing out more cards. Once she gave me my final card, her back jerked up and she let out a loud gasp.

"You have an iPhone!" She pointed at me, her jaw dropped and eyes wide.

I nodded. "I do."

"So do I!" she exclaimed, pointing to herself now.

"Amazing."

"So does Madeline, and so does Milo! SO!" She instantly dropped her cards and went to the kitchen island where her bag was. I heard keys hit the marble countertop and rustling of the contents on her bag. "Where's your phone?"

"In my pocket," I answered.

"Get it and FaceTime Milo. I'll FaceTime Maddie, and they can play with us!"

I furrowed my brow, twisting my torso to look at Jamie. She was already hunched over, the familiar ring of FaceTime echoing in the dining room. I quickly stood and walked over to her.

"That won't work Jamie . . ."

"Jamie?" I heard Madeline's tired voice come through the other end of the phone. It was followed by a grumble and some muffling. It was past midnight here, meaning Madeline and Milo were already fast asleep in Portland.

"Maddie!" Jamie yelled, loud enough to wake the entirety of Park City.

I tried to shush her, trying to get close enough to take the phone away, but Jamie pulled it away from me.

"Jamie, is everything okay?" Madeline asked.

"Yes! I'm wonderful, you want to play Clue with me and Daxton? I mean Elliot. Your name is still Elliot with me, right? I'd rather call you Elliot because you're an Elliot, you're not a Daxton." She turned her head and pinched her brow at me.

"Jamie . . ." Madeline yawned.

I grabbed the phone from her and looked at Madeline, laying down on her side, only her face illuminated by the phone's glow.

"Good night, Mads, I'll explain in the morning."

"Night, Elliot. You know she's a lightweight, right?" Madeline asked.

"I do now," I responded at the same time Jamie yelled, "I am not!"

I hung up and shoved her phone in my pocket. She plopped down on one of the stools and dropped her chin into her palm. Her eyes dropped and all the emotion drained from her face before she took a deep breath, held it for a few seconds and then let it out through her mouth.

"It would have worked," she mumbled softly. "I had it all worked out in my head . . ."

I dropped my shoulders and looked at the now-sad girl in front of me. Moments ago, she was full of energy, excited that everyone she loved in her life had an iPhone, ready to play a game of Clue, and now it looked like she was going to cry. I took a step forward and placed my hands on her shoulders, squeezing gently.

"I hate to tell you, but it really wouldn't have worked."

"Why did Jilly have to ask how we met? Why couldn't she have just taken your answer?" she asked, lifting her chin to look at me face on.

I shrugged. "Well, in her defense, I didn't know how you told her we met. I assumed we met with Milo and Madeline."

"What if she finds out you're not really Daxton?"

"I *am* Daxton though. Elliot Daxton Whittaker, remember?"

She hummed and licked her lips. Straightening up her back slightly, she looked at my shoulders, my biceps, before finally settling her eyes on my forearm. She grabbed my hand, turning it so my palm was down, and she slowly pulled my sleeve up, revealing my tattoo. Jamie studied it, running her fingers over the black ink.

"A part of me wishes you could just be Elliot," she whispered. "None of this stupid faking business. Just real dating. With the real Elliot and the real Jamie."

Real dating, with the real me, and the real her. Was that something I needed to pay attention to? Or was it the alcohol talking? I had been looking at Jamie for months now; ever since I saw her for the first time at the Piano Bar. When all she saw was

Clay, all I saw was her. I would give anything to be able to really, truly date her. Really, truly be able to call her mine. I was taking the three weeks as a trial period; hoping that maybe she would see it that way too. Jamie was something different, and I needed her to know she was truly remarkable.

I watched as her fingers traced the guitar strings that led to my elbow, her eyes following her finger's every move. She sighed, and finally looked up at me to meet my gaze.

God, she was stunning. I could kiss her . . .

I broke free from my trance and slowly pulled my arm away from her. Standing, I reached out a hand for her.

"Come on, you. Let's get you to bed."

"But we're going to play Clue," she said, still with sadness in her voice.

I laughed. "No, we never were. Come on, I'll help you up the stairs."

Finally, she nodded in agreement. Pushing herself to her feet, she fumbled, tripping over her own boots. I caught her, wrapping my arms around her waist and holding her close to my body. Her hands were flat on my chest as her chin raised to look at me.

"Elliot," she whispered.

I answered her with a hum.

"Kiss me, like you did that night after the wedding."

Taken aback, I leaned down ever so softly, my lips barely touching her, before I stopped.

"Not tonight," I whispered against her lips.

"But you said you would kiss me." She rested her chin on my chest, furrowing her eyebrows as she closed her eyes.

"Oh, trust me, I will."

Jamie let out a small groan. "Please, I always think about that kiss. I know you want to."

"I do, I really . . . really do, but Jamie . . ." I moved my hand and brushed the hair from her face, pulling it behind her ears, "I won't kiss you when you're not going to remember it. If you still want me to kiss you tomorrow, I will."

Heaving a sigh, she pushed herself off my chest. "Oh trust me, I've been wanting to kiss you all day. I'll definitely want you to kiss me tomorrow."

She stepped ever so lightly to the stairs; her palms parallel to the floor as she walked, almost as if they were her balance beam.

"Ask me in the morning, and I'll gladly kiss you," I answered, following her up the stairs to make sure she was safely tucked in, giving her a small kiss on her forehead before going back down to the living room. Leaving the board game on the rug, I grabbed my blanket and fell on the couch—there was no way I was going to sleep anytime soon.

The rustling of sheets and the creaky floorboard are what finally woke me from the little sleep I got. I tried to calm my mind, but no matter how hard I tried I couldn't shake what Jamie had said just hours before. She wanted me to kiss her. She was waiting for it. She asked for it. And I was too chicken shit to do it.

"Stupid demon stair . . ." she grumbled under her breath, just loud enough for me to hear.

I smiled, a breathy laugh leaving my lungs. "Good morning," I mumbled back at her, sitting up on the couch. I had slept in my clothes, something I rarely ever did.

Jamie appeared around the fireplace and groaned. Her hair was disheveled, and her shirt was wrinkly. She had managed to change into sleep shorts before I covered his with a blanket, but anyone could tell she had a "fun" night. Her makeup was smudged, her posture was terrible, and the look in her eyes could kill.

And yet, she was still stunning.

"How are you feeling?" I asked, standing to stretch and fold the blanket.

She held up a hand, stopping me from saying anything else. "Don't. Talk. I need coffee first."

"And a greasy breakfast. I think I have some sausages I can cook for you."

"I said . . ." she whispered.

"I know," I whispered back, "don't talk."

Coming up behind her, I ran my hand along her back. I leaned down and kissed her temple, causing her to stiffen. I could feel her eyes on me as I grabbed the coffee and started to work the pot. Did she remember what she said last night? Did she remember asking me to kiss her? A huge portion wanted her to remember, the other small—very small—part, hoped she didn't.

"Did I . . ." she grumbled, taking a seat at the island, dropping her head on the counter. I inhaled, holding my breath as I waited for her next question. "FaceTime Madeline to play a board game last night?"

Letting my breath out, I laughed. "Yes. You sure did."

She groaned louder, turning her head side to side on the cold marble. I just smiled as I made her sausages and coffee, setting them in front of her to cure her hangover.

All she had to do was ask me, but that small part of me knew she wouldn't.

Chapter Twenty

-Jamie-

I was never drinking again.

Avoiding Elliot all day was easy, for the most part. He, thankfully, busied himself with Harrison and my dad. They went for a hike, and then to the store, spending the majority of the day away from the cabins. Which was A-OK by me.

I would never—ever—let him know I remembered holding onto him with all my strength last night and practically begging him to kiss me. I know that if he did kiss me, more would have happened. I would have let so much more happen. But Elliot was too much of a gentleman. A gentleman who also said he would kiss me, said that he would show me *affection*. A gentleman that may have a different side to him. My mind couldn't help but wonder what he would be like if we were able to be the *real* Elliot and the *real* Jamie that I had so stupidly mentioned last night. How much affection was I missing by having him only pretend. The small kisses on my temple and touches on my back were one thing, but I was starting to crave more.

I tried to shake off any thought I had while I ate dinner with my siblings, immersing myself in the world of restaurants Holden owned. Listening to him talk about expanding his Italian chain made it a tad bit easier to not think about running my fingers over Elliot's tattoo. I could still feel his skin against my fingertips. This was not going well . . .

No more alcohol for me on this trip. Nope. It wasn't happening.

Elliot joined us around the table once he and Harrison had finished chopping the firewood. Before he sat down, he leaned down and kissed the top of my head, giving me a smile and sigh as he took his seat. Then he ate, enjoying the food Jillian had made, thanking her profusely. Then, when the kids were in bed and the day was done, we retreated back to the cabin, where I instantly ran upstairs and went to bed. I did not need any more alone time with Elliot Whittaker.

Just as fast as I closed my eyes, my alarm clock blared. It was Wednesday. The first "family day" where we all went to Woodward Adventure Park. There we could ski, the kids could jump on the indoor trampoline, or we could tube down the hill. It was supposed to be a fun day where we all hung out and did things we normally wouldn't do, but all I could think of was having to be close to Elliot.

I took a shower, giving myself a quick pep talk in the mirror before getting dressed and doing my hair. Elliot was already in the kitchen, the smell of coffee filling the small space. I could hear sizzling as well. Avoiding the demon stair, I attempted to quietly walk downstairs.

"There's no way of being quiet in this cabin is there?" I asked, loud enough for Elliot to hear me.

He let out a loud *"HA"* in response. "Pretty sure the creaks are permanent. Even if the floors get redone, they will still be there forever."

I came into the kitchen, noticing he was already dressed and ready for the day. His laptop was open, his emails there for the world to see. There was an email from Clay, one that had a lot of numbers that I couldn't make rhyme or reason out of.

"It gives it charm." I sat down on the barstool and watched as Elliot moved around the kitchen. *I could get used to . . . nope . . . stop thinking that right now.* I cleared my throat. "Did you get some work done this morning? How long have you been up?"

He rubbed his hand down his face, letting out a long, exasperated sigh.

"I didn't sleep well last night; I've been up since about five." He turned, a mug of coffee in his hand. He placed it in front of me. It looked perfect—the right ratio of coffee to creamer. I touched the handle and pulled it closer. "I got a few work emails out of the way. Clay gathered all the information for an appraisal."

"Oh, right." I sighed. "You're selling the company."

"Yes. There's also an email from Liam, that agent from Pacific Sound. There wasn't much to it, but I think he wants to get the ball rolling."

I widened my eyes. That was news I wasn't expecting to hear just yet. I figured he would sell before making the move on his band, and I knew selling could take years. "Elliot that's . . . that's . . ." I stumbled, unable to get the words out.

I wanted to jump up and give him a hug to congratulate him, but I forced myself to stay put.

He chuckled. "I know. I texted Bennett, but honestly, he's probably still sleeping. He had a game last night, so he is most likely out."

"A game?" I asked.

"He's a hockey player, and he's in season." He leaned on the counter, his palms flat against the marble, his shoulder hunching just enough as his eyes studied my face.

"I wouldn't have pegged Bennett for a hockey player. He seems all music."

"Music and hockey. That's all he does. He may call today. I know it's a big family day but if he calls I'll need to talk to him."

"Well, duh. When do they want to see you?"

He scoffed, turning back to the stove to remove the bacon from the pan. He tossed the towel over his shoulder, which, for me, was a move that basically sold me on a man. I blinked a few times and took a long drink from my coffee, instantly regretting how long I had let my eyes linger.

"They didn't say," he responded, turning back to me with a plate of bacon and scrambled eggs. "I asked your mom if I could make you breakfast, so don't worry, this is the only breakfast you'll have."

He needed to stop being so perfect.

"Thank you." I smiled. "But what do you mean 'They didn't say?'"

Shrugging his shoulders, he leaned his palms on the counter. "They were vague. Like I said, he didn't give much detail. But it seems like they are interested. I also gave them Bennett's information, letting them know that Bennett is just as much a lead guy as I am."

I took a bite of my eggs, the taste sitting perfectly on my tongue. Nodding, I tried to savor the taste while also trying to swallow to respond to him.

"Most labels want the front man, the face you register with the band, and that's you." I pointed my fork at him.

"True, but things have to happen before we can move forward with that, like today for instance." He raised a single eyebrow. "Your dad mentioned a place called Woodward."

I gave him a grin, biting the tip of my tongue.

"I hope you packed warm clothes. It's supposed to snow today."

Woodward was packed. The fresh powder on the ground only caused more people to come and enjoy the runs, which, for me, meant skiing was out of the question. I was more into the tubing hills anyway.

My parents paid for everyone, and volunteered to watch as the kids play in the indoor tramp park while everyone else picked their activity. Carrie, Holden, and Will all rented skis, and Jillian, Harrison, Elliot and I all went to the tubing park.

I lived for this. First, when it was Gorgoza Park, and then once Woodward came in—creating more tubing lanes—I was more stoked. I jumped up and down in line, my hair bouncing around my beanie as my boots crunched into the snow. I held onto my tube as we rode up to the top of the hill, the adrenaline filling my body. Ophelia had told me all about her new obsession with bungee jumping, how her heart rate would pick up and how she could feel the wind hit every nerve on her skin, I knew soaring down a mountain on an innertube wasn't the same, but man if the adrenaline wasn't coursing through me now.

"Easy tiger." Elliot chuckled as we got to the top of the hill.

"Hell no. This is my favorite thing. I am going to jump up and down like a five-year-old and live for it." I stuck my tongue out at him.

Jillian shook her head at us. "She acts like this every year. She must have told you."

Elliot looked at Jillian, thinking about his answer I could tell. Jillian had been giving us weird looks. Her eyebrows pinched, his eyes studying as we interacted. She would casually bring him up in conversation yesterday, asking random questions that I had to come up with answers to on the spot. I watched the two talk, Elliot giving her a simple answer as to how we've only been dating during the summer, and he'd rather sit and watch me paint. Jillian hummed, accepting the answer, but still not *liking* it.

"Miss," the attendant said, his arm held out to me.

I turned to Elliot, giving him a quick peck on the cheek before I jumped on my tube and was pushed down the hill. The air hit my face, my hair flapping against my shoulders. I caught some air over a jump and then the tube went up and started to slow down. The entire ride lasted twenty to thirty seconds tops, but I loved it. I cheered as I stood, raising my arms to the sky. I could feel my heart—my *heart*—pumping. Taking a deep breath, I turned to watch as Elliot's tube came barreling down the hill, his scream only getting louder. He met me at the bottom, his hair all out of sorts and his scruff covered with a light dusting of snow.

He stood, fumbled slightly, and then gave me a massive smile.

"Okay . . . we're doing that a million more times."

I laughed, grabbing his hand and my tube as we raced towards the lift again.

Chapter Twenty-One

-Elliot-

After flying down the hill fifteen times, I gave in. As much fun as it was—especially the ride where Jamie and I went down together, holding onto each other for dear life once the tube caught some air—I needed sustenance. Jamie danced her way to the tubing hill, promising me, after one more run, she'd meet me inside.

"I'll be the one with the hot chocolate," I responded, heading inside with Jillian.

The kids, along with Janet and Mr. Gaines (I still wasn't allowed to call him Howard *just* yet), had claimed a large table in the middle of the crowded room. Jillian wrapped her arms around her twins and asked what they wanted from the grill, then she followed me to the register.

I ordered some French fries, and two hot chocolates, shoving my frozen hands into my coat pockets while we waited. I had gloves but damn, they were useless.

"What do you think?" Jillian asked me, leaving against the counter.

"Of?" I responded, dumbfounded.

She laughed. "The place, and Jamie. It's amazing that Jamie can still have all this energy, isn't it?"

I furrowed my brow. "What do you mean? She's always high energy."

Tilting her head, she hummed. Shifting her gaze to the grill behind us she softly added, "She likes to pretend nothing is wrong you know, I'm sure you've noticed it. With her health . . . it still shocks me that she would exert herself like this."

I didn't respond. I wasn't sure how. Her health? I had known Jamie for a while now and she always seemed full of life, healthy—all the time. She worked every day, loving her job and seeing her friends at night. During Milo's Wedding she was a burst of energy, excited for everyone, even that night. That kiss.

Jillian noticed my silence, turning her head to me, her eyes wider. "She hasn't told you, has she?"

"Told me what?" My voice was low. My brain began to go over every health condition in the book that would make one's family nervous about them tubing down a hill. When Jillian didn't respond, only sighing, and turning back to the grill once her name was called, I dug into my snow pants for my phone. Jacob was the one person who came to my mind. He would be able to tell me all kinds of things WebMD wouldn't be able to.

"Hey!" Jamie's voice made me jump as she appeared by my side, the smile and look of pure *joy* on her face took the fear that she may be sick completely away. She was so happy, so *alive*. "Where's my hot chocolate?"

Stuffing my phone back into my pocket, I wrapped my arm around her waist, and gently pressed her into me, kissing her forehead. If something really was wrong, all I had to do was ask, and if she trusted me enough . . . she would tell me. She lifted her chin to me, her eyes narrow as her lips tightened into a smile.

"Hot chocolate?" she asked again.

"E. Daxton," came a shout from the grill.

"Right there. Fries and Hot Chocolate." I let her go to grab the food, instantly coming right back to her and handing her the paper cup.

Her shoulders danced as she lifted it to her lips and took a small sip. "You know, I love coming on this trip, but I think Woodward day is my favorite day."

"I can see why," I led her back to the table where everyone sat, taking the seat next to her as she removed her gloves and hat to pop a French fry in her mouth.

"So, where's the party moving to tonight?" Janet asked once we were all seated.

"Oh, it doesn't stop with Woodward?" I draped my arms around Jamie's chair, a position I've grown accustomed to since the first dinner.

Jamie shook her head.

"Oh, hell no," Holden answered. "Siblings and Spouse Night."

"Sibling . . . and Spouse Night?" I repeated, "So since I'm not a sibling or a spouse . . ."

Jamie began shaking her head vigorously, her hair flapping on her shoulders. "Oh no you don't. You're coming. Harrison comes."

"Yes, but I'm a sibling." Harrison raised a single finger, Jamie shot him a glare.

"My boyfriend may not be my spouse . . ."

"Yet," I mumbled. Jamie didn't hear, or rather she pretended not to hear.

". . . . but he's coming."

"And where are we going?" I ask, my fingers touching Jamie's shoulder.

She sat up straight to my touch, chin in the air and eyes closed. "You'll see," She responded.

"So many secrets." I tilted my head. "I thought we agreed I could choose the bar after skiing?"

"It's more fun that way, plus this isn't the ski trip." Jamie scrunched her nose and popped another fry in her mouth.

"Trust us, Dax, you'll have a blast. Just make sure Jamie sticks to one glass of wine." Will chuckled.

"One Mango-rita you mean," I correct him, my eyes never leaving the beautiful woman next to me.

Health secret or not, she was all I saw.

Chapter Twenty-Two

-Jamie-

"Thank God it stopped snowing!" I exclaimed as we left the cabin hours later.

"Well, when you decide stilettos are the shoe of choice in the middle of February . . . yea, I would be happy it stopped snowing too," Elliot joked, his eyes on me the entire time.

He had waited patiently for me to get ready for the night out. Sibling and Spouse Night was my second favorite activity, and I was more pumped to have someone to go with this year. I had even dressed for the occasion. My white high heels, that I never got to wear, a black short skirt, and a cream, long-sleeve, boat neck top. I even curled my hair and did my makeup. I felt gorgeous and, even though he was joking about my shoe choice, I could tell Elliot liked what he saw. Elliot dressed up too—as much as he could at least.

He wore a black, button-up shirt complete with his jeans and a pair of nice black boots.

Even the winter coats didn't throw off the feeling of . . . looking . . . good.

Elliot parked on Main Street, across from The Cabin Bar, paid the parking meter, and reached for my hand as we made our way to the entrance. Everyone was already there, holding out their arms as Elliot and I came up.

"Why didn't you park on the China Bridge!?" Holden asked as we got closer.

"What," Elliot defended, "And miss the thrill of parallel parking on Main Street? Nah. I want to gain the full Main Street experience."

We gathered in the entrance of the bar, gave our name for the reservation, and were led to our table. The lighting was dim, and the scene was perfect. We came here every year and it never got old. We always picked a night where there was a live band or karaoke, and tonight seemed like a karaoke night. Jillian always tried to get me on stage, maybe after a few drinks . . . no . . . maybe after *one* drink I would have the courage to go up.

The seven of us sat and ordered our first round of drinks. Once the Mango-rita was in front of me, Elliot raised a single eyebrow, bringing his beer to his lips.

"This is my only drink, I promise."

"I didn't mind taking care of a drunk Jamie, but you may need to call Madeline before to make sure she's ready to play Clue," he joked.

I pinched my brow, narrowed my eyes and gave him a tight smile. Two could play in this game. "Oh no, tonight I'll call Ophelia. She and Clay would play Clue on FaceTime with me."

"I'm sorry, what?" Harrison asked us, leaning across the table.

"Jamie got drunk the other night and tried to play a board game with people in a different state."

I brought the salted rim to my lips and licked. "I still say it would have worked."

Jillian laughed, rubbing her husband's bicep as she settled into her seat some more. "As much fun as that sounds, I need a night free of kids and phone calls from work. There have been way too many of those, this trip, and I am so ready for this night."

"That's why you need to just ditch that way of life, Jilly, and travel," Harrison said simply, his eyes roaming the crowd that had gathered in after us.

Jillian laughed. "No, thank you, Harry. I do love my job, my home, my family—the stability of it." Jillian's words were meant to stab him like a knife, instead Harrison just laughed.

"And I love the adventure that my life offers. Holden would agree. Wouldn't you Holden." Harrison tipped his beer towards our older brother.

"Don't pull me into this." Holden shook his head at Harrison, leaning back in his chair, his arm draped around Carrie's shoulders.

I smirked. There was no doubt that Holden picked up that move from Elliot. Sure, it was a move that men have done for years, but it had become something I expected from Elliot when he sat next to me. And to see my brother mimic him made me laugh inside. Elliot was leaning forward, his arms folded on the table as he watched my brothers talk, Will popping in every now and then. Once the lights dimmed and a man came on the small stage, the table quieted down and Elliot relaxed back in the seat, rolling the sleeves up on his shirt.

My eyes caught his tattoo right before he crossed his arms over his chest.

"Did you know they were doing karaoke tonight?" Elliot asked as the announcer began to talk about how the night would go and the massive selection of songs they had available.

I gave him a cheeky grin. "We always come on karaoke night, or live band night."

"Ooo . . . live bands?" Elliot's interest peaked.

"I think there is one later this week." Holden leaned forward, catching Elliot's attention, "We should try to get tickets. Carrie and I love coming to the shows."

Elliot raised his eyebrows, and I could tell he was doing his best to keep his love for the stage in. He was the one who said we would keep that under wraps, but I'd be lying if I said I wasn't secretly hoping he'd get on the stage and sing something stupid for karaoke night.

"That sounds great, Holden. What do you think, Jamie? Wanna see if we can go to a show?" Elliot looked over at me, his eyebrows still so high they were almost at his hairline.

I pursed my lips and nodded to him.

"Daxton." Jillian furrowed her brow and reached an arm across the table. "Is that a tattoo?" She grabbed Elliots arm and pulled it forward, revealing the guitar on his forearm. "A guitar?"

Elliot let out a breathy chuckle. "Yea, I used to play."

"Used to?" I added, "He still does."

From the corner of my eye, I saw Elliot tilt his body and look at me, pulling his arm back under the table. I kept my eyes on Jillian as I took a sip of my drink.

"You do? Jamie why didn't you mention that?"

"He doesn't like to talk about it. He has an amazing voice, too."

"You should sing karaoke!" Jillian screamed across the table to Elliot.

I could see it in his eyes that he wanted to say yes. He wanted to jump up and grab a guitar and just start singing. He didn't need his band to put on one hell of a show.

"I don't need to sing karaoke," was his simple, monotone response.

I rolled my eyes at him, accepting—but not liking—his answer. I wanted him to let loose. Be that real Elliot that I found myself paying more and more attention to. He pulled out his phone and chuckled, typing a quick response to a text before placing it face up on the table. Holden and Harrison started singing along with whoever was performing, terribly might I add, and all I could think of was how I could get Elliot on that stage.

If only I had Bennett's number . . . maybe, he would be able to convince him.

Elliot's phone lit up and he instantly picked it up, laughing once again before typing out his response.

"And who are you texting?" I leaned in and asked, instantly regretting becoming *that* girlfriend.

"Ha, you'll like this." He opened his phone, sliding it over in front of me. It was a group chart between him, Milo, and Clay, and it instantly made my stomach flip.

Elliot: *There's karaoke at the bar tonight - I think Jamie planned this.*

"I totally did," I said, before reading the rest of the chat.

Milo: *And that's a problem? Get up there and make her swoon even more.*

Elliot: *Ha - ya...no. My love for the stage didn't come to Park City. I'm an architect, remember?*

Clay: *Doesn't mean Daxton can't let loose. Get. On. That. Stage.*

Milo: *Sing that song that reminds you of Jamie - what's it called?*

Elliot: *That's not happening.*

Milo: *I'll ask Maddy, she knows.*

"You have a song that reminds you of me?" I asked, sliding his phone back to him. I slowly lifted my gaze to him, feeling my breath quicken. What was going on with me? Elliot was not the one I wanted to have these feelings for, yet, here they were seeming to get stronger and stronger with each passing moment. Ever since that first one, that first kiss on my doorstep . . . I was just having a harder time ignoring them now that he was in front of me.

Taking a deep breath, he nodded, taking his phone back. "I have a few actually."

"Sing it for me."

He scoffed, "Nah, not tonight."

"Who sings it?"

Elliot's eyes searched mine as the smile got wider on his lips.

"Elliot," I whispered, "who sings it?"

"Maybe I'll sing a different song," Elliot whispered back. "Do you want me to sing?"

Feeling the chills race up my spine, I nodded.

Without a beat, he slid his chair from the table and began to make his way to the stage. Butterflies grew in my stomach as he got closer and closer to the stage.

"Wait!" Jillian exclaimed. "He's singing!?"

My eyes never left Elliot as he talked to the man in charge, going through their list of songs and when he finally settled on one, he smiled. Then he waited for the others to go ahead of him, and then it was his turn. He looked relaxed, calm, his arms folded against his chest. He had rolled up his sleeves, his tattoo still visible from the distance. He exuded confidence—he was ready to get to the mic. If only they had a spare guitar for him. And just watching him, the butterflies grew. Was he going to sing the song that reminded him of me?

"Up next is a visitor from Oregon, Daxton Whittaker singing a country tune." The announcer let Elliot on the stage and when the music started—a song I instantly recognized, thanks to Madeline— I couldn't help but laugh.

"What is he singing?" Jillian shouted, leaning over the table to me.

"It's called *Craving You,* by Thomas Rhett." I smiled as the beat got louder.

"He's a country fan?"

"Not really, but Madeline loves country, so he had to learn a shit ton of Thomas Rhett songs for her wedding," I answered.

Her eyes narrowed as she tilted her head back and hummed, turning back to Elliot on stage.

He grabbed the mic and began to sing, his voice just as I remember it, so much better live than on the recorded tracks. He was in his element. The crowd cheered for him, and Jillian's jaw dropped. He wasn't even looking at the words on the screen, he knew them all by heart. I think the only thing he forgot about this song was that a woman joined in on the second verse.

When it came time for the woman, I joined in from the table, loud enough that my siblings could hear me, but Elliot couldn't. For the next line I sang louder, projecting my voice over the crowd, and this time, he noticed. His eyes met me as we sang the chorus together and when a mic appeared in front of me, Elliot wiggled his eyebrows.

I took the mic but stayed seated and Jillian's jaw went wide as my voice boomed over the crowd, joining him.

The music slowed, and soon it was just our voices, singing the lead up to the last chorus. The female was supposed to add her own vocal before he joined, and Elliot knew . . .

"This is all you, babe." He smiled, pointing at me and I hit the note perfectly. Well in my mind it was perfect, but who knows. It could have been completely off-key and absolutely terrible, but Elliot's attention was on me, and that was all I needed.

The song ended with Elliot, but he stayed firm on the stage, his eyes fixed on me.

I waved the mic around in my fingers, completely shocked that I just did that with him. I rolled my lips, trying to stay in the moment and be confident, completely shaking the nerves out of my body. I wasn't nervous when I started singing, so why was I getting nervous now?

The announcer walked up the stage and patted Elliot on the back, "I think it's safe to say we have a new favorite for the night!" The crowd cheered. "What do you say Daxton? Can you perform a few more for us?"

Elliot's smile grew. "Sure, I'd love to."

"I can't believe you just did that Jamie! And you kept that talent from us! He's amazing Jamie!" Jillian shouted.

I heaved a sigh, making sure the mic was off before I set it down on the table.

"Don't I know it."

Elliot had completely stolen karaoke from the rest of the crowd, but I don't think anyone else minded. He ended up singing at least six or seven more songs before he tapped out for the night, making his way back to the table. Full of confidence, his adrenaline boosted as he swooped me into his arms once I stood to meet him.

My siblings began to fawn over him, telling him exactly how amazing he was, but he had heard it all before. He thanked them, said he enjoyed every second of it, leaving to talk to the announcer once again before we all left the table after paying our tab. Elliot and I stepped out of the building first and greeted with a massive snowfall. The roads were covered with snow—one foot at least— and no cars were on the road. Elliot's Jeep was the only one I could really see, even though it was covered in snow.

"You've got to be kidding me!" I screamed. I could already feel the snow touching my feet, instantly regretting the high heels.

"I bet you're second guessing the stilettos . . . huh?" He laughed, wrapping his arm around my waist, bringing me close to his body. "I'll step in first, and then you can step in my footprints."

"Hell no," I said without hesitation. "Go get the car and bring it around to me."

"Oh, so you're a princess now?"

"I swear if you start calling me Princess . . ."

"Nah, you're my rockstar, so that's what I'll be calling you from now on. I didn't know you could sing. A painter *and* a singer . . . you are simply amazing." Elliot's voice softened as he said the last line. *You are simply amazing.*

My heart fluttered, but a quick clearing of my throat reminded me that we were in the middle of a snowstorm, and I wasn't wearing the proper footwear.

"Just go get the car and come get me."

Elliot's laugh boomed, "Yea, no, that's not happening."

He tightened his grip around my waist and lifted me off the ground. I bent my knees and reached for his coat, grabbing onto anything I could to help keep me stable, and once I was high enough, he trudged through. We laughed with each step, and I could feel myself falling, slipping through his grip.

"I'm falling!" I squealed.

"We're almost there," he replied, a laugh still hanging in the air. "I got you!"

Once we reached the Jeep, he kicked snow out of the way and dropped me down in front of him, his hands still on my waist. I could feel the heat from his palms through my layers. The pressure of them was enough to send my stomach in knots. I glanced at the bar, seeing my siblings finally leave the bar.

"See," Elliot's voice pulled me back to him, "semi-dry feet." He smiled.

I placed my hands on his chest, running them up to his shoulders, feeling his hair flutter between my fingers. Today was full of adventure—new experiences that I hadn't planned on having. All with Elliot. If he weren't standing in front of me, fake boyfriend or not, I wouldn't be feeling this way. I would have still flown down the mountain on that tube, alone, while my family went with their spouses. I would have still enjoyed my time tonight with them, but Elliot . . .

Elliot made it all feel different.

I had told him I had thought about our kiss, that I wanted it again. Who was to say he had to make the first move.

My heels already made it so I was closer to him, but I still lifted myself to the balls of my feet, pulling him down to me, and kissed him.

Just like on my front porch, his lips were soft and hesitant at first, but they relaxed as his arms wrapped around my body, fully enveloping me. With a deep breath he parted his lips, deepening the sweet kiss, becoming hungry—passionate. Our tongues began to dance with one another as the snow hit our cheeks, the chill from the flakes only making the heat between us stronger. Snow snuck its way into my stilettos, but even that chill was nothing compared to Elliot. Lacing my fingers through his hair, I finally broke the kiss, knowing very well I'd be coming back for more.

"Hi," he whispered against my lips.

"There's snow in my shoe."

He smiled. "You're simply amazing."

"Get. A. ROOM!" I heard Harrisons' voice from across the road. I jumped as Elliot spun his head quickly to look at them, almost as if he were nervous that we got caught. My siblings all stood at the sidewalk, waving at us as they began to make their way to their cars.

He waved his hand at them and turned back to me. Pursing my lips, I leaned my forehead on his chest.

"Did you know they were watching?" he asked, his voice hollow.

I swallowed. I could take this one of two ways, and I hated the response I gave him.

"Of course."

His grip on my waist loosened and he nodded, reaching over me to open the car door.

"Climb in, I'll get all the snow off, then we can get you back to the cabin."

I watched as the fire that was there drained from his face. I nodded at him, following his direction and sat down on the driver's seat, kicking my shoes off before crawling over the middle console to the passenger seat. I watched as Elliot removed all the snow from the car, wishing I had said something else instead of *"of course."*

Chapter Twenty-Three

-Elliot-

Of course . . .
> *Of course . . .*
> *Of course . . .*

Of course she knew her family was there.

We drove back in silence to our small cabin, taking turns and stopping slowly. The roads were covered in snow, the deep fluff untouched until I guided my tires through it. Everyone else was following me, their headlights hitting my rearview and side view mirrors just right. Even though I should have been one hundred percent focused on the road in front of me, all I could replay in my mind was Jamie.

Singing loudly from the audience, enough to get Pete's (the owner I found out, not just the man in charge of karaoke) attention to race a mic to her. Her voice matched mine and all I wanted to do was get her on that stage with me. I wanted to see her come loose, just like she did at the tubing park. I wanted to see all the adrenaline pump from her soul. Pete had told me to come back for the next karaoke night, and to bring my girl with me. I wanted so badly to get her on that stage with me. I had no idea she could sing like that. It clouded my mind . . .

But none of that mattered after Jamie kissed me.

She kissed me. *She* was the one who pressed her lips to mine, taking her time to explore what I had to offer. I would have kissed her again if Harrison hadn't interrupted the moment. And then of course she had to admit she knew they were there. That the kiss was for Daxton, not for *me.*

Then there were the looming words from Jillian earlier. *She hasn't told you, has she . . .*

The hours of the day seemed to mesh into one, making it hard to believe it was all in the past twenty-four hours.

I parked my Jeep in front of our cabin. Leaving Jamie in the car, I ran to the porch to get the shovel to clear a path for her. As much as I wanted to, I didn't think she would appreciate me carrying her into the house. Walking down her path with my boots, I opened her car door.

"You didn't have to do that." Jamie smiled as she slipped on her heels once more.

I shrugged.

"Night you two! See you in the morning!" Jillian called. I waved to them as they disappeared into their respective cabins, and instantly put my attention back on the girl in my Jeep.

Jamie quickly ran into the cabin, her heels crunching with each stab in the snow. Setting the shovel back down, and making sure the Jeep was locked, I followed her into the cabin and into the kitchen.

I could handle my emotions one of two ways here. I could ignore them, shaking it off as a part of the game that we were kind of playing. The kiss wasn't something to read into. The words she said while she was drunk meant nothing. The glances. The touches.

All of it was a part of the fake dating game. We hadn't even made it a week into it, and I wasn't sure I believed the performance anymore. Could I ignore the way she smiled when I came into a room, the way she would lean into my body whenever she could. Her lips against mine?

The second option—the option I liked better—was the one I decided to jump on.

I hung my coat on the rack next to hers and marched my way over to her. Standing at the sink she had poured herself a glass of water, and once the glass was down on the counter, once she let out that small breath of air and turned only to find me right up against her, I pinned her to the counter.

Jamie let out a small gasp, one that I wanted to capture.

"Jamie," I said, my voice low and heavy. "I doubt you remember this, but I told you all you had to do was ask for me to kiss you and I would. I'm going to take that kiss earlier as you asking."

I took her mouth in mine and kissed her, not a sweet and gentle kiss at first, as the rest of our kisses had been, but with the same hunger as I had on the street. And by the way she kissed me back, the way her hands found my skin, the way her fingers laced through my hair . . . she wanted to pick up right where we left off too.

She hummed into me, pressing her weight against me. A small moan was enough to send me over the edge. Gripping her waist, my lips never once leaving hers, I lifted her onto the counter. She spread her legs, allowing me to step closer. She escaped our kiss and smiled against my lips, only to keep kissing me a second later. Touching her waist, I slipped my fingers up the back of her shirt, feeling her skin twitch as my fingers explored her lower back.

Sighing, she tilted her head back and my lips found her neck. She let out a small giggle.

I would take her right here if she would let me.

"Elliot," she moaned, "I have a confession. A few actually."

"I'm listening," I replied, kissing her collarbone, my tongue gliding up her neck.

"I remember asking you to kiss me, I've been wanting to ask you again."

"Why didn't you?" I kissed right below her ear.

"Nerves . . ." she trailed off, letting out a small gasp as I bit her skin. "But I have another confession . . ."

I ran my hand through her hair, pulling it back as I lifted my head, my eyes meeting hers. I raised an eyebrow and waited for the secret I was hoping would escape her lips. That she meant to kiss me, that she wanted to, that it wasn't just for show.

"I knew they were watching, but that's not why I kissed you."

And that's all I needed.

Wrapping my arms around her waist I pulled her off the counter. With a laugh, one that I wanted to hear more of, she wrapped her arms around my neck, her legs around my waist as I walked over to the couch. I sat, Jamie straddling me as she kissed me again, her hands trailing down my chest. I could live in this moment, this first *real* moment between the real Elliot and the real Jamie. Our first moment truly together. I never wanted it to end.

But, as if a light switched on, I remembered earlier with Jillian. If she was accepting of this, maybe she'd be accepting of the other.

I broke our connection and licked my lips, tasting the mango from her drink still lingering. The glow from the kitchen hit her skin just right as she moved her hips over me, almost causing me to lose my train of thought.

I cleared my throat. "Before we take this any further . . ."

Her jaw dropped. "Just how far did you think you were getting tonight?"

Widening my eyes at her, I watched as her shoulders rolled. She was teasing me. "Keep moving and talking like that and we'll get a lot farther."

"Oh, you think so . . ." she bit her bottom lip.

"Stop distracting me." I grabbed her arms and forced her body to still. She smiled and giggled—that same giggle. I closed my eyes and dropped my head against the back of the couch. "I have a confession now."

"Is it that you've been thinking about this ever since we got here?"

"No . . . I mean, yes, I have thought about it a few times."

She bent down and kissed me. "I will say it's getting harder to ignore."

"Agreed, however, I have a really serious question."

She sat up, flipping her hair over her shoulder. She moved her hands to my stomach, resting just about my belt. "Okay, okay, in all seriousness, what's your question?"

I heaved a sigh, knowing all too well this was going to kill the moment, but if we got here already, we could get here again.

"Jillian mentioned something earlier today, at Woodward." My fingers traced down her arms, finding her hands. Jamie slumped her back, arching just slightly away from me. "She mentioned that she was still shocked that you would do that kind of activity. I think she said that she was surprised, 'with your health, you would still exert yourself'?"

Jamie let out a long, irritated groan. "I'm going to kill her."

And just like that, the mood was gone, and Jamie climbed off my lap. She kicked her heels off in front of the fireplace and ran her hands through her hair, coming together at the base of her neck.

"What else did she say?" she finally asked, complete annoyance radiating from her.

"She was shocked you hadn't told me yet. Tell me what, Jamie?"

She hesitated, battling internally with herself for what felt like forever before she finally moved, sitting next to me on the couch, one leg folded under her.

"When I was thirteen," she started, taking a deep breath, "I began feeling . . . different. I would get tired extremely fast, exhausted to the point where I was falling asleep in class. I fainted a few times in P.E. and when I found it hard to breathe . . . when I couldn't make it through a simple gym class, my mom finally believed me and took me to the doctor. After a few different doctors and multiple tests, they discovered a hole in my heart. It was . . ."

she swallowed and ran her hands up my chest, trying to find the words to keep going.

As if it would help, I lightly gripped her arms. I could tell, this wasn't something she openly shared. Feeling how tense she was I leaned forward and lightly brushed my lips against hers. "Jamie . . ." I whispered.

She took a deep breath. "It was big, and they told me I needed to have surgery to close it, or it could expand. So . . . twelve years ago I had open heart surgery, and the hole was fixed, I spent an entire year in the hospital and my family—especially my sister—always reminds me of it."

"Jamie . . ."

"Nope, you're not going to feel bad for me either. You're the only one I've told outside of family. Madeline doesn't even know about this. I go to the doctor once a year for a checkup and I have been in great health. I monitor my heart rate when I do things that exert a lot of energy, like running, hence why I don't run, I jog . . ." she joked, allowing me to have a small laugh with her. "But really, I'm healthy and I'm fine and I'm happy. Jillian was there for the whole thing; she was in the hospital with me a lot. She's the one who brought me my first canvas and oil paints. If it wasn't for my heart almost failing, I would have never started painting."

She shifted her weight on the couch, scooting closer to me. Reaching up she touched my neck, her thumb running along my jawline, my stubble creating a slight scratch.

"Oddly enough it felt good to tell you, but really, I don't want you to worry about my health because it's fine. My heart is stronger than ever."

I leaned in, kissing her sweetly. I believed her, she trusted me with this, trusted me enough to care for her heart. Realizing just how fragile it was, I cupped her jaw, deepening the kiss as she welcomed it.

"I would very much like to kiss you every day from now on," I admitted, feeling her nose brush against mine as she leaned her forehead against me.

"I kind of expect you to *from now on.*"
So, I did.

Chapter Twenty-Four

-Jamie-

Elliot's lips were a mix between gentle and soft, hungry and passionate, and when I said we needed to slow down and go to bed, he kissed me one last time and said goodnight as I left him on the couch. It took everything in me not to call him up to the bed. I could still feel him all over, and nothing had even happened. All it took was that one kiss. It was so much better than the first one.

I could still feel him when I woke up. I could hear Elliot moving around in the kitchen, and the smell of coffee wafted up to the loft. It felt cozy, it felt . . . right. I lightly crawled out of bed and tiptoed into the bathroom. I knew he could hear me, but pretending like he couldn't helped, somehow. I freshened up, taking a fast shower, brushing my teeth, and running my fingers through my hair. I changed quickly, and went to join him in the kitchen, grabbing my baggy gray sweater and a hair tie on the way downstairs. I skipped the demon stair and hit the living room floor with a creek.

"Good morning." Elliot was sitting at the island, his laptop out in front of him. He stopped working and pushed himself to a standing position. He reached his arm out, grabbing my sweater to pull me close, giving me the best morning kiss I could ask for.

I hummed and pulled away. "Good morning."

Just as his lips met mine again, there was a loud knock at the door. We both stopped and turned towards the glass door that led into the kitchen. Jillian stood on the other side, her arms wrapped close to her body, a stupid grin on her face and a wave that made me want to punch her.

"Apparently, my sister wants in." I placed my hands on Elliot's shoulders and ran them down his arms before walking over to let Jillian in.

"Good morning you two, Dax . . . do you mind if I steal my sister for a moment?" Jillian asked, grabbing my hand.

"Not at all, I have some work to get done and I need to call a friend." Elliot sat back down at the island.

I sighed and slipped my boots on my feet, wishing I could give him one more kiss before leaving. I took one step towards Jillian when I realized *I could*. I spun and took the three steps to kiss him before leaving him there on the island with his laptop and coffee.

"See you soon." I waved and followed Jillian back outside. "Did mom cook up too much breakfast or something?" I asked once I caught up to her.

"No, she's still with dad. I just needed to talk to you before the day got too crazy."

"If this is about what you told Daxton he asked me about it last night and I told him everything," I admitted.

"Oh good, but that's not what this is about." She opened the door to the cabin, and I stepped aside so I could walk in.

Phillip and Killian were already sitting on the couch, the two older kids had laptops out to complete their schoolwork, but Holden's youngest was nowhere to be seen. I'd assumed he was still asleep. Will was in the kitchen, pouring breakfast for his two boys and he waved as Jillian and I walked right past him into the family room on the opposite end of the cabin.

"Am I not allowed to say good morning to anyone?" I asked with a hint of sarcasm.

"Okay listen." Jillian closed the door to the family room, still in her winter coat and untied boots. She was starting to scare me. "I have to ask you something, and I don't want you to get all defensive and angry with me, I just want the truth."

I inhaled, holding my breath. "Okay," I stammered.

"Who the hell is Daxton? Because he's clearly not your boyfriend."

I blinked. *What?* "What? Of course he is . . ."

"Jamie. You two have been so stiff around each other. Your stories on how you met don't match up, he claims to be an architect, but I looked, there is no Daxton Whittaker in Portland working as an architect. There's a Graham Whittaker, who looks an awful lot like Daxton, but clearly is way older than him. At first I thought it could be his dad, but nowhere in his bio does it mention kids, so that I'm at a loss on. And that kiss last night . . ." She slapped her thighs, her eyebrows pinched. "If that wasn't the most uncomfortable kiss I had ever seen. *Daxton,*" she air quoted his name, "I could tell, was not into it. It's like you saw us on the sidewalk and told him to kiss you to make it look more believable. And this morning, he had to have seen me coming."

I was frozen, completely unsure as to how to react here. I thought we had done a pretty good job the past few days playing the roles of boyfriend and girlfriend, and our kiss last night was anything but uncomfortable. I twisted my lips and looked down, thinking to myself that if only she had seen us after the show last night she would know it wasn't fake. But then again, up until last night it was.

"His name is Elliot," I stammered.

"I knew it. You found some random guy on the internet and begged him to be your boyfriend for this trip, didn't you?"

I dropped my jaw and furrowed my brow at her. She knew me too well to have guessed my original plan.

"Oh, Jamie you didn't."

"No, that's not what I did. I actually did meet Elliot through Madeline and Milo; he sang at their wedding. We met a few times before, but just as friends."

"So, he's a friend that you begged to come here?"

"I didn't beg." I folded my arms over my chest. "He offered."

Jillian raised her eyebrows like she didn't believe a word I said. Folding her arms over her chest she gave me the ultimate mom look. The one I knew would send her twins into the spiral, the exact same one that mom would give us.

"He did," I reiterated.

No answer, her eyebrows just went higher, if that was at all possible.

"It gets funnier."

"I really don't know if I believe you."

Clenching my teeth, I plopped on the sofa.

Here we go.

"You and mom are always so concerned with me being alone in Portland, always fixating on my heart and how I have no one there to take care of me, even though I'm surrounded by my friends and people who love me." I glanced up at her. Her face relaxed as she listened, her shoulders easing as the reality hit her. When she didn't respond, I continued, "So to get you two off my back, I created Daxton, and it worked, until you invited him here. So yes, my first plan was to find someone online, but that date went wrong and guess who just happened to be at the Piano Bar performing and saved my ass from catfishing Rick? And then, when I told him the story, he offered. He laughed and said it was meant to be because his full name is Elliot *Daxton* Whittaker."

That got her response. She let out a small chuckle, covering her lips with her fingers before she composed herself, clearing her throat and coming to sit next to me on the couch.

"So, what does Elliot really do?" she finally asked.

"He really does own an architecture firm. His dad is Graham Whittaker, but Elliot's not an architect. He just owns it. He'd rather sing and be on stage."

"That was pretty obvious last night. That's where he belongs."

"He has a band; you should look them up." I turned and looked up at her, the mom glare completely gone. "Savaged Whittakers."

"I think you and I need to have a sister's day, listen to them in the car on the way? Screw the family plan."

She wrapped her arm around my shoulders and pulled me close. I leaned into her and nodded. "That sounds great."

"Oh, and don't worry," she rubbed my bicep, "I'm the only one who's figured it out and I won't tell anyone."

Tilting my body away I pinched my brow. "According to you it was obvious . . ."

"Oh no, that was just to get you to confess. That boy is madly in love with you."

Those words hanging in my head, I made my way back to the cabin. I could see Elliot in the kitchen still in front of his computer. Just the sight of him gave me butterflies. I didn't really believe Jillian that he was *madly in love with me*, but feelings were there. That much was obvious.

Opening the kitchen door, his attention turned to me and he smiled.

"I'm going to head out with Jilly, okay?" I walked over, placed my hand on his neck and pulling him in for a kiss. I was starting to really love kissing this man. "Oh, and Jillian knows who you really are." His eyes widened. I gave him a small peak on his nose. "But don't worry, she won't tell anyone."

"Oh, um . . . okay," he whispered as I ran my fingers along his shoulders to head upstairs.

"Hey, Jamie!" I heard another voice, one I didn't quite recognize. I stopped, coming back to look at his computer screen. Next to the documents from his firm, I saw his phone propped up, a FaceTime open.

"Jamie, Bennett. Bennett . . . Jamie."

I instantly turned red. "Hi, Bennett." I waved and then took off towards the stairs, hearing Elliot chuckle.

Having that time with Jillian was something I didn't know I desperately needed. We walked main street first, stopping at little shops to pick up things for friends and family. I found a few more magnets for Madeline, I still laughed at the memory of her throwing all the magnets away that came from her ex, each one hitting the trash can with a louder bang than the one before. I picked out simple ones that wouldn't create as loud of a bang, telling the story to Jillian.

"So, even though she hates magnets, you're getting her . . . magnets?"

I shrugged. "It's an inside joke."

We went to our favorite restaurant on Main Street and sat and talked—opening up about more than I thought we would. I told her about my health, and how I hated being constantly watched over. She agreed to lighten up, but still be the older sister. I had never thought of my hospital stay from her point of view. Seeing me hooked up to monitors, the constant beeping. No wonder why she became so protective. Jillian was one person, mom was the next. This trip she hadn't been so overbearing when it came to things, maybe it was the fact that Elliot was there with me. That, in her eyes, I was taken care of.

Which led to the topic of Elliot.

Or . . . Daxton.

Jillian didn't know what to call him. Every time she started saying the name Daxton, she quickly changed to Elliot, finally giving up and calling him "boyfriend."

"He's not my boyfriend though," I corrected. "He's just a friend."

"With the way he was kissing you . . ."

"You said we were stiff."

"Jamie, I also said that was just to get you to confess. He was into that kiss."

I smirked, feeling my cheeks blush.

"You were into it too."

"Well clearly, I was the one who kissed him."

Jillian smiled. "And this morning?"

My expression said it all. Less than a week with him and I was already twitterpated. As much fun as I was having with my sister, I couldn't wait to get back to the cabin to get to know Elliot a little better. There was a dinner planned tonight, and then we were going to go to the opening day of the art's fest tomorrow. There was still so much to do, and we had two weeks left. The first week flew by, I needed to savor the next two.

"All very . . . very real." I finally admitted.

Once we got back to the cabin, after a quick hug, we retreated to our respective cabins. I saw Elliot's Jeep in a different place, fresh tire marks on the snow. I pulled out my phone, thinking maybe he had texted me, but nothing was there. I shook my head at the thought.

The kitchen was empty when I walked in. His computer was on the island, his phone next to it. His shoes were by the door, and the upstairs wood floor was creaking. Taking my coat off and kicking off my boots, I quickly made my way upstairs. My mind began to wander. Maybe he was getting ready to take a shower, or better yet, just getting out. I could just envision him with a towel wrapped around his waist, his skin wet. Ever since I saw him the first morning I couldn't get him out of my mind. And after last night—touching his skin—I wanted to touch him again. I wanted more of Elliot.

Skipping the demon stair I looked into the loft, gasping when I saw Elliot there in the middle. He stood with his arms crossed, his feet lightly spread standing next to a gorgeous art easel. A blank canvas sat on it, a few more leaned against the wall behind him. A stool sat in front of the easel, an oil paint set complete with brushes on top.

Elliot smiled, clearly very proud of his gift. "I didn't know what colors you wanted, so I got a bunch, and I wasn't sure what brushes you would want or need, but the girl there helped me pick a few. We can always go back if you need more . . ."

"Elliot," I stopped him, walking up to him to slip my arms around his waist. "I love this."

"I want to see what you can do," he whispered. "I mean, I've seen your finished works, but I want to see your process."

"And what will you be doing as I paint?"

He laughed. "Bennett needs more songs for the agent so . . . I'll be writing lyrics."

"Oh, I love this. You'll see my process, and I'll see yours." I walked to the brushes and picked one up, my fingers bending the stiff hairs to make them flexible. There was nothing better than a blank canvas and fresh brushes. The possibilities were endless. Glancing up at Elliot, I whispered, "Thank you."

He nodded, his hands finding my waist. "Is Jillian . . ."

"She won't tell anyone else, so I hate to tell you, but you're still Daxton." I placed the brush back down on the chair and ran my hands up his arms, keeping him at a small distance even though I wanted to pull him.

Elliot heaved a sigh. "I can still be Daxton, but Daxton will be writing songs."

Chapter Twenty-Five

-Elliot-

As much as I loved writing lyrics, I was starting to love watching the creative juices flow from Jamie more.

She instantly opened the large windows that led out to the deck, letting the sun light in before she moved the easel for the best lighting. Setting herself up, she raised a pencil and tapped it to her bottom lip. Her eyes lit up when the idea came to her mind. She leaned into the canvas, giving me a sexy smirk before she began to sketch something onto it. Her concentration completely shifted once she opened the oil paints, and when she reached up to brush a piece of hair off her forehead, a yellow streak of paint smeared against her skin. And she didn't even notice.

I lifted my phone and snapped a picture of her painting, the perfect candid photo that would either make her really mad or make her want to kiss me. If I was being honest, I'd welcome either one.

The ding from my phone pulled my attention away from watching her, and the text from Clay instantly changed the mood in the room.

Clay: *I have the company's appraisal, I think you'll be happy. Meeting soon? Real soon.*

I glanced up at Jamie one last time, still so in the zone before I stood, and walked over to her to kiss her temple, but she popped up, lowering her canvas away and tilting her entire body as far away from me as possible.

"Not a chance." She glared.

"I was coming to give you a kiss before heading downstairs."

"Oh." Her posture relaxed. "Well, I will take a kiss . . . but you can't see the painting."

"Oh no, no." I raised my hands and stepped away. "I wouldn't want to interrupt your flow. I have to call Clay."

I left her in the loft, the yellow smear on her forehead making her seem more irresistible than before. I could spend the rest of this trip in this loft with her just watching her paint. The short moments we had only made me want more—I was craving it. I wanted to see her smile, I wanted to hear her laugh and taste her skin. I wanted so much more with Jamie, and it had only been a few days—I had plenty of time to get these moments.

And by the looks of it, I hoped they continued even after we got back to Portland. This wasn't Vegas. What happened in Park City didn't have to stay in Park City.

Slipping on my coat and shoes, I left the cabin, giving Jamie some peace and quiet. I knew I needed to call Clay, find out the appraisal of the company, but my feet took me right to the bigger cabin. I knew Janet was inside cooking dinner now, and Jamie's nieces and nephews were most likely on tablets or in front of some kind of screen. Jamie had told me that they had events planned, they did this every year - but the snow had stopped a few of the trips the kids would take. I still had a ski trip in the back of my mind, but when I walked into the cabin, I saw a different story.

The living room had been made into a giant blanket fort—the dining room chairs were being utilized to hold up the blankets. The oldest kid, Dustin, was in the kitchen with his grandmother, waiting for two large bowls of popcorn to be finished.

I laughed at the sight as I took my shoes and coat off. "What is going on in here? This is the fun cabin, isn't it?"

"Oh Daxton, we didn't expect you for a few more hours. Where's Jamie?" Janet asked, a smile on her face as she handed Dustin the bowls of popcorn. He went into the fort, only to resurface for more snacks.

"She's painting."

"She liked the surprise I take it?" Harrison asked. He sat on the island, a beer in his hand as he watched his nephew run back and forth from the fort to the kitchen.

I had asked Harrison if he wanted to go with me to the craft store earlier today. He helped me pick out things for his sister and it was nice to get to talk to him, again, about his travels. Out of all her siblings, he was the one who was more open to talk to me. It wasn't that Holden was closed off, but he was definitely focused on his kids—being the best dad he could be, while trying to run three restaurants from a different state. And Jillian was, well, now that she knew, I wasn't sure how to act around her. Did I tell her I knew she knew? At the risk of sounding like a *Friends* episode, I didn't know she knew I knew she knew.

"What are you doing?" I finally asked as Dustin made his third trip to the kitchen.

The eleven-year-old, who had been semi quiet with me since arriving, gave me a large smile and reached his hands out to grab the bottles of soda Janet had placed on the counter.

"Movie night."

"In the fort?" I asked, pointing towards the giant blanket that took up the entire living room.

He nodded. "Yea, wanna watch with us?"

"Depends, do you have poor man nachos?"

Dustin pinched his eyebrows at me and looked at his grandmother. Janet's eyes flipped from me to her grandson as she tried to contain any comment she may be holding in. Her lips were in a tight smile.

"What are poor man nachos?" Dustin finally asked, his voice completely monotone.

"Janet," I turned to Janet who instantly gave me her full attention. Jamie looked so much like her mom. Same eyes, same hair, same expressions. "You wouldn't happen to have potato chips and shredded cheese, would you?"

"Well yes, Daxton, I do." She turned, opening the fridge and pantry.

"Dustin, why don't you go take the drinks in the fort and come back and I'll show you how to make the best movie snack you're ever going to eat."

Dustin's eyes widened as he took off towards the fort, ducking his head inside to drop the sodas. I heard him say something to his cousins and siblings before making his way back to the kitchen. Janet had pulled out a large glass platter and the bag of potato chips. Once Dustin was back, I opened the bag.

"Now," I began, "The goal here is to get every single chip covered in cheese." I dumped the chips on the platter and then began to sprinkle the cheese on top. "Once every chip is covered, you pop it in the microwave."

"The microwave?" Dustin repeated.

"The microwave." I popped the platter in and set the timer. "I watch it, because the cheese will melt fast and you don't want it to burn."

"But burnt cheese is so good," Janet added in her own two cents.

"Not on chips Janet, trust me. Not. On. Chips." I opened the microwave before the timer was done and showed Dustin the platter of bubbling cheese and chips. I took a chip from the platter and pulled, watching as the cheese pulled off just like you see in pizza commercials. I couldn't tell if Dustin was in love with this idea or disgusted by it, but he took a chip and stuck the whole thing in his mouth, nodding as he chewed. My snack was approved by an eleven-year-old and it brought me great joy. "Poor man nachos."

"Not bad Daxton, not bad."

"Uncle Daxton!" Phillips' head popped out of the tent, "Come watch with us!"

"What are we watching?"

"How do you feel about treasure hunting?!" Dustin answered as Phillip's head vanished back into the fort.

"Is Nicolas Cage involved?"

Dustin rapidly nodded his head.

"Count me in. Dustin, can you grab me a coke?"

"Sure!" he exclaimed as he went back to the fridge.

Inside the fort were mounds of pillows, and a laptop sat propped up on a small table. The darkness of the blankets caused the right mood for a movie, and the snacks laid out in front of all the kids was a treasure trove. I placed the platter of chips next to the popcorn and candies and settled in next to Phillip, who instantly cuddled up to me. Once Dustin was in and all six of us were ready to go, they hit play on the movie, and we all watched as Ben Gates and his sidekick managed to survive a ship being blown up.

Close to the end of the movie, I had a sleeping Phillip laying on my lap, and the platter of chips was completely gone, as was all the popcorn. Out of the corner of my eye the blanket moved and Jamie's head appeared.

"What are you doing?" She laughed, taking in the sight of me amongst all the kids.

"Watching a movie, and you're letting all the light in." I reached up and pulled the blanket back down. I could hear her laugh, stronger at first but softening as she got further away.

I tried to listen as she talked to the others, all of them joking about how *"Daxton was in the fort, channeling his inner child."*

Jillian mentioned something about how she thinks it's sweet—how good I had been with all the kids. Then her dad's voice appeared, the one person I had yet to really win over. To be fair I hadn't spent that much alone time with the man. We had talked about my firm here and there, the new aspects to the field, but other than that we hadn't spoken much.

Granted, it hadn't been that long.

Maybe he would have opinions on selling my company, maybe I could go over a few things with him. Ask advice since my own father wasn't able to give it.

Right as the movie ended I pulled my phone out of my pocket, trying my hardest not to disturb Phillip. I hadn't called Clay like I was supposed to, I didn't even respond to his text.

Me: *I meant to call you - sorry man.*

He responded instantly, which wasn't his norm.

Clay: *You're on vacation, I didn't expect you to. However, I did send you an email. If you could look that over. It's the appraisal of the company. Once you see that, we can move forward with an broker.*
Me: *Ok, perfect. I'll check it now.*

Swiping out of the text, I went to my inbox. Clay's email was right there, right above the one from the talent agent. The two biggest things happening in my life right now have placed themselves together, all thanks to a tiny star.

I waited until the credits rolled and Phillip had woken up, relieving my leg of his head, before I opened the email. Clay's appraisal was there, and it took the air right out of my lungs.

Fifteen Million Dollars.

Fifteen.

Million.

Dollars.

Fifteen Fucking Million Dollars.
My phone dinged.

Clay: *Did you see it?*
Me: *You can't be serious?*
Clay: *Oh I am. That's all your assets and the building combined. And to think you were going to sell for only half a mill.*

I locked my phone, not having the brain capacity to respond to that number. No way had I thought it was going to be worth that much. Never in a million years. The thought of what I could do with that money ran through my head. I could pay off any debts my mom had. I could make sure my dad was comfortable. I could fund some of Jacob's research projects. I could give Sydney some money to expand her business, or at least pay off her schooling. I could buy a tour bus for the band. We could record on our own, no label needed. We could . . .

"Daxton?" I heard Jamie's voice from outside the fort. All the kids had left, leaving me alone in the pillows. "Are you coming out?"

"Yea," I said, crawling out of the fort. "You need to see this."

"What?" Jamie lightly touched my elbow as I stood. I unlocked my phone and opened the email, handing it to her before I completely left her be.

I didn't have to read the email again. I needed water. That or a stiff drink to help swallow the news. Since the kids were now in the kitchen with everyone else, I decided water would be the better option.

"Holy shit, really!?" Jamie shouted.

"Jamie . . ." Jillian's mom voice echoed through the room.

"Sorry, Jill . . . just . . ." Jamie stammered, waving my phone in my direction. "That's just . . ."

"What is it?" Mr. Gaines asked, furrowing his brow at us.

"Well, Dad . . ."

"I'm thinking about selling my company, Mr. Gaines, and I just got the appraisal. Kinda took us by surprise," I admitted. There was no use hiding it. If I was going to spend two more weeks with the man, the truth was going to have to come out eventually.

My first thought was he was going to be angry, seeing as we had only ever talked about our similar careers, but instead his interest seemed to peak.

"You're selling?"

"Thinking about it, sir."

"You'd be stupid not to sell with that number." Jamie handed my phone back to me and without thinking I locked it, shoving it in my pocket. "Fifteen million, Dad."

"Fifteen . . ." Mr. Gaines sounded shocked, almost as shocked as I was when I first saw the numbers, "What's your cash flow? How much, on average, do you bring in in a month?" He leaned forward on the counter.

Before I could answer, Janet spoke for me. "Oh Howard, let's not talk business at the table."

"We're not at the table, Janet, and I'm simply asking Daxton a question." Mr. Gaines looked at his wife, watching her shake her head. "Do you have an accountant?"

"Of course he has an accountant," Jamie answered, her hand sliding up my back and settling on my shoulder. "The best one New York can offer."

I looked over at Jamie, loving the feeling on her hand on me, but not loving where the conversation was going. "He worked in the office with me, but moved to New York, he works remotely from there," I added.

Her dad stood up, grabbing the pile of plates that Janet had set in front of him.

"Jamie, Daxton, could you please help the kids take down the fort so we can actually sit at the table for dinner?" Janet asked, diverting the topic at hand.

Mr. Gaines seemed to get the picture: no business at the dinner table. I welcomed the distraction that cleaning up brought, my mind still reeling from Clay's email. Fifteen million dollars was a lot . . . a hell of a lot more than what I was expecting.

"Hey." Jamie came up close to me. "Are you okay?"

Brushing away the uneasy feeling—or was it excitement—that had crept up since I opened my phone, I nodded, leaned in, and gave her a quick kiss. If anyone was going to bring me back to the present, it was Jamie.

"I'm perfect," I answered.

Chapter Twenty Six

-Jamie-

I could see Elliot's unease the moment we sat down so I linked my pinky with his, holding onto it for the entire dinner. Once he helped me put my coat, and we walked to our tiny cabin, and he was able to be Elliot again, he let out a deep, heavy sigh. He didn't even take his shoes off, he just went straight for the couch, flopping on it with all his weight. I swear I could hear the couch creek.

"Fifteen . . ." I began.

"Million dollars," he finished.

"Maybe you should talk to my dad, he may be able to help with the logistics of it?" I stood in front of him in the living room, tempted to straddle him and kiss him like the night before, but I could see the stress in his eyes—the weight that was being put onto his shoulders.

He scrunched his nose. "Yea, but if I talk to your dad, he'll know I'm not Daxton, architect boyfriend of the year, and that I'm simply just Elliot . . . the man who owns a company but really just wants to run off with his daughter."

Placing my hands on my hips and cocking my body to the side, I looked at Elliot with, what I hoped, was a sexy smirk. "You just want to run off me with me, huh?"

"Well, yea," he admitted. "I thought that was obvious."

A loud laugh escaped my lungs. "Only to Jillian, apparently." I turned, leaving him alone in the living room as I made my way back upstairs. "Now, don't bug me. I'm going to keep painting."

"Can I get a goodnight kiss at least?" he called, his voice bouncing off the walls into the loft.

"For fifteen million dollars," I replied, half-expecting him to run up the stairs and start something that I was too nervous to finish, but he stayed right where he was, laughing under his breath.

The next few days before the arts fest officially started were slow and relaxing. Elliot joined the kids for another blanket fort movie night, and this time they invited me. The pure thought of sitting next to Elliot, with my legs wrapped around his for two hours while we watched Captain Jack do stupid things was absolute bliss. And no one questioned it, because this is what boyfriends and girlfriends did. Jillian would smile at us as we acted like a couple. Between the small touches and glances, the kisses on my cheek or simply just letting the other know where the other was going to be, the line between dating and fake dating was starting to get very, very thin.

Each morning he would greet me with a kiss and a cup of coffee before returning back to his laptop or notebook for the morning. I knew a new song was forming, and as much as I tried to sneak a peek into the notebook, he always slid it away. He told me if he couldn't see the painting, then I couldn't hear the song he was working on. He and Bennett were working on a meeting with the record label, each wanting to give them something new. FaceTime calls with Bennett became a common occurrence as they worked through the rhythm and words. When he would say the lyrics out loud, he would leave the cabin altogether.

Meanwhile, I would paint. My painting was coming together better than I anticipated. A subject I had never tried to paint before came to life on the canvas as I worked. Imposter syndrome would always sneak in sometimes and I would tell myself my paintings were never as good as those in museums—that I would never be able to catch the attention of anyone. But as the brush moved along the pencil lines, that feeling never once occurred. It made me feel as if I should have waited to enter this into the festival, but then again, this one wasn't for me.

Each night I would cover the painting and join Elliot on the couch. I would make us hot chocolate and he would start a fire. I would drape my legs over his and he would rub his hands up and down my legs. We talked, we laughed, and we got to know each other. Once his mug was empty, he would lean in and kiss me. Those same kisses that made my heart flutter. The ones that sent sparks up my spine. The ones I never wanted to stop. He was beginning to get more adventurous with his hands, his fingers sliding up under my shirt, his calloused fingers rough, yet, so soft at the same time.

The morning of the arts fest, my stomach was in absolute knots. I had to be at the Arts Center to be presented with my painting. I had picked a black dress with my white heels, and planned to curl my hair and wear a black headband. I had to look sophisticated. Sophisticated enough that I could pass for a Park City artist.

My dress was hanging on the closet door with my heels underneath it and I glared at them from my bed. I knew I should get up, make a pot of coffee, take a shower . . . seize the day . . . but, hell, the knots in my stomach made me want to puke.

Why did I ever think I could enter a painting in the festival?

I rolled over, onto my back, letting a loud groan fill the air without even thinking that Elliot was still asleep on the couch. I hadn't heard him get up and move, in fact, all I heard was silence. If he wasn't awake then, he should be awake now, especially after that groan.

Slipping from my warm bed, I grabbed my robe and headed down the steps. Elliot lay on the couch still, a blanket only covering his waist and legs, his chest bare. His left arm was draped over his eyes, giving me a perfect view of his tattoo. His right arm hung off the side of the couch. He looked insanely comfortable, and insanely gorgeous. I suddenly wish I had my phone to sneak a photo of this sight. I would keep it forever.

An impulsive thought entered my mind.

Join him.

Normally, I never acted on impulse, but this one was too strong.

Making sure my robe was tight around my waist, I crawled on top of Elliot. He jumped, his right arm coming up quicker than I anticipated, but I didn't care. I laid my head on his chest and instantly found his heartbeat. He inhaled sharply and then his arm settled around my waist. Just the weight of his arm calmed my nerves.

At that moment, I was really glad I listened to my impulsive thoughts.

"Good morning," he mumbled as his arm lowered from his eyes to my shoulders. "What brought this on?"

I took a deep breath and closed my eyes. "Just an impulsive thought I chose to follow."

"Okay, yes, I know those. Clay likes to remind me I listen to those a lot."

"It seemed like a good idea."

He took a deep breath, his chin resting on the top of my head. "Embrace those thoughts. Clay may not like that I do impulsive things, but they can be refreshing sometimes."

"I'll keep that in mind." I laughed lightly, shifting my weight on top of him. "What are some of your impulsive thoughts?"

He hummed. "Offering to be your fake boyfriend for three weeks."

"I wouldn't consider that an impulsive thought."

"An impulsive offer."

I bit the inside of my lip, holding in a laugh. I was always laughing with him. Always smiling, always laughing. He made the world brighter.

"When do we need to be at the gallery?" he asked, sleep still in his voice.

I raised my head, resting my chin on his chest, his eyes were still closed, and his breathing was slower. His fingers began creating little circles on my shoulder. It was calming for both of us.

"I have to be there at two, the showing starts at four, and then the dinners and presentations at six."

"It's going to be a long day," he hummed. "Worth it, but long."

"I hope it will be worth it." Taking a deep breath, I began to lift myself from him. "I'll go make coffee."

His arm around my waist tightened. "Nah, just lay here a bit longer."

He didn't need to ask me twice. I settled back in, resting between the back of the couch and Elliot. I wasn't directly on top of him anymore, but his warmth was still there. I closed my eyes and forced my stomach and mind to calm down.

A loud banging startled both of us what felt like seconds later. Elliot fell off the couch, hitting the floor with a bang and I sat up, completely confused.

"Did we fall back asleep!?" I gaped.

Elliot grabbed his phone and let out a long sigh. "Yes, yes we did."

"What time is it?" I asked, looking towards the kitchen as the bang happened once again. Jillian stood at the patio door, banging her palm against the glass. Once she noticed I was looking at her, she waved like an idiot. "It's Jilly."

"It's ten . . ."

"Shit . . ." I drew out the word, scrambling to my feet. "I can't believe we fell back asleep." I walked over to the door and opened it for Jillian. "Hi . . . hey . . ."

"You two missed breakfast. I volunteered to come see what was going on. Oh, hey Elliot." She waved with a gawky smile as she stepped inside.

I glanced at the living room, Elliot was still on the floor, using his elbows to hold him up—bare chest and blanket wrapped around his waist. Then there was me. Wearing nothing but my robe. Well, my pajamas were under my robe, but I didn't really think a tank top and shorts would count as adequate pajamas. I looked at Jillian, trying to figure out what was going through her mind. I didn't have to wonder long because she finally blurted out . . .

"I thought this was a fake relationship?"

Elliot scoffed, "Yeah, well . . ."

"Elliot, why don't you go get dressed?" I stopped him before he could say anything . . . *impulsive.* He smiled at me, before standing and letting the blanket drop to the ground, revealing only his boxers. He flashed us a smile and then walked upstairs and into the bathroom. I looked back at Jillian with my eyes wide. "Nothing happened."

She pursed her lips and hummed. "If you say so. Mom was just wondering why you missed breakfast and, by the way, you and Elliot have been getting closer . . ."

"You know it's for show."

"Yeah, you keep saying that, but you were just canoodling on the couch."

"Sleeping. We were sleeping on the couch!" Elliot called from the balcony. "She came to wake me up and we fell back asleep."

Jillian's expression only got better and better. Her smile grew, and her eyes were basically sparkling.

"I need to get ready, and we will be over for lunch before I have to head to the gallery," I said sternly, ignoring her look.

"Is Elliot going with you?"

"Um, we haven't talked about it, but I don't see why he would want to. I just need to talk to the director, stand by my painting, and then go have dinner with all the fancy people who may, or may not, want to buy my painting." The knots were coming back just thinking about it. "He would just be bored."

"What would he do instead? I guarantee you he'd rather be with you than stuck with us."

"Actually . . ." Elliot came down the stairs wearing gray sweatpants and a white t-shirt while his hair was still an absolute mess from the couch. I never got the gray sweatpants thing, until this very moment. "I wouldn't mind going to that outlet mall for some nicer clothes. I saw your dress and think I should probably dress nicely for the occasion. I can meet you there before the showing starts, and I promise I'll be the perfect arm candy for you."

"Ooo, arm candy," Jillian fawned.

"He's joking."

"No, I'm not."

"Well, okay, as great as this is . . . we'll see you two at lunch?" Jillian wanted to so badly laugh, or say something else about how this was supposed to be fake. If she could, she would keep this going.

I nodded, grabbing onto her shoulders and pushing her out of the cabin. "Yes, lunch. See you soon."

As soon as she was gone, I spun on my heels and glared at Elliot.

"What?" His voice rose at least four octaves as he raised his hands in surrender.

"Arm candy?"

"Well, yeah."

"Maybe you need to keep some of those *impulsive* thoughts buried."

Chapter Twenty-Seven

-Elliot-

Harrison, Holden, Will and I took the boys to the small outlet mall that sat on the opposite end of Park City. We found the men's suit store, and all began taking turns trying on new "fancy" clothes for Aunt Jamie's first festival appearance. I settled on a simple, gray dress shirt, black tie, and black slacks. My Converse would be acceptable enough—add a bit of flair to the business-look. After deciding, I changed quickly, helped the kids pick out a nice set, and my stomach flipped when I saw the time—it was close to two. Jamie was most likely already at the gallery. She urged me to come here with her brothers, gave me a sweet kiss, and told me she'd see me at the gallery.

"Uncle Daxton." Killian pulled on my shirt as I paid the cashier. The use of the word "uncle" always tugged at my heart. This kid was in no way related to me, yet he adopted the term "uncle" on his own. "I want shoes like you."

I looked up at Will. "I can make that happen if your dad says it's okay."

Killian's eyes widened as he turned to his father. This kid was begging his dad, with every fiber of his being, for a pair of Converse.

"I wouldn't even know where to buy Converse," I admitted lightly to Holden as he appeared beside me.

He looked at his watch. "Showing starts at four, we have time to make it to the valley and back."

"Salt Lake?"

He shrugged his shoulders. "Why not. It may be fun."

"Or . . ." Will stepped in. "We can go to the shoe store next door, and get them some knock-offs because they are kids and will outgrow them eventually."

"Daddy no, I want to match Uncle Daxton." Killian gave him the best pouty lip of all time. It beat out my own nieces as she was begging Jacob. Jacob always—*always*—gave into his daughter. It was a wonder Will was holding on so strong.

"Ah, come on, we have time before Aunt Jamie's showing. Plus, the shoes are on me." I patted Killian's shoulder. "Who wants to ride with me?"

"I do! I do!" Killian and Phillip shouted at the same time.

"Did I just win your kids over?" I asked Will as we pushed the kids out to the parking lot.

"Seems like it. You sure you can drive to Salt Lake?"

"Not a problem, plus, Jamie will get a kick out of it."

"Tie, check. Chucks, check. Young Phillip"—I looked at the two kids next to me in my bathroom, dressed to the nines with their matching red converses—"Young Killian, I say we are ready to go woo your aunt."

"Woo her?" Killian stuck his tongue out. "Why would we want to woo Auntie Jamie?"

"Because, I really like your Auntie Jamie, and if you really like a girl you never ever stop wooing her." I grabbed my comb and ran it through my hair one last time.

"Like Daddy still woos Mommy." Phillip looked at his brother.

"Exactly. Now, are you boys going to help me woo your Auntie?"

They both nodded at the same time at the exact same speed.

"Alright then, let's go."

Like most of the days here in Park City, it was snowing. Large, big flakes fell from the sky, creating the perfect magical feel as we walked into the gallery. There were already so many people there for the opening day of the festival, but my eyes landed on the only important person in the room.

Jamie stood next to her painting with her hands clasped together in front of her as she spoke with someone. Every now and then she would turn her body to look at the sunflowers and mountain landscape.

She was absolutely, without a doubt, the sexiest person in the room. The black dress she wore left little to the imagination, and her hair cascaded down her shoulders, the black headband creating that certain waterfall effect. The heels that I knew all too well accentuated her gorgeous legs, making everything about her simply flawless.

I couldn't help but remember the first time I ever saw her. Then the second. Then the night at Milo's wedding. All those small seconds led me to this point and it took all my strength not to go to her, wrap her in my arms, and kiss her.

I felt a familiar tug on my shirt, and looked down to see Killian staring up at me. "Uncle Daxton, go woo her."

I chuckled. "You coming with me?"

He nodded, grabbed my hand, and led me over to Jamie. The couple she was talking with said their goodbyes as we approached, and her attention turned to us. Her eyes lit up as we got closer. She was the star of the gallery, everything about her shined. This was her night.

"You came!" She smiled as she took Killian in her arms for a hug.

"Did you doubt we would?"

"No, not at all, but, man, you were cutting it close." She stood back up, releasing her nephew to lean towards me, giving me the smallest kiss on the lips. Just the softest touch and my body lit up.

"We had to go to the city," Killian exclaimed. "Look!" His entire body bent at his waist and he looked at his feet, wiggling the red shoes. He scooted his attention over to my black ones and then looked back up at Jamie. The smallest thing made these kids happy. "We came to woo you."

Jamie looked at our shoes, but then her eyes met mine. "Woo me?"

I nodded, cocking a shoulder. "When you really like a girl, you never stop wooing her."

Her lips parted slightly as her eyes studied me. The room around us froze, and it was just her and I. The noise around us vanished and I watched her breathe. I saw something in her eyes— a want, a need—the same need I felt.

"Jamie!" Janet and Mr. Gaines appeared out of nowhere, wrapping Jamie up in their arms. Jamie jumped, and the noise filled the room once again. "We're so proud of you! Look at you . . ." Janet held Jamie at arm's length and then looked at her painting on the wall.

They have set it up so the light would hit it just right, making the colors more vibrant and breathtaking. The yellow of the sunflowers popped, and the green of the mountains almost looked real. There were so many other landscape paintings around, but Jamie's had a certain feel to it, and I didn't think I was being biased. Jamie's painting was stunning, almost as much as her. Every stroke, every color was Jamie, and I knew I wanted this painting as much as I wanted her.

"Thanks, Mama," she sighed into her mothers shoulder. "I hope I picked the right one. I had so many others—"

"You definitely picked the right one," I answered, coming up behind her and wrapping an arm around her waist. I kissed her temple, my lips lingering there a little longer than they should for a public setting, but I didn't care. I wanted the entire room to know she was mine.

Well . . . sort of.

"You really did, Jamie." Mr. Gaines walked over to the painting, getting up close and personal with it. "And it's for sale? Actually for sale?"

"Well if someone bids on it, yes." Jamie explained. "It will hang here for two weeks before the awards ceremony is held. I have the option of taking it out of the bid."

"I'll bid on it," I instantly said.

"Ell—Daxton." she sighed, correcting herself. "I can paint you another one."

"Nah, I want this one." I walked up beside Mr. Gaines.

"Well then you'll have to bid on it." Jamie smiled, but her attention was pulled away once another group of people came to look at her masterpiece and talk to the artist herself.

Mr. Gaines and I stepped back, my fingers trailing on Jamie's lower back as we left her there. I tried to focus on the other paintings, the photographs, and sculptures of other amazing artists that were in the room, but none compared to Jamie.

Nothing would ever compare to her.

My mind swam, knowing I had been watching this woman for months, had her on my mind even when she was avoiding me completely, and now she was here, in front of me, exuding confidence from every pore, showing the world who she was meant to be.

And I couldn't help but fall farther than I already had.

After the long, successful dinner with other artists and potential buyers, Jamie was exhausted. I saw it on her face as we pulled up to the cabin. She had traded her heels for snow boots, had draped her thick coat over her shoulders, and her head rested on the headrest of her seat. And when the Jeep came to a stop, she lifted her head and took a deep breath.

"Thank God that's over." She sighed.

"You did great."

She hummed and laid her head back down. "Do you think I should put the painting in the auction?"

I turned the Jeep off and pulled the key from the ignition. "A part of me thinks you should keep it, it has meaning now, doesn't it? But the other part of me really wants to see you make millions."

"My painting is not worth fifteen million like someone's company."

"Oh hell no." I opened the car door. "It's worth so much more."

I walked around to the passenger side of the Jeep, opening the door for Jamie and offering her my hand. She took it without hesitation, the heels in her hands swaying back and forth as we walked into the cabin. I had purposefully left a light on, causing a soft glow around the kitchen. Jamie dropped her heels and kicked off her boots, wiggling her toes before she walked into the kitchen. She pulled two wine flutes down from the cabinet and turned to get a bottle of wine from the fridge.

A pink Moscato. Simple and sweet, just like her.

She poured the wine, tilting her head to allow my eyes to search her skin. She took a deep breath, her chest rising and falling gracefully. She turned to the fridge, bending over slightly to put the wine back, the dress she was wearing hugged her body just right. I wanted to feel her in my arms, I wanted *her*.

She picked up the flute, but before it could reach her lips, I took it from her, placing it back on the counter. I gripped her neck, pulled her closer to me and crashed my lips to hers. She gave me a moan, one that I longed to hear again. Her fingers found my hair and her palms slid up my chest while my hands ran down her back, sinking lower and lower.

I wanted this woman. I wanted her to be mine.

"Jamie," I broke the kiss and whispered her name. Her breathing had picked up, in sync with my own and I could feel her heartbeat. The rhythm of it was one I could write a song to. "Jamie I—"

"Elliot," she rasped my name and my lips instantly moved to her collarbone.

My hands began to wander, memorizing every inch of her. The fabric of her dress caught on my fingertips as I explored, a gasp escaping her lungs once I found her breast. She leaned her head back, and in an instant my tongue trailed up her neck to her lips again. She didn't need the Moscato to taste sweet, that was just Jamie. It was a taste I would never get used to—one I would always crave.

Her fingers began tugging and pulling at my shirt, loosening my tie, and fumbling with the buttons. Grasping onto her hands I stopped her.

"We don't have to do anything Jamie," I whispered as I kissed her palms.

This woman was finding her way into my mind in more ways than just one. After that first kiss a few days ago I admit I had a hard time sleeping on the couch. I wanted to be next to her, to feel her against me in every way possible. Just as my fingers wanted to memorize her skin, the way my eyes studied hers as she stared at me, I desperately wanted every part of her.

With heavy eyes, she licked her lips. The warmth from her hands moved to my neck as she kissed me, gently.

"Take me upstairs, Elliot," she whispered against my lips. "I want you to take me upstairs."

I lifted her off the ground, her legs wrapping around my waist as her lips found me again. Carefully, I carried her up the stairs and to the bed. Half of me wanted to throw her on the mattress, completely have my way with her, but the other half wanted to take it slower—savor this moment. If this was happening now, it was definitely happening again.

Gently placing her on the bed, my fingers began to lift her dress up her thighs, while my lips covered hers, and my tongue slipped right into place. Her moans drove me wild, almost as if she was begging for more. Just my touch sent electricity through her skin, I could feel each and every twitch. I could feel her want, her need. My fingers found her lace panties with ease. She was already wet for me. I could feel the heat and, without any hesitation, I began to pull them down, standing at the edge of the bed to pull them off her feet, taking in the sight in front of me. Never in my life had I seen a woman like Jamie. Everything about her was perfect, down to the small creases by her eyes as she smiled. I could stare at her all day.

She would always take my breath away.

"You're very broody, Mr. Whittaker." Jamie leaned up on her elbows, crossing her legs at the knees. Her pose was taunting me. Her dress was wrinkled around hips, her black panties still in my hands as I felt the lace between my fingers. "You should see yourself."

I raised my eyebrows at her, forcing myself to stay put. I wanted this to last. "Mr. Whittaker? Broody? I should see myself? Jamie, all I see is you. Absolutely gorgeous. Stunning. Perfect. Wet for me. Teasing me without even trying."

"I'm not teasing you," she *teased*.

"You most definitely are, Miss Gaines."

I dropped her panties on the ground and crawled on top of her, her body falling back onto the bed. Her hands found my belt the same time her mouth found my neck. She undid my pants but left them on as her hands began to trail up my stomach, tickling my abs. The only thing that was on my mind was getting her bare skin against me. She was opening up, becoming more and more relaxed, but the moment I began to lift her dress further up her body, my fingers brushing against her stomach, she froze back up.

I stopped, keeping the pressure of my palm on her, holding her in place as I watched her mind start to reel. "What is it," I whispered, kissing her neck.

"It's just um . . ." she hesitated, her hands leaving my body. "I haven't . . . no one . . ." She lifted her hands to cover her face. ". . . no one has ever seen my scar."

Nerves settled in her body as she tensed. Hovering above her, I slowly continued to lift her dress up. Her scar came into view faster than I thought, her lace bra covering most of it.

"Sit up," I commanded, gently taking her arms from her face, and pulling her towards me. "Jamie, nothing is going to make me stop this," I said as I pulled the dress over her head, "Nothing is going to make me think twice about you." I trailed my fingers through her hair and down her spine. She shivered as I reached the clasp of her bra. "Nothing is going to stop the way I've been feeling about you. Ever since the first time I saw you at the Piano Bar, it's only been you."

The lace strap fell from her arms. Slowly and with new found confidence, Jamie tossed her bra off to the side. She heaved a shaky sigh and laid back down on the bed, completely bare in front of me, the nerves that were there just seconds before were now completely gone. Her scar started right below her collar bone and traveled in-between her breasts, the skin was slightly raised, and slightly lighter than the rest of her body.

With one finger I traced it, mimicking the way she would trace my ink.

"I don't know why you're worried." I leaned down and kissed her scar, starting at the bottom giving simple kisses until I reached the top. Her breathing began to pick up again. "It's a part of you, and since I've been falling for you since day one , I love it. I love—" she stopped me, wrapping her hands around my neck, pulling me in for a hungry kiss.

"Elliot . . ." she whispered. "You can have me tonight."

Chapter Twenty-Eight

-Jamie-

Three different times Elliot made me feel more than any man ever had. Once he kissed my scar, every fear, every self-conscious thought vanished, and it was just him and I. After a shower we laid in bed, wrapped up in each other's arms, Elliot giving me sweet kisses until I finally fell asleep.

I woke up before him, and found his arm resting around my waist. I knew he was a heavier sleeper than most—hell, he slept through the cabin's many creaks and noises every morning—so I wasn't even worried I'd wake him up as I twisted to face him. His hair was mussed, and his scruff was a tiny bit thicker than it was last night.

I couldn't help but reach my hand up to his face, my thumb tracing his jaw line. Elliot Whittaker was something different, the man I had told myself I had no business with, was the only man I wanted to continue with. He was unexpected, especially now.

Last night only proved how much I wanted him.

I scooted closer, wrapping my arm around his waist. Closing my eyes as I nuzzled into him, his arm tightening around me. His heart rate picked up as he stirred, and his hips shifted, causing me to feel more than his heart rate.

"Good morning," he sighed.

I kissed his collarbone, pressing my body up to his. He felt so good, every inch of him. Even after seeing him every morning, he still managed to take my breath away as he removed each piece of clothing last night. His body was made for mine, and, even though I wouldn't admit it out loud, I never wanted to have sex with another man again. No one could ever compare to the way Elliot made me feel. With others, I had kept a tank top on, never letting them see that aspect of my life. But Elliot . . . He made me feel like it was the best part of my body . . . one I shouldn't cover up.

"Good morning," I whispered against his lips.

He hummed in response, keeping his eyes closed as his hands slipped up my bare back. "I'll go make coffee as soon as I'm more awake."

I held back a laugh. "You *are* awake. I can feel it."

"I'm trying *not* to get further awake . . . there."

"Maybe I am," I whispered, taking the moment to crawl on top of him. Never in my life did I think I would love being on top, but I *loved* riding Elliot last night. He was dominating, but he gave me full control here, and I loved it.

His hands found my waist as we began to move together. He tilted his head back, pushing himself into the pillow.

"Jamie," he growled. I loved it when he growled. There were so many different sides to this man. "I hate to stop this, but there's a reason why I was trying not to let this go any further."

Circling my hips, I ran my hands up his chest. "And why's that."

"I only brought so many condoms . . . and we used them all last night."

I stopped, slouching my back.

"I know, I'm sorry. I'll go to the store." He closed his eyes and began touching my arms again, sending shivers through my skin. Goosebumps formed at his touch. "Come here."

I let him take me in his arms, the pure weight of them relaxing me back into him. I held in my chuckle at the realization that he even thought to bring condoms on this trip.

"You mean you only brought three?"

"Well, I didn't expect this to happen so soon."

"I think it's funny you thought it was going to happen at all."

"It was inevitable, Jamie. I've wanted you for a long time." He kissed the top of my head. "Even when you were ghosting me."

"Yeah, let's not talk about that lapse in judgment."

"Okay, I'll never mention it again." He kissed the tip of my nose. "Now, I'll go make coffee, you rest." Crawling out of bed with the smirk on his face telling me a different story than *"never mentioning it again."* I had a feeling the "ghosting" would be exactly like Milo and Madeline's first kiss. I watched as he went downstairs, completely naked—a wonderful sight to see.

After a few cups of coffee, we slipped on our boots and headed over to the big cabin. I had completely lost track of the time and I was sure I was still glowing. That look that said "just slept with someone" plastered all over my face. The way Elliot's hand felt in mine was different now. I knew what those fingers could do, and I could not wait to have them to myself again.

As soon as we got to the porch, I could feel him squeeze my hand, his body language shifting into Daxton. I had a feeling my dad would bring up his business, and Elliot—being the amazing man he was—would talk to him about it more. I shook his arm to get his attention.

"I wonder what my mom cooked for breakfast," I said, leaning my chin on his shoulder.

He hummed. "I wonder if we'll get in trouble for being late?"

He opened the front door, and the chaos that was my family greeted us.

It wasn't a shock to see Main Street so packed. Park City, Utah went through many seasons, each bringing in different crowds. There was Sundance in January, where the movie stars and movie goers enjoyed the small city and snow. Ski season was perfect this year, from what I've heard. Spring and Summer brought the hikers and mountain bikers, adding races to the mix. But this festival was new—it's first year—so, when I saw a crowd of people in front of my painting, completely fawning over it, my mind was blown.

I couldn't even make it to my painting, there were so many people.

I tugged at Elliot's hand. "Come on, let's go skiing. It's too crowded here."

"You don't ski, plus I want to see your painting."

"I can ice skate," I mumbled. "The resort has . . . well used to have—I'm not sure if they still do, but they had a rink there. My family would go skiing and I would ice skate with my mom."

"I told Milo I'd take a photo with you and the painting. They want to see, then we can leave." Elliot leaned down and whispered in my ear, kissing my cheek before he stood back up. "Now the question is how do we get to it?"

We weaseled our way in and once the crowd dispersed to go see another painting, Elliot raised his phone and snapped a photo of me, smiling like a complete idiot next to my giant sunflowers. Once the awkwardness of standing there was over, I rushed back to him. I didn't want anyone to notice me as the artist. My picture was right next to my painting. If they were paying attention, it would be like last night all over again.

"Let me see." I leaned my body over, and the instant he locked his phone screen, my phone buzzed in my pocket. "You sent it to me?"

"Started a group chat." He wiggled his eyebrows before going to look at my painting once again. I pulled out my phone to see a new chat started, six circles sat up top—my people all right there.

Elliot: *Check out my girl next to her million dollar painting.*

My.
Girl.
I inhaled, sharp and quick. I wasn't sure how to react to that. His girl. Elliot called me *his girl* to our mutual friend group. My heart began to race as I became completely frozen in my spot. I probably looked like a lovesick fool, the heat in my cheeks pointing out the obvious.

My phone buzzed again, this time only Madeline's photo looked back at me. Not in the group, a private message.

Madeline: *Did Elliot just say what I think he just said?*

And then a few seconds later . . .

Madeline: *Absolutely stunning photo - but he did just call you his girl!?*

I held back a smile, feeling like all I did these days was laugh or smile, I looked up at Elliot. He had moved on to the next painting, following the crowd of people as they jumped from landscape to landscape.

Me: *Well - things have...happened.*
Madeline: *It's been a week!*
Me: *Well...*
Madeline: *Jamie! I. Need. Details.*
Me: *All in good time Mads, let me enjoy him a little longer.*

I wanted to enjoy all of Elliot for a little longer. At that moment I was his girl, and I was going to bask in that glow. Moments later my phone dinged and dinged again . . . and again.

Clay: *Holy shit, Jamie that's amazing.*
Phe: *JAMIE! That's gorgeous!*
Milo: *Madeline wants to hang it above the fireplace.*
Elliot: *Hell no, that's my painting.*
Madeline: *Is NO ONE going to mention that Elliot called Jamie "his girl"???*
Elliot: *Well, she is. And Maddy - it's my painting.*
Clay: *Jamie's being awfully quiet.*
Elliot: *Maybe in the chat - but man her eyes are telling me a whole different story.*

Dropping my arm to my side, my phone hitting my thigh with a thump, I pursed my lips and looked at Elliot. There I was, again, smiling for no reason.

"Madeline is already after me, so can you please stop the cryptic texts?" There was a hint of sarcasm in my tone, and with the way he flinched his eyebrows and took a step towards me I knew he caught it. "My eyes weren't saying anything."

"Oh, but they were."

"What are they saying now?" Our eyes locked. The darkness of his eyes began to search mine, heaviness filling them as he leaned in and kissed me, right there in the middle of the gallery.

I melted as his hands cupped my face, his kiss lingering for only a second longer. The world stopped spinning and the only thing that was in front of me was Elliot.

"They were asking for a kiss," he finally answered. "And a coffee. Let's go grab one before we meet your family at the resort, yeah?"

Taking a deep breath, and coming back down to earth, I nodded. "That sounds perfect."

He wiggled his eyebrows once, a corner of his mouth raising. "Let's go."

Walking down to the coffee shop, Elliot's hand was firm in mine, never once faltering in his grasp. He wasn't pulling me along, but we walked together. I remembered when he first really, truly talked to me. He stumbled over his words, and was as stiff as a board. His band mates were joking with him, most likely making it worse, but he wasn't the same Elliot that was with me now. His knuckles were white as he gripped his steering wheel that first time. Now they were full of confidence as he gripped my palm. Then it hit me. He was nervous all those months ago.

He ordered our coffees while I looked at the books that lined the walls, trying to find one for Madeline. And just as I had focused my mind on something other than Elliot, he appeared next to me, a paper coffee mug extended to me.

"Do you remember when you drove me home from the wedding?" I asked, taking the cup from him.

His shoulders slumped and he let out a small groan. "How about this," he took a sip of his drink, "I won't mention you ghosting me for five months if you don't mention how awkward I was."

I grabbed a book off the shelf and looked at the cover. "Well, now that I think of it, it was kinda cute."

"No, it wasn't."

I turned the book over to read the blurb. "I mean it got you a kiss at the end of the night, didn't it? Do you think Madeline would like this book?" I showed him the cover.

"My awkwardness is what made you kiss me?"

I shook my head. "No, but I remember thinking you were stiff because you didn't want to be there. Like you felt obligated to drive me home maybe . . . and sure, Madeline and Ophelia had told me you were interested in me, but you sure didn't show it. But now . . . now that I've spent time with you, felt your hand in mine, and have seen who, I think, is the real you . . . well, you were nervous. And it was kinda cute." I looked up at him as I drank from my cup.

"Jamie . . ."

"You turned down those girls and treated me like I was the only girl in the room. Then you told me you wanted to kiss me and I just . . . thought it would be a good idea." I put the book back on the shelf. "Then I got nervous, and ghosted you. I convinced myself you were someone completely different than you really are. If I could change that . . ." I gave him a gentle kiss. "I would. I could have been kissing you longer." I looked over at him, tempted to give him a small kiss. Instead, I turned back to the shelf, grabbing the book once again. "Now . . . this book . . ."

"Jamie . . ." Raising a single eyebrow, Elliot took a drink of his coffee, his eyes on me the entire time. "Your eyes are talking really loud now, Jamie, and yeah . . . I do think Madeline would like that book." Giving his eyebrows another wiggle, he took a sip of his drink and walked away, leaving me alone by the bookshelf.

Chapter Twenty-Nine

-Elliot-

Clay: *I found a good broker that has handled firms as large as yours before. I know I'm just the numbers guy but...*

Clay: *I was thinking about flying out to Portland to meet with you. Phe's coming too.*

Clay: *She's actually really excited about this now. I can check in on the law firm too.*

Clay: *Hey...you.*

Clay: *Oh Eeellliot.*

Clay: *ELLIOT!*

Me: *Can't a guy go skiing?*

Clay: *Ha. No.*

Me: *Well, that's too damn bad.*

Clay: *I'm kidding – just, I found a broker. When will you be back in Portland?*

"Who are you talking to at the speed of light?" Harrison came up behind me. We had just gotten to the bottom of the run and, even though I was strapped to my snowboard, I could feel my phone going off in my pocket. There were even more messages to look at, not just Clay's, his was just the first one I had opened.

Other messages included Jamie, Milo, and Bennett.

"My accountant. He wants to fly out and take a look at the company." I used my teeth to pull off my other glove. "And your sister, and my friend."

"You're an important man." Harrison chuckled. Pulling off his hat and goggles, Harrison didn't even look tired. Snow was stuck to his beard in certain places, and his messy brown hair was sticking up in all directions – but the man looked happy. "Is Jamie still at the rink?"

I opened up her message thread to see a picture of her and her nephews, all with large smiles on their faces in the middle of the ice-skating rink. Just seeing her happy made my breath stop.

"Yeah, she is," I replied. Typing a quick response before opening Bennett's text next.

Bennett*: I need you to check your email ASAP. AND THEN CALL ME.*

Following his directions, I opened my email.

"Holy shit . . ." I mumbled, reading the email subject five times over.

Harrison twisted his head at me. "What?"

I shook my head, closing out the email before reading the body. With a subject like *Savaged Whittakers Proposal – time sensitive* my brain went on full anxiety mode. I opened the messages back to Bennett's.

Me: *On the mountain, call you as soon as I get back to the cabin.*

Swiping up I texted Jamie the second after.

Me: *Meet for coffee. Big news.*
Jamie: *Of course. Where are you?*
Me: *Just got off the run. Let me unhook and meet you at Roasters?*
Jamie: *See you there.*

Stuffing my phone back into my coat pocket, I bent over to unhook my boots from the snowboard before hoisting it over my shoulder.

"Going to meet Jamie?" Harrison asked, twisting his body back towards the lift.

"Yeah, you coming?" *Please say no . . .*

"Nah, I'm going down a few more times."

Yes!

"Alright man, see you soon," I said over my shoulder as I took off towards the coffee house.

I dropped my snowboard outside the door, pulled my beanie from my head and walked inside. It was crowded, but I spotted Jamie instantly. She was with Jillian and the twins, sitting at a booth with her hands wrapped around her paper cup of coffee. She had a huge smile on her face as she talked to her sister, laughing and nodding along with Jillian's story. I didn't even hesitate or consider going to the counter, I went directly to her—the email burning its way through my phone, just waiting to be read.

"Hey, Elliot." Jillian smiled up at me. Jamie's attention turned to me, and her smile widened, if possible. "How were the runs?"

"Great! It was great to be snowboarding again. Jamie . . ." I spoke quickly, looking at Jillian and then back to Jamie. "Big news . . . and I haven't opened the email yet."

Jamie sat up, her attention peaked. Jillian watched our exchange, growing curious in it as well. "Good, big news?" Jamie asked, her eyebrows raising.

"Well, I haven't read the email yet, but Bennett says I need to call him right away and the subject line is promising."

"Okay I'm invested, read the damn email." Jillian shifted in her seat.

I sat next to Jamie and dug my phone from my pocket, flying to my email. Another text from Bennett popped up. Swiping it away, I opened the email and read aloud . . .

"Elliot Whittaker and the Savaged Whittakers—"

"Savaged Whittakers?" Jillian interrupted.

"His band, shush," Jamie snapped.

I cleared my throat and continued, "My name is Carson Bently, the owner, and CEO, of Pacific Sound Records. One of my agents, Liam, had the pleasure of meeting with you at The Piano Bar in Portland Oregon a few weeks ago. Needless to say, he is thrilled to work with you in the future. And, from what I've heard, so am I. We think your sound is the perfect fit for our label and would love to set up a meeting with you and the rest of your band. Please respond with five original tracks for us to sample and we will reach out with timing to meet. If this goes further, we will fly the band out to our studio for a performance and, if we really like what we hear, discuss the contract situation. I look forward to your response and hope to meet with you soon. Sincerely, Carson Bently, CEO, Pacific Sound Records."

I dropped my hand down, my phone going dark, exhaling a breath through my mouth.

"Elliot . . ." Jamie spoke softly. "That's . . . that's . . . holy shit! First your company and now this! This is crazy!"

"I need to call Bennett, he has all the tracks, he can send over a few of our popular ones—"

"Why doesn't this Carson Bently guy just go on Spotify, they're all there, aren't they?" Jillian asked.

I furrowed my brow at her. "You listened?"

"Jamie played them for me, but I didn't know what the band was called. I get the Whittakers . . . but Savaged?"

"Bennett Savage. It meshed."

"No, I like it." Jillian smiled, taking a sip of her coffee. "It fits."

A corner of my lips raised in a small smile in response to Jillian.

"So, Bennett will send over some tracks . . ." Jamie prodded.

"And then we wait for a date to go to California." I turned to her, resisting the urge to pull her in for a kiss in front of her sister and nephews.

"Daxton?"

Everyone at the table froze at the sound of my middle name. When Jillian was in the room, I was Elliot. Everyone else in her family still called me Daxton, or Dax, but with Jillian being the only one who knew our secret, I could be myself around her. I turned to the sound and saw Pete, the owner of The Cabin, standing at the end of our table.

"Oh, hey, Pete." I settled, remembering that he was introduced to me as Daxton. "Good to see you, man."

"Likewise, I couldn't help but overhear, you have a band . . . and Pacific Sound is interested?" He smiled, shifting his weight as he folded his arms over his chest.

"Yes, sir. I do."

"He's the lead singer." Jamie smiled as she slid her hand up my back.

Pete's smile grew. "You know, I've had a few people ask about you after karaoke that night. Just solo you put on a show. Thursday and Friday's I have band come and play; I'd love to see you again, and then, maybe your entire band, up on my stage."

Jillian gasped and spun her head to look at me across the table. "Elliot, you have to."

"I'd love to, but I don't have a guitar here and my band is in Portland."

Pete gave me a slight nod. "If you can get a guitar, I can get your band here."

"Seriously?" Jamie's voice rang in my ear as I studied the man in front of me.

"Yes, seriously. You're visiting, how long are you here till?" Pete asked.

"Um, we leave on the 26th to head back to Portland."

"Come play on the 23rd with your band, and this Thursday solo. Can you get a guitar by then?" Pete asked, his eyes narrowing.

"Yes," Jamie answered for me. "There are plenty of music shops around, we can get a guitar."

"Perfect, here . . ." He dug in his pocket and pulled out a business card. "I'm serious. I'll fly your band members out for the night. I'd love to have you guys play. Just call me when you talk to your band okay. Sounds like you need to call them about the label anyway. Talk to you soon, Elliot."

I smiled at his use of my real name and waved as he walked off.

"Well then." I sighed, looking at the car in my hand.

"I have one request," Jamie said, leaning into me.

"What's that?"

"You need to sing the song that reminds you of me."

I approached Jamie's dad with caution that night. After talking to Bennett, who was, with no surprise, extremely elated to send tracks to the CEO of the record label, I knew I had to talk to someone about my company. It was a weight on my shoulders I had been able to ignore thanks to Jamie, but fact of the matter was I was avoiding the topic. Her father had shown interest in the company ever since we mentioned how much it was worth. He had brought the topic up a few times, and Jamie was able to divert the conversation. But now I needed to talk to him.

If Clay was serious about coming to Portland to actually put the company for sale, I figured I should talk to a man who has sold his business before. Since my father—and Jacob—were out of the question, Mr. Gaines was my best bet.

I left Jamie at the dinner table with her siblings and nephew as I went to join Mr. Gaines in the living room. I felt myself go stiff, turning into that awkward Elliot that Jamie had mentioned before.

Except here, I was awkward Daxton, and I wasn't quite sure how to act. Do I tell him I'm not actually an architect? Do I tell him why I'm selling? I had no idea how to approach him. Thankfully I didn't have to speak first, Mr. Gaines took care of that.

"Something on your mind, Daxton?" he asked, setting his glass on the side table next to the chair he had settled on.

I took a deep breath and looked over my shoulder. I could feel Jamie's eyes on me as I sat on the couch across from her dad. I rested my elbows on my knees, not the most professional stance I could take, but I tried to force myself to relax.

"Yes, sir, I was actually wondering if you could help me with something in regard to my company."

"Made the decision to sell?" He raised a single eyebrow.

I nodded. "Yes, sir, I think I have. An opportunity was tossed my way today and I don't want to miss it, but to take it I need to sell the company."

"This is a company you inherited, correct?"

I took another deep breath. That was two. How many deep breaths would I take during this conversation? "Yes, sir, it was my fathers, I took control . . ."

"After he passed? I'm sorry to hear that Dax . . ."

"No, sir, he's alive. He was diagnosed with Alzheimer's a few years ago. He worked until he couldn't anymore and then I took over. I went to school for business, sir, not for architecture." I mumbled, almost afraid to tell him the truth. I didn't have to let the cat out of the bag with Jamie and how I'm "fake dating" her, but at least he could know the truth there.

Narrowing his eyes, he lifted his chin before giving me a slight nod. He hummed. "For someone who's not an architect, you knew a lot about it."

"Well, sir." I chuckled. "I've been working with him for three years and showing clients their projects. I work closely with my team and I do enjoy the work, I just . . . I'd rather do something I love, not something that is from nine-to-five."

"And what's that?"

"I have a band, sir. I'm the lead singer and we may get offered a record deal soon. I love being on the stage more than behind a desk. It's where I really think I'm meant to be, and . . . the company . . ."

"Is just in the way." He finished my thought for me.

I looked up at Mr. Gaines through my eyelashes, fearing that his reaction was going to be the same as my dad's, as Jacobs, but instead, he was smiling. I nodded, looking back down at my feet.

"Have you talked to your family about the desire to sell?" he asked, breaking the awkward silence that sat between us.

I nodded. "Yes, my dad . . . well, he's not in control of the company anymore. I am . . . solely. My mother accepted and gave me her blessing, and my brother, well, he wasn't too happy about it, but I think he will live." I rubbed my palms together. "I decided before this trip I was going to sell. Jamie and I didn't know how to bring it up to you, but now that my accountant found a broker and is going to travel to help close the finances, it's getting real . . . and I was hoping . . ."

"I could give you some guidance?"

I met his gaze and gave him a soft nod. "Yes, sir. I'm a fish out of water selling a company. I just want to be on stage. I want this to go smoothly and be stress free and I just . . . I want it to be simple. I don't want the weight on my shoulders anymore."

"Selling a company is no easy task."

I pursed my lips, looking over my shoulder to Jamie, who was still watching us like a hawk. "I know," I finally mumbled.

"Well then, Daxton, I think you and I have a lot to go over. Do you have that email from your accountant?"

I gave him a slight smile. "I do."

Reaching in my pocket I pulled out my phone. Clay had sent me all the information Mr. Gaines was asking about the other night and I was ready to lay it all on the table. My confidence slowly came back as I sat across from him. Jamie joined us after the dishes were done, as we discussed my options and the path I should take while selling. It was the conversation I needed—the push to know everything I was doing was right, that I was on the correct path for *me*.

And at the end, as Jamie and I pulled on our coats to go back to our cabin, Mr. Gaines shook my hand.

"Thank you, Mr. Gaines, I really appreciate it."

"Please Daxton, call me Howard."

Chapter Thirty

-Jamie-

Waking up next to Elliot was going to be my favorite thing, I could feel it.

Elliot had managed to make me feel alive once again before enveloping me in his arms. I traced his tattoo and kissed his knuckles as he lightly stirred awake. He kissed my temple when he woke up, leaving the bed to make coffee and a light breakfast. If I had my days right, today was the day we went down to Salt Lake.

As much as I loved Park City, I was beginning to miss the hustle and bustle of a big city. Park City sure had grown in the years since coming here, but it was still small compared to the city. Salt Lake City had everything you could want to keep yourself occupied during the day, and today we planned to go to the outdoor mall in the heart of downtown.

When I finally made my way downstairs, Elliot was perched on a stool with his laptop open and chin resting in his palm. Still shirtless, but wearing his gray sweatpants. He looked relaxed in front of his computer. I wrapped my hands around his waist and rested my chin on his shoulder.

"I heard from Pete," he mumbled, turning his head slightly towards me.

"Already, it's still early." Which reminded me that as awake as Elliot made me feel, I still required coffee. I left his warmth and went to the coffee pot, pouring myself a cup.

"It's official, the guys are going to fly out next week for a show and he wants me to play this week. So . . ."—he shut his laptop—"I'll need a guitar."

"Is it possible to have Bennett ship you yours?" I asked, turning to face him, leaning on the counter. I took a sip of my coffee, humming as the caffeine hit just right.

He laughed. "I would not trust my baby with any shipping handler."

I raised an eyebrow at him. "You sound like Clay and his car."

"Except my guitar is way better than his Tesla. I found a shop down in the city, do you think your family would mind the detour?" he asked, grabbing the handle of his own coffee mug.

He had one eyebrow raised, his stare focused on me as he raised his mug to his lips. Not once did he break contact as he took a sip of his coffee.

I inhaled, looking down at my mug to force myself to stay where I was. I didn't need to make us late for the family plans. I simply smiled, responding with, "Not at all."

It didn't feel "fake" anymore. I mean, it hadn't been "fake" for a while with us, but for my family . . . I think they could tell there was a difference. Jillian would give us small glances, small smirks as she saw us interact. Holden and Harrison would try to take Elliot to show him something, but his grip on my hand would force me to come along. Even my mom would give us these little looks, making me wonder if she knew all along. And my dad was beginning to treat Elliot like he did Will, or Carrie—as part of the family.

The only thing that still proved to me it was fake was when they called him Daxton.

He wasn't Daxton.

I wanted to tell them everything, I wanted them to know everything. How we met, how he convinced me into letting him come here, and how his life was about to change. How much I was growing to care for him more and more, and how I hoped that after this trip we would still be . . . *this*.

The last stop of the mall was the craft store, a large building that had everything an artist would dream of. Elliot made the mistake of letting go of my hand. I was lost in the aisle of paint and brushes. I ran my finger along the bristles, my unfinished work coming to mind as I thought about how I could make it even more remarkable. Picking a few of the things I knew I would need, I flinched when two hands found my shoulders, and lips found my cheeks.

"Finding things?" Elliot whispered.

"So many things," I answered, picking up another paint brush.

"Just let me know when you're ready. Your parents went to get us a table for lunch and Jillian dragged the kids to the Disney Store again." Elliot's hand slid past my shoulders as he stepped to the side, taking the same paintbrush off the shelf.

I rolled my eyes and let out a sarcastic laugh. "I bet they dragged *her*."

"Nah, it was definitely the other way around. Are you almost done in here?"

"Yeah, I'm done. I have what I need. I could stay longer though, for sure. I'm assuming me in this store is going to be you in the music store after lunch, am I right?" I tilted my head and looked at him.

He furrowed his eyebrows, and his lips created a small line. The temptation to kiss that small line was extremely strong. Hell, every temptation was with him.

"Oh no," he finally said, "it will be much . . . much worse." He put the paintbrush in the wrong container, and I gave him a playful glare before I placed it in its correct spot, and, once my fingers were finally free, he grabbed my hand. "Come on VanGogh, we need to meet your parents for lunch."

The restaurant was quiet for the lunch hour, which made for a pleasant afternoon, and then we all traveled to the other side of the city to join Elliot in picking out a guitar for his upcoming show. He made good on his statement that it would be much worse than me in the craft store, he didn't even grab my hand, he just took off towards the entrance. What brought a smile to my face, however, was the five kids following him at top speed.

Loud rock music greeted us as we entered, Elliot was already lost in the back of the store. Drum sets sat on high shelves all around the large room, keyboards and band instruments sat in small alcoves, and all the guitars lined the back wall. That's where I headed, knowing very well he would be next to the flashiest guitar there was. I tried to think of what Elliot's guitar looked like back home. I never really paid attention to it that much—I was always avoiding watching him on the stage, but I knew it was an electric guitar. Maybe it was red? Or was it blue? Orange?

Stopping and scrunching my nose, I instantly felt terrible because I couldn't answer this question about my "boyfriend." I looked around to see where my family was before pulling out my phone to look at the band's Instagram, scrolling through until I found a photo of Elliot, his hand gripping the microphone, his eyes closed as he sang, and a white guitar around his neck.

White.

I would have never pegged him to have a white guitar. But after taking a screenshot and cropping the photo down, I couldn't see him holding anything else.

Scanning the wall, I found the white electric guitars, but Elliot wasn't near them. Neither were any of the kids.

"Hey," Harrison said behind me, "we lost your boyfriend."

I chuckled. "Yeah, so did I."

"Jamie," Jillian called from across the wall, "I see him." She smiled.

I walked over to her, folding my arms as I got closer to a small closed-off room filled with acoustic guitars. Once the door closed behind us, the sound from the main part of the store faded, and all I heard was Elliot's voice along with the strumming of a guitar. He was in a smaller portion of the room, a glass door keeping him separate from everyone else. He sat on a stool in the middle of the room, with all the kids gathered around him. He had a brown, simple, acoustic guitar perched on his leg—his fingers moved flawlessly as he sang.

My heart skipped a beat.

"She painted their beauty, but little did she know, the love in my world was continuing to grow. Sunflowers bloomed beneath her skilled hand, the golden light enchanting a love so grand . . ."

I had never heard these lyrics before, and I had listened to a lot of his music on my phone before we left. I had heard him sing originals and covers, but nothing hit my ears like this.

A painter.

Sunflowers.

Falling in love.

Butterflies grew in my stomach. I was certain he was singing about me but I kept out of view, worried that if he were to see me, he'd stop, and I desperately wanted to hear the rest of the song.

"Together they danced and swayed, the bristles capturing the summer's day. He whispered his love into her heart . . ."

"Jamie?"

I jumped. I was so focused on Elliot, the world around me seemed to mesh together and I didn't hear Jillian sneak up on me. Everything was blurry, except him, until Jillian pulled me out of the trance.

"I think he's singing about you," she whispered.

I licked my lips and turned back to him. He had finished singing, but his fingers were still focused on the strings. Dustin was closest to him, watching him with the guitar, his eyes completely focused on Elliot's fingers on the neck. Just like me, Dustin was enchanted by Elliot on the guitar.

Elliot did one final strum before placing his hand over the strings to silence the guitar. He looked up at Dustin and smiled, then an employee came into view. She had her arms folded, a blush on her cheeks.

"Yeah, this is the one." Elliot stood, holding onto the guitar's neck.

The girl smiled and then gently took the guitar from him. "I'll have it waiting for you up front. Beautiful song, Daxton, absolutely gorgeous."

"Thank you." He nodded.

I backed further away, pretending to focus my attention on the guitars on the wall when the glass door opened, and they all came out of the small room. The kids were louder than I wanted, but they all dispersed, each heading towards a different guitar. Jillian followed her twins, and Dustin went directly to a guitar just like the one Elliot had picked. I watched them for a moment, but my eyes landed on Elliot as he smirked at me.

"You found me," he whispered, his arm slinking around my waist.

"I did," I whispered back. "You found a guitar?"

Raising his eyebrows and chin, he gave me a small nod. "I did. Do you think Park City will like an acoustic set?"

"Sing that song and yes, they would."

Scrunching his nose he shook his head, pulling away slightly. "Nah, that song isn't finished yet."

Mimicking his expression, I added an eyebrow wiggle and turned my back, only to feel his hand slip into mine, keeping me from going too far.

"Come on, let's go find everyone else. Believe it or not, I think I'm done here. I just need to get a case and a few picks." Elliot picked up his pace to walk next to me. "I think I sparked something in Dustin, you should have seen him as I was playing."

"If only they were old enough to come to the shows. I doubt Holden will want his eleven-year-old in a bar." I laughed, spinning my head to see Dustin looking at the acoustic guitar that he had picked up.

We left the room and walked over to the cases, Elliot's eyes moving to the electric guitars as we passed. "I can teach him a few things if he'd like, and I'm pretty sure the bar is an all-ages type of place . . . isn't it?"

"Not sure." I reached out to touch one of the guitars as Elliot's hand led me towards the small alcove. "But lessons would be cool, give that kid something to focus on other than video games."

With no response Elliot dropped my hand to open a guitar case, both hands feeling the velvety fabric inside. Closing it, he picked up the case and reached for my hand again. An entire two minutes felt like so much longer, and without his hand, I was missing those sparks he always gave me.

He grabbed a pack of guitar picks, being pickier on these than he was on anything else, we cashed out and met my family at the front of the store.

"When is the show?" My dad asked, the sounds of the street filling the void that was left from the store.

"Thursday, and then the one with my band is next week. Pete wants me every night if he could."

"We'll make sure to contact a sitter for the night your band is here. We're all coming," my mom added.

Elliot raised his eyebrows and turned to look at me. "I'll make sure to tell the guys. They will be thrilled."

Chapter Thirty-One

-Elliot-

The days before the show started to go slower and slower. I had picked songs to fit the time limit Pete had given me, and was able to run through the set in private, while Jamie had left for the gallery. I had Bennett on FaceTime as I ran through all the songs, and sent him over the final lyrics for the new one I had been working on.

"We all got our plane tickets the other day. This Pete guy is really into it, huh?" Bennett asked as I packed up the guitar.

"He's excited, that's for sure. Do you think you guys can get that new song down before next week?"

"You're really determined about playing it in a week? I mean, yeah, we can work on it for sure but maybe save it for the studio?"

I shook my head and locked the case. Running my hands through my hair, I leaned on the counter where the phone was propped up. "No, we have to play it that night. In case you haven't guessed—"

"It's for Jamie. We figured. Interested to see where the sunflowers come into play. You don't like flowers."

"I'll send you the photo, but it would be better to go see it at the gallery. It's stunning. And she's working on something upstairs but she won't let me see it until it's finished." I glanced upstairs, as if I suddenly gained x-ray vision and could see the canvas through the flooring and cloth that covered it.

Each night, before we climbed into bed, she would cover the painting and turn the easel away from the bed, taking no chance in the fact that I'll see it. We even made a bet one night that I could send her over the edge using just my fingers and tongue, and if I won, she had to show me the painting. And even though I won the bet, she distracted me, and I forgot about the painting altogether. Jamie had a way of doing that, she could clear my mind in seconds. She could help me forget about selling my company and playing a solo gig in front of a crowd when I had no idea how they would react. She only made me think of the moment we were in.

"Go up and sneak a peek, it wouldn't hurt," Bennett's voice snapped me back to reality.

"Yeah, no. It would. She's only heard a few lines of the song, and I can't see that painting until she's ready. She spends a lot of time on it though. I'll play and she'll paint, it's becoming our rhythm." I racked my teeth on my bottom lip. "Jamie has a way of making me focus. I don't think I've ever been this into a song before, or enjoyed simply watching someone as they did what they love."

Bennett smirked, his eyes narrowing. I knew the look. I knew what he wanted to say, but he was stopping himself.

"Say it."

"I've never seen you this worked up over a girl. You were a mess the night of the wedding. Sure, the set was good, but you had a hard time concentrating on some of the lyrics *because* of her, but now she helps you focus?"

"How the tables have turned," I joked.

Bennett chuckled. "We'll work on the song, keep practicing the tempo and I'll send over the sheet music for you. I take it you want me to bring your guitar?"

"Please, I'd rather have electric for our show. Milo has a key to my place, just carry it on the plane. If I find out you checked it—" I glared at him. He knew how important that guitar was. It was my first electric, and, even though I had a few, it was the one that carried our shows.

"I know, you'll leave the band and kill me. Got it." He waved me off with his hand. "I'll take good care of her. Chase needs to know if the guy has a drum set or if he has to pack it up?"

"Pack it up and check it, Pete mentioned bringing our own instruments, but said hotel accommodations would be taken care of."

"And he delivered on that too. We all got our confirmations. Looks fancy." Bennett wiggled his eyebrows. "Something called Stein Erikson."

"Hell yeah, and this is Park City, everything is fancy here."

"Yeah well, we will have to add it to our tour list. I better get going, you have a family function and I need to get back to work. I'll shoot over that sheet music." Bennett grinned.

Waving goodbye I locked my phone down. I had a few minutes before we left for the mountain. I really should contact Clay and get some work done, but I had zero motivation for it. Instead, I slipped on my coat and boots and went outside to see Jamie with her nephews. They had worked hard all morning on another snowman to add to their growing family of snow people, and the fort was still standing from our first snowball fight.

Zipping up my coat, I wandered towards them. Killian noticed me first, giving me a large smile and wave. Phillip ran over to give me a quick hug, allowing me to throw him over my shoulder as I took the remaining few steps over to them. Jamie's beanie was covered in the fresh snow that fell from the clouds, her blonde hair an absolute mess around her shoulders, but she didn't care, she was focused on that snowman.

"Uncle Daxton, put me down!" Phillip began to punch my back.

"Phillip, don't hit," Jillian corrected him as I put him down in the snow.

Jamie stood up straight, using her sleeve to wipe her forehead. "I think this is our best one yet, don't you," she asked her nephews as she stepped back to admire her work on the snowman. So far, they had a huge snowman who was dubbed the "daddy," and two little ones, who were rightfully dubbed the "twins." This one must be the "mom."

I set Phillip down on the ground as he gave me one last punch and then took off towards the cabin.

"Best one yet, Jamie." I smiled, sticking my hands in my pockets. "What's on the agenda today?"

"Relaxing," Jamie responded, stretching her arms out to the side, her eyes closed as she lifted her head to the sky.

"Snowball fight!" Killian screamed.

The small human reached down and gathered snow in his hands, packing it down into a ball and aiming right at his mother. Jillian held her hand out, one finger raised and that motherly look on her face. "I don't think so Killian, drop it."

Furrowing his brow, Killian dropped the snowball. "Come on, Mom, we need to have another one." He slumped.

"Yeah, Mom . . ." Phillip whined.

"I'm out," Jamie raised her hands in surrender. "This snowman is done, the family is complete. I am going to go start that fire on the back deck and sit with some hot chocolate. I. Am. Relaxing."

"It's snowing." I pinched my eyebrows and looked towards the white clouds that covered the sky. "I don't think I've seen the sun since I've been here."

"It has been a wet winter," Jillian agreed. "However, that fire pit and a hot chocolate sounds perfect."

Jamie walked over to me and slid her arm around my waist, pulling me close to her body. Her hair was wet and the tip of her nose was bright red. She scrunched her nose and looked up at me.

"Are you going to join us by the fire, or are you going to be all boring and broody alone in the cabin?"

I kept in my chuckle. *Broody.* That wasn't the first time she had called me that, and the sheer memory of it made the heat rise. Raising my hand, I brush some snow from her cheeks.

"I need to get this set list, and Bennett is demanding lyrics."

"So, in other words," Jillian said as she came up to us, "your fake boyfriend is ditching you."

"That's fine, he can go be boring. More hot chocolate for us." Jamie pushed herself away and grabbed onto her nephews shoulders. "Go and be boring, Mr. Music Man."

I shoved my hands in my pockets and watched the two sisters head towards the main cabin. "If only I had my rockstar to inspire me," I called.

Jamie spun and narrowed her eyes at me. "Please don't . . ."

"See you soon, Rockstar."

"Rockstar?" Jillian stopped and looked over her shoulder at me, only to be stopped by Jamie, pushing her forward up the steps.

"Just ignore him. He's got music on the brain," Jamie grumbled, giving me one final wave before the door closed behind them.

Music and Jamie, the two things that consumed me.

Chapter Thirty-Two

-Jamie-

"Will wants another baby." Jillian said, out of the blue. We had moved to our cabin once the hot chocolate was gone and the fire had failed to keep us warm, and Jillian had taken over the armchair that Elliot normally played his guitar in while I painted. He was downstairs, his light strumming filling the entire cabin, but Jillian's words were able to drown them out in an instant.

I looked up at my sister from the canvas, lingering only a moment before dipping my brush in the water. The yellow paint had stained my fingers and my white t-shirt was covered in brown and black. I wiped my hands on my stomach and sighed. "I thought you were done after the twins?"

"I thought so too, but Will really wants another. He keeps saying this time it would be a girl, and nothing would change in our lives," she said softly, pulling at thread from her sweater.

"*Everything* would change," I corrected her.

"Well, I mean with jobs and the house and . . . all of that adulty stuff." She waved her hand around in the air.

"Adulty stuff," I repeated, grabbing my paint brush in the cup of water and swirling it around.

"I think he was kind of hoping this trip would ignite something. It's hard sharing a cabin with Holden and Carrie because, well, you know they are trying for number four, so Will is thinking we could try for number three."

"Remember earlier when you said there were some things you didn't need to know?" I raised my eyebrows and looked over at her.

"That was between you and Elliot. I don't need to know you and your fake boyfriend are using this as your sex cabin." She raised an eyebrow at me.

"We're not using it as our sex cabin. He's been sleeping on the couch," I lied, avoiding looking at her as I attempted to concentrate on the painting.

She let out a *Mmm Hmm*. "I'll believe that when I see it."

I heaved a sigh, choosing my words wisely, when in fact, he had been sleeping in the bed with me ever since our first night together. I didn't want him back on that couch. "He moves whenever *someone* decides to randomly stop by."

"Who's stopped by?"

"You," Elliot and I said together. His voice was faint, but loud enough that we heard it, and both of us broke out in laughter.

"Jilly, I'm serious. You know how I feel about sex, and I'm not one to just go sleeping with random guys, but if you and Will really want to make that cabin your sex cabin"—I used my brush to point toward the main cabin—"just let me know so I don't come barging in."

"We're not. We have five kids, Holden, and Carrie under the same roof, and the walls are thin. Plus, I don't know if I want another baby. In all honesty, Will and I haven't even touched each other since coming here." She sighed.

"Make it special, don't just have sex to have sex."

"Oh, and do you think *making love* will help Will get me pregnant?"

"Probably. Sex and making love are two different things. Sex is just a roll in the hay, having fun, doesn't matter who you're doing it with. Making love is . . . well, making love. You care for the person, and you want to be with that person, so you give that person your all. Your body, your heart, your mind—every piece of you. And if they love you back, then you're making love. It takes a certain person to want to make love with, and not just have fun." I stroked the paintbrush on the canvas, filling in the small void that caught my eye.

"So, what are we doing then?" Elliot's voice carried up to the loft. I didn't even notice the music had stopped. I looked over at Jillian whose jaw had dropped. We were both frozen, and I found myself completely unable to answer the question in front of my sister.

What *were* Elliot and I doing?

I cleared my throat, put the paintbrush in the water and walked over to the balcony. Elliot was standing in the middle of the living room, his new guitar propped up against the couch, his hand in his pockets.

I thought, and thought, and finally said, "I don't know, having fun?"

Raising an eyebrow, he let out a small grunt and nodded. "Good to know." Then he grabbed his guitar and left the living room, the side door closing behind him.

"What did I say?" I asked, turning to look over at Jillian. She stood and folded her arms.

"He's not just having fun, Jamie." Her voice was flat, scolding me almost. "I get your opinion on sex verses making love, but have you thought about what that means to Elliot?"

"We're not—"

"Don't try to admit you haven't slept together, your answer was obvious enough. Elliot is a good guy. He's fun, he's great with the kids, he's creative and he's head over heels for you. You may be having fun, but he's not." Jillian's eye bore into mine. I swallowed, taking a deep breath after before picking my paintbrush back up again. "Do you want to be more than his fake girlfriend?"

The streak of yellow hit the canvas, but my hand faltered. Pulling away slightly, I looked back at my sister.

"I don't know what I want. I enjoy my time with him, and I really like him, but I'm still nervous."

"Of what?"

I didn't answer. I didn't know how to answer. When I looked at Elliot the nerves and reservations about him flew away, but when we were apart, that's all I could concentrate on. I pushed the brush into the canvas, creating an effect that didn't belong on the painting. The paint was thick in that area, not meshing with the rest of the stroke at all. I used my thumb to smear it away, furrowing my brow at the mess I created.

"It's easier being fake, but that doesn't mean I don't want it to continue once we're home. I really . . . really . . . *really*"—I sighed—"want it to continue when we get home."

Jillian plopped on the edge of my bed, her arms still crossed over her chest. "You may want to tell him that, but I have a suspicion he wants that too."

"Let's just get through his show tomorrow, and the festival, and we still have to do the Christmas shindig . . ."

"I don't think that's happening this year."

"A gift exchange always happens. We just need to draw names."

Jillian shook her head at me, her gaze falling to my painting. Up until now no one had seen it. I had kept it secret from everyone. I wasn't used to having others around as I painted. Normally they were for my eyes only until they were done. Jillian smiled as she studied it, finally looking back at me—her smile growing.

"If you draw Elliot's name, are you going to give that to him?" she asked, her voice low.

I turned and looked at the painting, "I think, either way it's going to be his, don't you think?"

"I think"—Jillian stood and placed her hands on my shoulders—"you and him need to have a talk about what is happening here, and I bet you fifty bucks, if you don't, he sleeps on the couch tonight."

"He's been sleeping . . ."

"No, he hasn't."

I rolled my eyes. "Okay, he hasn't."

She scrunched her nose at me, a smile growing once it relaxed. "I'll remind Mom and Dad about the gift exchange tonight and we'll draw names at dinner. You paint, I'll go make sure Elliot's not crying in the ditch."

She shook my shoulders before giving me a slight push. She skipped the demon stairs and I listened to the creaks until the cabin went silent.

"Every year," my dad began, holding a cowboy hat that he pulled from his bedroom, "the adults draw names to give gifts at Christmas. Janet and I take care of the grandkids, so you guys only need to focus on each other and us. So . . ." he held the hat out to Jillian, "pick a name."

Jillian reached for the hat and pulled a piece of paper, then Holden and Will followed suit. Harrison and Carrie went next, and finally Elliot and me. I pulled a piece of paper and opened it, smiling when I saw the upper-case *D*. Elliot took a piece and furrowed his eyebrows at it. I tried to sneak a look, but he was quick to take the paper away. We would always try to figure out who each other had, but this year we all held our papers in our palms. Harrison stuck his in his pocket and Jillian smiled at her husband.

"Did anyone draw their own name?" my mom asked.

We all shook our heads.

"Great, now the dollar limit . . . let's say . . . fifty?"

"Fifty is good for me." Elliot stood and patted my shoulder. "If anyone knows what a certain mother figure would want, please let me know."

"Hey!" Jillian screamed. "You just gave away who you got."

"No, I didn't. I count three mothers in the room. So . . . if anyone knows any hints, shoot them my way." He squeezed my shoulder. "I need to call Bennett and make sure their flights are settled, see you back at the cabin?"

I gave him a hum in response. He leaned down and gave me a quick kiss before telling everyone goodnight and leaving. I pretended to ignore Jillian's look that stabbed me from across the room.

"Is Dax okay?" Harrison asked.

"Yeah, I think . . ." I muttered. "I think he's just nervous for his band coming out. They've only really played in Oregon. Maybe Washington. Park City is a different crowd."

"I'm sure that's it," Jillian said, leaning back into her chair.

"I'll talk to him before we go to bed." I stood and walked into the kitchen. "Do you have any more of that Mango Moscato, Mom?"

"No . . ." She sighed. "You drank it all."

I settled on a sweeter white wine as we talked by the fire. I could see the light glow from our cabin. Knowing Elliot was there by himself put a sour taste in my mouth. I saw small movements every now and then, nothing that could help me determine what he was doing, but enough to know he wasn't comfortable. I gave him a few hours of space, and once the kids had all gone to bed, and my parents and Harrison walked to their cabin, I said goodnight to Jillian and Holden and made my way over to Elliot.

The kitchen stove light was on, creating that soft glow, and the balcony light was on. He was sitting on the couch, his guitar next to him and a notebook on his lap. I walked up to the living room, noticing the blanket and pillow on the couch.

"Are you sleeping down here?" I asked softly.

He looked up at me. "Yeah, I thought I would tonight. I need to finish this song, so I'll be up for a bit longer."

I gave him a hum and nod. "Alright then. I guess I'll go to bed."

"Goodnight."

"Goodnight . . ." I elongated the *i*, trying to figure out if he was being mad or just considerate that he needed the light a little longer. "I'll just . . . get ready and turn the light off?"

He looked up at the balcony. "Oh, right." He reached over and turned the lamp on. "The overhead light is too strong so I put the balcony light on. You can turn it off."

"Okay . . ." I wasn't going to draw it out any further. I didn't say anything else. I swiftly turned and went upstairs, a stronger thump with each step. I slammed—not on purpose—the door to the bathroom, causing myself to flinch. "Good one, Jamie," I muttered to myself. "Let's just piss him off even more. It's not like he's the best non-boyfriend you've ever had and gives you all the swoony kisses and looks, and you had to go and piss him off." I glared at myself in the mirror before waving myself off and climbing in the shower.

I braided my wet hair and brushed my teeth, taking longer in the bathroom than planned. I knew Elliot, most likely, was waiting for his chance to shower, so, rolling my eyes I left the bathroom, only to be greeted by a dark cabin. He had turned off the lights. I was tempted to go peek over the balcony, but thought better of it. Instead, I let out a long breath and walked over to the bed.

Over the past week Elliot had taken the right side of the bed, always lying on his right to scoop me up, but the empty bed confirmed the fact that he was on the couch. I climbed in and attempted to get comfortable, but the bed seemed bigger without him in it.

Pull yourself together, it's only been a week.

"Elliot," I finally gave in. "This is ridiculous, come to bed."

"I'm fine, Jamie," he muttered.

"Yeah, well, I'm not, so get up here." I sat up and watched the stairs, trying to be quiet, waiting for any sign of movement from him.

After a few moments of silence, I heard him heave a sigh and then the couch groaned. The floorboards began to creak and then he was skipping the demon stair, walking around to his side of the bed. I watched as he pulled the covers down and laid flat on his back. He placed his hands on his bare chest and closed his eyes.

Even pissed off he was stunning.

"I'm sorry," I muttered.

He opened one eye and turned his head. "For?"

"The sex comment I made today."

He hummed and turned his head back again, closing his eyes. "I have a question for you Jamie."

I swallowed and laid down on the bed, facing him. "Okay."

"How many people do you think I've slept with?" Elliot's voice was monotone, and when I didn't answer right away he turned his head to look at me.

"What?"

"I'm being serious, I would really like to know how many people you think I've slept with."

"Um, well . . ." I turned to lay on my back. I didn't want to answer this question facing him. I knew my answer, obviously: two men, including Elliot. But I could only imagine his number to be so much larger. He was Elliot Whittaker after all—lead singer of Savaged Whittakers, owner of a multimillion-dollar company— women would be lining up to get a piece of him. "I'm going to guess . . ." I trailed off. "Twelve."

"Twelve?" He shot up, using his hands to help his body twist towards me. "You think I've slept with twelve people?"

"Well . . ." I hesitated. "You're Elliot Whittaker."

He let out a long groan and slumped his shoulders. "My name has nothing to do with how many people I've slept with."

"Okay," I said meekly. I sat up, bunching the comforter around my waist, stopping myself from touching him. "Maybe I just assumed . . ."

"So, when you said we were 'just having fun,' it made me wonder how you saw me. Do you really think I'm just some playboy?"

I pursed my lips, forcing them into a tight line. That never even came to my mind. I didn't know what to say, how to tell him what I really felt about him. Instead, I sat in silence, listening to his breath.

"Jamie," he finally said, "I've slept with four women—including you. I don't sleep with someone just to have sex . . . for me, there has to be feeling and emotion. A hint of a promise to the act. I wouldn't have slept with you if you didn't mean something to me." Even in the dark I could tell his eyes were firm on mine. "If you're just 'having fun' then I'll stop this, I'll go back down to the couch and finish out the week . . ."

"I don't want you to do that," I shot out, faster than intended. "I wasn't sure what to say earlier when you asked, I froze and said the first thing that came to my mind. You're more than that, Elliot. I'm not entirely sure what this is yet, but I know you're more than what I thought you would be. I've told you that. I wouldn't have slept with you if there wasn't a . . ." I smiled, trying to pull his exact words. "Hint of something more."

He scoffed and turned his head away from me. I scooted closer, wrapping my arms through his and resting my chin on his shoulder. His shoulders moved with every breath, and he began to play with his fingers. Even though he was more confident, there was still that nervous side to him. I began to trace his tattoo; it was becoming a habit to do so. Following the line of the neck down to the body of the guitar. His breathing slowed the more I traced.

"I'm sorry I guessed twelve . . ."

"Yeah, where did twelve come from?" His head turned slightly.

I let out a small laugh. "Do you remember, at the bar, when those girls came up and you said you would meet them after the show . . ."

"I told you that wasn't my thing . . ."

"I know, but maybe it used to be. So, I guessed high."

"Way too high," he whispered. After a moment of silence, he moved his hand and touched my forearm. Just his touch was enough to pull me back to him. "So then, what are we?"

"I told you; I don't know quite yet. But I know I like you," I admitted. "I know I don't really want this to end."

"I'll take that," He answered, turning his body just enough to kiss me. I melted into him knowing it wasn't going to be the last time.

Chapter Thirty-Three

-Elliot-

There wasn't a label yet, but that didn't mean there wouldn't be. Come morning I could still feel Jamie's lips as she kissed me everywhere she could. Any other morning I would have scooped her back up against me until the need for coffee pulled me out of the bed, but I knew that wasn't an option today.

Today I had to call Clay, set up the final date with an agent once we got back to Portland, and then I had to make that setlist one hundred percent perfect for my show tonight. Pete had said he posted on his website and all social media platforms that the "karaoke sensation" would be performing an acoustic set, and that he had already sold out on tickets (keeping a table reserved for my "family" of course). My mind was blown, I wasn't aware this was an event that required tickets to get in.

This would be my first one.

All the events at the Piano Bar and surrounding areas were just for fun. We played while people had a good time with their friends and family. It had been that way for years. Only within the past year did we start to gain traction and a larger crowd, but our events were still free and open to the public.

So, the knowledge that people were paying to see me shocked me. It was a feeling I would have to get used to, no doubt about that, especially once we met in front of the label.

I climbed in the shower while Jamie still slept, my mind buzzing with my to-do list, hoping there wasn't anything pressing with the family today to interrupt it. If I had my way I'd sit in the arm chair and play while Jamie painted. I just wanted to simply *be* in the same room as the woman I was falling in love with.

And there it was.

The thought popped into my head faster than I had meant it to, but it was out there in the "open" now. I had always teased Milo for being too quick to love. First with Madeline in college, fretting over when she would call after his botched first kiss. Then with Hannah and their relationship. Love was a word Milo would say even to me or Clay. And Clay, well he always knew he loved Ophelia, they just had to figure out their little game. Then there was me. I had only ever told one woman I loved her, besides my mother. I never really had the desire to. But with Jamie, I wanted to tell her that from the first moment I ever saw her.

And now it was really happening.

I was falling in love with Jamie Gaines.

I'm pretty sure I was falling first and falling hard.

"What are you thinking about?" Jamie's voice made me jump. I thought I was alone in the shower, only to find her right next to me.

The shower had two heads and an open doorway, making a sneaky entrance easy for anyone. The grin on her face as she stepped into the stream of water was taunting me as her fingers found my waist. I held her elbows in my palms and pulled her slightly towards me, the water hitting her hair just enough to cause small beads of drops.

"You," I answered softly, not wanting to hide anything from her anymore.

"Oh really?" she whispered back, her fingers moving from my hips to below my waistline. "Nothing else?"

I shuddered, taking in a quick breath. "Nothing else . . . ever. It's only you." I kissed her, completely skipping the sweet kisses and going right for the gusto, my tongue dancing with hers.

The to-do list flew from my mind as Jamie became my only train of thought, the warm water covering our skin and amplifying everything right up until it turned cold.

"So, other than a FaceTime with Clay and perfecting your set list, what do you have planned today?" Jamie asked after our shower. Her hair was still wet as she floated through the kitchen, a white t-shirt and black leggings hugging her in all the right places.

"The show's at eight," I reminded her.

"Oh, right, I forgot."

I raised my eyebrows at her.

"I'm being sarcastic," she added.

I sat at the island chair and leaned my elbow on the counter, resting my chin on my fist, keeping my eyebrows raised. I bit my cheek to keep from saying anything. I knew she was being sarcastic, but I wanted to see her reaction. I wanted to see all of her reactions.

"Oh, come on." She began to bounce on her toes. "You know I'm being sarcastic. You know I'm kidding—you know I'm coming."

"Yeah, at eight," I said in a monotone voice.

She stopped bouncing and quickly turned her body to the coffee maker, her wet hair hitting her shoulder with a tad more *oomph* than normal. I chuckled under my breath and reached for my laptop, pulling it close to me.

"Clay should be calling any minute now. If it were up to that man, he'd call me at 5 a.m."

"But . . . sleep." Jamie twisted her body, the coffee pot raised in the air. "That man is a workaholic."

"I can't deny that, but he's a hell of an accountant—more so."

"Yeah, why is your accountant helping you with selling the business?" Jamie put a cup of coffee in front of me, with creamer, exactly how I like it, before she slid onto the chair next to me. "Shouldn't you have a real estate agent help with that?"

I picked up my mug, taking a gulp before answering. "Well, we'll need a broker, but Clay knows my company inside and out. He knows it's worth, he knows my employees, and he knows how much it means to my family. Since Jacob wasn't a fan of me selling, Clay stepped in. He's found an agent, and will work closely with the numbers, while I show potential buyers what an amazing investment it would be."

"Jacob . . . your brother?"

I nodded. "Older brother. If it were up to him we would never sell the company and just keep passing it down from kid to kid. But, I don't want to sit at that desk anymore. He's a doctor—he's working on a research project, and Sydney just opened her salon. Selling the company would allow me to do so much more than become a full-time musician. I would be able to help them too."

She scrunched her nose. "They don't see it that way, huh?"

"Jacob doesn't."

My phone began to sing as a photo of Clay and I at Milo's wedding showed up on my screen. Not caring what Jamie heard, I swiped to answer.

"Good morning," I began.

"Morning, Clay!" Jamie shouted beside me.

"Is that Jamie!?" I heard in the background.

Clay simply pursed his lips and waved at the screen as Ophelia became larger in the background. Once she was behind him she swooped his phone away, the screen becoming a giant blur.

"Jamie!"

"Hey, Phe!" Jamie reached for my phone and held it up to her.

"I guess I'll talk to you later, Clay!" I shouted.

"I'll call you on Zoom." I heard his faint voice as Jamie took my phone to the couch, plopping down as she and Ophelia began a conversation.

Laughing, I opened my computer and waited for Clay to start a Zoom meeting.

With things falling into place—a firm date on Clay coming to Portland and the broker hired—I gave Jamie a quick kiss, grabbed my new guitar, and headed toward The Cabin for tonight's show. Once parked in the garage on Main Street I pulled out my phone to look at the screen.

During my talk with Clay it hit me that I hadn't talked to Jacob about any of this. As much as he hated it, and me at the moment, he had every right to know what was going on.

I opened his text thread, and quickly typed.

Me: *Clay's coming to Portland to help with the sale. Hired a great agent and we are confident in this move. Park City has been a blast, actually playing a show tonight and next week. Talk to you soon Jake.*

The message swooped away and I locked the screen, the text thread turning black. I leaned and shoved my phone in my jean pocket, grabbing my coat on the passenger seat before stepping out of the Jeep. Before I could grab my guitar and lock the door, my phone began to ring. Jacob's name flashed on the screen, the green circle to answer him staring me in the face.

"Alright then," I mumbled before answering. "Hey, Jake," I said, hoping my enthusiasm was there.

"So, you're selling? You're really selling to play guitar on a dingy bar stage?"

"Yes, Jake, I'm selling. Mom gave her blessing and dad . . . kinda did."

"Dad did no such thing." I could hear his teeth clamp down on each other, the strong *tap* that came whenever he clenched his teeth. "I talked to him . . ."

"He told me that he would be supportive—"

"He has no idea what he talked to you about. When I'm there he talks about Mom and the company. He asks how you're doing with it and then asks if you're still wasting your life with that dumb guitar." Jacob's voice was getting louder and louder with every syllable, reminding me of our dad. He would always say I was wasting my time, that I belonged at the firm to make sure everything there was run smoothly—that music would never be a career.

I had begun to drown him out as he rambled on about how Dad was wrong to leave me in charge of the firm, how he would have gladly run it on the side and how I was just too naive to see that it was just as important as anything else in the family.

I slammed the door to my Jeep shut, setting the guitar on the ground, feeling the anger and fire rise in my chest until I finally couldn't hold it in anymore. Jacob may be older than me, but he didn't need to make me feel this way, especially when he was putting down everything I loved and everything I had worked for my entire life. Music was *me*, sitting behind a desk was . . . not.

"You just don't seem to give a shit about your family. All you care about is that fucking guitar!" Jacob shouted.

"And how the hell would you know what I care about, Jacob? Have you even seen me on stage? No. Have you seen me at that firm? No! I put my all into that office while I'm there and I *do* care about it, but it's not what I *want*. You have never been to one of my shows—not even when I first started. I guarantee you've never even listened to my music online." Now I was shouting. People passed, giving me a look as they left the parking garage, but even through their stares I laid into my brother. "Music is my passion, Jake, not managing people who went to school longer than I did and have a passion for that. I want to give them someone better than me. Someone who can help the company grow bigger than it is. Dad told me that all I had to do was ask my *father,* and I may be surprised by how supportive he actually is.

"So, *Jacob,*" I spat him name, "until you can accept that I'm doing whats best for me, and the fucking company, you can just lay off. And maybe . . . just maybe . . . support your little brother from time to time."

I hung up on him before he could say anything. I heard a faint sound before I slammed on that red button. I didn't care what he had to say—let him be angry, let him hate me, let him throw a tantrum like a five-year-old.

Taking a deep breath, I relaxed my shoulders and bent to pick up the guitar case. I had a show to perform.

Chapter Thirty-Four

-Jamie-

The stage was dark when we got there. Jillian grabbed us some drinks, handing me my signature Mango-rita, and placing a few beers on the table for everyone else. Harrison ran his hand through his messy hair and Holden wrapped his arm around his wife's chair. Everyone had gone skiing before the show, you could see it in their eyes that they were tired and probably wished they could just crawl into bed. But since the kids were with the grandparents, seeing a movie, it was another sibling's night—this time in full support of Elliot.

The show was supposed to start at eight, and with only five minutes until showtime, the place was starting to get crowded. It wasn't at full capacity—I had seen this place more cramped during a karaoke night—but everyone was here for the purpose of seeing Elliot. Just the thought made the knots in my stomach grow.

I regretted not going to his shows with Madeline. I hated that I missed five months of this. If I could take it all back . . . but that wasn't an option. From now on, though, I'll be at every one of his shows. Even if it meant staying out until late to make sure he enjoyed himself, or leaving work a little early to help him set up. I wanted to be there for all of it. I loved this feeling it created—the butterflies. The thrill of knowing he was going to be on that stage with just him and his guitar . . . I shuddered.

Was it time yet?

I pulled my phone out of my bag, a small smile gracing my lips as I saw a text from Elliot.

Elliot: *The first song is yours, ok – don't judge me for it later.*

Without hesitation, I swiped to Madeline's name, hitting the green camera.

"Hey . . ." Madeline smiled. "Where are you?"

"I'm at a bar, Ell . . . Daxton is about to play." I raised my eyebrows, hoping she'd catch on.

Her smile widened and second later Milo appeared in the camera.

"We're *so* here for that," he shouted.

"He said the first one was for me . . . Milo, what song is it?"

Milo's smile grew, while Madeline looked over her shoulder at her husband, her jaw dropping. Closing his mouth and biting on his bottom lip, Milo wiggled his eyebrows and walked away.

"No . . . Maddy, what is it?"

"What time is the show?" she asked.

Tapping on the screen, the small clock appeared. "In three minutes."

"Flip the screen, I want to watch."

"You gotta tell me what the song is."

"Jamie . . . just listen." She gave me a slight nod. "Now, flip the camera. I want to see."

I did as she asked, holding the phone on the table in a spot where she could see the stage. The lights dimmed and a small cheer came from the crowd. Harrison slapped my shoulder and twisted in his chair to face the stage while Jillian settled into Will's side and Madeline was focused on her screen, Milo, once again with her.

Seconds later, Elliot came out and gave the crowd a wave, taking his seat on the stool that was provided, he propped his guitar on his knee and, without saying anything, he began to play.

I knew the song, it was one that played at my work, one that I knew he had learned, thanks to Madeline's wedding. One that wasn't his normal sound, one that mentioned mango-ritas and kissing on the dance floor. This song, without doubt, was us. *Unforgettable,* by none other than Thomas Rhett, had written our relationship before we were even a thought, and it reminded Elliot of me.

The entire time he sang, his eyes were on me and, when he sang the line about marrying, his smile grew, and he raised an eyebrow. He could ask me tonight, and I would say yes. This man had me wrapped around his pinky finger and I don't think he even knows.

I couldn't say exactly what I was feeling, but I knew it was a lot stronger than I gave it credit for. Elliot Whittaker had me . . . all of me.

The song ended and the audience clapped, Elliot smiled into the mic and knocked on the body of the guitar.

"Hey, everyone," he said, his voice filling the room. "I always like to start off with a song to gain your attention and, even though that song was for a certain person, I hope it worked. I'm Daxton Whittaker, and I'm here from Portland, Oregon. A week ago, I was dragged up for karaoke night and Pete then hunted me down and asked me if I'd like to play. So here I am, with a new, fancy guitar and a set list. I hope you don't mind hearing a slow, easy set tonight." He winked, and the only thing that kept me from falling to the floor was the chair I was sitting on.

A few other girls whooped, making Elliot look their way, giving them a chuckle.

"Back in Portland, I'm the lead singer of a band called Savaged Whittakers—who will be playing here next Thursday, so tonight, I'll give you a glimpse of a few of our songs. I have a few covers to sing, and a few of my own, but I promise not to bore you. And, if you like what you hear, you can find us online and make sure to come see us on Thursday, that will be a hell of a show, I can guarantee that." He situated his guitar and used his pick to strum through the cords. "So, without further ado . . ."

"Jamie . . ." I heard Madeline's voice faintly. I hunched my shoulders to look at the screen, flipping her back around to see me. "That song has always reminded him of you, ever since he first saw you drinking a Mango-rita."

"Funny how fitting it is . . . isn't it?"

"Enjoy the show! Send videos and pictures, okay!"

I scrunched my nose and waved at the screen, turning it off to give Elliot my full attention.

The sound of his guitar calmed the entire area. The normally noisy bar was quiet, save for the claps that followed every song. People were watching Elliot intently as he sang—all eyes were focused on him. And when he sang Savage Whittakers' original songs, their attention was caught. I looked around the room and watched as a few people pulled out their phones, pulling up their music apps. He sang songs I knew, ones I had listened to before coming to Utah, even the covers that he sang I had recognized. I swayed with the music, taking in each and every note. I waited for a song that I hoped he would play, even though I wouldn't know the words . . . I would remember the sunflowers.

But it never came.

Elliot sang an original as his last song, his eyes closed as he focused on the chords, and when the final strum rang through the room, the crowd cheered. They all knew Elliot was made for the stage.

He stood and thanked everyone, waving, and giving a small bow before turning to look at me. He winked and lifted the corner of his lips to a smirk before turning to walk off the small stage. I shot up from my chair and ran to meet him. Others had stood and walked to the side of the stage, but I ran around them – wrapping my arms around Elliot's neck the second I made it to him.

"How was it?" He laughed in my neck, his free arm wrapping around my waist. "No one sang along."

"They were too focused to sing along, but I swear I saw people looking up the band." Pulling away to look at him I placed my hands on his shoulders. "I sang every song."

"I know." He smiled. "I had my eyes on you the entire time."

"Daxton!" Pete's voice boomed behind me. Turning to look, I saw more than just Pete—Elliot had a crowd of people waiting to talk to him.

Stepping to the side, my arm still firmly around his waist, I let Pete come closer. Elliot's fingers pressed into my hip.

"Amazing show! If that's what just you and a guitar is like, I can't wait to see what the band sounds like next week. I've already had people come up and make sure tickets were still on sale."

Elliot gave him a nod, his expression beaming. He was trying to not let the fame and attention get to him, I could tell, but there was that small sliver that snuck in and it showed in his eyes. I had thought it before, and I would definitely be thinking it again: this is where Elliot belonged.

"They're looking forward to it. Bennett and I talked this morning about the set list, it's going to be about a seventy-minute show . . ."

"As long as you sing those . . . Whittakers . . ."

"Savaged Whittakers," I corrected, my gaze turning to Elliot.

Pete let out a loud chuckle. "Sing every one of your band's songs and I guarantee I'll have you back." Peter slapped his hand on Elliot's shoulder, giving him another proud smile. "I'll let you get to these new fans of yours. Come see me before you leave, okay?"

"Sure thing, Pete."

Running my fingers along his shoulder blades, I slowly stepped away from him, letting him take in the moment. Who knew people would be so smitten over an acoustic set from someone they had never heard of? Slowly, I made my way back to the table, watching as he shook hands and took a few photos with new fans.

Reaching out to grip the stem of my glass, I raised it to my lips, taking the final sip of the Mango-rita that had managed to last me his entire performance. Jillian nudged my shoulder, and I gave her a small smile, not saying a single word.

"How was the show?" My mom asked as soon as we arrived back at the cabin. The kids were all in bed already and she had wine and glasses set out to celebrate.

Everyone removed their coats and brushed the snow from our hair. Harrison shook his head like a dog—the snow flying everywhere.

"Harry, you need a haircut," Holden grumbled, slapping him on the back as he made his way to the kitchen. "It was great, Mom. You and Dad missed a fantastic show. Daxton is really talented."

"I'm sure he is." She smiled. "Your father and I are planning on coming to the show Thursday to see his band. We already have a sitter in place for the kids."

"Dustin can come, he's old enough and he's shown an interest in music ever since he watched Dax at the guitar shop. He's been asking for a guitar ever since." Holden pulled out one of the island stools and took a seat, grabbing a bottle of red wine and glass—popping the cork with ease.

Elliot leaned against the counter next to him, his palms holding all of his weight. I knew he enjoyed the show, but I could also see he was getting tired. I wanted to grab his wrist and yank him to our cabin. Snuggle up next to him in our bed and just listen to him breathe. That wasn't creepy at all to think of, was it?

"I told Jamie I'd be happy to show him a few things before we leave. Learning the guitar can be simple if you're really into it and he seemed into it." Elliot sighed, straightening his shoulders slightly.

"Yeah." Holden raised his glass. "I'm sure he'd love that. I'll send him your way tomorrow if you're not too busy."

"Not at all. My accountant has figured out the sale, but I need to be in Portland for that, and we've already set the playlist for next Thursday, I have plenty of time." He pushed himself off the counter and reached for the bottle of wine, pouring himself a small amount in one of the glasses. "What's the plan for the rest of the week? We have a Christmas celebration coming up, right?"

"Yes," my mom said, loudly, her eyes beginning to sparkle. It was her favorite part of the trip, and I was still upset that we almost didn't do it this year. "I think we'll do that on Wednesday."

"Oh, the guys will be here. Can they join us?" Elliot asked.

"Of course, the more the merrier."

"They didn't choose a name?" Holden chuckled.

"Eh they'll survive." Elliot raised his glass and drank the contents in one gulp. Once he set the glass on the counter he pulled out a stool and sat down, his shoulders slumped slightly.

"We'll ski again," my mom continued, "and walk Main Street one last time before we all pack up and leave. Oh, and the festival is ending. We need to get a few more looks at Jamie's painting."

I shuddered and walked up behind Elliot. I wrapped my arms around him and rested my chin on his shoulder. "Let's not talk about my painting. I had forgotten it was there. Honestly, it's been nice not stressing about what's going to happen."

My mom took a sip of her drink. "It's officially in the auction."

I nodded, my chin stabbing Elliot's shoulder. "Ouch," he mumbled.

"Oh, that doesn't hurt." I lifted my chin and took a deep breath. "Let's keep the focus on the real star of the show, Daxton is the center of attention tonight . . . okay?"

He tilted his torso. "I want to see the painting again."

I scrunched my nose at him. "Don't get me wrong I love it, but it's still nerve-racking to think it's there, with people looking at it every single day."

"It's no different than going on stage."

"It's very different."

Shaking his head, Elliot turned to my mom and nodded towards the bottle of wine. She lifted it and poured him a glass, picking it up by the stem and handing it to him.

"The lights are focused on you, Jamie, whether you're next to your painting, or not. Every light is aimed at that painting and more and more people see it every day. It's a masterpiece and you need to give yourself more credit." He lifted his glass, giving me a silent toast before taking a sip of the wine. "It's no different than when I'm on stage, except I'm only on their mind for an hour or so. Your painting is never leaving their mind."

My mom hummed. "I like this one, Jamie. I hope you keep him around."

Rolling my lips, I looked at Elliot. "I don't think he's going anywhere."

Chapter Thirty-Five

-Elliot-

"You need to just tell me who you have, and I can help you pick a better gift." Jamie walked around me, her fingers lightly brushing my back as she passed.

It was just us in the store and I was currently holding up a candle and bath bomb set. I had drawn Janet's name from the hat and, seeing as I had no idea what to gift my own mother for Christmas and birthdays, picking something for Janet was going to be worse. I would have been better off with Jillian or Carrie.

I put the set back down and gave Jamie a side eye. I knew she cooked, but I had already gifted her the oil and vinegar which she used every night. Getting a gift she would enjoy even after the trip was proving to be a challenge.

"If I tell you, it would be breaking the rules of the gift exchange. All you need to know is it's a mother."

"So, neither of my brothers and obviously not me. Give me some more hints."

"Brown hair," I mumbled.

"They all have brown hair," Jamie shot back. "I'm the only one with blonde hair."

Cocking my head to the side, I wiggled my eyebrows at her. She had her mother's eyes and nose, but her father's hair. She and Holden were the ones to carry the blonde through the family, and I'm sure her dad was happy about that.

"That's not a good hint." She crossed her arms and cocked her hip. She was clearly annoyed, and even annoyed she was sexy as hell.

"And yet, it's the only hint you're going to get." I bent down and gave her a fleeting kiss on her lips. "Just think about what a mother might like."

Her lips were twitching, wanting to form a smirk but she kept it at bay. She didn't want to give me the satisfaction of knowing that a small kiss was able to get rid of her annoyance. Her lips still in tight line, she took a sharp inhale, and then turned her body away from me, her eyes looking at the shelves.

The small shop on Main Street offered an array of gifts, from tourist attractions to high end clothes. When Jamie asked where I wanted to go to get a gift, my thought process was that Main Street would offer a better selection than the Wal-Mart on the other side of town. Even though this shop seemed to attract a wide audience, I didn't think Janet would like a gift basket.

"Well," Jamie sighed, "what would you get your mother?"

I shrugged my shoulders. "Sydney normally takes care of the gift for mom. She'll bounce ideas off of Jacob and I, and then we give her the cash and sign a card. My mom is simple though. A vase of flowers or a candle would make her smile, especially if it was from me."

She narrowed her eyes at me, "My mom loves roses, white ones. But she also loves to read, and chocolates. There's a bookstore that way, and it's connected to the Rocky Mountain Chocolate

Factory. Jillian would love the candle set and bath bomb, maybe some bath salts as well. She's a working mother so she doesn't get a lot of time to herself. Carrie is a stay at home mom—Holden is mainly held up at the restaurants—and as a married couple, they don't get a lot of time together. Sure, they're connected at the hip here, but once the vacation ends, it's back to being busy, busy, busy. Carrie would probably like something for her and her husband. A date night maybe? Or something specifically for couples. You could offer to take the kids off their hands while they go spend an evening together before it's back to normal." She picked up a leather book, turning it over in her hand. "A card with a gift card somewhere on Main, and then just hang out with the kids."

"That's all it would take to make Carrie happy?"

Jamie gave me a small hum. "Did that just give you an easy gift idea? You have Carrie, don't you?"

I chuckled. "No, I don't have Carrie."

"That's a bummer, she would have loved a date night."

"Who do you have?" I reached out for her hand, and, to my great joy she took it, her fingers sending those zings up my arm, "Do we need to get white roses and a book for your mom?"

"My gift is already done, and I won't be telling you who I have." She smirked. "But if chocolates and books are now added to your list, let's head to Dolly's."

She pulled me from the store, and into the snowy street, the storm overhead brewing as the street bustled with people still.

"But before we do that, let's go see your painting."

"We already went to go see it before we started shopping." She laughed. "You've seen it a million times."

"Then seeing it again won't hurt . . . will it? Come on, let's go."

Milo: What's the set list for Thursday?
  Me: A few covers, but mainly ours.
  Clay: Thomas Rhett covers?
  Me: And others.

Milo: *Madeline has completely ruined country music for you, hasn't she?*

Clay: *Elliot has the voice for country, I say his band go that route.*

Me: *Bennett wouldn't go for that. A few covers for sure, but our sound is what's getting us noticed. I think we'll stick with that.*

Milo: *And what did you get her mom?*

Me: *A book Jamie helped me pick and a few chocolate bars with an I Love Lucy theme.*

Clay: *I Love Lucy?*

Me: *You know the one where she and her friend work in the chocolate factory – here I'll send a picture.*

Clay: *No no... I can picture it.*

Milo: *Well, I want to see. SEND IT.*

"Who the hell are you talking to?" Jamie leaned her head back on my shoulder as we sat on the couch together. "That *whoop* noise is happening way too fast."

"Milo and Clay."

"I love that you guys have a group chat."

"What? Are you saying that you, Ophelia, and Madeline don't?"

"Never said we didn't." She reached over her head to the back of the couch, opening up her phone and pulling up her messages. The circle of pinned messages hit me. Her mom, Jillian, a group that was named "Bridesmaids" and then . . . me. "We started it during the wedding and just kept it going. What?" her voice changed as she tilted away from me, no doubt taking in my expression.

"I'm pinned to the top?" I asked, keeping a hiccup down. "We don't text that much."

"We will," she calmly said once she closed her phone down. "I expect that our new group chat is going to continue when we get back to Oregon. Don't you think?"

I kissed her temple. "I hope so." Setting my phone on the arm of the couch, ignoring chimes from the incoming texts, I shifted my body and wrapped my arm around Jamie. "Don't you think we should tell your family my real name? I know we don't have an official label yet, but even you can admit we haven't been faking for a while now."

"I will"—she settled into my side—"soon. It's just a little embarrassing. Faking a boyfriend so my family will stay off my back, only to start really liking the fake boyfriend." She laughed. "Madeline would have predicted this."

"Are you saying we are officially a book trope?"

"I'm saying . . . Madeline called it." Stretching her back she kissed my jaw, only to leap off the couch. "I'll tell them, and then when Bennett and the guys come in, they can call you Elliot instead of Daxton."

A knock on the door shifted her attention. Leaving me in the living room, she went to the kitchen, opening the door seconds later. "Hey, Dustin," I heard her. I twisted my back and looked at Jamie and her nephew.

"Hey, Aunt Jamie, is Daxton here?"

"I'm right here, bud." I stood from the couch, folding my arms. "What's up?"

He swallowed. "I was wondering if you would show me . . . if you would want to . . . I mean . . ."

"Yea." I smiled. "My guitar's upstairs, I'll go grab it."

"Really?" His eyes sparkled as his gaze followed my every move.

My eyes met Jamie for a moment, noticing the smile on her lips, before I dashed up the stairs.

An hour later, Dustin had my guitar on his knee, his arm draped over the side with the pick sturdy in his fingers. He was a quick learner, and picked up the cords easily. Once he had the first few down, I moved on to a song—one he requested—one that wasn't quite ready but he picked it up and was able to begin playing with ease. He wouldn't sing the lyrics, but knowing that would help him keep the tune, I sang softly.

"She painted their beauty, but little did she know – the love in my world was continuing to grow. Sunflowers bloomed beneath her skilled hand – the golden light enchanting a love so grand . . ."

Dustin stopped playing and looked at me, his eyebrows furrowing. "Is that . . ." he mumbled. "Did you write this for Aunt Jamie?"

I gave him a soft nod, hoping I could trust him with this secret. I knew Jamie had heard some of the lyrics, and she had heard the cords, but I still hoped to surprise her. My hope was to sing it in its entirety on Thursday. Bennett had gotten the guys on board, and they had been practicing the melody. It was a slower song than Bennett wanted but for Jamie, but she needed a song that I could sway her too, one I could whisper in her ears as we danced. I smiled softly.

"Don't tell her, okay?" I asked.

Dustin nodded and his focus went back to the strings. My phone dinged as he continued to play. I stood, leaving him in the living room, the strumming and soft hum filling the room.

Jamie: Hey look, using your pin in my messages.

I chuckled.

Me: And you're only in the house with your mom. You could come over here you know.
Jamie: And miss out on using the pin, nah. How's Dustin?
Me: He's playing a song, humming the tune.
Jamie: What song?
Me: Wouldn't you like to know.
*Jamie: *angry emoji* Tell me, or I'll tell my mom what you got her for Christmas.*

I shook my head and looked towards Dustin, his eyes still focused on his fingers.

Me: *You'll hear it soon. And I don't have your mom.*
Jamie: *A book written by one of her favorite actors and I Love Lucy chocolates. You definitely have my mom.*

Chapter Thirty-Six

-Jamie-

Elliot: *Still not telling you what song he's singing.*
This man.

Even through text he could make me laugh. He was just fifty feet away in our cabin, and I wished I was over there with him as he played with Dustin. Or I wanted him here with me in the main cabin, the music filling these walls. Instead, I was here with my mom, Jillian, and Carrie as we wrapped gifts for the kids. My mom, as usual, went overboard on the gifts for her grandchildren, but Carrie drew the line at getting Dustin his own guitar.

"He has to prove he wants to do it first," she mumbled as she stuck tape to the side of the island. "You know Dustin, he was into karate for a moment too but didn't stick with that."

"Maybe karate wasn't his thing, but maybe the guitar is. I saw his face as he watched Elliot play—" I stopped, literally feeling my heart stop beating as I waited for their response. Maybe they didn't catch that I just called *Daxton,* Elliot. Maybe it would slide off their shoulders.

"I'm sure he enjoys playing with Dax, but I can't afford to put him in another lesson if he's not going to stick with it. Karate was expensive." Carrie finished with the tape, setting it down on the countertop harder than she intended.

"I wish you lived closer. I'm sure Daxton would teach him for free. Dax is good with kids." I used my fingernail to create a stronger crease in the wrapping paper.

"Yeah, well, I don't like Portland, and I'm sure Dax wouldn't drive to our neck of the woods."

"You only live a few hours away. Daxton and I could take trips to see you once a month or so."

Carrie shook her head. "If Dustin is really into it, Holden and I will talk about it later."

"He was really cute when he came over and asked for Daxton." I smiled, counting in my head how many times I had said "Daxton" since slipping "Elliot" earlier. Four times? Maybe five . . . if I kept going it was going to become obvious I was purposefully saying his name.

Maybe he was right, maybe I should tell them sooner rather than later. Goodness knows I wanted to. It was obvious to me that Elliot was in my life for longer than the three-week mark we had originally planned on. Just the thought of being separate from him again once we got back to Portland . . . pretending this never happened . . . I didn't like that. I wanted to be near him constantly. I wanted to hear his voice and feel his lips against mine. But he couldn't be "Daxton" to my family forever. It's not like he changed the way he acted, he was himself around them, one hundred percent. It was just the name that was different.

"Hey, Mom," I heard myself say before I could stop it. I guess I was telling them *now.* In the midst of them talking about Dustin and how he wanted to play the guitar, I was telling them about Elliot. "I really need—"

Just then, the front door flew open. My two brothers and all the kids flew through the door, my dad following them slowly. They trampled in with the ski boots still firmly on their feet, the banging on the wood floor caused my mom to drop the wrapping paper and march towards them.

"If you ruin the flooring and we have to pay for it when we leave . . ." she scolded.

Jillian and I laughed as we gathered the wrapped gifts. Thankfully, all had been wrapped. Placing them by the fireplace—missing the giant tree we normally would have—I sighed and looked at Jillian.

"I almost let something slip," I whispered.

"I was wondering how many more times you were going to say 'Daxton' after you called him 'Elliot,'" she whispered back. "You're going to tell them, then?"

I shrugged a shoulder. "Eventually. He wants to tell everyone."

"Well, I'm on his side. You aren't pretending with him so why pretend with us?"

"I don't want to, it's just . . ."

"Awkward."

I nodded. "I don't want Mom to bring my health into it, you know?"

Jillian scrunched her nose. "She won't. She'll understand." Lifting her arm she rubbed my shoulder, forcing me to move, "How does Elliot react to it? Is he as worried as we've been?"

Thinking of Elliot, mainly his lips on my scar, I blushed and shook my head. "No, he doesn't even take notice of it very much. It's just . . . me."

Jillian dropped her hand. "It *is* just you." She smirked. "You know I'm still reeling over it, but I think mom will take it easier than you think. Dad on the other hand . . . he really . . . really likes *Daxton.*"

I chuckled and looked over at everyone in the entrance, still removing their snow gear, "Well then, he will really, really like Elliot. Seeing as they are the exact same person."

"I even heard him talking to Mom," her voice lowered as she leaned into me. "He's interested in Elliot's company."

"How? He doesn't know much about it?"

"I guess Elliot told him more than we know, I think Dad wants to buy it."

I dropped my jaw. "But he's retired."

Raising her shoulders only to drop them quickly, she smiled. "Doesn't seem that way."

I furrowed my brow, taking yet another quick glance at dad. "You don't think that will change once he finds out he's not really my boyfriend, will it?"

Jillian pinched her brow, her eyes piercing in me. "If he's not your boyfriend then I'm not Killian and Phillip's mom."

Wednesday came faster than I wanted it to, the days got busier as the time in Park City came to a close. We spent another night in the bar, one that Elliot picked after taking the day skiing and teaching Dustin more guitar. We walked Main Street again with the entire family, stopping in the Chocolate Factory once more, and getting the best pizza in town. It snowed—of course it did. This had been the most snow I had seen in a long time, and I loved grabbing Elliot's hand to pull him close to me for a kiss. Romantic kisses in the snow, what could be better?

My painting officially had an auction number next to it. Now that I saw it, it felt official. It already had a white ribbon next to it, labeling it as one of the most visited entries in the festival. I still couldn't believe it—my painting was hanging on a wall in Park City, Utah, in a high-end gallery, with that fancy white ribbon next to it. Elliot made sure to take a photo, keeping the group chat going. It was officially labeled "All of Us."

Madeline: *I love this so much!!*

Ophelia: *How much are we going to bet that goes for!? I say two million!!*

Clay: *More than that Phe.*
Milo: *I still want it above our fireplace.*
Elliot: *Back off, it's mine.*
Me: *Technically it's no one's until someone bids on it Saturday night.*
Elliot: *Wrong. Mine.*

I chuckled, loving the fact that, even though Elliot was right next to me, he was texting the group, laying claim to my painting. With the look he was giving me I knew it was more than the painting he was laying claim to.

Wednesday afternoon, Elliot and I traveled to the Salt Lake City Airport to pick up Bennet, Jameson, and Chase, and all of their instruments. I felt terrible with the fact that they all had to cram in the backseat of Elliot's Jeep, but with how little Chase was, he didn't seem too terribly uncomfortable. I twisted my body to face Elliot as he drove, allowing myself to see the boys in the backseat. I had seen them plenty of times before, but never up close like this.

Bennett had dark brown hair that was shaggier than I remember it being, and a decent build with bright blue eyes. Jameson was stoic as he looked at his phone, most likely telling his girlfriend that he arrived safely. He had short, buzzed black hair and a strong jawline. He was intimidating, that was for sure. And then there was Chase, with shaggy blonde hair and a scrawny build—the exact opposite of the two next to him.

"You guys must be excited to play?" I asked, breaking the silence.

"In Park City? You bet! I can't wait for you to hear—"

"The set list," Elliot interrupted, looking back at Bennett in the rearview mirror. "The set list, right?"

Bennett chuckled. "Yeah, of course. We got a great line up."

"Really?" I smiled and looked at Bennett. "What am I going to hear?"

"Nope." Elliot shook his head. "You'll find out at the gig. Are you guys coming to the Christmas shindig? Or am I taking you directly to the hotel? Just remember . . ."

"We know, you're Daxton," Jameson mumbled.

He speaks! My jaw dropped slightly as I stopped myself from shouting that out loud, although Elliot saw my reaction and chuckled softly.

Elliot gave a slight nod. "Until you're told otherwise, yes, I'm Daxton. But . . . hotel or cabin?"

"My mom already invited them to dinner tonight, and they wouldn't be imposing on Christmas." I looked at Elliot, tempted to reach my hand over to touch his arm, but refrained. I wasn't sure how much the guys knew about our relationship, so I didn't want to press the matter. Hell, I was still unsure as to exactly what we were. All I knew is we were going to define it before we got back to Portland.

"I'm sure Janet would be happy to feed more people." Elliot laughed.

"If your family wouldn't mind us being there, I'm sure we can find a way up after we settle into the hotel. Jameson needs to call the wife."

"She's not my wife . . . yet," Jameson mumbled.

"Yet?!" Elliot twisted his head to look at Jameson for a split second. "Are you proposing!?"

Jameson nodded. "I plan to once we get back from California."

"If we go to California," Chase added, his voice a little softer as he looked down at his fingers.

"We haven't heard anything yet," Elliot said to me, "But I'm sure we will soon, and then we have a proposal to plan apparently."

"I already have the ring and the plan in motion, I just want the stress of a possible record deal out of the way, then we can go from there."

"And if you don't get a record deal?" I asked, my eyes focused on Elliot.

A part of me wanted him to answer the question. I knew Elliot's plan to sell his company was part of the bigger picture, and would enable him to get on the road and focus more on his music. But I hadn't thought about where I fit into that plan. I didn't need to before now. I wanted to be a part of it, and maybe in Jameson's answer I would have a small, smidgen of hope that I could be. Record deal or no record deal, where did I fit into Elliot's life?

I guess that was just another piece of the puzzle he and I would have to figure out together.

"Either way, I'm marrying her," Jameson finally answered. "I just can't be thinking about proposing on top of figuring out if we are flying to California or not. One thing at a time, and regardless, I know my girl is solid."

Solid.

I gave Elliot a small smirk. He glanced at me from the corner of his eye, mirroring my smirk.

Solid.

Later that night we sat in the living room that was lit by a fire, Elliot's band sitting at the dining room table as we all began to exchange gifts. Elliot gave my Mom (shocker) the book I helped him pick out, and the chocolates. She instantly blushed and gave Elliot a hug, telling him how much she loved *I Love Lucy* and the book. He chuckled and smiled as she kept giving him thanks. Jillian and Carrie, oddly enough, got each other, and in a twist of fate got each other the exact same thing, a self-care kit complete with lavender essential oils. Harrison had my dad, and got him new fishing lines and lures. Holden picked my name, gifting me with a set of oil paints and new brushes. My dad picked Holden and gave him a new leather-bound journal. My mom got Harrison, and as a gag gift, she got him a shaving kit. Everyone laughed except Harrison, who just shook his head and mumbled *"yeah, yeah yeah,"* as he put the shaving kit off to the side.

Once everyone had opened their gifts I stood and went to the closet.

"I take it everyone knows I got Daxton." I smiled as I pulled out the canvas from the closet.

"It was rigged," Elliot whispered.

"No, it wasn't, but I will say I was extremely happy to pull your name." I walked up to him, standing in front of him as I held the painting close to my body. "I know you want the one I entered in the festival, but I hope you like this one just as much." I spun the painting around and watched as his expression changed.

"Jamie . . ." he whispered.

I had painted an abstract portrait of him sitting on a chair, his head dipped as his fingers strummed his guitar. There were very few details to his face, but he could tell it was him. The shades of brown in his hair, his jeans, and signature converse shoes. I captured him playing his music, hoping you could hear it through the painting, and by the silence in the room, and the look he was giving me, I think it did exactly that. He stood and took the painting from me, looking at it closely, taking it all in before he turned to set it on the couch. Before I knew it, his lips were on mine—soft, warm and absolutely perfect. Holding my face in his hands he kissed me as if we were the only people in the room; not caring that every pair of eyes were on us. He just kissed me, living completely in the moment. A moment I could stay in forever.

He broke the kiss sooner than I wanted, but once his forehead touched mine, my mind came rushing back to earth.

"I love it," he whispered against my lips.

So many sensations found their way into my body as his thumbs traced my jaw. Reminding myself that I couldn't take him right here, that there were other people watching, I took a deep breath and ignored the butterflies that fluttered around. Gently grabbing his hands and pulling them from me, I gave him one last fleeting kiss. His eyes were heavy on me as I pulled away to look at him, a look I had seen before.

"I'm glad you do," I finally answered back.

"Can we see?" Harrison's voice brought me back to earth.

Elliot blinked, letting out a small chuckle, his eyes returning to his normal weight. "I figured she would have shown you."

"Nope, I'm the only one who's seen it!" Jillian shouted, complete and utter joy in her voice. Jillian was—at least for this trip—the queen of keeping secrets.

"You didn't show anyone?" Elliot smiled, reaching for the painting, taking one long look before showing everyone else.

I wrapped my arm around his waist. "You had to see it first, but Jillian weaseled her way in."

He gave a light chuckle, bending down to kiss the top of my head while my family, and Elliot's band, came over to look at the painting. It was weird. This felt different than when I was standing at the gallery next to my piece there. This felt more real, more intimate, more . . . alive. The gallery was an amazing experience, but nothing would amount to how I was feeling at this moment— appreciated and seen for what I could do with a paint brush, but most of all, loved.

A few hours later, well after the sun had gone down, Elliot drove the guys back to their hotel and I made my way to the cabin, alone. I knew Elliot would be back faster than it felt, but I wished he was holding my hand as I opened the door, and gently set his painting up against the wall. I placed it so he would see it first thing when he got back.

Leaving the entry light on, I made my way upstairs and got ready for bed, falling into the covers and sinking in, not realizing how tired I was until my head hit the pillow. I could fall asleep in seconds if my mind wasn't going a million miles an hour. I kept replaying every kiss Elliot had given me. That very first one on my front porch, where his hands and lips were stiff until he finally sank into it all the way up to tonight—surrounded by everyone, but by far the most intimate kiss we've shared. When he whispered, "*I love it*," I half expected him to say "*I love you.*" And I would have said it back.

I heard the door open and softly shut. A soft chuckle and the sound of shoes being dropped, then there was the groan of the floorboard and the creek in each step. Elliot's silhouette came into view, his arms moving to remove his jacket before he crawled onto the bed. He kissed my shoulder and my neck, my temple, and, finally, my lips. I rolled my shoulders, my fingers finding the hem of his shirt with ease.

"The guys love you," he whispered, a shake in his voice as my fingers touched his skin.

"Oh yeah?" I kissed his lips.

"Bennett told me I needed to keep you around."

"Oh really?" I laughed. His lips moved against my collar bone, the warmth of them bringing chills up my spine.

I pulled on his shirt, forcing him to sit up so I could pull it over his head, my fingers instantly finding his abs. He was defined, perfect to touch and feel—to kiss. I sat up, wrapping my arms around his waist as I kissed my way up to his lips. He let out a long sigh before I kissed his lips again wanting every inch of him to be mine.

"Tell me what you want, Jamie," he said, his voice husky and full of need. He shifted his weight on the bed so he was sitting next to me, his hand moving quickly to remove my pajamas, his lips instantly finding my scar and his hands finding my breasts.

I shuddered under his touch, melting into him.

"Elliot . . ." I let out a soft moan, trying to find the exact words to tell him what I wanted from him. I hadn't ever asked for it before because I was nervous. Honestly, a part of me was scared, but I knew with Elliot . . . with Elliot it was what I wanted—more than anything.

"I can kiss you here," he whispered as he kissed my collar bone, gently using his palm to push me down on the mattress. "Or here." I could feel his smile against my hips as his kisses trailed further and further down my body. "Or here . . . this spot made you jump last time." He kissed my hips, making me laugh and twitch again. "Tell me, Jamie . . . tell me what you want, and I'll give it to you."

I sighed. "Elliot, I . . ."

"Tell me, Jamie. I'm yours in whatever way . . ."

"Elliot," I said, with a bit more force than intended, but it got him to stop kissing my stomach, and look up at me. I met his eyes as my fingers ran through his hair. I swallowed and finally said aloud, "I want you to make love to me."

Elliot's breath stopped as his entire demeanor changed. He gave my scar one final kiss before hovering over me on the bed, his elbows hoisting him up as his fingers found my hair. The air in the room shifted when he kissed me, the same kiss as earlier filled with passion, heat, love. And then, when he took over, we blended in a way we hadn't before, and I knew . . . I knew, I was madly in love with Elliot Whittaker.

Chapter Thirty-Seven

-Elliot-

I woke up the next morning to an empty bed, something I didn't expect after last night. The way Jamie asked me to make love to her, and then, after she allowed me to do just that . . . I figured I would wake up with her next to me, my arm draped around her, holding her close to me. I pinched my brow when I saw the indented pillow and messy sheets. I sat up and looked around the room, our clothes were still a mess on the floor, even her robe was still on the armchair.

I climbed out of bed, grabbing my sweats to pull on. Rubbing the back of my neck I made my way downstairs, hoping to find Jamie on the couch with a book and coffee mug. Instead I found her in the kitchen. She swayed as she danced to the soft music. *My* music. She was dancing in the kitchen to my band's music wearing nothing but *my* t-shirt.

The fact that she didn't turn as I approached told me she was completely into the song as she emptied the coffee grounds. She didn't hear me coming. I slipped my arms around her waist, causing her to jump slightly and giggle before she leaned her head back against me. I bent down and kissed her neck.

"Did I wake you?" she asked.

"No, you look good in my t-shirt." I kissed her neck again, only lifting my head to move her hair from her skin.

"I'm pretty sure that's a song."

"No, it's not." *Kiss, kiss.*

"Pretty sure it is." She giggled again. She ran her hands along my arms, bringing herself closer to me—if that was even possible.

"No, I would know. I'm a singer. I know every song on the face of the earth, and I'm one hundred and eighty-nine percent sure that it's not a song."

She twisted her body to face me, kissing me fiercely. "Pretty sure it's a song. Pretty sure it's by Thomas Rhett. Pretty sure I've heard your band cover it before. And I'm pretty sure it plays at my office . . ."

I silenced her with another kiss. "No, no it's not. You're hugely mistaken."

She laughed against my lips, her hands running up my bare chest to wrap around my neck. Her hands began to wander as she kissed me, completely forgetting the tasks she was doing. She was my only train of thought. That is, until my phone rang, disrupting everything. I broke the kiss and let out a growl, causing Jamie to laugh again. God I loved her laugh. I looked at my phone, which was almost dead after not plugging it in last night, to see Bennett's name flashing.

"Well, good morning," I answered, half-annoyed he interrupted my moment with Jamie.

"Please tell me you checked your email this morning." His voice was quick as he got straight to the point.

"I just woke up," I admitted.

"Well, check it. They want us. Pacific Sound wants us. This weekend. Elliot . . ."

"What?" I shouted, pulling my phone down to switch him to speaker. I opened my email, only to be greeted first thing with the subject line: *Savage Whittaker Performance* . . . "You're shitting me."

"Elliot!" Bennett screamed. "They're purchasing plane tickets, hotel rooms, accommodations . . . they want us there, Elliot! This weekend!!"

While Bennett rambled, I read the email. He was right. They wanted us to come this Saturday to perform original works with the possibility of signing a contract. They wanted us to stay a few days, meet with agents, possibly *record*. That word hit like a thousand knives. Record. We had to get in touch with them today, and then—if we accepted—we'd fly out tomorrow. It was all happening so fast, so many things were piling up. My heart began to race. With excitement? Nerves? At this point I couldn't tell the difference. It wasn't until Jamie touched my back that I slowly came back to reality.

"Seriously?" she asked, her voice low.

"Jamie!" Bennett shouted. "Can you believe this!?"

"Oh, I can . . ." Jamie smiled. "But I'm afraid Elliot has turned into a statue."

"No, I'm here . . . I'm . . ." I'm what? What *exactly* was going through my head.

Jamie. That's what.

Jamie was the only thought process I seemed to hold.

"It's unbelievable. Jameson is calling his girl. Chase almost fainted! A show tonight and then off to California tomorrow. It's happening, Elliot, it's really happening." Bennett's words were becoming louder and louder as his excitement grew. I could hear him pacing, I could hear Chase saying something in the background. Jameson's voice was faint as well, they were bustling over there, and all I could think of was the woman next to me.

"Okay, Bennett, slow down. I'm picking you guys up in an hour, right? We'll go to the bar, set up, and do our sound check, then call the label. We'll get this squared away."

"Come on man, why don't you sound as excited as all of us? We have a shot of getting signed, Elliot! It's happening!"

I looked at Jamie. Her eyes were wide as she watched and waited. Even *she* seemed more excited than I was. I was excited. Deep down I knew it. This was what we were working towards, this is what I wanted for the band. But this weekend . . . it was too soon. I wasn't done here. There were still things in Park City I had to do.

"Bennett, I'll call you back soon, I, uh . . ."

"Elliot . . ."

"I'll call you back." I hung up the phone, placing it face down on the marble counter, and looked at Jamie.

"What's wrong?" she asked, jumping right to the point. "Elliot . . ." She touched my arm, her fingers trailing down to my tattoo. She had gotten used to tracing it, and I'd admit it had a calming effect on me, one I welcomed.

I leaned against the counter, still trying to focus on her fingers. "I can't fly out this weekend."

"Sure, you can, this is your break, this is what you wanted."

"The gallery auction is on Saturday." I met her gaze.

"So?"

"So . . . I need to be there for that."

"Unless you're planning on bidding on it, no you don't. You need to be in California getting yourself a record deal." Her eyes lit up, wide—full of excitement. There was a slight grin on her face, bringing a warmth into the room. She was so sure of it, so sure of herself, so sure of *me*. "Why are you so focused on being at the auction?" she asked, her fingers still tracing my tattoo. I watched as they moved with the ink.

"Because it's yours . . ." I mumbled.

"Elliot." Her fingers stopped as she gripped onto my forearm, the pressure of her fingers tight against my skin. "I'd rather you be there, performing for that label than sitting in a chair watching some rich assholes bid on my painting. Hell, I'd go to California with you if I could, but I'm assuming I'm going to have to drive your car back to Portland."

"You'd drive the Jeep back?"

"Well, the plan was to head home on Sunday, right? I'm assuming you'd still be in California on Sunday. So . . . Elliot . . . here's what you're going to do." Her hands relaxed, sliding up to my neck, her fingers finding my hair with ease. "You're going to kiss me, and then you're going to go upstairs and get ready to pick up the guys. You're going to call the label from the hotel room and set up anything you need to. Then you're going to go to the bar and set up. I'll meet you there and you can tell me all about the plans. You'll kiss me again and then you're going to put on the best show of your life, here in Park City, Utah."

I smirked, totally in awe of the woman in front of me. I kissed her, breathing her in, intending to follow all of her directions.

"You're something else, Jamie Gaines," I mumbled against her lips, kissing her again before she stepped away.

"Go get ready, and you're not changing your mind. You get your ass to California." She lifted a finger and pointed at me, still looking sexy as hell in my t-shirt.

I twisted my lips. "It's not a song." I chuckled, taking her all in before I pushed myself off the counter to make my way upstairs.

"Yes!" she shouted after me. "It is! I'll even play it right now!"

I laughed as I went into the bathroom, shaking my head as Thomas Rhett's *T-Shirt* began playing on all the Bluetooth speakers.

"Check, check . . ." I spoke into the mic, that familiar feeling on my lips.

"Are you sure you want to start the show with a Thomas Rhett song?" Bennett asked.

"Yes," I said into the mic, singing out the "e."

"People are going to think that's all we sing."

"If I recall correctly, there are only two Thomas Rhett songs on that set list." I turned towards Bennett, my voice fading as the mic got further away. "And one Ben Rector song, and a Chord Overstreet . . ."

He rolled his eyes. "It's mostly our stuff, plus this new one, but really . . . opening with him? Madeline isn't even here."

"No, but Jamie will be on FaceTime with her, I guarantee it. Check your mic." I pointed to Bennett's mic. "Jameson, check yours too."

They both made their way to my sides, Jameson to my left, Bennett to my right.

"Check," Jameson grumbled. "Still don't know why I have a mic."

"Because you sing," Bennett sang.

I chuckled as I went to the mic and puffed a breath of air in it, finding Pete up behind the bar with the sound board. I gave him a thumbs up and turned back to the guys.

"Two Thomas Rhett songs, one Ben Rector, two Chord Overstreet, one brand spanking new song that only a kid has heard, and sixty minutes of our original works and yes, Jameson, you have to sing back up on a few of them." I opened my arms to the stage in front of me. "Last show being indie, you guys."

Jameson rolled his eyes, "Just promise me I won't have to sing on the record."

I pointed at him. "No promises." I gave him a quick wink. "Get your instruments, let's get this check going."

The moment Jamie snapped me back to reality, the moment I took control. We made the call the second I stepped into their hotel room. The entire time the agent spoke to us on the phone, giving details about what to expect, my mind was thinking about Jamie and how I so desperately wanted her in that room listening in on the phone call. The plan was to leave tomorrow afternoon, have a car meet us in California and take us to the hotel. Then we would meet with the agent on Saturday and talk about what they wanted and expected from us. Sunday was a prep day for us, when we would pick our top five favorite songs to preform and perfect before we walked into the studio on Monday. Monday was the day we would find out if they wanted to sign us, and if they did . . . we would sign a contract Tuesday and be out the door and back home on Wednesday.

Reaching down I grabbed my guitar, slinging it over my shoulder. Jameson had his bass situated, his keyboard to his left, and Bennett was already strumming a few chords while Chase tapped on his cymbal. I watched as Pete left the sound bar, leaving it up to me and the guys to make sure we sounded good. Normally I knew the man behind the sound bar, I knew his signals as he would help direct us, but this man didn't even look up from the controls.

"Chorus," I looked over at Bennett, "of *Pilgrim.*"

Chase tapped his drumsticks together, counting us down and then—all in sync, all perfectly timed—we picked up and played one of our most upbeat songs as if we had started from the beginning.

Just hearing the music, I came to life.

Chase kept rhythm, Bennett carried the tempo, and Jameson led the beat, all the while my voice brought the entire thing together. I could hear a few tweaks to be made to the sound but all in all, this was us. We sounded great no matter the imperfections and just holding this simple sound check, I could feel it in my gut that the label would sign us. As Bennett kept saying, it was happening.

Once the chorus was over and the sound died, I reached up and adjusted my mic.

"Sounds great," I spoke into the mic. "Jameson I need your amp turned up just a tad, and Bennett, yours needs lowered. Chase, adjust the mic near your footing . . ."

"Daxton," Pete's voice came from behind me, forcing me to stop directing Chase and go to the edge of the stage. "Sounds great, but you . . ." he smiled at me, "have a visitor."

My first thought went right to Jamie. Even though she had said she would see me tonight, the fact that she was constantly on my mind—wishing she was here, I had hoped she was feeling the same.

"My girl?" I asked, that glimmer of hope.

Pete chuckled. "No, sorry to tell ya. It's a man. Your brother?"

My back stiffened and I stood straight, ice flooding my entire body. Jacob? Jacob was here? I looked over at Bennett and let out a puff of air. "Make those tweaks . . ."

"Yeah, we got it, you go see what's up." Bennett nodded towards the bar top.

I followed his nod, catching sight of Jacob right away. He leaned on the bar top, his legs crossed as if he had been standing there for longer than anticipated. I could see the annoyance on his face as he watched. I lifted my guitar over my shoulder and set it on the stand, jumping off the small stage. I shoved my hands in my jeans pockets and slowly made my way towards my brother. What I didn't expect to see was Jacob, standing there, with a smile on his face.

"Sounds good," he said once I was in ear shot.

I clenched my teeth, trying to force myself to form the words, any words at the point, that wouldn't end up becoming a fight between Jacob and I.

I cleared my throat and settled with, "What are you doing here?"

He took a deep breath, shoving himself off the bar top, "Well, you told me you were playing, so I figured I may as well come out and see what you do up there."

"So you flew to Park City . . . even though I've played in Portland millions of times – you decided to come to Utah to watch me play instead of just watching me at home?" I asked, trying to keep my voice calm.

Jacob didn't respond. He blinked, gave me a nod and looked at the floor. "Dad was lucid."

"What?" I asked, shocked by the change in subject.

He met my gaze. "Yeah, a few days ago. Right after we spoke on the phone."

"You could have called. You didn't need to fly out here to tell me that."

He shrugged. "He asked about you. When mom told him you were making moves to sell the company . . . he, uh . . ." he trailed off, kicking his feet, and mimicking my stance as he shoved his hands into his pockets.

"He was mad?" I filled in the blanks. I may have taken that moment between us as him giving me his blessing, but I could have been wrong. Honestly, I probably was.

Jacob however, stopped my train of thought.. "No. He said he was shocked you didn't sell it sooner. Mom played him a few songs—songs I hadn't heard before—and then pulled up a YouTube video of you guys performing at the Piano Bar. He seemed . . . impressed."

I raised my eyebrows. "What?"

"Yeah, we all were. So . . . dad and I talked. We want this for you Elliot, we want you to follow . . ." he waved his hand around, "this, wherever it may take you."

"You mean that?"

Jacob nodded. "Yeah. Of course, I do. I looked up your site the next day and saw this listed as a show. Andrea and I bought tickets and here we are. She's excited for a few nights away from the kids, and I'm excited to see my little brother play."

"You're serious? One hundred percent serious?"

He let out a chuckle and nodded his head. "Yeah, Elliot. I know I haven't given you the best reason to believe me, but really. Watching your band online and even that sound check . . . that's where you belong."

Relaxing my shoulders for the first time since I laid eyes on my brother, I turned back to the stage. Bennett still has his guitar on his shoulders, Chase was flipping a stick between his fingers, and Jameson was strumming a few chords.

"They seem like fun guys," Jacob added.

"Want to meet them?" I asked, turning back to him.

He smiled. "I'd love to. That is, if they don't hate me."

"Nah, don't take it personally. Jameson hates everyone."

We both removed our hands from our pockets at the same time, the tension between us lifting completely. All the years of fighting seemed to vanish as he followed me over to the stage. It was coming together—perfectly.

Chapter Thirty-Eight

-Jamie-

The day without Elliot went slow. I had to stop myself from looking at my phone, and fight the urge to text him—knowing how busy he was. He didn't need a text from me to disrupt his flow.

Jillian attempted to keep me busy, but even though she tried her hardest at the cabin, she failed. I wanted Elliot there. I wanted to hear the guitar play as I started a new painting. I wanted him to throw a snowball at Killian and Phillip, and I desperately wanted to be in his arms.

Last night changed things, changed *us*. I had felt it for a while now, but last night made it real. Really, really real. Jillian, seeing my brain move at a million miles an hour, pulled me from the cabin. Piling me and her twins in the car, we went to the Newpark Shopping Center in Kimball Junction, stopping at a local clothing store where we each picked out a new outfit for tonight. The owner was one of the sweetest ladies I had ever met, and when I found out her husband was a dentist . . . well, that gave us something to talk about. Something to distract my mind. Even though she knew nothing of the profession, just the familiarity of something so close to home made me smile. It helped take my mind off the looming thought that Elliot still hadn't texted me.

Jillian had to pry me away from talking with her, telling her we would come back on our next visit. She waved with the brightest smile.

"Why are you so weird? You don't need to talk about teeth all the time," Jillian grumbled.

"I don't, that's Madeline. Not once have I talked about teeth on this trip."

"What do you call *that*?" Jillian used her thumb to point behind her at the store.

"What?" I laughed. "Her husband is a dentist! I had to."

"Mommy!" Phillip shouted, his arm held out in front of him. "A pottery place! Can we go paint!!"

Jillian looked at me and then to her phone. "What time is the show?"

"Late . . . eight. He's most likely doing his sound check right now," I said softly, taking a deep breath as I looked at my sister. "Let's go paint some pottery."

She wrapped her arm around my shoulder. "You really like him, don't you?"

I gave a harsh laugh. "Isn't it obvious?"

"Very." She nudged me with her hip. "And it's obvious he really, really likes you too. And you're sure you're okay with him leaving tomorrow?"

I grabbed the door handle and held it open for the boys and Jillian. "Yes, why wouldn't I be? He's worked so hard for this; he can't miss this opportunity."

My phone dinged in my bag, and as Jillian and the boys went to look for their piece to paint, I fumbled to grab it. Almost as if he knew we were talking about him, a text from Elliot sat on my screen.

Elliot: Two Thomas Rhett songs – acceptable?

I smiled.

Me: As long as one of them is my song.
Elliot: Sadly no – but I guarantee one will make you smile. Or hate me. One of the two.
Me: Then three Thomas Rhett songs. Come on. Make Madeline proud.

I watched as the three dots danced on the screen, butterflies growing each time they bounced.

Elliot: Two. That's all Bennett will give me. See you tonight?
Me: Wouldn't miss it.

"Auntie Jamie!" Phillip yelled. "You should paint this for Uncle Daxton!" He turned quickly, holding a small guitar. "If you don't, I will!"

I took the guitar from him. "We can both paint one."

His eyes went wide. "Let's do it!"

We each had a small piece painted in an hour, and handed them in to be fired in the kiln with the promise of pick-up before we left Park City. Then we piled into the car and made our way back to the cabin, just as the snow began to fall.

I showered and got ready for the night, simply excited to see Elliot on stage again. Walking into the main cabin, I saw the kids in the living room and all the adults, ready to go. Everyone looked like they were ready for a night out, especially my parents. They had gone skiing and participated in all the family events, but they hadn't been out without kids since they arrived. My mom was particularly excited to see Elliot play. They kept talking about

Daxton and his band, Daxton and his business, Daxton . . . Daxton . . . Daxton. He had become a part of the family in the three short weeks he had been here.

"You keep that one, Jamie. He's something different and we can tell . . . Daxton loves you." My mom smiled as she gathered her coat.

Daxton.

"Uncle Daxton said he could keep teaching me guitar!" Dustin came up behind us, hoping we would change our minds and let him come to the show. "He said we can have Zoom sessions or he could visit. Auntie Jamie, you need to marry him."

Daxton.

"I was talking to . . . Bennett . . . last night?" my dad sighed, slipping on his shoes, "He said Daxton has been wanting to sell his company for a long time and finally decided to take the plunge. Something about a record label?"

Daxton.

"Just wait until Dax sees you in that dress, Jamie . . ." Jillian began, her voice growing faint, after the word "Dax"—that was all I heard. He wasn't Daxton.

"Okay I have something I need to tell you guys, and it's a little weird, but I hope you'll understand," I blurted out.

Everyone stopped and looked at me, their eyes wide. Jillian grew a small smirk on her lips and every man in the room folded their arms over their chest. My mom stood still, causing me to lose my train of thought.

I heaved a sigh and looked at my feet.

Oh yes . . .

My fake relationship, that turned into a real relationship.

"Daxton's name isn't really Daxton. And he's not really my boyfriend . . . well . . . he wasn't . . . I'm not one hundred percent sure what he is, but he's not *Daxton*." I was talking faster than intended, and I could tell if I didn't stop talking now, I would ramble and tell them everything—word vomit to the extreme—and I didn't want that to be how I told them.

"It's about *time* you tell us," Harrison grumbled.

Wait . . .

"What?" I instantly looked over at Jillian. She shrugged her shoulders and bit her bottom lip. "You know?"

"I promise I didn't tell them," Jillian instantly defended.

"One Google search was all it took. We've all known since karaoke night." Holden chuckled.

I looked at my mom and dad. They were being oddly quiet.

"Did you two know?" I finally asked.

"Well," Dad sighed, "like Holden said, one Google search. Especially after talking with him about his company. Elliot . . . isn't it?" I answered my dad by nodding. "He looks like an Elliot. How on earth did you come up with the name Daxton?"

"Well . . ." I looked at Jillian. She was the first one to hear that lie all those months ago. "I don't exactly remember, but would you believe me that Elliot's middle name *is* Daxton."

"Ah." Holden laughed. "We were wondering what the 'D' stood for!"

"I said it was Daniel, Holden was trying to say Derek or something like that. Elliot Daniel Whittaker just has a nice ring to it." Harrison laughed, opening the front door for everyone. "That's actually hilarious that Daxton is part of his name. No wonder why he answered to it easily enough."

"So, you guys aren't mad at me?" I finally asked, wrapping my arms around my stomach as we stepped into the snow.

"Of course not." My mom wrapped her arm around my shoulders. "I mean, I can't wait to hear the reason why you thought you had to invent a boyfriend. But it must have been a good one. And then to find a guy to play the part? Sounds like something out of a Rom-Com."

"He volunteered," I added. "I really did meet him at Madeline's wedding."

"He volunteered as tribute!" Jillian raised a fist in the air.

"Don't make it weird," I grumbled.

"Oh Jamie, it's already weird." My mom rubbed my shoulder. "We adore him, but can we call him Elliot now?"

"He'd like that."

Hearing my family call Elliot by his real name on the drive to the bar, made all the difference in the world. Made it more . . . real . . . if that was even possible. The illusion of Daxton was erased, and the reality of Elliot became common knowledge—no longer a secret I had to keep.

The Cabin was already packed when we got there, but the table Pete promised was there waiting for us. My parents took their seats first, my siblings slipping in next to them. I stayed standing, looking around hoping to catch a glimpse of Elliot before the show. I hated to admit that I never saw him getting ready for a show, I wasn't sure what his routine was or if he did anything for luck. A part of me, a very large part, wanted to hunt him down and kiss him good luck. I knew he didn't need it, but maybe he wanted it.

But he was nowhere to be found.

We sat impatiently as the clock ticked closer and closer to when Savaged Whittakers would take the stage, and there was still no sign of Elliot. I glanced at my phone, seeing a text from Madeline (*FaceTime when the show starts! Milo and I want to watch!*), and one from Ophelia (*Promise me I get to design your wedding dress – I already have the perfect design picked out*), and, thankfully, one from Elliot.

Elliot: *I don't think I've ever been this nervous for a show before.*

I quickly responded.

Me: *Well come out from wherever you're hiding, and I'll give you a kiss for good luck.*

And just as I hit that blue arrow, the lights dimmed. Harrison began clapping loudly and my parents got situated in their seats.

People began to cheer and clap, moving from their tables close to the stage.

"Ladies and gentlemen," I heard over a speaker—the voice of Pete—one I had grown to recognize. "It's my pleasure to introduce to you a band from Portland, Oregon. Please help me in welcoming, Savaged Whittakers!" He drew out their name, hyping up the crowd more and more. It even created butterflies in *my* stomach.

There was a cheer, a few claps, and once the spotlights hit the stage—Chase's drum set showing the most perfect SW above a guitar—the crowd's cheers got louder. Jameson came out first, giving the crowd a soft wave, then Chase, who rushed to his drum set, his sticks already flying through his fingers. Bennett and Elliot came out last, with Bennett reaching his microphone before Elliot. I watched Elliot nod to Chase and then, once the guitar started, my stomach grew knots. The butterflies fluttered up higher, making my heart beat faster and faster and once he finally turned to face the microphone, looking sexier than I'd ever seen him, I was able to breathe.

I knew the song they started with, it was one of Madeline's favorites. *Like It's The Last Time* by, none other than, Thomas Rhett.

I loved watching Elliot play, the way he would move with the music and the way the words flowed from him effortlessly. He said he was nervous, but it didn't show. He exuded confidence. Just his body language alone showed pride and excitement, and the crowd could see it. I remembered seeing him the few times I went to the Piano Bar, and the performance at Madeline's wedding. I thought he was good there, but those shows had nothing on this.

If only that label agent was here to see this.

I snapped back to reality after the song was over, pulling my phone out to FaceTime Madeline. I turned the camera to him, not even saying hello to her once she answered.

"Jamie!" my mom shouted. "I really can't believe that's him singing."

I scrunched my nose and turned back to Elliot.

"Helllllll-o Park City," he said into the mic, his voice carrying over the cheers. "I promise that's only one of the few covers you'll hear from us tonight, the majority of our set tonight is going to be one hundred percent ours and we can't wait. But before we begin, let me introduce the band. To my left is Jameson, the amazing bassist and keyboardist that hates to sing, even though I force him to. Behind me is Chase, the baby drummer who joined us unwillingly. Bennett is off to my right, he's the one who keeps me on my toes and I . . ." Elliot searched the crowd, nothing but silence coming from him as he looked for me.

Our eyes met faster than I expected. I stood and shouted, "Elliot Whittaker!!" Cupping my hands around my lips to create a louder sound. People turned to look at me, but my focus was on Elliot as his smile grew.

"Well, I'm Elliot Whittaker, lead singer and that amazing woman's boyfriend." He pointed at me, giving me a wink before returning his hands to his guitar. "My goal is to give you guys a good time, so without further ado . . ." He turned and nodded to Bennett. "I do love it when you guys get up and dance."

Chapter Thirty-Nine

-Elliot-

I belonged on the stage.

Nothing compared to this, knowing my band was with me, and my fingers were on the guitar strings with my lips against the mic—the spotlight on us. That was normally my favorite part, the lights. But tonight, the part that kept me going was knowing Jamie's eyes were on me.

I was on top of the world.

I made sure to constantly keep her gaze, using her to keep me steady. I knew where Jacob was in the crowd, he was hard to miss, but I chose to ignore him. If I even thought about him being here, my entire groove would be thrown off. Just like at the wedding, when I was more focused on a certain female who was standing alone . . . but this time it was that exact same female who helped me lock onto this moment.

There was no doubt in my mind that I was in love with Jamie Gaines. She was everything to me and I couldn't wait to tell her that simple fact. Before the show I had texted Milo, letting him know that I officially joined the "dark side" when it came to falling in love. I got a FaceTime back, involving Clay of course, of the two of them acting like teenage girls over a crush. Even Madeline was in the background putting in her two cents.

"Love isn't something to be nervous about," Milo had told me. "When you find that right person, it just makes sense. You and Jamie . . . make sense."

After his call I texted Jamie, the nerves shooting through my fingers. I wasn't nervous about the show, I was nervous for these feelings that seemed to creep up without notice. A part of me wanted to tell her through text, get those three simple words out in the open, but that wasn't the way to do it. When she offered a kiss for good luck, I was tempted to run out and take her in my arms in the five seconds we had before Pete dimmed the lights.

But now, here on the stage, the words flowing effortlessly, and the band not missing a single beat, she was my only focus. I was no longer nervous about the way I felt for her. Jamie Gaines was my world, my life, my heart . . . Jamie Gaines was my everything.

After a lot of upbeat songs, with the crowd dancing and even singing along, I turned to Bennett and gave him a quick nod. Slipping my white electric guitar off my neck, I casually walked to the stand next to Chase, setting it down gingerly while using my other free hand to grab the new acoustic guitar. Bennett came up to my side, grabbing a bottle of water.

"We're ready for it." He smiled. "She's ready for it too."

Wiping the sweat from my brow, I looked over at Chase. The grin and stick flip that followed was his classic move. Once the stick was still he lightly began to tap the cymbal. Jameson gave the crowd a wave, reaching down to shake a few hands. The moment lasted less than a minute before I was back at the mic, situating my guitar over my shoulder.

"You having fun so far?" I asked, getting a loud cheer in response. "We're slowing it down for just a second to bring you a new song, and I mean *new*. Basically, so new I wrote it here in Park City and we've only played it once as a band, but there's no better place to bring this song to the world."

I locked onto Jamie's eyes, slowly starting to begin the song. She knew the melody, I had played it multiple times while she painted, but she still hadn't heard the lyrics. They were her, in a song—completely inspired by her painting that hung in the gallery. The looks she had as she painted, full concentration with each stroke. The beauty, the elegance she created with her craft, I had to immortalize it in a song. One that I would sing to her every night if she let me.

"She painted their beauty, but little did she know – the love in my world was continuing to grow. Sunflowers bloomed beneath her skilled hand – the golden light enchanting a love so grand... Together they danced and swayed, the bristles capturing the summer's day. He whispered his love into her heart...The sunflowers that came alive sang, Open your heart, for love will find you, let the light guide you."

Jamie was frozen, I couldn't even tell if she was blinking, she was just transfixed on me. Her family that surrounded her looked from me to her, their looks telling me they knew my feelings simply from my song. It was hard to miss. Surely, she knew exactly what was going through my mind.

None of this was pretend for me, ever. My hope was always to have Jamie in my arms for the rest of my life, and here I was.

When the song ended, the last strum melting from the guitar, I gave Jamie a wink. Her body relaxed and she took a breath through her mouth. If I didn't have to play a few more songs I would have jumped off that stage and kissed her, telling her the words I so desperately wanted to. But alas, Bennett pulled me back, handing me my white electric, and taking the acoustic from me.

I turned around from the mic. "We gotta switch it up." I smiled.

"To . . . ?" Bennett raised his eyebrows. Deviating from the set list was never his favorite thing.

"T-Shirt."

"Seriously?" one eyebrow lowered as he cocked a smile. He hated—and I mean hated—this song.

I chuckled. "Oh, yeah."

"I hate you."

"I know . . ." I turned back to the mic as Bennett went to tell Jameson and Chase the change in plans. I heard Chase laugh as he started the song with his drums. Unlike Bennett, he loved the song.

"Now, this next one . . ." I said into the mic. "Is going to embarrass the shit out of my girl, but after this morning . . . well . . . hot damn she just looked so damn hot in my t-shirt."

Even in the low-lighting I could see Jamie's cheeks turned red. She covered her face with her hands and shook her head, slinking down into her chair slowly. Jillian laughed and turned to her, nudging her with her shoulder and her brothers just bobbed to the music. Howard and Janet clapped and stood up from their seats, enjoying every moment of the song. All while Jamie gave me soft glares as she tried her hardest to hold back her grins.

I keep her gaze as I sang

During a bass solo I called Jameson out, stepping away from the mic to give him his moment. He was truly a god of the bass. He looked over at me and bobbed his head, a rare smile forming as he took the solo and ended it as I stepped up again with lyrics. The song references Gun's n Roses, but I had another plan. I changed Gun's n Roses to Savaged Whittakers, which made Jamie jump and cheer. The crowd laughed and I knew I had caught their attention. Jameson even let out a laugh that was caught by his mic.

Nothing would ever beat this.

The song ended and the crowd screamed.

"That was supposed to be our last song . . ." Bennett said into the mic, the banter between us only just starting. "But he decided to mix things up."

"Hey, I had to." I laughed. "After singing the most perfect love song, seeing the woman of my dreams melting in her chair, I had to give her exactly the opposite reaction."

The crowd laughed.

"We can do some more covers . . . ?" I asked.

"You promised me only two Thomas Rhett . . ."

"Sing *Unforgettable*!!" I heard Jamie scream, somehow managing to carry her voice over everyone that stood in front of her.

I pointed at her. "You heard the lady." I looked over at Bennett, my finger still aimed at Jamie. She threw her head back and laughed. "What do you guys say? One more then back to the SW originals?"

The reaction from everyone made Bennett shake his head, turning back around to grab my acoustic guitar. Normally I would step away and switch guitars myself, but I welcomed the hand off.

"Last. One," Bennett grumbled as I started the song.

Once that first line left my lips, I met Jamie's gaze again, knowing damn well that I would be holding on to it for the rest of the show . . . if not the rest of my life.

After an encore which wasn't planned, we made our way backstage. We had about thirty minutes back here to let the people leave the bar, but all I wanted to do was run out into the crowd and be with Jamie. Screw the fact that Jacob was most likely still waiting for me, all I wanted was her. I set my guitar's down, patted Jameson on the back, and rushed back out to the main room.

I was met quicker than I thought by Jamie's arms around my neck. She pulled me close, laughing into my shoulder.

"You were phenomenal!" she exclaimed as she pulled away. "Best show yet. I can't believe how many people were here, and"— she slapped my shoulder—"why the hell did you sing *T-shirt*!? You were so adamant it wasn't a song."

I pulled her back to me. "I had to. You just looked so damn hot . . ."

"I get it. I get it." She laughed as she kissed me. "But you could have picked a different song so my parents wouldn't be embarrassed."

"Your parents? Or you?" I raised an eyebrow. "'Cause by the looks of it, your parents enjoyed that one."

"Everyone loved the show Elliot, they loved *you*." She gave me a small kiss.

"Even me." My brother smiled as he came up to us.

Jamie spun around once she heard my brother's voice. She kept close to me, my arm still around her waist. Jacob and Andrea appeared, both with a smile on their face, excitement filling my sister-in-law's eyes.

She came up, basically forcing Jamie to step aside as she gave me a hug. "I can't believe we've never seen you play before. Jacob has been regretting it since you first started. And that song about the painter . . . Elliot that was . . ."

"Fantastic. Beautiful. Amazing. Elliot . . . you are amazing," Jacob finished his wife's sentence.

Andrea stepped back, and Jamie instantly filled the gap between us.

"Thank you," I said softly, completely unsure how to take my brother being here . . . talking about the show. "That song wouldn't have been written if it wasn't for Jamie." I pulled her closer to me, looking down on her, kissing the top of her head softly.

Jacob smiled. "So, you're the girl he followed out here, huh?"

Jamie let out a soft chuckle. "I guess so. I kind of forced him to."

"Well, I'm glad you did." Jacob held out his hand. "I'm Jake, Elliot's older brother."

Jamie looked up at me and smiled. "Nice to meet you, Jacob." She turned back to him and shook his hand. "I'm . . ."

"Jamie, the girlfriend, the one who looks 'damn hot in his t-shirt.'"

Jamie responded to Jacob by slapping my stomach. "You *had* to sing that song."

Jacob laughed, pulling Andrea into his shoulder, mimicking Jamie and I. "Listen, we're here for another day, we'd love to take you two out to dinner. I'd love to get to know Jamie more and talk to you about your upcoming adventure Elliot."

"Oh . . ." I began.

"We'd love to," Jamie stopped me, "but Elliot is flying out to California tomorrow. He's meeting with the label."

Jacob's eyes widened. "Wait . . . seriously?"

"I leave tomorrow afternoon."

"I can't . . . really . . . Elliot . . . that's . . . seriously?" Jacob stammered. I had never seen him this way. He always knew exactly what to say and he wasn't afraid to speak his mind—ever. But now he was stunned. He was, dare I say, speechless? Does this mean he was proud?

"Yeah, the guys and I meet with the label on Saturday and then Monday we perform for them. We're hoping for a record deal."

Jamie hadn't heard that news yet, so when she lightly touched my chin, pulling it down to her to give me a kiss, I took it as she accepted and was just as excited as I was. My girl.

"That's amazing. Does Mom know? Does Syd? . . . Dad?"

"Dad wouldn't care even if I told him."

"He would. He's proud of you. Next time I visit I'll show him the videos I took today. I got one of the new song, and then a few others."

"You recorded the new song?" Jamie asked, taking a small step forward. "I had FaceTime with Madeline up, so I didn't. If I give you my number . . ."

"I'll send it."

"I need it as a ringtone." Jamie smiled. "What's it called?" she asked, looking back up at me.

I gave her a smirk. "It doesn't have an official title, but I'm thinking of calling it *Jamie*."

Chapter Forty

-Jamie-

Elliot was called back to the stage once everyone had left, so I took a seat with Jacob and Andrea while he cleaned up the stage. Pete had approached him, welcoming him and the band back anytime and, by the sounds of it, they would be returning within the year. That is, if all went well with the label.

My family had left, making sure I was good to get a ride with Elliot first, and then told me they would be ready for us when we got back. They wanted to meet Elliot . . . actually *meet* him as Elliot—not Daxton.

Jacob was easy to talk to, telling me about their family back in Portland and how I would get along with their sister. He was a doctor, focused on an Alzheimer study which sparked his interest after their dad's diagnosis. He said he was also eager for me to meet their dad and claimed that we would get along great. Meeting

Elliot's family never crossed my mind before Jacob had sat across from me. This was supposed to be a three-week and done kind of deal, but now that Elliot had turned into a . . . forever . . . kind of deal, meeting his family was something that would happen soon. And I couldn't wait.

Elliot and Bennett were singing lyrics to songs as they packed up and wrapped the wires. I could hear the familiar lyrics of the songs they performed tonight, even *T-Shirt*. Jacob laughed as he watched his brother.

"You'd never guess that he was close to forty, huh? He acts like he's twenty."

"Age is just a number. I have a feeling I'm never going to escape that song though." I leaned my chin on my fist and just watched. I had never had these feelings for a man the way I had for Elliot. Just watching him created new sparks, new butterflies, that I never wanted to fade.

"Knowing my brother . . ." Jacob chuckled. ". . . never. That's going to be your theme song."

We said goodbye to Jacob and Andrea as we all piled up in Elliot's jeep, with Chase, once again, shoved between the two in the backseat. It was a quick drive, and we only hopped out to give the guys a hug goodbye, congratulated them on the show, and then—finally—it was just Elliot and me. He grasped my hand over the middle console, the warmth of his palm sending chills up my spine. The warmth . . . sending chills, a feeling I would never get used to.

We pulled up to the cabin and instead of going to the main house where I knew everyone was still awake, he pulled me to our balcony and took me in his arms. The snow fell around us as we kissed, completely immersed in each other.

I couldn't deny it now. Elliot Whittaker held my entire heart.

That night we slept, wrapped in each other. As much as I wanted to do more, I could tell Elliot was exhausted. He fell asleep the second his head hit the pillow, waking only slightly to allow me to cuddle up next to him. His heartbeat was fast, still coming down from the high that was the stage. Or maybe the high from seeing and spending time with his brother? Or maybe a high from simply lying next to me. I knew *that* was what was making *my* heart race.

But we slept surprisingly well for the night, and I woke up to his lips on my neck, his fingers searching my body. We made love, slow and intimate, completely focused on the other. Once our heart rates and breathing had returned to normal, he kissed me, humming against my lips. We showered, teasing each other more. Almost as if we didn't have any more time, like I wouldn't see him again in five days and that this time with him was coming to an end. In the back of my head, I knew it wasn't true, but I wanted—needed—to feel closer to him, and I knew he felt the same.

His flight to California was at three, giving us just enough time to go have brunch with my family and pick up the guys. On our way over to the main house, Elliot grasped my hand, looking at the snow-covered trees, the family of snowmen, and the forts used for snowball fights.

"I think we need to come here next year," he said softly.

"Well . . ." I brushed my hair behind my ear and took a step closer to him, bumping into his shoulder as we walked. "Lucky for you, we come back every. Single. Year."

"If you'll have me, I'd love to come back."

"Oh . . . I'll have you." I took a step ahead of him, still holding his hand but turning to face him, walking backwards.

The corner of his lips raised, giving me a cocky smirk that I had grown to love. One that made my knees weak.

"When's the auction?" he asked softly.

"Tonight, I'll text you updates throughout, I promise."

He stopped, his arm pulling me to him. "You better," he said sternly. "Please," he added.

"Hey, you two, get in here! You skipped out on us last night and we all stayed up. Mom has brunch ready, and we are all starving waiting for you," Harrison called from behind me.

I turned to look at him, freezing when I saw his clean-shaven face.

"Harry . . . what the hell?"

"Yeah, yeah, yeah, my face is cold, get your asses in here."

Elliot broke out in laughter as Harrison turned away and went back into the house. He took a step before I did, pulling me towards the house. The moment we entered everyone cheered, my mom being the loudest clapper in the room. Elliot jumped and turned towards them.

"Elliot!" My mom clapped her hands together in front of her. "The show last night . . . was just . . . wonderful!"

"Thank you, Janet . . . I . . ." he stopped, his brow twitching as he turned to look at me.

"Oh," my mom grumbled, waving her hand in front of her, reaching out for Elliot's shoulders pulling him in for a hug. "Jamie told us last night, we're just happy she finally told us."

"Well . . . I figured after she screamed my name last night, but it's still weird to hear you call me 'Elliot.'" He hugged her back, his eyes on me as I passed them heading into the kitchen.

"Would you rather us call you 'Daxton'?" Harrison asked, his fingers gently touching his smooth chin.

"No . . . no . . ." Elliot fumbled. "I'd prefer 'Elliot.'"

"I still think it's comical that Daxton is your middle name. I need proof." Jillian chuckled.

"Can I still call you Uncle Daxton? Daxton sounds cooler than Elliot." Killian came up to him and grasped onto his hand, gently tugging on it.

Elliot knelt down to Killian, meeting him at eye level, "You can call me whatever you want. But only you and Phillip."

Killian grinned and wrapped his arms around his neck. Elliot returned his hug, melting Jillian and my heart just a little bit more.

"Well, brunch is ready, and I want to hear all about Elliot." My mom clapped her hands again, gaining everyone's attention. She turned towards the kitchen, and mostly everyone followed to help her transfer the food to the table. "Where's your band?" she asked Elliot as he grabbed the stack of plates.

"Most likely still sleeping at the hotel. I'd be sleeping too if Jamie hadn't woken me up." Elliot chuckled.

"Excuse me, you woke *me* up," I corrected him. "I met his brother last night."

"Your brother!" My mom's voice was filled with more excitement than necessary.

"Yeah, Jacob surprised me last night. He has never seen me play. He . . . uh . . . wasn't too happy about me selling our dad's company." Elliot pulled out my chair and waited until I was sitting to take the seat next to me.

"You father . . . Graham Whittaker?" My dad asked, taking his seat at the head of the table.

Elliot nodded. "I was wondering if you were going to put that together." He laughed.

"It took me a bit longer than planned, but I figured it out. I knew your father briefly—amazing architect, and man."

Elliot pinched his brow. "You knew my dad?"

"We met once at a conference, maybe ten or so years ago."

"Sounds legit. He dragged me to a few of those when I first started getting my degree in business. I wonder if we ever crossed paths there." Elliot filled his mug with the fresh coffee that Holden placed in front of him, then he filled my mug.

I took a look around the table, noticing there was absolutely no creamer. Knowing Elliot would want creamer in his coffee I stood and left, coming back moments later with the vanilla creamer, before adding it to his mug. I sat back down and smiled over at him, before I was rewarded with a light kiss.

"Thank you," he whispered.

"Well, Elliot, I was actually hoping to talk to you about your company today before you left. I'd like to be considered when you put it up for sale . . . to buy it from you." My dad laced his fingers together and rested his elbows on the table in front of him.

Elliot's jaw slightly dropped, and his hand found my knee under the table. He gave my thigh a soft squeeze. I grasped his fingers with mine and looked at my dad. Jillian gave me a slight inkling that this was coming, but I had no idea he would bring it up now.

"I'm sorry, sir, you . . . you want to buy the company?" Elliot stammered.

"I'd like to be considered. I understand your accountant is going to be meeting with you to finalize everything, but once things are established with an agent, I'd like to put in an offer."

My dad's voice was steady, his eyes locked onto Elliot. Elliot's leg was beginning to shake and his grip on my hand tightened.

"Yes . . . yes . . . I'd um . . ." he stammered. "I'd be honored. I'm sure my dad would rather the company be in the hands of someone he knew and trusted, versus a complete stranger. Plus, I know my employees would be well taken care of."

"They would," my mom added softly. "He's been talking about coming out of retirement for a while now and when you mentioned selling your company . . . he hasn't stopped talking about it."

"You guys could really afford to buy a fifteen-million-dollar company?" I asked.

"Jamie." My dad chuckled, reaching for his coffee. "It's worth way more than fifteen million dollars. That's just the value. But there's so much more to buying a company, and I'm willing—and ready honestly—to put in an offer."

Elliot froze, his eyes wide.

"Let the boy meet with his agent and accountant first." My mom glared across the table at my dad. "No more business talk, I really want to get to know Elliot."

Elliot relaxed as the conversation started up again, no more talking about buying a company, just simple talk. He told us stories about how he first met Bennett and Milo. Dustin was interested in hearing how Savaged Whittakers became a band, how they formed and how they got their name. The kid really was into the musical aspect, and was still rather annoyed that he had to miss the show last night.

Elliot even talked about the time he first met me, how I didn't show him any interest but all he saw was me. So, when he heard that I needed a boyfriend he jumped at the chance. Like he had said to me before, it was inevitable that we would eventually get together, he just had to be patient.

"It was so much fun being ghosted for five months after our first kiss, and then for a week after I agreed to this play." He raised an eyebrow and gave me a side eye.

"I already apologized for that," I defended myself.

"You were worth the wait," Elliot whispered, creating those flutters I would never get used to.

Elliot's phone dinged, causing a rift in what I hoped would be a moment. He shifted in his seat, pulling his phone from his pocket.

"Bennett . . ." he mumbled. "We need to get going," he sighed.

I scrunched my nose, not wanting the morning to end. I wanted him to stay here, come to the auction, and sit next to me if, and when, I won an award. I wanted his help in packing up the car, and I wanted to sit next to him in the Jeep as I forced him to listen to my music. But I knew he was right. We had to go get Bennett and the others and I had to get them to the airport. He had packed his bag already, and he was ready to go—I just didn't want him to.

Elliot said goodbye to my family, and each of them gave him a hug. The twins begged "Uncle Daxton" to stay longer, but with tears forming in their eyes they understood why he couldn't. We packed up the car and rode to the hotel where the guys were waiting for us and then we began the forty-minute drive to the airport.

It was the fastest forty minutes of my life.

Bennett was the first to jump out of the car, a skip in his step as he began to unload the guitars and drums. Jameson was next, followed by Chase. The two said a quick goodbye to me and then ran to get their bags checked. Elliot slowly climbed from the car, and slowly shut the door, shoving his hands in his coat pockets.

Nerves.

I was starting to notice when he was nervous about something. He had his easy tells, and even though they didn't show very often, especially when he was in his element and comfortable, there were times when the emotions got the better of him.

I took a step forward, sliding my hands along his waist, grasping them together once his body was pressed into me.

"You'll text me when you get there?" I asked softly.

He raised his chin slightly, giving me that smirk I loved so much.

"I'll let you know the moment I land, it's not a long flight."

"And you fly into Portland on Wednesday?"

He nodded.

"I'll pick you up, just send me flight details, okay?"

He nodded again. I could feel his breathing quicken and his heart rate increase. His hands slid up my back then he drew in a sharp breath. He wanted to say something, and simply by the look in his eyes I had a feeling I knew what he was going to say.

I wanted to say it too, but I knew it was too soon to utter those words. Three weeks wasn't enough time to bring it out in the world. I *loved* him. I knew it, but I didn't know if I was ready to hear it. Or if I was ready to say them out loud.

Nerves.

"Jamie I . . ."

"No," I stopped him.

"No?" He repeated.

I swallowed, finding the courage to say the words. "I think I know what you're wanting to say, but I don't think you should say it just yet."

He heaved a sigh and closed his lips tight, his jaw clenching.

"It's been three weeks . . ."

"Not for me it hasn't," he debated. "It's been a lot longer for me."

"Okay, then listen." I met his eyes. "If you still want to tell me when I see you in Portland, you can tell me then."

"I'll want to say it in Portland too," he whispered.

I raised up on my toes, pressing my lips to his, and kissing him with all the fire I had in me. *Just let him say it*, I thought to myself. It wouldn't hurt anything, it would only make the connection stronger, even if I didn't know if I had the courage to say it myself.

"Elliot! Come on!" Bennett called from behind us.

Elliot cupped my face, giving me one last fleeting kiss.

"Then tell me in Portland, when I pick you up at the airport. Okay?"

A corner of his lips raised as he nodded once again. "Deal."

"Elliot!" This time it was Jameson.

He scoffed and dropped his hands. "Drive back safe to Park City, and I'll let you know when I land."

"*You* be safe, and good luck. They're going to love you."

Just like I do.

Chapter Forty-One

-Elliot-

California was hot compared to Utah, and I found myself preferring the snow.

"It's hot," I grumbled as the driver helped us pile our luggage into the van.

"It's gorgeous! I say, after we check into the hotel we head to the beach." Chase looked up to the sky, closing his eyes, taking in the sun.

I furrowed my brow, wishing my sunglasses weren't in my Jeep. In Utah. With Jamie. "I'll need to find a store. I left my sunglasses in the car." I sighed, taking a look at the black van that sat on the side of the street. The label for Pacific Sounds made it quite obvious to anyone where we were going.

"I'm sure there's plenty of places where we can find sunglasses, but you need to get your mind here . . . now." Bennett slapped my shoulder.

I looked over at my friend, knowing that I wasn't fully giving him, or the band, my all. I heaved a sigh and closed my eyes.

Get out of your head.

"Where's the hotel from here?" I asked, digging in my pockets for my phone.

Bennett looked up, squinting his eyes. Ha. He would want sunglasses too. "I think we're staying close to the studio. I want to say in a Hilton . . . Maybe a Marriott?"

"Simple, yet fancy." Chase smiled.

"A Hilton," the driver answered us. "Two rooms, you'll enjoy yourself."

I chuckled and shook my head. "Fancy . . ." I would take that cabin any day now over a fancy hotel.

Opening my phone and switching from airplane mode, I instantly opened Jamie's text thread.

Me: *Landed, and it's hot.*

Less than a second later, those three dots appeared.

Jamie: *It's snowing...*

Bennett shoved his hands in his pockets as the driver shut the hatch on the SUV. "That Jamie?"

I nodded, answering her text quickly. Letting her know I'd much rather be in a snowstorm than here in the heat. "It's snowing in Park City again," I answered him, mimicking his motion of putting my phone away. As much as my heart was in Utah, he was right, I needed to get my mind here, with them. Even if that meant putting Jamie away for a little bit.

"And it's gorgeous here." Chase opened his arms. Jameson shoved him forward, his body flying towards the van.

Jameson laughed as we piled in. My phone dinged in my pocket as I took the front seat, sitting next to the driver. He was more stoic than Jameson was, focused completely on his job: getting us to the hotel.

Jamie: We're heading to the gallery. I'll send photos, ok!
Me: Send as many photos as you can and update me on the auction. I lov...

I stopped. She wanted me to wait. She didn't want to hear it just yet. So I deleted the last four letters and hit send.

We checked into the hotel quickly, Bennett pushing us along as he was more excited to get to the label, even though we didn't have to be there until morning. I wanted to find food, call Jamie, and talk about the auction. I wanted to play a few songs with the guys in the hotel room to relax and get my mind on what I was here for. But Bennett had convinced the guys we needed to at least find the label and then go out for dinner before returning for a decent night's sleep.

As promised, we had two rooms, Bennett and I in one, Jameson and Chase across the hall, and before I even got a good look at the room Bennett had pushed us out of the hotel.

I checked my phone again—nothing from Jamie yet.

We found a small food truck on the boardwalk of the beach and settled in the sand.

I raised my phone and took a photo of the water, the sun setting creating that perfect picture to send to Jamie.

Me: I'm tired...

I sent, along with the photo.

Moments later I got a photo of the gallery, packed with Jamie's painting in the background.

Jamie: *I can't even get to the painting! There's too many people.*

I looked closer at the photo, zooming in to see a white ribbon and a red one hanging next to the painting.

Me: *Another ribbon I see? You'll win both no doubt.*
Jamie: *Auction is starting.*

The three dots still danced, more was coming. They danced, but they stopped, and nothing came. Did she type words she longed to say too—but remembered that they were to come later?

Me: *Have Harrison put a bid in for me, fifteen million dollars.*
Jamie: *HA! Yea...no...*

"So," Bennett sighed next to me, crumpling his taco wrappers, "tell me about this three-week adventure. Tell me about Jamie."

I scoffed, "*Now* you want to know more? After rushing us to the hotel and then a walk past the label, and the taco truck . . . can't we just enjoy the view?" I asked, motioning towards the sea.

"I would love to, except my best friend is trying too hard to pretend to want to be here." Bennett slouched, his elbows resting on his knees. "You don't want to be here."

"I do," I admitted, "you know I do. This is a dream. What we've worked for, what we've wanted for a long time so, yeah . . . I want to be here,"

"Except . . ." he urged.

"I wish Jamie was here too. Or I wish I was there with her during her auction."

"Auction?"

"Her painting, the sunflowers? It's up at the festival's auction. It has two ribbons next to it and I'm not there to see how much it goes for. Instead, I'm here. Sitting in the heat, on the sand, waiting to be told we're either going to be the next big hit for Pacific Sounds, or if they'd rather skip on us." I sighed, my eyes focused on the horizon. "So, yeah, I'd rather be in Park City."

Bennett was silent for a moment, his long sigh filling the void. Chase had his feet stuck in the water, Jameson was perched on a rock, looking stoic as always. Bennett's eyebrows were furrowed, his jaw clenching over and over.

"I'm sorry, man," I added softly. "I'll be more *present* tomorrow, I promise."

He shook his head. "You don't need to promise anything. I know when you get in that booth and have that guitar in your hands you'll come to life, you always do. I just didn't think I'd ever see the day when you were more in love with a girl than the music."

I chuckled. "Me either, to be honest. But then she had to come waltzing in the Piano Bar."

"You love her?" Bennett said quickly, not even skipping a beat.

I looked over at him "I really . . . really do."

"I think we need to sing that song, the one about her, for the label."

"Really?" I wasn't expecting that. To me, that song belonged to Jamie, and I knew it wasn't up to Bennett's standards. We had practiced it and made it sound fantastic for the show, but did Bennett love it?

"It was a hit last night, maybe single worthy?"

I pinched my eyebrows at him and gave him a soft smile. There was my answer. He had to have loved it as much as I did. "That's saying we get a single."

"We will. They'd be stupid not to sign us. They wouldn't have sought us out if they didn't already want to sign us."

I smirked. "They did find *us*, didn't they?"

Bennett nodded and then instantly changed the subject. He motioned towards my phone in my hand. "Have you checked on the auction?"

"I don't think it's started." I lifted the screen, and was greeted by a blank screen with no notifications.

"Only one way to find out."

My heart beat picked up, I opened Jamie's thread.

Me: *Auction time??*
Jamie: *Auction time, mine's the third piece. Are you still at the beach?*
Me: *Sadly.*

A FaceTime call came through, joining so Bennett could be a part of it too.

Jamie's smile instantly eased my nerves. Not only about the label, but everything, "I have to be quiet," she whispered.

"JAMIE!" Bennett replied, so loud that he caught attention from people passing us. Even Chase turned to look at us.

"I'm pretty sure she said we need to be quiet." I looked over at my friend.

"No, you're fine." She moved her hair over, showing me the white earbud. "You can be as loud as you want, I just have to be quiet."

"When is your painting up?" Bennett squeezed his way into the screen.

Jamie's gaze went behind the camera, "Mine's up next. The first one went for fifteen thousand . . . I'm nervous."

"If one sold for fifteen, yours would go for fifty," I said, optimistically. I was coming back to *me*; I could feel it. Just being on the phone with Jamie brought me back to life. I guess I didn't realize how low I've been since setting foot in California.

Jamie let out a soft laugh. "Fifty bucks maybe."

"Fifty Million."

Jamie gave the camera a perfect scowl, tilting her head and pursing her lips. If she were in front of me, I'd kiss her with that glare, turning it promptly into a smile.

"Elliot . . . it's not going to sell for fifty million dollars," she grumbled.

"It might."

Shaking her head, she looked back up at the auction that was happening behind the phone. Her eyes went wide and her shoulders slumped. "That one went for twenty thousand."

"Jamie . . ." Jillian's voice came from off camera. "Shh, yours is next!"

"Elliot, I'm scared."

"Tell Harrison to put a bid in for me."

"No."

In the distant background I faintly heard, "Up next is a first time painting, artist Jamie Gaines. Her debut painting won Landscape and got third in Breakthrough—"

"You didn't tell me that!" I shouted, louder than intended.

"Shhh," Jamie looked at the camera for a millisecond before her eyes went right back to the stage. A part of me wished she would turn the camera so I could see too. Maybe I could place a bid through FaceTime.

"We will start the bidding off at ten."

"Ten," Jamie whispered as she closed her eyes.

"And you said fifty bucks."

"Shhh." She shushed me again.

I brought the phone closer to my ear, hoping to hear any announcement on the auction. Bennet leaned in, furrowing his brow at the screen.

"What are you thinking?" he whispered to me.

I shrugged. "Jamie, update."

"It's at fifteen." Her eyes were still closed and I could see a hand rubbing her shoulders, most likely Jillian.

"Fifteen!" I looked over at Bennett.

"Elliot, it just hit twenty." Jamie slumped in her chair.

I waited and tried to listen, and then *bang*.

"I thought she was at an auction, not a trial?" Bennett grumbled.

"Sold!" I heard faintly. "Jamie Gaines, *Sunflower Stars*, sold for twenty-nine thousand..."

"Twenty . . . nine . . ." Jamie opened her eyes and her jaw dropped.

"Twenty-nine thousand dollars!? Jamie!" I shot up from my sand, placing my hand on the top of my head in an attempt to stop myself from jumping in the air, which, let's face it, I totally would have done. "Jamie . . ."

"Elliot . . ." She looked at the camera, tears welling up in her eyes. "I need to go talk to the person who just spent twenty-nine thousand dollars, we need to figure out payment and, Elliot . . . twenty-nine thousand!"

"Jamie . . ."

I wanted to shout it at the top of my lungs. I wanted—needed—her to know that she had my whole heart, my whole world . . . she was the center of it.

"I'll talk to you tonight, okay? I have to go."

"Okay, bye . . ." I said instead. She waved at the screen and then a final *whoop* brought my home screen back to view.

I dropped my phone and looked back at the horizon. The sun had gone completely down now, the soft twilight cascading over the waters.

"So . . ." Bennett came up next to me, dusting the sand from his pants. "If you love her, why didn't you tell her?"

I scoffed and shook my head. "She asked me not to."

"Seriously?"

I nodded. "I tried to tell her this morning, right before we got on the plane, and she told me that it was too soon and that I could tell her if I felt the same when she picked us up in Portland."

Bennett hummed, squinting his eyes to look off into the horizon. "She does know that when you set your mind to something you don't give it up . . . doesn't she?" he asked. "You would think she would get that after five months of ghosting you and you are still thinking about her."

I chuckled and turned to look at my friend. "She's aware. I told her I would still tell her. I bet you fifty bucks that when I see her next that's the first thing I say to her."

Bennett let out a loud belly laugh. "Yeah, no, I will not be taking that bet because you will most definitely win." He slapped my shoulder, turning his body toward the street. "Come on, we need to get back to the hotel. We have a label to meet with tomorrow, so . . . sleep."

"And by sleep, you mean pacing the room trying to figure out the best songs to play?" I laughed, following him. Chase and Jameson were already up by the car, leaning on the hood. Jameson had his arms crossed and Chase just looked tired.

"Exactly," Bennett responded.

Chapter Forty-Two

-Jamie-

I was frozen as I stood next to the woman who bought my painting. I had met her on the first day of the festival, but I couldn't remember her name to save my life. I was still in awe that someone had bid so much on a silly painting that was simply brush strokes on a canvas. One of my biggest goals was just to have a painting in a festival . . . I never imagined standing next to a woman who had spent over twenty thousand dollars on something I created.

The woman shook my hand and told me a story about how her husband always gave her sunflowers before he passed, so she knew she had to have the painting, and then left.

"We'd love to have you back this spring, Miss. Gaines, and again next winter, if you're able," the gallery owner said to me once the financial end of things was complete. I wasn't walking away with the total auction money, there were the fees and the gallery claimed some, but I was walking away with more money than I had ever seen before.

I looked at the owner of the gallery.

"What do you say, Miss Gaines? Would you be able to join us again next year? I'd even love to keep something of yours on my walls year-round. You were quite the rage here this year."

I'm sorry . . . what did he say?

"I'm sorry, you want to hang my work year-round?" I stuttered.

He nodded. "Yes, I'd love to. I'll commission you for two to four paintings a year, and then one at the spring arts fest, and one at the winter fest. This festival did better than they thought it would, I guarantee you they will bring it back next year."

Speak, Jamie, speak. "I . . . I . . ." *Use your words, Jamie . . .* "I'd be honored."

He smiled and nodded. "Meet me after the auction, then, we will draw up a contract."

Contract.

Oh . . . that was serious.

My breath shook as he handed me an envelope with my portion of the sale. I took it gingerly, trying to remain as normal as possible. The next purchase stepped up to the desk, and I stepped aside. I looked around for Jillian, Harrison, Holden . . . anyone. I stopped when I found my eyes searching for Elliot. He wasn't here. I had just gotten off the phone with him, yet I still looked for him.

With a smile and a wave to the woman, I left the gallery and met my family on the street, all greeting me with hugs and cheers.

"How much did you end up with?" Harrison asked.

"I don't know, I haven't looked, but he wants me to meet him after the auction so we can discuss a contract." My voice was still shaky. Why the hell was I shaking?

"What!" Jillian shouted. "What does that mean?"

"He wants two or three paintings to keep on his walls for the year and then he wants me back for the spring arts fest and the one in February."

Jillian's reaction was how mine should have been in the beginning. She gasped, covering her mouth with her hands, her eyes wide as she held back a scream.

"I'm not sure what's going to come of it, I'm just going to talk to him and see . . ."

"You better sign it," Jillian urged.

"Only if it's worthwhile," Harrison added.

"Call Elliot. I'm sure he will have all the answers."

I shook my head. "Elliot's busy. He's working on his set for the label and Bennett is probably hounding him. This is the last thing he needs to hear about."

"How do you know he wouldn't want to hear about it?"

"I bet he does, but I'm not going to let this get in the way of him meeting the label." I looked down at the envelope in my hand, running my thumb over the thick paper. "Mom, will you take this back to the cabin? I can get an Uber once I'm done here."

My mom took the envelope and placed it in her purse. "Harrison will stay."

"I'm twenty-six, not six. Park City is safe enough that I can manage to get back to the cabin by myself. I'll be fine, Mama."

"Yeah, Mom, plus I've had more to drink than Jamie," Harrison grumbled.

Pursing her lips and squinting her eyes, she gave me that signature "mom" glare before her lips curved to a smile. "You're right. I may have been a little too protective of you."

I tilted my head and looked from her to Jillian. "You two have been talking."

My mom reached out and touched my shoulder, gripping it slightly, her fingers pushing comfort into my muscles. "I'm sorry, Jamie. But we are so proud of everything you've accomplished in spite of your health complications. So, go in there and settle it and we will see you at the cabin."

I pulled her in for a hug, feeling my mother's warmth fill my entire body. Jillian joined in on the hug a second before we let go of each other, prolonging the hug to last longer than expected.

They let me go, each offering a kind look.

"Oh, hey, don't open the envelope until I get home. I don't know how much is in there," I added as they all began to step away.

"No promises!" Harrison shouted.

Rolling her eyes, my mother patted him on the back and pushed him down the sidewalk. I smiled as they all left, and watched as Jillian gave me another glance over her shoulder before I turned back into the gallery. I pulled out my phone and opened Elliot's messages. The last thing he had sent was a photo of the sunset on the beach, with a caption: *Missing the snow...*

I quickly texted him back:

Me: *You're never going to believe what I'm about to do. It's late and you have a big day tomorrow. I'll call you soon with all the details.*

I didn't hear much from Elliot on Saturday—just a quick text saying he couldn't wait to hear my news, that he was about to go meet with the label, and we'd share news together later that night. But the phone call never came. I didn't blame him, and I didn't press the matter, instead I busied myself with packing up his Jeep, making sure everything was ready for the next morning.

The contract I had signed sat on the kitchen island, all put together nicely in a manila folder, signed and ready to go. It was simple. Two paintings being bought by him from me, to be sold by him, and one painting for the next festival in February. I decided to skip out on the spring arts fest, knowing I was still way out of my league with that one, but with the knowledge that one day I'd get there.

I had dinner with my family, another snowball fight with the nephews, and then curled up in my bed all alone, wishing that Elliot was with me. My phone dinged on the nightstand, and still wide awake, I reached over for it.

It was a text.

Elliot: Bennett wants to play Pilgrim, Marsh Land, Cosmic, and Jamie at the show on Monday for the label. They wanted three – but he thinks we can sneak in the other.

Swiping out of the text, I pulled up Spotify, clicking on Savaged Whittakers photo that had landed a permanent spot on my home screen, I chose *Cosmic,* smiling when I already knew the words to the song.

Me: Definitely Cosmic, it's my favorite.
Elliot: I miss Park City.
Me: Park City misses you. You'll come back next year.
Elliot: Maybe before that if Pete wants us to play again. Apparently we were a hit.
Me: Oh you were. It's late. You need to sleep – tomorrow's prep day right?
Elliot: Yup… and you're driving?
Me: All day.
Elliot: Be safe, and tell me the moment you get back into Portland.
Me: I will.
Elliot: Sleep well, Jamie. See you soon.
Me: Goodnight Dax.
Elliot: Well now…

I chuckled, locking my phone down and sticking it back on the charger on the nightstand before rolling over to the empty side of the bed, wishing Elliot was there next to me.

Everyone packed up their cars and said their goodbyes, while mom cried harder than anyone. We locked up the cabins, placing the keys in the lock boxes. I couldn't help running my hand on the balcony railing one last time, taking in the mountain scenery before climbing into Elliot's Jeep. He was fancy with a MagSafe car mount, which I instantly stuck my phone on.

I chuckled as I looked at my iPhone, remembering the second night we were here.

"You have an iPhone!"

"I do."

"So do I!"

"Amazing."

I waved to Jillian as she and her family drove off, with Holden and Carrie following them. Harrison waved me in front of him, so I put the Jeep in drive and off I went, beginning the twelve-hour journey, alone.

Surprisingly, it went well. I listened to music, Savaged Whittakers mostly, and chose an audiobook to enjoy in-between other albums. I ate at crappy fast food joints, loving the grease and sodas I didn't normally enjoy and when I was stopped, I texted Elliot.

I sent him mostly selfies. I took a photo of myself in front of the Idaho sign, giving him a goofy grin. I took a photo of Boise, telling him I was stopping at Walmart for some snacks, and then I took a photo of the Welcome to Oregon sign off of I-84, with the caption: *Missed these mountains!*

Elliot: *Make sure you eat something decent, stay away from McDonalds.*

Elliot: *How's the Jeep – I'll Venmo you gas money.*

Elliot: *Ah Oregon... I can't wait to get home to you.*

I pulled up to my apartment complex later than planned, and tired as hell. I wanted my bed more than anything, although maybe not as much as I wanted Elliot. But the moment I locked my door and went to my bedroom, I plopped down on my bed, closed my eyes, and instantly fell asleep.

The loud ringtone woke me a second later. The living room light was still on, but the daylight that came through the living room told me it was the next day.

"What the . . ." I grumbled, rubbing the sleep from my eyes as I reached for my phone.

Elliot's name lit up the background, and my heart fluttered. I answered, clearing my throat before trying to talk.

"Hello . . ." I said, sounding like a frog, "Oh geez . . . hi . . ." I cleared my throat again.

"Well good morning, sleeping beauty. I was wondering how many phone calls it would take to wake you." I could almost hear his smile.

"How many times did you call? What time is it?"

"This is the third try, and it's ten."

"TEN!" I shouted.

"You didn't have to work today, did you?" Elliot asked, a chuckle to his voice.

"No, thank the Lord. But tomorrow is back to normal for me." I looked down at my legs, still in the leggings I had worn the day before. I was honestly surprised I had taken off my coat before I hit the bed. At least remembered to do that. "Where are you? The hotel?"

"No, I'm at the label." His voice dropped. "Everyone else is inside but I'm on the street. I needed to call you before I went in."

I took a deep breath. "Why? Get in there? Sing those songs and get that deal."

"I just . . . I need to tell you something or it's going to continue to eat at me the entire time I'm here, and Jamie . . . I can't wait until Wednesday."

Elliot . . .

"Nope. Don't screw it up for you. You need to concentrate . . ."

"Jamie. I'm going to tell you and then you can hang up on me if you want to, but I want to . . . need to tell you. So please . . . just let me say the words and then I can go in there with confidence and land this, but I need you to know this."

I stayed silent. I wasn't sure what to say. I wanted to hear him say those words, and I desperately wanted to say them back to him, but a part of me still thought it was too soon.

"Jamie...you can hang up the phone after I say it."

I swallowed. "Okay."

"I love you, Jamie. I have ever since I first saw you in the Piano Bar. Even when you were dancing with Clay. Even when you ghosted me for five months and then again for another week. I loved you when you sang during karaoke, and when you kissed me. Then when you asked me to make love to you . . . Jamie . . . I love you."

I took a deep breath, my heart racing a million miles an hour and then I lowered the phone and hit the red button . . . ending the call.

Chapter Forty-Three

-Elliot-

The line went silent and when I looked at my phone screen all I saw was my home screen—my apps staring me in the face. I didn't know what I expected, I told her she could hang up the phone, but I guess a small—okay, not so small—part of me wanted her to say it back.

But she wasn't ready.

She said it herself; it had been only three weeks for her. Even though, for me, it was six . . . going on seven months of thinking about Jamie and how to get the nerve to drive over to her house to ask her out, wanting so much more than just friendship.

I stared at my phone screen, my guitar case firm in my other hand, the weight of it becoming more and more heavy with each passing second.

I'd wait for her, as long as it takes. She was worth waiting for.

The small vibration caught my attention, but Jacob's name made my stomach twist. Yes, he and I had been talking more since he came to my show, but there was still the lingering "he's my brother, what does he want" feeling. I opened the message, sighing when it was a simple: *You'll kill them, call me after! Break a leg.*

At least he was supporting me *now*.

I took a deep breath, responding with a quick: *We got this, thanks Jake,* before shoving my phone in my back pocket and opening the door to the label, the air conditioning hitting my skin immediately.

"Did you tell her?" Bennett quietly asked once I reached them.

I gave him a quick nod. "Yeah, and just like I thought she would, she hung up the phone."

"Hey . . . that's not bad. You said so last night that you just needed to tell her."

"She has something to tell me, she hasn't yet."

"You don't think you freaked her out, did you?"

I shook my head. "No, she's in this just as much as I am. She just hasn't been pining for seven months."

"Well, you'll find out on Wednesday, right?" he asked, his tone trying to add excitement. "Come on, we gotta get checked in. You ready for this?"

"Bring it on."

We checked in and waited . . . and waited . . . and waited, for what seemed like forever until a familiar face emerged from the glass door. It was Liam, the same agent we had seen at the Piano Bar. He opened his arms wide before bringing his hands together in a loud clap. His dark hair was neatly styled and his suit was pressed to the nines. I did a quick look at the group. I was wearing a black button up, jeans and converse, and the other guys were wearing their signature styles (t-shirts and jeans . . . Chase looked like he didn't even brush his hair). We probably could have taken more effort to present ourselves better, but this was who we were.

"Savaged Whittakers!" Liam exclaimed. "You have no idea how excited I am that you guys are here, that you were able to make it on such short notice. I take it the show in Utah went well?"

"Hey, Liam, was it?" I asked, even though I knew his name. I grasped his hand, giving it a good, firm handshake. "Utah was great, thank you, and we are probably more excited than you."

Liam shook his head. "I think I told you, but I've been following you guys on YouTube for a while, and I've been talking you up to my boss for about a year now. I made the move to come out and see you in Portland, and thank God the big man loved you as much as I do." He rubbed his hand together and looked at Bennett. "Are you guys ready to hear the plan?"

I looked at my friends behind me. "Bring it on."

Liam chuckled at my comment, leading into a laugh. I could see Jameson roll his eyes from the corner of my eye, which made me only want to say even more ridiculous comments.

"Ha!" Liam said, turning his body towards the glass door, waving at us to follow me. "Now I'm sure you guys understand this, but we will need all cell phones to be turned off while in the studio. First we're meeting with Carson, showing him a few videos of your sound, going over what we would expect from you etcetera, etcetera. Then after everything logistical is out of the way we head into the studio and record the three tracks, I'm assuming you picked your tracks right?"

"Yes, sir," Bennett answered for me. "Picked our best ones, plus a new one."

"That's fantastic, I love new stuff. I'm sure Carson will too. Those tracks will be recorded and then it goes to our audience."

"What happens after the audience?" Jameson asked, his voice void of emotion as always.

"We'll talk about that after. I just want to make sure you're prepared to spend the day here. Lunch will be provided, of course, and we do have other bands we're hearing today . . . you'll meet them later." Liam glanced at us over his shoulder. "Just keep in mind how much I'm rooting for you. I'd love to represent you guys and I'll try my hardest to get you signed. But, first . . . let's meet Carson. Phones off please. This is where magic happens."

We all stopped, and pulled out our phones. I had a text, which I would have ignored if it wasn't from Jamie.

I stared at the words on the screen, my breath being to pick up as I read them over and over again before I switched my phone completely off.

Jamie: You're absolutely amazing, Elliot, I can't stop thinking about you. I miss you – it's not just a three week fling. I'll see you on Wednesday and I'll tell you everything then. Knock 'em dead – they are going to love you...just like I do.

"Now,"—Carson leaned back into his seat, raising his thumb and finger to his chin—"Liam won't stop talking about you guys, hell, even I'm excited, but let's talk about what you want here."

I looked at Bennett who sat across the table from me. He and I had been doing the majority of the talking, with Chase and Jameson mainly nodding—following along with the plan.

"Well," I started, "having a label represent us has been something we've always dreamed of. Records, tours, a bigger way to get our music to the world without having to rely on Instagram or YouTube. This is something we've worked towards for a long time. I mean, we've been together for five years."

"You've put in the work."

"Yes, sir."

"I see it on your Instagram page and especially on your YouTube. I've contacted a man named Craig . . . he says that when you play at his bar they have the biggest crowds. So much so that there is a standing day you play."

"Yeah, usually once . . . sometimes twice a month." Bennett nodded.

"Tell me about this," he picked up a remote that was on the table and aimed it towards the giant flatscreen on the wall. Once he turned the TV on and I saw a video from our night in Park City, a chuckle left my lungs. "This has been all over TikTok and YouTube, did you know you were being recorded?"

I shook my head. "No, we had no clue."

It was when we were performing *T-Shirt*, when the crowd went the wildest. You could just tell by looking at us that we were in our element. Jameson was focused on his bass, Chase was smiling and bobbing to the beat, and Bennett and I were dancing and moving, completely immersed in the song.

This was *Savaged Whittakers* at its finest. It brought a thrill to my body, just knowing this is what we were meant to do, and that Jamie had been there for that entire show. She was the one who inspired me to do that cover, and she cheered and danced along with everyone else—even more so. That night felt like a lifetime ago already when it was really only days ago.

I used to think the time I spent between holding my guitar and singing was wasted space. The time spent running a company I had no interest in, wishing for more. Now I was here, my entire future being laid out on the table, and I just wished that Jamie was in this building with me. I came more alive with her in the crowd, I knew that no matter what happened I would need her next to me. As I glanced back up at the screen, the cover came to an end with Bennett and I beginning our banter, then Jamie screaming *"Unforgettable"* which made me bust out laughing.

"A friend?" Carson asked, a smirk on his lips as he gave me a side eye.

"My girl," I replied. "That song always reminds me of her."

He hummed softly. "Give me an idea of your past, how many covers have you guys done? Any you want to record if we could get access?"

Bennett raised his eyebrows. "We talked last night actually, we would like to keep records to our music and only do covers for live shows."

"We did a wedding for my best friend last summer; his wife is a huge country fan. Our set list then was mainly Thomas Rhett,

Josh Turner, and Jordan Davis. We've kept a few of them in rotation with our live shows and they seem to do great, but I'm with Bennett, I'd love for our records to be just us," I added.

Carson narrowed his eyes and gave us a nod. "That's the answer I was hoping for." He leaned up on the desk. "Those covers that you've done, they're a hit. People like them a lot, maybe just as much as your original stuff, so I'm totally okay with you performing covers at live shows. Especially if they have meaning like that." He pointed at the screen. "And with the crowd requesting their favorite covers . . . that's what I love to see."

"That's what we love to give." I locked onto his gaze.

Carson looked at Liam and nodded. "Let's get you guys in the studio."

Still on a high from performing, the guys and I headed out to a bar. We were in full celebratory mode, and we didn't even have an answer from them yet. That would come later, but from what we could tell, they loved us. We were able to play the four songs we had planned, explaining to them why we wanted to show them Jamie's song, and two covers. It just so happened that the female producers loved that one. I swear I even heard one whisper to Carson, "I call him," to which he responded, "I think he's already taken."

Heading out earlier than the rest of the guys, I unlocked the hotel room and plopped on the edge of the bed. I held my phone, circling my thumb over Jamie's contact. There was no hesitation as I clicked on her name and listened to the FaceTime jingle, waiting to see her face.

It appeared with a smile, the tip of her tongue sticking out between her teeth. "Hey, you." Jamie smiled.

God, I loved that smile. "Hey, back," I mumbled, twisting my back to turn on the light so she wasn't looking at me in the dark.

"How did it go? It took everything in me not to text you all day."

"Nope." I shook my head. "You said you had news and you still haven't told me."

"That's what you want to talk about?"

I nodded, raising an eyebrow.

She bit her bottom lip. "The Gallery . . . they signed a contract with me. They want me back for the next winter festival, and they want two paintings to sell."

I dropped my jaw. "Jamie, that's . . . that . . . Jamie."

"I know. It's crazy—it's insane. I can't believe it. I just . . . signed a five-thousand-dollar commission contract. It's totally unbelievable." She laughed, causing a chill to run up my spine.

I wish I could kiss her.

"Five thousand dollars?"

"Per painting."

"Damn. I wish I could kiss you right now," I admitted—the words pretty much falling from my lips.

"Wednesday. Now . . . *you* tell me about *your* day. How did it go?"

"No, I want to keep talking about this contract . . ."

Her lips formed a smile. "I need to do two paintings and a third for February. If he sells them then he'll order more, but for now . . . two paintings."

"Just don't give them mine."

"Oh, hell no. That one is yours and yours alone. Like my song."

I raised my eyebrows. "I sang it today." I expected her to scrunch her nose and fight back, but instead, she blushed. "They loved it. It's still just as special as you."

Licking her lips she looked off to the side, her blonde hair falling in her face, covering her blush. If I were there I would reach up and put it behind her ear, only to kiss her again. I wanted to kiss her every second of every day, but this damn screen.

"Tell me about it," she finally whispered, looking back up at the screen.

"We don't know yet, but we'll find out soon. We recorded the four songs and two covers . . ."

"Let me guess . . ."

"Only one Thomas Rhett." I chuckled, holding up a finger. "I plan on giving the CD to Madeline once we're done with it."

"She'll love that."

"But now we wait. Carson and Liam are pretty positive their audience will love it. But . . ."

"We wait."

"We wait," I parroted.

"A gallery contract and a record label. Look. At. Us."

"I love you, Jamie," I spilled, not meaning to say it out loud to her like this yet. On the phone this morning was one thing, but over FaceTime, I instantly regretted saying it. Wishing I could pull my words in like a fishing line. It was something that needed to be said in person - my lips close to hers.

Her lips formed a tight smile, and her eyes . . . I swear they sparkled.

"I can't wait to see you."

"I can't wait to kiss you."

Chapter Forty-Four

-Jamie-

Ding, ding, ding.

You'd think being away from that annoying doorbell for three weeks would have made it less annoying. If anything, it made it worse. I loved being back in the office, but the catch up was real. Drew had taken over for me while I was away, so not only had the front desk gotten behind on a few tasks, but the second I walked in the door, Madeline gave me a huge hug and told me I could never leave again. We ate lunch in her office, and I filled her in on my gallery contract, which Dr. Brenner overheard and then promptly asked for a painting for the office. Once I was caught up from the morning madness and my brain was more focused, I thought I would be able to breathe in and out.

But that damn doorbell.

I rushed into Dr. Brenner's operatory, thinking that's where the dinging came from, but Claudia looked up at me through her glasses and shook her head.

"Whatcha need, Octopus?" Dr. Brenner looked up at me, his light attached to his loupes blinding me for a moment.

"You didn't ring the bell?"

"Nope. Kelli, maybe?" he sighed, going back to the patient in his chair.

"It was me!" I heard from Madeline's office.

I chuckled. I should have known. I always forgot about the bell she kept in her office. I made sure the office had everything it needed before I went and leaned on Madeline's door frame. She sat at her desk, her chin resting on the heels of her hands, her wedding rings shinning brighter than I remember.

"Yes, Maddie?"

"I know we just had lunch together, but our last patient canceled, so sit. I need to know all about Elliot."

Taking a step into her office, I plopped on the chair in front of her desk. I loved coming to her office, we had many venting sessions, and talked about a few breakups (mostly mine) in here. My eyes caught a glimpse of her whiteboard which was full of magnets from her travels, as well as from friends and family which made me remember . . .

"Oh!" I shouted and ran out of the room.

"If you got me a magnet . . ." she screamed as I dashed away. I had a feeling the end of that sentence was "I will kill you," even though I knew she'd proudly stick it on her board.

I grabbed the tissue paper in my bag and then went back to her office, placing it gently on the desk. "You don't have one from Park City yet." I smiled while taking a seat in front of her again.

Shaking her head, she opened the paper to reveal the gondola magnet I had picked out that first trip to Main Street with Elliot.

"Elliot told me you didn't need a magnet . . ."

She scoffed, turning to place it with the others on her board. "You know I love it, but seriously, I need to know about Elliot. When does he come home?"

"Tonight," I said, feeling my heart begin to race just thinking about seeing him again. "I have to leave work at five to get to the airport by six. He texted me a few hours ago saying he was at the airport."

"So, you're his girlfriend then?" Madeline raised her eyebrows and looked at me, a grin growing on her lips.

Shaking my head, I looked down at my lap, "Yeah, I guess I am."

She let out a small squeal. "I knew it would happen."

"No, you didn't," I grumbled. "*I* had no idea it would happen. But Elliot . . . he's something else."

"Milo and I called it before you even left for Park City, before you even had this wild idea of fake dating him."

"When did you call it?"

"Our wedding. The way Elliot was looking at you, we knew he had fallen hard. Milo's known him for years and he knows when something is getting to him, and Jamie . . . you got to him." Madeline leaned back in her chair. "We just had to wait for you to figure it all out. Glad you finally did."

"Took me long enough," I admitted, "He told me he loved me, twice."

Madeline's eyes grew wide and she leaned forward in her chair. "And what did you say?"

"Well, the first time I hung up on him . . ." her jaw dropped and she almost jumped out of her chair. "Wait, stop . . . he told me to— he knew I wasn't ready to say it. But then he did it again over FaceTime the other night. I think he just let it slip but . . . he said it."

"How do you feel?" Madeline asked softly.

She knew I wasn't one to take love lightly. My boyfriends in the past had been easy, but none of them were "I love you" worthy. I never felt for them the way I feel for Elliot. I never had heat rise in my body thinking about them, or have tingles everywhere from my toes to my fingertips. My heart did little flips when I thought of Elliot. Even just the way he looked sleeping on the couch caused my pulse to pick up—the way he held me in his arms and refused to kiss me when I was drunk, and then the way he finally kissed me after that first show . . . in the snow. The way he finally let loose . . . Everything about him made me feel passion and desire.

Love. Not Lust.

"I love him," I finally admitted out loud.

She raked her teeth on her bottom lip. "And you're going to tell him?"

I nodded, my breath beginning to shake. "The moment I see him."

The second the clock turned five, and that last patient was checked out, I gave Madeline a quick hug and ran down the stairs, not stopping for anything.

The drive to the airport was, thankfully, uneventful in Portland traffic, and I found a spot close to baggage claim in no time. Checking my phone for any sign of life from him, I wasn't shocked to see no messages had arrived.

Families had started to arrive, and passengers came up to their baggage claim carousels. It wasn't crowded as people walked past me, but I suddenly wished I had a way to make myself more visible to him. I didn't want him to miss me.

I saw Bennett first, with his guitar case strapped to his back, and then Chase, carrying his drumsticks and a large black bag on his back which I assumed was part of his drum set. I swallowed. If they were here, Elliot had to be close. Jameson came into view next, his cell phone up to his ear, most likely talking to Macy. But still no sign of Elliot.

"Jamie!" Bennett called, making his way over to me. "You made it."

He wrapped his arms around me, giving me a hug, which was completely unexpected.

"Did you expect me to be late?"

"Ha, no . . . I just thought you would pick us up outside, not come in the airport."

I narrowed my eyes to him. "You obviously don't know me very well."

"I guess I'll be getting to know you more though . . . right?"

"I hope."

He wiggled his eyebrows at me and nodded toward the hallway, "He's coming. The plane had no room for his guitar, so they had to put it under, he was waiting for it at the gate."

"He let them take his guitar?"

"I know, right? Shocked us too. Meet you at baggage claim?"

I nodded, and then turned my attention back to the hallway, right in time to see Elliot walking out. His hair was a mess, just like I liked it, and his black button up shirt had the sleeves rolled up with his tattoo fully visible. He wore his signature jeans and converse shoes, with his guitar swinging at his side, and I swear the moment our eyes locked, I stopped breathing. His smile grew when he saw me, and his pace picked up from a casual walk to a jog.

Go to him you idiot, meet him halfway.

But my legs were frozen, watching the man I was madly in love with weave through people to come up to me. He put his guitar on the ground first, not stopping for a moment but bending just enough to grab my waist as he stood, lifting me and spinning me around. My arms wrapped around his neck, and I buried my face in his neck. His smell—I didn't think I'd ever miss his smell.

"You're here," he whispered as he gently set me back down on the floor, his lips instantly meeting mine. How I lived all this time without his kiss I'd never know. The way he melted into me, his hands cupping my face and bringing me closer to him, the chills that ran up my spine and the warmth that came with him. I loved this man—all of him.

I broke the kiss to tell him those exact words, but he spoke first.

"I've missed you," he whispered.

"Elliot," I muttered back, hoping I had enough breath left in me to tell him I loved him.

"I love you, Jamie," he said, making my knees turn to butter. If he wasn't still holding onto me, I would have melted onto the floor. "I love you; I love you."

"Elliot shut up," I laughed, loving the words he was saying. "Let me say it too."

He stopped, pinched his eyebrows, and put his forehead against mine. He took a deep breath, ready and waiting.

I touched his hands on my neck, moving them to his shoulders before whispering, "I love you."

Not a second later he kissed me with everything he had, the kiss that I had had all those months ago, the kiss that brought me to him in the first place. He broke the kiss, leaving me wanting more, as he gently gave me a butterfly kiss.

"I have so much to tell you," he said. "Please tell me I can take you out tonight?"

I slumped my shoulders. "Or we can order Flying Pie and go to my apartment and never leave my bed."

"Ooo." His lips twisted. "I love that idea too."

"I want you to tell me everything."

"Then there's no time to waste."

"Elliot Daxton!" A bag hit his feet. He pulled far enough away to make me miss the warmth, but the glare at the duffel bag and Bennett's chuckle pulled me back to reality as the sounds of the airport came back into full volume. "I know you have your girl now, but there's your bag. Can we please go home?"

Elliot raised a single eyebrow and turned to look at me before bending over to get his guitar and duffle bag.

"Let's get out of here."

Chapter Forty-Five

-Elliot-

The plan from here on out was simple. The next year Bennett and I would start to work on new tracks, sending sounds to the label to start a debut album, and then we would tour. First, we would be an opener for a larger band, touring with them to gain some traction, but the label was certain we would have our own headlining tour in the next two years. To me, that seemed crazy, but I trusted their timeline.

Clay was planning on flying out, but I knew I already had a buyer for the company. Howard Gaines was the right fit—I knew he was—so the weight of selling the company was completely off my shoulders. The only thing I had to focus on now was the future . . . and Jamie.

We bought a bottle of wine to have with our pizza and we talked about everything. Jamie told me everything about the painting that she had in her head, and how she was excited to start painting them for the gallery and now her office. I requested one for my place, but she assured me I was going to be sick of her paintings before too long.

"Impossible," I whispered as I kissed her neck.

Jamie knew how to bring me to life in the best way possible. Just being in the same room as her made the entire world make sense. She assured me that we'd make my commute to and from California work, and then when the tour began, she would come. There was no way she would miss it.

"I can't be away from you for too long, I'd go insane."

"So, no more ghosting?"

"Are we always going to bring that up?"

"It's like Milo's first kiss with Madeline . . . it's never leaving."

She pushed my shoulder first and then crawled on my lap, her hands running up my chest as she kissed me.

"I'm so in love with you, Elliot Whittaker," she whispered against my lips.

"I'm in love with *you*, Jamie Gaines."

"Can I be yours forever?" she asked, her eyes heavy as she looked at me.

I stood, holding onto her as she wrapped her legs around my waist. I kissed her as I walked towards her bedroom, her body pressing against mine with heat radiating off of it.

"Forever," I whispered back, laying her on the bed. "Forever."

I awoke with Jamie's back pressed against me, her alarm clock blaring. I knew it was only Thursday and that normal life had to resume someday, but I wanted to stay here just a little longer. Grumbling, I pulled her closer to me, completely ignoring the alarm clock.

"I have to get up," she groaned.

"Nah . . . call in sick."

She hummed a chuckle, turning over in the bed to face me, giving my nose a small kiss. She touched my cheek and lightly rubbed her thumb on my bottom lip. Everything this woman did drove me crazy, made my body buzz and I knew that this was it. *She* was it, she always was. Her gray eyes looked deep into mine, as if she was searching for something. I could look at her forever and never grow tired of her eyes, her lips, her hair . . . everything about her would be a new experience, every time.

I kissed her softly as she took a deep breath, her shoulders rising as she pressed into me. She began to pull away slightly, knowing she had to leave for work soon, but I held her close, not wanting to give her up just yet.

I never wanted to give her up.

"Elliot, I need to go to work."

"Marry me, Jamie," I said softly.

"What? No." She laughed.

"No!" I protested. "I'm being serious."

"I know you are, and I love you for it, but Elliot . . . it's been three weeks."

"It's been a lot longer for me."

"You keep saying that." She narrowed her eyes and pushed my shoulder, plopping my back on the mattress as she climbed on top of me. I held her waist, my fingers pressing into her skin.

"Marry me," I said again.

She shook her head. "Ask me again in . . ." she closed her eyes and scrunched her nose. Damn she was cute. I'd ask her every day for the rest of our lives, and she could keep saying no, but I knew she was mine. "Twenty-four months."

I used my elbows and propped myself up. "Two years!"

"Two years, and I promise you I'll say yes." She placed her hands on the back of my neck, giving me the most sexy smile as she looked down at me.

I sighed, slumping my shoulders in defeat. "Okay, in two years you better be ready. I'm starting a countdown on my phone. I'm buying the ring. I'm planning a huge ass wedding."

"Elliot!" She laughed. "We have so much to focus on, we can't be thinking about that now. Let's just . . . be together."

"Together?" I asked. She gave me a small hum and a nod for an answer. "Okay," I said, "move in with me then."

She smiled, a blush rose in her cheeks and her eyes sparkled.

I loved this woman.

"I can do that," she finally replied. "I can do that now."

"Perfect." I kissed her. "Together."

"Forever."

Epilogue

-Jamie-

Eighteen Months Later

The Piano Bar. Back where it all started.

It's only fitting they do their last performance of the tour here.

The last year and half had been crazy busy, but somehow, we had managed to make the most of it. I had two paintings in Park City—my second set. My first had sold quicker than we had planned, and I was commissioned for another two. We went to Park City with my family again in February where I had another piece in the festival. This year they begged me to come back for the Spring Festival, but I, yet again, declined. I had other plans.

Elliot and Bennett had been back and forth between Oregon and California, making sure their debut album was one hundred percent perfect. Not to mention, during that time Elliot was busy selling his company . . . to my dad. My dad had flown out not long after we got home and took a tour of the building, instantly offering Elliot what it was worth, plus more. My dad agreed to keep the entire staff—plus Clay—on, and assured Elliot the company was in good hands. Once that was off the table, Elliot was able to focus more on his music.

Savaged Whittakers was the opening act for a big label band on their tour. Elliot even being invited on stage to sing with them. And when the label saw how much SW Merch was being sold at the events, and how people were excited to see them, they began to plan a solo tour on the east coast. The only deal breaker they had was the final show had to take place at The Piano Bar.

The instruments were set, and the crowd was beginning to gather in. I had a table on the side, reserved for the show, for the five people that mattered most to Elliot. They hadn't arrived yet, but I was shocked to see Jacob and his wife, Sydney following them.

"You came!" I shouted, giving Jacob and Sydney both a hug.

"We wouldn't miss it." Jacob smiled. "Where are they?"

"In the back . . . well, upstairs. They start at nine and it's only eight, they have time."

"Yeah, but doesn't he normally mingle?"

"Jake," Sydney looked at her brother, "He's a big name now, he can't mingle anymore."

"I'll let him know you're here, I go back before every show. Your table's here, but can you keep an eye out for Madeline? They said they were coming but I need to get up to Elliot." I turned to look at the table with the reserved sign on it and Jacob gave me a quick smile, Sydney moving back to their seat.

"Yeah, I'll look out for them, go get him." Jacob patted my shoulder and I left, making my way towards the stairs that led up to the dressing rooms.

I passed Jameson on the way up, stopping to give him a quick hug, as he promised me he'd be back before they had time to miss him. Chase was in the lounge, laid out on the couch with his trusty drumsticks on his stomach. He had an arm over his eyes and his breathing was deep, no doubt getting in his final nap before the show. Bennett had left the dressing room, wiggling his eyebrows at me before he gave me a quick hug.

"Good luck in there," he whispered.

"Good luck to me?" I asked, furrowing my eyebrows at him.

He wiggled his eyebrows again and turned his back.

I opened the dressing room and saw Elliot standing in the middle of the room, his acoustic guitar on his back and his hands in his pockets. Behind him sat the small guitar I had painted in Park City. It came to every show and always brought a smile to my face.

"Why is Bennett telling me good luck?" I looked at him as I shut the door to the dressing room.

He raised his eyebrows. "Because he knows what's coming."

My heart rate picked up. I think I knew what was coming too.

"I know it hasn't been two years yet, but . . . I couldn't think of a better way to do this. I love you, Jamie." He took a step towards me, pulling his hands out of his pockets, his right hand still in a fist. I began to move my leg, nerves shooting through me. He was doing this . . .

"I love you so much, Jamie Gaines, more than anything in the entire world. I couldn't have gotten through this past year without you and now that we're literally where it all began . . ."

"Yes." I stopped him, taking a step towards him, trying to keep in the tears that I knew were coming.

"I didn't even ask it yet."

"Okay, okay, okay . . . ask." I waved my hands in the air, closing my eyes, allowing a few tears to fall. "But my answer is yes. Yes. Yes. Yes."

He laughed and dropped his head, sighing before he lifted his head and looked at me through his eyelashes. He waited for my breathing to slow and my hands to stop waving around. Then he simply said, "Can I ask now?"

"Yes."

"Marry me, Jamie Gaines?" He opened his right hand to reveal the most perfect, simple, princess cut ring. His eyes never left me as I looked from the ring to him.

"Can I answer now?" I asked, parroting him.

"Yes."

"Yes." I wrapped my arms around his neck. "Yes, yes, yes, yes." I kissed him, the idea of Elliot being my fiancé filling my entire soul as he pulled away to slip the ring on my finger. The perfect fit. Tears began to well in my eyes as Elliot kissed my forehead.

Clearing my throat, I blinked, "Are you ready for this show?" I asked, my forehead pressed against him. "Hate to break it to you but I don't think you can top this moment for me no matter what you sing."

Elliot laughed as he nodded. "Is Milo here? Clay?"

"They should be, Jacob and Sydney are." I gasped. "Do they know?"

He laughed. "Jacob did, but you get to tell the others." He kissed my nose. "What should we sing first?"

I loved this new tradition we had developed over the past year, the guys always let me choose the opening song. "The one that makes you think of me," I whispered, stopping myself from kissing him again. I had my entire life to kiss him, I could skip one. "I love you, Elliot." I ran my hands down his chest and took a step back. "See you on the stage."

I floated down the stairs, passing Bennett one last time, and giving him a longer hug as he whispered congratulations in my ear. Then I skipped to the table, where my excitement picked up even more when I saw my four best friends sitting at the table.

"Jamie!" Ophelia shouted, standing up from the table to bring me into her arms. "How is he? Nervous?"

"This is Elliot you're talking about. That man has only been nervous once in his entire life."

Clay let out a loud laugh. "Yeah, when he was trying to land you."

I looked over at Clay. He had cut his long brown hair, his beard fuller than before, but still handsome as ever. "Nice to see you too, Clay," I grumbled, pulling him in for a hug.

"Jamie . . ." Madeline's voice caught me, and I turned to look at my friend. "Is that what I think it is . . ." She reached for my left hand, pulling it closer to look at my new ring. "Jamie!"

Milo leaned in, his hand on his wife's shoulder. "Damn, do you know how long he's been carrying that around?"

"Jamie!" Madeline shouted again. She stood to give me a hug but hugging her these days had become a little difficult, with her pregnant belly pushing into me, and I swear I felt a kick. She was due any day now with their first baby—a little boy. Milo was ecstatic and Holly couldn't wait to be a big sister. She had read more pregnancy books than Madeline. "Congratulations! When did he ask?"

"Just now, but I think he's been holding it in for a long time." I smiled, still in shock I was engaged.

"Please tell me I get to make your dress." Ophelia wrapped her arm around me as I took my seat next to her.

Ophelia was even more radiant than ever. She and Clay had really grown. She had another store front, with seasonal items filling the shelves, and Clay was now working out of his own office, complete with his own employees. Of course, he still handled Elliot's finances, and my dad's new architecture firm. Without Clay, Elliot would be lost when it came to the tour's finances. Clay was even looking to sign a contract with Elliot's label.

"If you don't, I will be quite upset. Custom, but . . ."

"I know, I'll make sure to cover the scar." Ophelia smiled, leaning into her husband.

I raised my hand to touch my skin above my scar. Since telling my friends about my surgery, I had tried to get more comfortable in my own skin. The fear that they would have the same fear my family once had completely vanished. Just like Elliot had said, it was simply a part of me.

"I think you should show the scar." Madeline leaned over. "Elliot loves it doesn't he."

"Well yeah, but I don't need to advertise it."

"I'm sure Elliot will see it that night anyway," Milo added, taking my hand to look at the ring again.

"I'm sure he'll see it tonight," Clay mumbled.

"That's enough." I pulled my hand away, and turned to look back at Jacob and Sydney, who both gave me a giant smile. Sydney mouthed *"congratulations"* my way and then, before I could even turn back to my friends, the lights dimmed, and the crowd began to cheer.

Chase was out first, and, as always, he waved and sat down at his drums. Jameson was next—completely emotionless as he plugged in his bass. Then Bennett, jumping to rile up the crowd a tiny bit and of course, the best for last, Elliot walked out, his white guitar in his hand and his acoustic on his back. The cheer got louder and people began to move closer to the stage.

Normally Elliot began right away with a song, but tonight he changed things up. He sat his electric guitar on the stand and with a bright smile, walked up to his mic.

"How's everyone doing tonight!"

Milo stood and cupped his hands over his lips, letting out the loudest cheer. Elliot looked our way and waved his hand.

"Pay no attention to the yahoo in the corner," he said and the crowd laughed, all looking towards Milo. Milo sat down and draped his arm around Madeline's shoulders. "We normally start right with a song, something to hype y'all up, but tonight—and she's going to hate me—I want everyone to look back at the yahoo . . ." The entire crowd turned their heads towards our table. "And to the beautiful blonde there. The love of my life, my bride to be, Jamie Gaines . . . this show is for you. I love you."

I wanted to both punch him and jump up and make love to him right there on the stage, but instead I decided to blow him a kiss and give him a small wave, mouthing *"I love you"* as I pretended every eye wasn't on me.

"She normally tells me the song to start with, and tonight she chose the one that always reminds me of her. So . . ."

He grabbed his guitar on his back, flipping to his stomach, strumming his fingers on the chords.

Thomas Rhett's *Unforgettable* began to play and Elliot locked his eyes with me, the warmth and love in his eyes was something I felt across the entire room. I still couldn't believe he was mine. I still couldn't believe I was his. And I still couldn't believe all it took was three weeks to fall in love with him.

And when the lyrics about a Mango-rita fell from his lips, I swear I fell even harder.

The End

Acknowledgements

Elliot and Jamie were the couple that were never supposed to be, but they have become my favorite. The Moments of Us Series was supposed to be a duology, Milo and Madeline and Clay and Ophelia...but then Elliot entered the chat.

It takes a lot of people to bring a book to life and bringing Elliot and Jamie to life was probably my favorite experience. So many people to thank...so without further ado...

My family. My wonderful husband put up with a lot while I was writing this book and he supported me all the way. My kids even asked me what Elliot was up to. They are my true cheerleaders in all of this, and I couldn't do any of this without them.

My new editor – Caitlin, man I don't know what I would do without you here. My panic was real, but you made sure to calm the storm and prove to me that we had this. Elliot and Jamie are your babies just as much as they are mine and I am so grateful for every unhinged comment, every edit and every single time we watched and quoted *National Treasure*. You. Are. Amazing. (Elliot should totally be thrown in the baby name hat btw...)

Erika Plum and Melody Jefferies. The wonderful artists who brought my characters to life on paper, inspiring me along the way.

Erika, the character art was everything I ever dreamed – it always is, and I couldn't have asked for a better Elliot and Jamie. Melody, you brought Jamie's painting to life. I cried when I saw it because it was absolutely perfect. I couldn't have envisioned it done by any other artist. You two are amazing and here is to many more projects together.

My tribe on bookstagram. Shawn, Allie, Courtney, Jessee, Jamie, Shannon, Katherine, Chelly, Kate, Lorissa, Cayla, Alyssa, Hannah, Lindsey....all of you (I know I'm forgetting tons!) – you guys are the best support system and friends I could ever have in the booksta community. You take a place that could be dark and dreadful and turn into an escape. Thank you for being with me since the beginning – I am so grateful for all of you!!!

Michelle and Tessa. Michelle. I love you. Forever and always. You are my solid and I would never ever not include in one of these. I. Love. You. Tessa: Why did it take us long to find each other!? Thank you for taking on a random proofreading job and loving my cozy stories as much as I do, and giving me all the comments along the way. Sorry Jamie made the fake dating a little too real when they first kissed – but I'm glad Elliot made up for it.

Fifth book down....so many more to go. Here's to all the other stories floating in my brain. Thank you all so, so much!

Love,
Stefanie K Steck

Also by Stefanie K. Steck

Standalones

All Because of Elowin
Under the Marble Sky

Moments of Us Series

That Right Moment
That Next Moment
That First Moment

Coming soon...

Hartwell Hills Series
Summer 2024

About the Author

Stefanie K. Steck is a romance writer, full-time dental assistant, army wife and mom of three small humans and six fur babies. In the little spare time she has, you can find her writing, reading, cuddling with her dogs, or watching the entire Marvel Cinematic Universe in one sitting. She is the author of *All Because of Elowin, Under the Marble Sky* and *The Moments of Us Series*.